THE HOUSE OF OLDENBURG

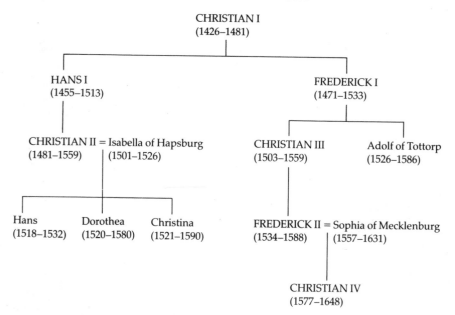

CHRISTIAN I
(1426–1481)

HANS I
(1455–1513)

FREDERICK I
(1471–1533)

CHRISTIAN II = Isabella of Hapsburg
(1481–1559)   (1501–1526)

CHRISTIAN III
(1503–1559)

Adolf of Tottorp
(1526–1586)

Hans
(1518–1532)

Dorothea
(1520–1580)

Christina
(1521–1590)

FREDERICK II = Sophia of Mecklenburg
(1534–1588)   (1557–1631)

CHRISTIAN IV
(1577–1648)

IN
THE COURTS
OF POWER

IN THE COURTS OF POWER

Helle Stangerup

Translated from the Danish by Anne Born

MACMILLAN LONDON

First published in the United Kingdom 1987 by
MACMILLAN LONDON LIMITED
4 Little Essex Street London WC2R 3LF
and Basingstoke

Associated companies in Auckland, Delhi, Dublin, Gaborone,
Hamburg, Harare, Hong Kong, Johannesburg, Kuala Lumpur,
Lagos, Manzini, Melbourne, Mexico City, Nairobi, New York,
Singapore and Tokyo.

First published in Denmark 1985 by Gyldendalske Boghandel,
Nordisk Forlag A/S Copenhagen, Denmark.

Title in Danish: Christine

British Library Cataloguing in Publication Data

Stangerup, Helle
  In The Courts of Power
  I. Title   II. Christine. *English*
  839'.8'1374[F] PT8176.29.T28

  ISBN 0-333-45222-4

Typeset by Wyvern Typesetting Limited, Bristol
Printed in Hong Kong

Contents

Copenhagen, April 1523

I

It was the day after Low Sunday 1523. The sun came up over the Sound and the coast of Skåne. In moments it had pierced a grey cloud cover and cast warm golden light over Copenhagen. It gilded the huge heavy spire of Our Lady's Cathedral from above, moved downwards to the royal palace and stepped gables of St Peter's before falling on the more modest bulk of the Greyfriars' monastery and Nicholas' church.

Only then did it light on merchants' houses, workshops, streets and alleyways. The sun crept in through little windows and cracks in the walls and threw painted shafts and squares on the earthen floors in Klaedebo Rodemål, where work had long since been under way in the Shopkeepers' red house.

But Maren Shopkeeper was in a bad mood that morning. First it was Ana, dratted child. She had bungled lighting the fire so Maren was cross when she smelt smoke from the neighbours' houses wafting in through her kitchen hatch. While everyone else kept deft serving-girls with deft fingers, Ana just stood there banging away at the flint without raising a spark.

Then there had been a rat at the pork. Maren grabbed the poker and swung it at the brute. The first time she missed, but the next blow fell with such violence that the head flew off and landed in the cabbage.

The last straw was that Ole Shopkeeper had stayed out all night. It wasn't the first time but Maren doubted he had got home long after nine merely because he'd been drunk. He had it coming to him; this time she'd make sure and drag the truth out of him.

3

But it was more than just Ana and the rat and Ole and who he was sleeping with. For Maren and the other folk in the Clothiers – and in the whole of Copenhagen, for that matter – this Monday morning was unlike other mornings. Not that there weren't the everyday sounds of the workshops and the pigs grunting and chomping in the rubbish dumps out in the street. But the usual yelling and shouting were absent. Even Mette Beltcutter in the yellow thatch was keeping her sharp tongue still today. And Ana escaped a slapping. For the wind had gone round to the South, and that gave Maren something else to think about.

Folk said the king was going away. Maren had heard about it at Anders Paviour's; his sister was in service with Jesper Brochmand himself, so it must be true. When the wind changed, the king would set sail for the Low Countries to fetch the queen's dowry and then return with a mighty army. Maren did not really know what it all meant but she was wise to signs and portents and there had certainly been plenty of those.

That thunderclap, for instance. It had been the worst she could remember, and on a day of clear blue sky. That couldn't have happened naturally. Sure enough, rumours began to circulate around town. Prince Hans had been playing in Mother Sigbrit's house. And when no one was keeping an eye on him he had gone in to where Sigbrit kept her flasks and bottles and dropped one of them on the floor so that it shattered. That same instant came the thunderclap, for Sigbrit had imprisoned it in the bottle and the poor boy had let it escape.

But Maren didn't believe that story. Nobody could doubt that Sigbrit was a witch, but even a witch couldn't manage to bottle up a whole thunderstorm. What had happened was an omen, a bad omen, like the pig born with its legs turned the wrong way so that it could only run backwards, stern first and head at the back. Or when the weather-vane fell down from the Blue Tower in completely windless weather. It was said the king himself had been frightened by that; he had ordered it to be put up again during the night, so that people would not talk too much. But they talked anyway.

4

The most recent thing had been a child born in North Rodemål with a tail, and fur on its back; and that had been the worst portent of all.

Then the Nobles' Day in November had been postponed. Not that anyone had missed the noble lords, who made themselves free of the citizens' houses and often had the arrogance to go off without paying. Now they were scheming with Duke Friederich and the Holsteiners. That was something that was bound to bring hardship to the Danish people. Even though spring had come at last, and a mild southerly wind caressed the town, the omens were not to be gainsaid, nor would there be any compensation for the nobility's betrayal of their oath and their king.

Not that Maren had ever cared for King Christian. It was common knowledge that, ordinarily enough, he'd been wild as a lad. But people felt it was too much that he should have returned from Bergen bringing that Dyveka hussy, much less that having married – and a princess of such noble birth – he should keep her on.

Maren was a simple soul who judged everything in life according to the tribulation it brought her. She had never forgotten the night Ole took Abelona into his bed, and with all the children round him too. It was a wonder Abelona hadn't stifled the baby while she was going at it with Ole, for she'd been anything but sober. Neither had Ole, nor Maren for that matter. If it hadn't been for the darkness, and the children being pushed about in the straw by Abelona's pudgy body so that you couldn't make out who was who, Abelona might well have met the same fate as the rat had done this morning.

Maren had to be content with throwing Abelona out, threatening Ole with no meals and getting that nitwit Ana instead. Ever since then Maren had had strong views on Christian, even after Dyveka died. Watching the queen walking back to the castle from mass at Our Lady's, Maren found all her maternal feelings aroused by the sight of that slight, frail figure. A woman's lot was not easy, far less that of a queen. She felt they had something in common. Queen Isabella of Denmark and Maren from the Clothiers'.

5

Maren took an interest in the royal children too. Prince Hans was a handsome lad – never mind that he was allowed too much freedom – and Princess Dorothea, with her fair curls, was a sweet little girl. The only one she had never seen was the youngest, Christina. She was by all accounts a singular child: the best-looking of the three, and clever too.

While Maren was thinking about Dyveka and Abelona, two of a kind and no mistake, and about warming up the pork stew, and her husband's leather hose that were torn at the heel, something extraordinary was taking place throughout the city of Copenhagen.

It had begun in districts like Bremerholmen, where work at the anchor smithy had come to a halt, and at the rope-walk, where men were emerging, having downed tools. In Mag Street and Snare Street, too, the din from the workshops was falling silent. From across the canal, people were gathering to gaze at the sombre pile of the castle, and at the ships below that were preparing to embark.

Throughout the crowd, silence gave way to an uneasy murmur of disbelief. There, riding at anchor, was a fleet of twenty vessels, including the *Maria*, the pride of the fleet. Mirrored in the water, masts, rigging and cannon gleamed in the spring sunlight. Outwardly the sight was magnificent. It reflected pride, wealth and power. Thus did the king of the North set out to sea.

The spectators knew better. Perhaps better than the king himself. They had no say in government; but nonetheless they felt the burden of taxation. They suffered oppression, too, from the nobility, with its arrogance and power-seeking; and they knew that even now the forces of their lordships were on their way to Copenhagen. But they also realised that it was neither the king, nor his nobles who were going to rule over Denmark. In the eyes of the populace, the fleet as it prepared to set sail was not a sign of wealth, nor of strength, but of weakness and fear. And, as the whisper went about, 'The king is setting sail', what people really meant was 'The king is taking flight'.

Among the crowd the murmurs grew. The rumours they bore spread, house by house, through streets and alleyways.

The whole city was streaming towards the waterfront: old women, and young gallants in hose and slashed sleeves; beggars and merchants; pert serving-maids and drunken hags; students, scholars and runaway serfs. One feeling was uppermost. He had exasperated and disgusted them; public feeling had judged him and found him at fault; privately he was spoken of with an oath. But in spite of Dyveka, in spite of Sigbrit and high taxation, he was still their man. Their friend. Their king.

As the ships weighed anchor and made sail, the populace, knowing they had been deserted, looked out over the Sound, all too aware of their potential foes. Lübeck ships by sea; by land the armies of Holstein. News of what was happening ran through the crowd like the terminal shuddering of a fever. The queen and the royal children were embarking; they were even now aboard the *Lion*, on the point of sailing to the Low Countries together with the state treasure and most of the king's trusted courtiers.

Among the people the murmurs ceased. Gulls flew screaming over the Sound and about the fleet as it put to sea. Beneath the king's standard flying in the breeze, the ships set course towards the North.

Maren was one of the last spectators to reach the shore. She had left home in such haste that she had forgotten to put down her wooden spoon, and had carried it down to the harbour. There, the rumour was also afoot that Sigbrit had left as well, smuggled on board, some said, in a coffin. The mention of her name provoked gestures of anger. She should have been sent to the stake as a witch. She belonged with Didrik Slagheck and those others who thought they could rule the king. But such resentments were too late now. Yes, Sigbrit was to blame, and the nobles and the treacherous Swedes. Most people had little trust in the king's promise to return, but they knew Copenhagen must be defended. They would hold their own against the Lübeckers and the Holsteiners and after three or four months the king, having got help from the emperor, would return with a new army.

But as she stood there holding her wooden spoon Maren, for all her limited powers of reasoning, could see that it

7

would not be like that. Tears ran down her cheeks. If the queen, noble soul, had kept faith with Christian, so could Maren. She wept in despair, from fear but also from sorrow. It was like losing her own family, even though she had never got to see Princess Christina, the little girl about whom it was said there was something remarkable. What was to become of the poor princess and the queen? And what was to become of her and Ole and the children and everyone else in the Clothiers' and the rest of the town?

The ships grew smaller, and one after another, beneath their shining sails, they vanished beyond Skovshoved point. On the waterfront the crowds lingered in silent bewilderment. At length people began to drift off; the citizens of Copenhagen made their melancholy way home.

The Low Countries, 1526–1533

II

In the early hours of morning a thick wintry fog swept across Flanders. It came in from the sea, rolling over dykes and canals and enveloping fields. Soon after, daybreak wrapped its cold veil around the city of Ghent.

It did nothing, later that afternoon, to discourage the townsfolk who were gathering along the streets leading to St Pieter's church. Something important was about to happen. People stamped to keep their feet warm; the weak-chested kept up a chorus of coughing, to the annoyance of others passing the time exchanging news, opinions and gossip. All over Ghent the church bells were tolling. From St Baaf's huge tower, from St Jacob's church, from St Elizabeth's, even from little St John the Baptist, their voices rang out in the fog whose layers filled the spaces between rows of pointed gables and blanketed the green waters of the canals.

As the arrival of the procession became imminent, impatience mounted. It was the funeral of Queen Isabella of Denmark.

But what would there be to look at, after all, when there might be no one to pay for it? The king of Denmark hadn't a guilder to his name; but perhaps the emperor would provide fitting obsequies. Some thought he could hardly do otherwise, considering the deceased was his sister, and he could afford it.

'Why did they have to marry her to that daft barbarian?' a seaman wanted to know, pushing his way to the front.

'Because a princess of the house of Hapsburg can only marry a king,' replied a woman's husky voice. 'No one else is good enough. And all the other kings already had wives.'

The sailor persisted. He knew the country Isabella had been sent to. He had sailed with a cargo of salted herring and anchored up at Elsinore in one of King Christian's kingdoms and had learned the strangest things. Folk in Denmark could neither read nor write, hardly ever washed themselves and mice and slow-worms nested in the bed-straw. And there could never be a court sitting after eight o'clock in the morning for by then everyone was so drunk they couldn't utter a word of sense. The bit about drinking brought a smile to some faces, for the seaman himself was having trouble keeping on his feet.

'Is it an honour, then, to be queen of a country like that?' he shouted, but nobody wanted to listen to his talk about the king's vast debts – to the emperor, to the regent and to the German electors and the merchants of Lier . . .

That was all-too familiar and while the sailor began a monologue on the subject of North Sea gales, other bystanders turned to wondering what the regent could do to get rid of King Christian.

The bells went on tolling, and the crowds grew, some of them too busy to take any interest in the king of Denmark: the pickpockets knew that where enough people were gathered the plunder would be good. Several were mere children, bedraggled little creatures whom the pains of hunger had equipped with nimble fingers and keen eyes. Beggars were more open about getting hold of what didn't belong to them. One hobbled around with his stunted legs bound in rags, and a sign bearing the words 'Give alms for the love of God'. A young man raised a laugh as he kicked the beggar into the gutter; but the beggar got up again as if nothing had happened.

Some there were in the crowd who just stood silently and waited. They wondered whether the queen had only lived to twenty-four because her evangelical faith had brought her such great misery. While others talked of the building of the Town Hall and whether England would raise the price of wool in the spring, such dangerous opinions went unspoken, for both here and in Antwerp and Brussels the new faith had left not a few languishing in prison.

Suddenly a silence ran through the crowd and people were craning to see. Hoofbeats rang on the cobblestones, and out of the foggy streets emerged the imperial heralds. A buzz of delight ran through the crowd at the sight of their emblazoned shields and the ranks of torchbearers whose flames lit up the dark winter afternoon. It was obvious to all with what pomp they were burying this daughter of the world's greatest royal house. The people were not to be cheated of their spectacle after all.

As the coffin passed by, every eye was on the extraordinary man who had once ruled over the Nordic kingdoms – and who had fled from them even while he had a fleet and an army and control over his capital city.

The king of Denmark rode immediately behind the coffin. He was very tall, and dressed entirely in black except for the glitter from the Order of the Golden Fleece slung from his shoulder. As one, the spectators pushed forward to see his face more clearly. But it revealed nothing. They saw the prominent nose and full beard, and the bushy eyebrows – and a gaze that looked as if he were far removed from the world and all its sorrows.

At the king's side rode Prince Hans, heir to those kingdoms his father had lost. Although only seven years old he sat his horse with confidence. At the sight of the comely boy, and his two little sisters following him, a whisper rose from the crowd. Little Princess Christina had tears in her eyes. Even more than her extraordinary father, powerful once, and now in debt to both German electors and Flemish merchants, she was the object of all eyes. She was so small and looked so unhappy. Then followed the rest of the procession: the nobles and clergy on horseback, and seven fine abbots and several monks could be counted.

The queen of Denmark, wife of Christian the Second, was buried surrounded by representatives of the Roman Catholic church. But there were some who knew better, who silently disbelieved she had ever gone back to 'Papist antiChristianity' before God took her pious soul to Himself.

The voices of the choir sounded from St Pieter's. The daylight faded. The coffin was carried into the church, and the pickpockets made for their lairs to look over the day's takings. For the people at large, the show was over, and they were content. Whatever Isabella had missed out on in her life, they made up to her now with a lavish funeral.

Last to leave was the beggar stumping off. His pennant begging alms for the love of God had been folded away for future use and the stick that bore it was now a crutch. It was nothing to him whether Isabella had died in one faith or another. Nor that he had suffered kicks in abundance and been made to crawl in the gutter's filth. The money in his purse made up for that. He counted his coins. It had been a good day.

Christina's mother was dead and now she was with God. But as God was good and as He knew Christina loved her mother more than anything in the world He would be sure to send her mother back soon. He had just borrowed her, the little girl said to herself. Of course He wanted to see her and talk to her before she came back to earth again.

But even though Christina missed her mother, that was not why she had nearly cried when she rode behind the coffin. It was because of the crowd. They had frightened her. They stared up at her, pushing closer and closer, all those grey, threatening faces with their noses and mouths and eyes, all strange to her, and she did not understand what it was they wanted.

In a way Christina was used to being among a lot of people. In Lier it had been the halberdiers; but they were there to look after her. There were secretaries and her mother's ladies and the gentlemen and the servants; people who did the washing and those who cooked and the candle-makers. But they always smiled at her, not stared like this. And when her mother grew very ill and they moved to Zwynaerde, the monks there would sometimes treat her to something nice to eat, though they whispered to her not to tell anyone.

When Christina had been led into the church she had felt calm again. She was quite at home among monks, candles and the music of the choir. Behind her the doors closed, shutting out the faces in the fog. Afterwards, as the days passed, Christina ceased to think about those silent, expressionless faces. Instead she became preoccupied with thoughts of her father.

Before Christina's mother died her father had paid little attention to his children. On the rare occasions when he was at home he would have them sent to him. He would lift them up and kiss them and ask solemn questions about whether they loved and feared God. When they answered Yes, he would put them down, beckon to the ladies-in-waiting and send them away again.

But since Christina's mother had gone up to God in Heaven her father had seemed transformed. Each evening when it was getting dark he sat by the fire in a small room and put Christina and her sister on his knee and told them stories. He told them about the northern countries where their home was. There the forests were so huge that you could travel for days without meeting anyone; there the cliffs were so high they towered above the clouds; and rivers fell over precipices and the sunlight turned them into a flood of diamonds. 'What is that called?' he would ask. He always looked first at Dorothea, but she only laughed shyly and buried her head in her father's shoulder.

'A waterfall,' Christina said prettily and got an extra hug from her father.

She was given one too when she recited the names of the largest towns up there or retold stories of bear hunts in Norway and elk hunts in Sweden and wild rides through beautiful verdant Denmark. For a whole month they sat evening after evening by the same fireside hearing about the lands they would return to one day. Dorothea still giggled shyly but Christina was more apt to remember what she was told. Each time her father held her close she felt his beard scratch her forehead.

'Why don't we go there now?' she asked him one day. Then he told the story of how his uncle had stolen the throne, and how they must first gather an army before the traitor could be thrown out.

'He doesn't even speak Danish,' their father said. 'You

must never forget how to speak Danish. It's good that you can speak Dutch well and are beginning to learn French. But you must never forget the Danish language, for it is your own.' And every evening ended with their father asking for Hans, whom he talked to alone.

One evening there was a pile of boxes and chests on the floor. Their father told them they were packing because they were soon going to Saxony, where he would muster an army. He went on to tell them some more about the northern countries. Christina began to feel as if each one of them had its own sound, its own smell and its own colour. As they sat there close to the stove, with all the boxes around them, she dared to say so.

Her father's laughter rang through the room. Dorothea nestled against him while he asked Christina, 'And what colour does Norway have, then?'

'White,' she answered. 'White as snow.'

He laughed again and asked, 'And Denmark?'

'Green,' she replied, 'as the grass and the forest in summertime.'

She felt this pleased her father too, and he said, 'And Sweden?'

Christina hesitated, then chose the loveliest colour she knew. 'Red.'

Her father said nothing, and she repeated eagerly, 'Red. Like blood.'

Silence. Christina heard only the hiss of a log burning. Her father's embrace slackened. His hand fell heavily and gripped the arm of her chair. She hugged him, upset at having said the wrong thing, but not understanding. The only sound was his breathing. At length he said, 'It is late.'

Slowly he put down the two girls, rose and rubbed his brow as if something in his head pained him. For a moment she thought he had forgotten they were there. But then he bent and kissed them goodnight and they were led away.

A month after the funeral the girls were with their father when a secretary hurried into the room, out of breath. 'Her Grace the regent is on her way.'

Christina's father let out a roar, sprang up, and the girls

16

slipped off his knees like a couple of lapdogs. The secretary did not dare to say more. From the courtyard came the sound of hooves.

'What does that female want?' shouted Christina's father, going with long strides to the window. The secretary trembled as the king turned to him with a threatening look.

'Does she think she can take my children away from me? *Does she?*'

He shouted into the terrified man's face, while ladies-in-waiting came running. Christina and her sister were seized, lifted up and carried out. The last thing she saw was her father taking dishes and silver from the crates. She heard the sound of breaking glass, of metal crashing on the floor and chairs being overturned. Suddenly there was silence throughout the castle. Her Grace the regent of the Low Countries had arrived and desired an audience with King Christian.

That night Christina cried. She wept in earnest, not as at the funeral when she had merely had tears in her eyes. She lay alone in the big bed behind the curtains and suddenly realised that she would never see her mother again. And she understood that if you could lose your mother you could lose everything else you loved too.

There was not a sound to be heard in the great house. Through the crack in the curtains she could see the servant girl in the chair by the door. Flames from the fire lit up the room. But in the hidden world of her bed Christina folded her hands and said a prayer to the Holy Mother. She prayed silently and fervently that God would wait a while before taking any more away from her. 'For I am such a little one,' she whispered under her quilt.

Next morning before sunrise Christina and Dorothea were taken to their father. He stood leaning against the stove with his arm resting on its shelf. At their approach he did not turn round. Behind him on a stool, among the packed chests and boxes, sat a lady. For a moment Christina thought her mother had come back after all and was sitting there in the torchlight.

Then the lady slowly turned towards them. She was

heavily built and dressed in black with a starched white headdress. 'Come over here,' she said in an authoritative tone. As she did so Christina could see what had caused her mistake. She had the same mouth as Christina's mother – but bigger. Everything about her was broader, quite twice so.

'Let me look at you both,' she said. Christina and Dorothea looked askance at their father's back, uncertain whether they ought to go to her.

Their father just stood there. The lady looked at him. After a moment's silence she turned again at the girls. 'I am your mother's aunt, and I have arranged with your father for you to live with me while he is away.'

Christina heard her sister start to cry. The lady, who was short and heavy, rose slowly and came towards them. Christina looked up at her. She was afraid of this woman and could not understand why her father turned his back instead of protecting them.

The lady stretched out her hand and with a curtsy they kissed it. She folded her hands against her black robe, drew in her chin and said, 'I had a little child once. It died. You had a mother who died. I will love you as my own children.'

Dorothea stopped crying and Christina looked more closely at the lady. She knew the person sitting before her was 'Her Grace', whom everyone feared, and whose presence made everyone move soundlessly and speak only in whispers. Everything she saw was heavy. Her eyes and nose bulged and her underlip was thick. Never before had Christina felt herself so alone in the world.

Suddenly her father turned round. He walked slowly towards them, lifted them up one on each arm, held them to him and looked into their eyes. 'Your aunt will love you. It is probably all for the best. Put your trust in God and do not forget the Danish tongue.'

The girls gave no answer, for his voice was thick and tears ran down the furrows in his cheeks into his beard. For a moment he stood there holding them in his arms without speaking, then he set them gently down.

'I will have Prince Hans sent in,' said the lady. She took Christina and Dorothea by the hand and led them out.

III

The sun came out, but it was only early March. The air was cold and damp and Christina felt wretched, as they arrived at the palace in Mechelen. No one was able to tell her when her father would return from Saxony, or when he would regain his lands and throw out his wicked uncle. She had had her father with her and now suddenly he too was gone. Their aunt had hardly spoken during the journey, only bowing slightly to the people who doffed their caps to her by the wayside.

In the courtyard was a long arcade with slender white columns and in the corner by the great staircase servants and grooms were standing, with ladies-in-waiting who curtsied low. Christina was quickly lifted down.

'Come along,' said their aunt, folding her hands while she hurried the children along. 'I'm going to show you the house. First the library; there's something you'll like there.'

While the servants in livery and velvet opened and closed doors for them, Christina and her brother and sister were led into a dimly lit room full of books, manuscripts and paintings. Her aunt gestured at a picture on the wall saying, 'Well, Christina, now who is that?'

'It's Mother.'

Christina's voice was stifled with sobs. Her mother was the most beautiful sight she had ever seen. She wore a white dress embroidered with pearls. Its bodice had laced sleeves, and a brooch fastened at its centre. Her face was framed with curls.

'Yes,' said her aunt 'And who is that, Dorothea?' turning to another portrait.

'Father,' answered Dorothea, and could say no more.

'Good,' she said. She put an arm round Hans's shoulders and addressed all three of them. 'Your mother is with God in Heaven and your father is away on a journey. But they are here as well, so that you can always come and see them. And your mother in Heaven and your father on his journeys will be happy if they know you are obedient, Godfearing children who are a credit to them.'

'Yes, Madame,' said the children in small voices.

'Good,' said their aunt again. She walked heavily across the room and paused. 'Come along. There is much more for you to see.'

They were shown around the rest of the house. They saw tapestries depicting the story of David and Goliath, and hunting scenes and Greek myths. There were paintings and great silver mirrors and enormous chandeliers; and, not least, there were animals.

First there was the Italian greyhound. Christina saw her aunt smile as she leaned down to pat it. Then they looked at the birds. There were songbirds in big cages, and cockatoos from the new world, and lastly the green parrot. It had been bought to replace the old one that died. Their aunt told them about the dead parrot.

It was so clever that it could speak three languages, and it could answer any question. But it was unbelievably old, for it had formerly belonged to their aunt's mother at her court in Burgundy, which was a long time ago. This one was friendly and just as bright green but unfortunately not nearly so clever.

The bed in Christina's room had golden hangings, with blankets instead of the quilts she was used to; and at night there were two women to watch over her. 'One of them always falls asleep,' their aunt explained with a little smile.

Once Christina was in bed she felt happier than on their arrival at the palace. Her mother really was there in the painting and her father, too, and she was quite sure her aunt really did love all three of them. But she still couldn't help wondering how God could allow a green parrot to live on earth so long when her mother had to die so young. After the long journey she was very tired, and soon fell asleep.

*　　*　　*

The children became quickly familiar with their everyday
life in Mechelen. After Mass they sat down to their lesson in
Latin, which was followed by French, Bible study, history,
geography and mathematics. They also had to learn deportment, dancing and riding. Whatever the weather they went
out every day. 'Fresh air gives you backbone,' their aunt said
and refused all their pleas to be let off when the snow made
their cheeks smart and the canals froze up.

For Christina and her brother and sister, the daylight
hours were carefully divided. No time was to be wasted.
From the moment the children opened their eyes behind the
bed hangings until, tired and rosy-cheeked, they fell asleep
at night, every moment was filled.

'Idle hours encourage gloomy thoughts,' said their aunt.
But one hour was set aside for play, even so.

During that time she would sit in her chair looking on at
them with her heavy eyes under her white headdress. She
watched them while they played with the animals, romped
around beneath the tapestries, sent arrows flying towards a
large target or were allowed to adorn the little wooden
images of saints with flowers. Stout and heavy, with her
hands folded in her lap, she merely smiled, whatever they
did and however rough they were on their clothes. This was
the period when they were 'allowed to', and only important
councils of state or journeys kept her away from the children. Their games, their rough-and-tumbles and mishaps,
were quite as important as their Latin studies in the bitter
cold morning hours.

Christina grew up surrounded by people. When she was
bounding about around her aunt, liveried servants stood and
watched. Women attendants were in every room, and from
the basement windows came the chatter and laughter of the
kitchen staff busy with preserving and salting, cleaning fish
and cooking. They could hear the girls in the linen room or
making candles in great vats, and the stable-boys grooming
the horses. The ladies-in-waiting were subdued and dignified; but the young noblewomen staying at court to finish
their education were always full of chatter as they made
their way through the rooms and apartments of the building.

21

Pages bowed to Christina, footmen opened doors for her; the governess supervised her manners, the teachers her education, ladies-in-waiting her clothes, dancing and singing. But Christina was attached most closely of all to her sister. There was only a year's difference in age between them. And as Dorothea had grown a little more slowly they felt as if they were twins. Their brother Hans was taught separately because he was the son, the heir, and also the eldest. Although easily moved to tears Dorothea always bubbled with merriment. She could collapse into giggles over the least thing. After she had lost her milk teeth and the permanent ones grew, rather disappointingly, with little points, her aunt and the ladies-in-waiting tried to wean her from these wild outbursts of laughter. She must learn to show herself to the best advantage, to be a pleasure to those around her, and her teeth were certainly not her best feature. She tried to control herself, and, instead of laughing, sank the pointed teeth in her underlip, while her whole head shook under her fair curls.

Dorothea opened the door to life's comedy for Christina, as for Dorothea Christina showed the way to a knowledge of Latin, theology and mathematics. It came easily to Christina to understand, construe and learn the lessons of the day, and she helped her slower sister with verbs and inflections.

Both the girls loved Aesop's *Fables*, but differed in their favourite female saints. Of them all Dorothea preferred her namesake Saint Dorothea, who was so gentle, and the miracle of the rose that took place when she suffered death for Christ, her bridegroom.

Christina preferred holy Saint Brigitta, partly because she was Nordic, but also she was both noble and just, a lady of high birth who cared for the sick and powerless and who at the same time was always aware of what went on in the great world. Of course it was all very beautiful to get God to send a basket of fragrant roses and apples down to earth in February. But to be as wise as Brigitta, whose advice was sought by heads of state and by the pope himself, was after all far more exciting.

Christina and her sister shared both joys and sins. They whispered their secrets to each other, about how when their aunt was away Dorothea had poured some hock into the parrot's water bowl, or when Christina had hit one of the images of a saint with her arrow, or when they'd laughed at a monk during Mass because his nose, being covered with warts, had looked so funny. They confessed that to Father Antonius, since they were not specially afraid of him. He simply told them how many candles to light, and never scolded them.

But just as there were people who merely bowed, curtsied and tried to meet their requests, so there were some who towered over them and filled them with trembling and respect.

Above all, naturally, was God, to whom they prayed morning and evening. But immediately under him, not very far down, was the emperor, whom they heard about every day but had never seen.

For Christina the most exciting lessons in geography were when they were allowed to borrow the great globe with the handle and point out all the countries their mother's brother ruled over. He was emperor of the German–Roman empire, king of Spain and Naples, and ruler of the Low Countries, which their aunt governed in his name. And as well as all this he possessed the new lands across the sea, which they had to turn the globe round to find.

The emperor was good, almost as good as God, and in any case better than any other person in the world. The greatness of his power, stretching right round to the other side of the world, was due to his mother's parents, King Ferdinand and Queen Isabella. It was they who had sent Captain Columbus off to discover the sea route to India.

The idea of people once believing the earth was flat made Dorothea smile. 'How would it have come to an end, then? With a garden fence?'

Like the notion of the earth being flat, everything in 'the old days' seemed comical and outdated. Then, you lived in palaces like the one on the opposite side of the street, with fortifications and no running water. Most people had been

23

unable either to read or write; they hadn't known how to print books but wrote them by hand, and scientists had been so ignorant that both girls laughed at their foolishness.

Christina felt that Hans soared far above her. He would put his arm affectionately around his sisters, joke with them, and laugh at their talk. He was their protector and their knight. He helped them over problems with Latin, and kept quiet about their small misdeeds – even the time when the parrot got so dreadfully drunk that it couldn't talk properly but flapped around its cage in confusion, hitting its green wings against the bars, without the ladies-in-waiting having the least idea why.

He was their friend, their brother. They relied on him and admired him enormously.

It was in her geography lessons that Christina learned about the countries of the North. She knew where they were, and could point to them on the globe. But she heard nothing of her father.

Christina had not forgotten him, however. When she stood in the dimness of the library looking up at his face he was as alive and present to her as when she had sat on his lap, felt his beard scratch her face and listened to his fantastic stories. There were bears in Norway, elks in Sweden, she reminded herself, in order to remember it for the day when he would come and take them home with him to his kingdom. When she was in the library she felt she was talking to him. She could hear his voice, his laughter, his step. And after she left the room she felt herself strengthened. Even though he was probably far away he shielded her from dangers. He was a wall built of gigantic blocks and she would always be able to reach out and lean against it, put her hands on it and feel its power.

Dorothea in particular had come to love the green parrot. It must have come from Germany because it always said 'Jawohl, Gnädige Frau', and no matter how hard she tried she could never get it to speak a word of French.

The children also got to know something about life outside the palace. They heard most through Johanna, in spite of the fact that Johanna's lowly standing forbade her to talk to the royal princesses.

It started the day Dorothea was feeding the sparrows from the cloisters. Heedlessly, she leaned further and further out, and Christina screamed as she saw her sister disappearing out of the open window.

But down in the courtyard one of the women must have foreseen what was about to happen, for she threw down her basket of bedclothes, spread out her fat arms, caught Dorothea and put her down between two pillars as she exclaimed, 'The fool gets the trump card!'

Just at that moment the regent rode into the courtyard with her train. But she was unaware of Dorothea's offence, for as swiftly as she had acted in catching Dorothea the woman smoothed down her bodice and straightened her cap.

That woman was Johanna, and the girls did not forget her kindness. Johanna worked at the linen but even though she had several girls under her she was still a woman as opposed to a lady, a situation that could not be changed. First they smuggled two oranges to her but later they grew bolder and spoke to her, and unlike the others Johanna answered their questions. They managed to get permission for Johanna to look after their rooms and clothes, and in this way Johanna was promoted from the basement to the young ladies' quarters. This meant she was moved up to a higher position in the servants' hall and sat at table with the chief house-keeper, although her official place was at the lowest end.

Johanna could tell stories as well as she could look after clothes and it was from her that Christina learned about things not taught in the schoolroom. Johanna talked about 'the old days', which meant the time when she had lived on a small farm in north-west Brabant. She had had five chil-dren. First there were three boys and then God had blessed her with the girls, all of them healthy and well formed. In the old days there had been the kermis, or fair, and weddings with bagpipe music, and Johanna talked about how to milk a cow, what the inside of a mill looked like and what went on at a cattle market. But in the old days, too, 'God gave. And God took away.'

25

The Year of Our Lord 1520 was when the plague came. The eldest girl fell ill on St Valentine's Day. Before the week was out she was dead and before the month was out the plague had taken her husband and the four remaining children. The gravedigger died and the priest and the people on the other farms. But she managed to bury her family in consecrated ground. She pulled them along on a small sledge, first one little corpse and then the others.

Christina and Dorothea were frightened, and Johanna reassured them by saying that if the plague came to Mechelen the court would move away at once to a place where there was no infection. The emperor had other castles, even though her own family had not had another farm to move to.

Then Johanna would hustle them off, 'Madame Dorothée' and 'Madame Chrétienne,' as she always called them, although she could not speak a word of French. There was no more time for talking; they had to get dressed for the evening meal.

When their aunt shared her meal with them something exciting always happened – a troupe of trained bears, or singers and musicians from England. Johanna would sometimes describe how they had been sent out to wash before they performed, because they stank so badly Her Grace could not stand them near her table. Johanna thought Her Grace liked the king of England's sonnets better than the king himself, but they must not tell anyone that. They watched marionette plays and jugglers, and sometimes Christina wished she dared write a letter to her father. If he would come and live with them the world would be really wonderful and she herself the happiest child in the world, for she was almost that already. If he would join them they could speak Danish again as he wished them to, and he could share their life in Mechelen.

Between the visits from troupes and musicians there was always something to amuse them. The little alabaster reliefs in their gilded papier-mâché frames, or processions, or the guard marching in with flowering hawthorns and planting them in the courtyard. Sometimes Florentine merchants appeared, bringing choice silks. In the bargaining, their aunt knew exactly what was becoming for the two girls, how many yards would be needed and how much to allow for growing. It was important that they dressed to suit their royal station, but there was no need to be extravagant.

Everyone was friendly. The noble people talked to them; and servants and soldiers just smiled but showed their affection for Christina and her sister and their brother Hans. All except one.

That was Kiki.

Kiki was a dwarf. But Kiki was also a changeling. It was the general opinion, at least among the staff and servants at court, that Kiki would probably have been a few inches taller if she had not had so many thrashings that her back was damaged and stopped growing.

You couldn't really blame anyone for doing that, for it was the only way of getting the goblins to take back their off-spring and replace it with the rightful human child. But as the creature with her wiry red hair was so ugly, even the goblins felt no sympathy for her over the blows she suffered and they never exchanged the children again. So Kiki grew up among human beings even though her rightful place was underground, while the real child led a wretched existence among goblins and other mobs and was never seen again.

But whatever her origins may have been, Kiki ran away from home. She roamed around for several years and arrived in Antwerp just when the authorities were rounding up homeless children in the streets. They were to be sent to institutions to learn to read and write and become honest citizens, and not to steal and beg until they ended up in the hands of the hangman and his assistants.

In the haste and the darkness Kiki was dragged along with them, but when her captors had taken a good look at her and discovered that she was much more than six or eight years old someone had the bright idea that the regent might find a use for her. So Kiki was sent to the court as a gift from the town of Antwerp.

It was a stroke of luck for Kiki. For the first time in her life someone found her useful, and that someone was the regent herself.

Kiki was sent in to the diminutive lady, who asked her to talk about life in the village. And even though Kiki was shaking with fright she described everything she had seen and heard during her existence in hiding behind haystacks and barn doors or in mills and stables. In the whole of her life Kiki had learned only one thing: to hide herself away from the rain of blows that awaited her, and she had whiled away the time in hiding by listening and watching.

Her Grace laughed at what Kiki said. Her heavy head shook under her veil, and the more daring Kiki grew in her descriptions the more the great lady laughed. But then the regent stopped, folded her hands in her lap, glanced down and asked quietly, 'What are the peasants saying about the taxes?'

She lifted her gaze, looked inquiringly into Kiki's wrinkled little face, and Kiki smiled back happily. At last here was a use for her special talents.

From then on Kiki left the palace in Mechelen every morning at sunrise and did not return before darkness had fallen over the town. She was often sent for to talk to Her Grace. Sometimes she had little to report, but when strolling players brought crowds to the square and the ale flowed to loosen tongues, she could tell hour-long tales of whoring and thieving, and anger over taxes, and gossip from English merchants about doings at the court in London.

Her Grace listened in the dusk with her hands folded and head slightly bent. She did not say a word other than 'Good evening, Kiki' and 'Goodnight, Kiki.' But she had ways of rewarding Kiki for her services and Kiki had plenty of gold coins sewn into her dress lining. Kiki was not by any means the only person who provided information for the regent, but she was the only one who lived at the palace and reported directly to her.

Kiki had a prodigious talent for hearing without being seen. Just as she knew what went on outside the walls, so everything within the narrow confines of the court was familiar to her. Kiki knew who stole from the olive crock, and who was scented with Her Grace's oils when Her Grace was absent. What is more she even knew what had happened when the king of Denmark had fled his country to seek help to regain his kingdoms.

On that day Kiki had hidden herself in one of the big chests, and she was there when the regent came in to hear the message. Through a crack in the wood she saw her lady fly into such a rage that all her blood collected itself in her underlip so that it turned blue.

'What has he got an army for?' hissed the regent. 'What does he want here?'

But she controlled herself and issued orders for her niece the queen of Denmark, and the children, to be received with all the honour due to their rank. Money was allocated for the subsistence of the exiles and inside her chest Kiki rejoiced to learn how small a sum it was considering the persons concerned were royalty. Two thousand guilders a year for the queen and five hundred a month for the whole household. Not much more than a crust.

So Kiki was all the more vexed on the day barely three years later when Her Grace rode into the palace courtyard in Mechelen with the children. What had they come here for? She felt her position, her times alone with the regent, in danger; and her suspicions were all too soon confirmed. There was still a use for her information. But the gifts of guilders grew rarer, for now the gracious lady spent all her spare moments with the children of an exiled king and a dead queen, as if she, Kiki, were not far more useful.

The regent was not the only one who liked Kiki. There was the green parrot too. When Kiki opened the cage the parrot put his head on one side, looked at her out of one eye, then flew out and settled himself on top of her head.

The only part of Kiki that never stopped growing was her hair. It grew out of her head like a huge flaming mane, flowed down her deformed back and fell to the ground like a train. It was a grotesque sight to see Kiki walking around the halls and apartments and under the arcades of the courtyard with her hair like a blazing cloak, and the green parrot above it like a phosphorous torch screaming continually its 'Jawohl, Gnädige Frau, Jawohl, Gnädige Frau . . .'

One day Kiki heard two servants laughing scornfully at

her and she resolved to give them a fright. She jumped up among the beer tankards and wooden dishes on one of the tables in the servants' hall. She was then on a level with their eyes and she told them she was no changeling and she was certainly not so small because she had been beaten.

'I have always been little like this,' she said, 'ever since I was born.'

She gazed around, looked gleefully at the footmen and maidservants and other staff and said cunningly, 'You see, I can remember my christening. I was only one week old and so small that my godmother put me in her fur-lined glove when she took me to church. I can still remember feeling the lambskin that day, it was so nice and warm.'

She saw the terror in their eyes as she said that, and enjoyed it. They stared at her open-mouthed. To know what had happened when you were only one week old couldn't be natural. It was one thing to be a changeling and goblins' offspring, but a witch was something quite different. Kiki knew it was dangerous talk, but safeguarded herself by telling Her Grace what thorough fools she'd made of them all.

Her Grace laughed her weighty laughter and asked to hear more about the glove, and how much fur there was in it. And Kiki felt quite secure, for Her Grace was not afraid of witches. Her Grace was afraid of something else. Heretics.

Kiki was aware of her own increasing influence in the war waged by the emperor and the regent against Lutherans and Anabaptists. If she had had to forgo time with Her Grace because of the hours the regent spent with those worthless children, a German monk and his seditious writings certainly kept her fully occupied.

When Kiki walked through the gateway and mixed with the crowd she felt aware of her own importance and more sure of herself than ever before. And who knew? If she waited long enough perhaps she would regain her place beside the regent.

Kiki understood all about human beings. She realised that Her Grace with two husbands and a child in the grave was a lonely woman despite being surrounded by so many people. At one time she had filled the emptiness by bringing up the children's mother and her siblings, but they had been sent away to Austria, Portugal, Hungary and Denmark. It would not be too many years before the Danish princesses took their places in some royal marriage bed or other and then Her Grace would be left lonely again and would need a little laughter sometimes.

Kiki tried to hide her hatred of the children. She would bide her time; one day she would have more power than anyone could imagine. All her life Kiki had met nothing but spite, injustice, blows, cold and hunger. Now she was dressed in silk but her little legs were still blue from the frostbite she suffered sleeping in Antwerp gutters and her body was a mere lump. She wore a starched cap, but beneath it her face was as wizened as months-old fruit. Kiki wanted power, she hated everyone, all those with smooth skin and tall, healthy bodies. She hated those children and most of all the Princess Christina, for although she was the youngest she stood out above all.

'How she does grow,' thought Kiki one October morning as she stood under the columns and felt the parrot's claws on her scalp. 'But then no one has ever taken a hand to her delicate cheek.'

She stared at the little girl as she was lifted on to her horse. Kiki saw the pearl-embroidered cap and fur-lined sleeves; she saw the princess push her long legs into the stirrups and wished with all her heart that she really was a witch. For then she would turn Princess Christina into a dwarf, no, a reptile, so scaly and horrible that everyone would rush screaming away from her.

But Kiki was no witch. The Princess Christina rode out of the courtyard erect and proud and Kiki stayed behind the columns while the parrot on her head squawked out its 'Jawohl, Gnädige Frau, Jawohl, Gnädige Frau . . .'

IV

As Christina mounted her pony, she saw Kiki standing under the arcade staring. But she did not let it affect her even though she detested the dwarf.

It was not because Kiki was unpleasant to look at. Christina could just remember that her mother had once had a dwarf. Her name was Karine and she was good at somersaults. And Hans had already been given his own dwarf, whom everyone liked because he said funny things and ran errands.

But each time Christina saw Kiki's red hair sweeping over the tiled floors she felt she was in a waking nightmare. Kiki was the only living creature Christina could not bear. To Christina Kiki's staring eyes were a repetition of all the silent threatening glances that followed her during her mother's funeral. She shivered under Kiki's gaze and her greedy curiosity. When Christina saw that spiky red hair sticking out from behind a door or heard small, stealthy footsteps disappearing along a corridor, or opened a chest to meet the toothless grin in the wrinkled face it was like being entwined in the grip of a cold slimy snake.

When Christina rode through the gateway out into the lovely clear autumn day she forgot Kiki. The heavens were high and the day was young, she felt her pony's muscular body beneath her, it was strong and she was in control. She determined speed and direction, she was almost nine years old and the world around her grew bigger and more exciting every day. It was more beautiful, more wonderful, and on this bright morning when the first leaves were falling on to the waters of the canals she felt like stretching out her arms and embracing the whole round world. Christina felt that life belonged to her. Every window stood wide open. She had only to lean out to see it all, sparkling, colourful, freshly painted.

After her ride it was time to try on clothes. She was shortly going to a banquet for the first time and while Johanna and the ladies-in-waiting looked on, dressmakers bustled about her. When she was able to look down at herself she felt a surge of delight at the sight of the golden overdress drawn aside to reveal her red velvet underskirt. The sleeves, which were velvet, hung halfway down to the floor over narrow lace cuffs. Her hair was parted in the middle, combed back and almost covered by a delicate pearl-embroidered net. The only disappointment was in not being allowed to follow the new fashion of narrower waists. The ladies told her that Her Grace had strictly forbidden it because she thought it unhealthy, especially for such a young lady.

Christina soon forgot her vexation over this and turned to watch Dorothea try on her costume of green and silver.

The regent sat under the gold-embroidered canopy she had received as a gift from the Doge, dressed as usual in her black widow's weeds. Prince Hans sat on her right and the cardinal on her left, while Christina and Dorothea still had to be content with their seats at the ladies' table.

The weather outside was stormy. The first gales of autumn were sweeping over the land and although the palace was new and well-built it was draughty in the hall. There was a fire in the great stove in the centre and the torchbearers were positioned along the walls, but the heat of the flames was insufficient to combat the chill rising from the floor.

Although her fur lining came right up to her neck and covered her sleeves, Christina was cold. She could hear the window-panes shake at each gust of wind. But the glasses were filled with Rhenish wine that was warming. The fat carp had been eaten, and the nut sorbet, and in front of her the carver was at work.

The young man held up the haunch of wild boar in front of him on a roasting fork while he sliced the meat with long sweeping movements of his knife.

'Higher,' said the regent sharply, 'and swing the knife more.'

The regent turned to the cardinal. 'I saw a carver in Toledo who was a pleasure to watch.'

The cardinal leaned forward, smiled amiably and said, 'They tell me even the king of France cannot find one to satisfy him.'

'And the king of England?' she asked.

'I think . . .' The cardinal hesitated and went on, 'I think the king of England has more to think about than his carver.'

Then he sucked his fingers clean, leaned his plump scarlet-clad body towards the regent and whispered something in her ear. And while Christina felt the cold creeping up her legs and the gale strengthened, she heard her aunt say, 'I see.'

There was a moment's silence. The cupbearer replenished the goblets while the regent said, 'I have been given to understand that the king has wearied of that whore.'

The cardinal shook his head regretfully. The company fell silent and listened, and Christina wriggled her toes in their velvet stockings. The regent went on, 'I had the care of her sister once, many years ago now, but she was soon sent away to be brought up at the French court. And this – ' she caught her breath – 'this Anne Boleyn grew up there too, and that is the kind of thing they teach you at that place.'

The cardinal was open-mouthed but the regent held up an imperious hand. 'I know we are at peace with France now, but I am an old lady and must be allowed to voice my opinion, and those Boleyn girls are nothing but scum.'

She turned her face to the cardinal. 'Anyway, the king tired of the eldest. When will he have had enough of whoring with the youngest?'

Christina stopped wriggling her toes. There was that word again that she did not really understand.

The cardinal looked down dejectedly and his reply came so low that Christina could not hear it. The servants started to move about; the roast meat was finished, the dishes carried out and others brought in for the game, and a spicy perfume rose from juniper twigs thrown on the fire. The torches still flickered, throwing a confused glimmer of light and shadow over tapestries and ruddy polished walls. The cardinal was speaking again.

'They are afraid the king will marry her if she becomes pregnant. It is no longer a dream, it is an obsession. The king of England wants a son.'

The regent's voice came mildly. 'But he already has a good and virtuous daughter, and she has reached the age of discretion, too.'

'Only a prince . . .' The cardinal dug into his duck. 'Only a prince can safeguard England's future.'

He stuffed his mouth full, grew aware of the silence and said as clearly as he could with a mouthful of food, 'That is the king of England's opinion, of course.'

While Christina struggled to get the contents of a plate of sauce into her mouth without the liquid running into her sleeves the regent said sharply, 'But Castile could be inherited by a woman, and my blessed mother inherited Burgundy, and moreover . . .'

She smiled and laid her hand on the cardinal's red sleeve. 'Does King Henry not have his mother, Elizabeth of York, to thank for the crown? For when all is said and done, who was this Richmond?'

This last sentence brought all munching jaws to a halt at the ladies' table. The English envoy was sitting only five places away from the regent and had heard every word.

Huge dishes were arriving laden with candied fruits, oranges and peaches sent up from Spain, and bananas, dates and figs from North Africa. But all eyes were trained on the dried-up little Englishman, who calmly went on eating without showing the least reaction to the insult.

'The emperor will give his full support to Princess Mary on the day she ascends the throne of England,' the regent said loudly.

'My lord the king is not in the least doubt about that,' replied the Englishman, dropping his last duck bone into the sauce. He finished his mouthful and stretched out for the fruit.

'And the king of England will be happy to have that support,' essayed the regent.

The Englishman looked in front of him, smiling. 'Your Grace may be sure that my Lord appreciates all the joys life grants to him.'

Total silence. The Englishman swallowed a date, sucked his teeth and proposed a toast to the emperor. The regent suddenly relaxed and smiled broadly, granted the Englishman that honour, and the lively general conversation began again.

During the remainder of the meal Christina sat pondering over all these surprising new things. Much of what had been said was beyond her understanding, but beneath the words she apprehended something sharp, almost hostile, but also thrilling. She felt that the wine had gone to her head and she was tired from sitting so long at table. But above all was this bewilderment, confusion, at entering into the adult world, the grown-ups' words and atmosphere, and she made up her mind that in the morning when she was rested and wide awake she would think over every word she had heard that evening.

Next morning the gale had blown itself out. Early in the day the regent trod on the fragments of a broken crystal goblet and had to take to her bed immediately to stop the bleeding. The court physician examined her. He did not foresee any particular danger but nevertheless a silence fell over the great house. Even Dorothea could find nothing to laugh at.

The next day blood poisoning set in. The regent was bled, but this did not improve her condition and neither did the herbal remedies sent from the French court. For a few days she fought against death, but it was impossible to save her. Father Antonius watched over the sick woman, who wished to bid farewell to all who had served her and were close to her. The children were taken to her in the afternoon, first Hans, then Dorothea and lastly Christina.

Christina found her aunt too weak to lift her head from

37

the pillow. She wore a nightcap over her steel-grey hair, and slowly raising one hand laid it on Christina's head and said, 'My beautiful child . . .

Her voice broke, but she went on with difficulty. 'The emperor will take care of you all. You must obey him always, and . . .

The thick lips went on moving but all that came from them was a faint mumbling. Christina bent down, tears streaming down her cheeks, and kissed the old lady's hand while she whispered, 'Yes, Madame.'

On the same evening, the 30th of November 1530, Margaret of Austria, regent of the Low Countries and Christina's second mother, died.

In the desolation of the moment Christina could only wonder how God found room for all the people he took to himself. But at once the church bells began to toll.

The news spread all round the town and on to the next town and the next, the regent was dead; and couriers were despatched to the wide world. The news travelled from mouth to mouth, from church tower to church tower, and suddenly Christina realised what had happened. Her aunt seemed so little as she lay in the huge bed surrounded by weeping ladies and doctors and Father Antonius waiting to give her divine unction. She had been still alive when Christina kissed her hand. But now Death's merciless sickle had again swung close; once again she had to accept that something had gone for ever.

Christina wanted to hide herself away, safe behind her bed hangings, to be alone, to weep, but the court ladies were waiting. It was time for her, her sister and brother to go to Mass. By keeping to routine their mentors were carrying out their deceased lady's behest not to let the children be idle, for idle hours encourage gloomy thoughts.

Next day Christina went into the library. It was December now and the room was still darker than when she had seen it for the first time five years ago.

Christina stood in the middle of the floor and felt as if she had stepped back into that day. She heard her aunt's voice saying, 'Come,' and again, 'Come along,' curt and authoritative but also filled with all the love her aunt could express only in that way. It was so curt, almost like a signal, something you could understand if you wanted, or merely take literally. She had once had a little child who died. 'Come,' the voice whispered from carved wooden panelling, from leaded panes, from rows of books. 'Come' – all-embracing, but fervent too in its tenderness.

The voice came from everywhere, just one word repeated, a word that held almost five years of boundless love. Christina had not understood it until now. For her aunt merely sat heavily in her chair watching them while they played. Christina felt pain as she realised that they had never sat on her lap, put their arms round her neck and told her how much they loved her. But it had seemed enough for her that they had kissed her hand and that she had sat there watching them, in her heart remembering the voice of a little child who had once been hers.

Christina recalled their first meeting with the greyhound, and the birds. She felt a dog's muzzle against her hand, heard a parrot's squawk and the sounds of animals perhaps acquired solely to give a voice to all their mistress did not express for herself.

But it was past, too late, gone for ever. At only nine years old Christina sensed that she had lost more than her dead aunt, that she was the loser in those hours of tenderness that could never be recaptured.

Why hadn't they made more of her aunt? she wondered, standing in the sombre room, as once, long, long ago they had done, when they hung round a grown-up, hugged him close, felt his beard scratch their cheeks and stroked his neck.

Christina looked up. She gazed at her mother's portrait. In the dim light the white dress looked so real she felt she could touch it. But the human being had gone. The pearl embroidery, the twisted sleeves, the curls around a face, all without life, without strength. Christina could no longer remember her voice, her movements, her skin. She hung there on the wall over the bookcase and was as dead as if she had never been alive. In the twilight Christina's mother changed into a guardian angel or a figure from legend. A white angel, pure and virtuous, far above earthly life.

But Christina had had only one father, and he was real. She remembered the lines in his face, she remembered his beard and his laughter, his voice and step. In that short spell between their first and second mothers he had been there, and no other father could take his place. As he looked down on her that afternoon she thought the melancholy eyes were set in a head filled with foreboding. She had no knowledge of his life and of what made him so sad. He was there, alive in the picture as in reality, wherever he might be.

The bells tolled on and hooves rang on the cobbles outside, but Christina knew only silence. And she was suddenly conscience-stricken at not having remembered the Danish language as he had told them to. She and Hans and Dorothea had forgotten it; it was gone and lost like the memory of their crib, their rattle, their first spring. Christina wanted to call to him: he must come, he must step out of his frame, lift her up onto his horse and take her home to Denmark with him, so the people would rejoice to see their rightful king come back bringing his three children with him.

In her imagination Christina was far away many hundreds of miles to the North – when she heard a sound.

Suddenly she was back in the present, hearing what sounded like a hiss. She glanced to both sides but nothing was there. Then she turned right round.

Kiki was standing over by the door. The last of the daylight fell on her small face and its wrinkles. Her eyes rested on Christina, expectant, appraising. Then her hands took hold of the silk of her skirt and held it out as she curtsied deep. She was nothing but a bundle of silk with a head on top; at last she straightened herself up, with her body twisted as if she were on a stage. 'The king of Denmark has been here in Mechelen begging for money.'

Her words came low and hoarse, each one like a blow. Christina stared at the deformed creature. She could not take in what Kiki said, but had no time to think before the dwarf spoke again. 'He wants four and twenty thousand florins.'

She stopped, waiting for the effect. After a pause, she said, 'He had crawled to the emperor.'

She lowered her voice still more. It became a hoarse, gleeful whisper. 'And crawled to the cardinal.'

Kiki licked her lips with a huge red tongue and began to speak very quickly as if hurrying to get the words out. 'But Her Grace knew that he had also sent a letter to friends of that heretic Luther. And he did not ask to see his children.'

She held her breath tensely and stood there with open mouth. Christina could see her red tongue. She knew she ought to go. In the silence the tolling bells were the only sound. But could her father have been here in the summer without seeing her? Kiki's words resounded in her ears like dull blows. Sudden fury came over her. 'I am the king's daughter. He would never come here and not see me.'

She could say no more; the few words had exhausted her. But the dwarf laughed. It was a crackling sound like rows of icicles breaking and falling to the floor. Quickly she said, 'It was in June. Why would he want to see his children when he had sold them to Her Grace to pay his bills? He owed for the queen's funeral, and to the innkeeper in Lier for . . .' The dwarf nearly doubled up with laughter. 'For Rhenish wine and roast pork.'

The dwarf wriggled about in glee, her foot stamping the floor. Christina saw a wall in front of her. Great cracks opened in it; it swayed and fell on top of her. It should have protected her against all evil, and now she was crushed under its torture. The dwarf stopped her contortions, stamped hard and said, 'The king of Denmark preferred a plain wench called Dyveka to his own queen.'

And she shouted, again curtsying to the ground, 'If they had been Dyveka's children he probably wouldn't have sold them.'

Christina seized a pewter candlestick from the mantelpiece and hurled it at the dwarf. As it struck Kiki's head there was a sound of metal hitting stone. But Kiki merely laughed, making short jerking sounds, even while

41

she still lay crouched on the floor. 'He cut off the Swedes' heads and the Danes knew his word was worth nothing.' She straightened up, stretched her short arms up into the darkness and uttered a long derisive yell. 'For wine and roast pork!'

Christina rushed at her, but Kiki, quick as lightning, as if she had planned her escape in advance, tore out of the library, giving a last hoarse scream as the door slammed behind her.

Christina stopped short a few steps from the door. Suddenly she turned and walked back so soundlessly that she could hear her own breathing. She picked up the candlestick, went closer and closer to him, and stopped.

The candlestick was still in her hand and her father still looked down at her. She pictured him in the inn at Lier, at a table with wine in great goblets and dishes of roast meat.

She shrieked like a wild animal as with all her strength she threw the candlestick at the face that had to be obliterated.

It struck the wall, fell heavily and rolled across the floor. The eyes and the beard and the lined cheeks were still there.

Christina ran to pick up the candlestick and throw it again when a sound intervened. Something in her memory, the sound of metal and porcelain striking another stone floor in another house, long, long ago.

She let her arm drop slowly and stood there. After a long time she put the candlestick back in its place.

Then she pressed her hands against her temples as if to squeeze all the pain and all the evil words from her consciousness. She swayed to and fro, shaken by feelings she had never known before.

Suddenly all that too, had passed. Christina heard the bells again and distant noise from the street. She stood there tired and drained. Slowly she looked up at her white mother and her sombre father. It was all over. They were both dead.

In March 1531 the emperor Charles the Fifth rode into Mechelen with his enormous train. He was greeted by crowds of people standing along the streets and leaning out of windows. Before the council hall he was received by the town council, and by a boy of twelve with curly brown hair and bright eyes.

The boy was Prince Hans of Denmark. Standing in front of his two smaller sisters he described in simple terms and impeccable Latin the sorrow that had befallen them, and begged that they be allowed to stay on at the Netherlands court until his father had regained his kingdoms.

The emperor was deeply moved. He embraced his nephew and nieces and straightway promised them that they could remain in the Low Countries. It was not a hasty decision. In all his life he had never made up his mind in a hurry. It was some time since the emperor had chosen the person who should take charge of the Danish children and the Low Countries' problems.

In her last years his aunt, despite her great abilities, had been fatigued, and the country he was revisiting now was markedly unwilling to pay taxes and increasingly influenced by heresy. It was also time finally to rid himself of that troublesome uninvited guest the king of Denmark, who was harrying the northern provinces with freebooters and piracy. By the time he was ready to undertake his current travels through his mighty empire the person who could undertake the task better than anyone else was already waiting to begin, and she was with him on his arrival in Mechelen. She was his younger sister, Marie.

The emperor had admired Marie from childhood and with the passage of time she had become the only person for whom he felt the same respect in which he'd held his now dead aunt. The lessons that had been so hard for him to understand and learn had been assimilated with ease by Marie.

Marie was the widow of the king of Hungary. It would be her task to rule the Low Countries while he dealt with the Turks, the French, the papacy and the German heretics. It was thus as their future ruler that Charles the Fifth presented his sister to the city councillors of Mechelen.

But Marie had had her hesitations, and had made conditions. She demanded that she should not have a new husband forced upon her, for, as she expressed it, 'she had been so completely happy in her first marriage that she did not wish to try another'. Whatever she may have meant by this, the emperor bowed to her wish.

The next problem was what Marie called her 'Lutheran tendencies'. However, the emperor found it hard to take these seriously. His sister had always been addicted to reading and attracted by new ideas. But studying Erasmus and other humanists would not hinder her in carrying out her task as regent.

Seeing her there against the background of tapestries in the great council chamber, a small, brisk, childless woman in her black widow's weeds and white veil, the emperor was proud of his sister. He was less satisfied when his thoughts moved to the king of Denmark.

King Christian was a burden. His demands for money, and dowry for a wife long since dead, were a constant irritation. Marie thought it would be better to pay him off and get rid of him once and for all. The emperor wished him dead, indeed considered him as such. But at the same time he could not allow the nobility unconcernedly to renounce their oath, throw out their king, then set another man on the throne. That kind of treachery could have serious consequences for other rulers, and could not be suffered.

The longer the emperor cogitated the more clearly did the twelve-year-old prince seem the solution to the Scandinavian problem. Had not the great Danish nobles at one time expressed a wish for the boy and his mother to remain in Denmark? Elizabeth was dead; but the prince, the heir and rightful future ruler of the kingdoms of the North, was alive, and had been brought up in the true faith. Perhaps they still wanted him in Denmark. Moreover the prince was his, the emperor's, nephew.

The emperor stroked his chin as he regarded the straight-backed boy. He was moved to a feeling of warmth at the sight of the boy and his sisters Dorothea and Christina. As an emperor too, he sensed that a prince who at only twelve years old had mastered Latin fluently would also be capable of solving more difficult problems.

The emperor stroked his chin again and returned to the difficult art of thinking.

Christina had lost her beloved aunt. But now she had a new one. The dead aunt had been sister to her maternal grand-father, and the new one was her mother's sister. But on the very first day Christina and her brother and sister discovered that she was quite another sort of aunt.

She was slim and young where the first one had seemed old and solicitous. She did not take them to look at portraits but asked them, 'Do you want to come hunting?' And she rushed out as fast as she could to join the horses and the court waiting in the courtyard.

When Her Grace the queen dowager of Hungary, now the regent of the Low Countries, hunted red deer, wild boar or wolves, no one could keep up with her. She could spend a whole day in the saddle without the least sign of fatigue, and she loved to make her lords and ladies go searching for her in the depths of forest thickets or in villages. They gradually grew used to the distant sight of Her Grace's black robes fluttering around her horse, and knew she would always be first at the kill, and home before anyone else. When they returned, breathless and exhausted after a day in the saddle, they told each other it must be inherited from life on the vast plains of Hungary. True or not, none of them could keep up with Her Grace on horseback. The children found they had an aunt so young she might well have been their elder sister. She jumped ditches, spurred her horse across canals and streaked across the sodden fields at a wild gallop. Nothing was fast enough, nothing could stop her; there was game in abundance. The widow of Hungary had arrived.

It was a tremendous experience, meanwhile, for the children to meet the emperor. They had known about him for as long as they could remember, and it was an incredible honour when he put his arm around them and told them he loved them. Naturally he had paid most attention to Hans. Christina and Dorothea were proud of their brother, and the fact that he could make a speech without faltering. They

45

wished they could do the same – could stand outside a council hall, unconcerned about crowds, councillors and nobles and clerics, and express their wishes freely and frankly in Latin.

They saw little of the emperor during his visit. But their new aunt plunged them into a life of youthful excitement. When her ladies complained that the queen lived dangerously she laughed merrily and danced lightly away. 'I will never be accused of not enjoying every hour on this earth.' Then she would send for Monseigneur, and Mesdames Dorothée and Chrétienne. Herds of wild boar had been sighted in the nearby forest.

In other ways everyday life went on as before. They were surrounded by the same faces – but now Johanna would bemoan the state of the girls' clothes, torn in the violence of the chase.

Kiki alone had gone. She vanished without trace the night following the death of the old regent. Nobody heard anything further about her, and soon everyone except Christina had forgotten her.

Christina had tried to wipe out the memory of what had happened that late afternoon, when the bells had been tolling throughout the Low Countries. She had sought to deceive herself as to the meaning of the dwarf's words. But their import and their reality could not be erased from her mind. Christina never told her brother and sister about what had happened. It was her knowledge and her burden alone. And all the while the feeling grew in her of having been robbed, her roots unjustly severed.

V

On a frosty January day in 1532 a tournament was in progress in front of the Portuguese envoy's house in Brussels. The queen of Portugal had been delivered of a son and celebrations were in progress.

The emperor and his family were watching the spectacle from a balcony decked with green and white velvet. Christina laughed as knights in armour were thrown from their horses, and she stared in wonderment at fire-eaters and sword dancers, while all around her the crowds clapped delightedly. Everywhere the great square was adorned with flags and banners. As the trumpets were sounding to announce the next item Hans leaned towards her and whispered, 'I have just heard that . . .'

He glanced at his aunt and again turned his face to Christina. 'Our father landed in Norway a month ago. The Norwegians acclaimed him. They have renewed their oath to him as their king.'

Bears came in. Christina looked straight ahead of her and Hans said, 'It's true. Father has already reconquered one of his kingdoms, and they have taken an oath of fealty to me up there.'

Christina retained her interested gaze. She was too big to forget who she was and that she had a duty to be seen. She was the emperor's and regent's niece.

But only that. Since that day in the library over a year ago she had sought to ignore the part of herself that had its origin in a man who broke faith for money's sake. Who ravaged and plundered, begged, lied, and chopped the heads off Swedish nobles, and who preferred a common wench and sold his own children. She had snuggled under her Hapsburg family as if beneath warm blankets to keep out the northern chill and had tried to forget she was 'of Denmark'. Hans would win back the realms, and put the crowns of Scandinavia on his own head. To Christina Hans was already king of Denmark. She smiled admiringly at him but said nothing.

In the evening a banquet was held at the castle. The emperor sat midway down the table with the regent on one side of him and Dorothea, the eldest niece, on the other. Hans was seated between the regent and Christina, who had the Portuguese envoy on her left. In front of Christina were the other tables and the light and warmth of the fireplace. Her table was the highest; even Prince René of Orange, who had just inherited his uncle's country, had to eat with the ladies, and he was three years older than she was.

Christina was enjoying making the Portuguese laugh. She felt warmed, not by the wine or the fire but by the sensation of being popular. With a certain measure of defiance she wished her father could see her at the high table. Perhaps then he would understand what it was he had cast aside. But she must not forget herself, for all eyes were resting on those of her own distinguished rank. Christina took a cautious sip of her Rhenish wine, met a smile from fair-haired René and continued her conversation with the Portuguese.

The banquet ended at eleven o'clock. An Italian comedy followed and later there was a buffet with wine from Madeira and Valencia and sweetmeats served in dishes and bowls of silver, gold and porcelain.

The festivities for the birth of the Portuguese prince lasted a whole week. Dances and concerts, dinners and perform-ances filled the hours and banished Christina's gloomy thoughts.

The court had now moved to Brussels, and it was there that one day Christina and Dorothea met a new relative of their own age. Her name was Margaret. The sisters had already heard that she was their cousin, and no less than the emperor's daughter. They were naturally eager to meet a relation they had never heard of before. But they did not know quite what to think when they saw her. She was a plodding, heavily-built girl whose big feet were easily visible under her skirts.

'I am the emperor's daughter, Margaret,' were the first words she said. But then she had seemed unable to say more. She remained standing before them as if waiting for them to do something. But Dorothea merely broke into one of her wicked giggles and asked, 'Why are you wearing so many pearls? Are you going to sit for a painting?'

'I have been painted,' the girl answered solemnly.

'Really?' said Dorothea. She bit her lip with her pointed teeth and looked her cousin up and down as if counting the precious stones and other adornments.

But Christina controlled herself, partly because her nature differed from her sister's laughter-prone temperament, and partly because of her deep respect for the emperor, and her dependence on him, and all that belonged to him, rooted in her knowledge of their family which Dorothea did not possess. Christina saw her cousin's overdressed appearance, in a brocade dress in the middle of the morning, with pearls and golden chains, and diamonds in her hair instead of a decent cap. But there was something behind all this that she knew she did not understand. Full of her budding feeling for her fellow beings and her wish to appraise their desires, she leaned forward and asked, 'Would you like to go for a ride?'

At last Margaret smiled. As her face lit up, she nodded and her strange air of uncertainty disappeared. Christina gave orders for the horses to be saddled.

When the sisters were alone again Christina could restrain her curiosity no longer. Especially when Dorothea, hands in the air, reminded her that the emperor was still unmarried when their own mother had died. So how could he have a daughter who was as old as they were? First you were married, and then you had children as a gift from God. If, that is, God willed it and did not cheat as he had cheated their aunt Marie.

49

'But how could the emperor have had a daughter when he wasn't married to anybody at that time?'

Christina looked at her sister framed in the damask bed-hangings as she pondered the problem. She lay down across the bed and looked up at its ceiling. Suddenly a thought struck her. 'She is Margaret. But not Margaret of anything at all.'

'Something must be wrong somewhere,' said Dorothea. 'We'll ask Johanna.'

Johanna was reluctant to talk about it. She twisted her fingers in her apron as was her habit when she felt herself off guard; but Dorothea would not let her off.

'How can the emperor have a daughter when he wasn't married when she was born?' she asked persistently.

'It was a misfortune.' The words slipped out before Johanna could stop them. She hid her face in her hands as if she had said something sinful.

'We won't tell anyone. Go on, do,' begged Christina.

But Johanna still stood in the middle of the room with her hands covering her face. She shook her head and kept silent.

'She certainly looks like a misfortune,' came artfully from Dorothea with her arm round the bed-post.

'That's true enough. Margaret is one great big misfortune.'

'Madame,' said Johanna reprovingly.

'Margaret of what?' asked Christina mildly, feeling she must help her sister to get to the bottom of the mysterious matter.

But they got no further with Johanna. Soon, though, they remembered the business of whoring. Despite the fact that they did not know what the word meant, it was clearly something wrong and forbidden and what the king of England did with a certain Anne Boleyn. And most important of all: it was something that could get you with child.

The children thought and thought; but Johanna would not answer, and they could not think of anyone else they dared ask. The strange fact remained that the emperor had a daughter who was not the daughter of the empress, and they had the feeling that just as God took, while people could take too, so God gave, while people could obviously bring about situations that were not entirely intentional.

A fortnight later the emperor left for Regensburg, taking Prince Hans with him. It was no secret that the great man took pleasure in his nephew's company, and made time to talk to the boy.

The news that Hans was taking part in the electors' meeting came at the same time as another, more down-to-earth event.

Christina and Dorothea had new stockings. The sisters were surprised at first, for they were not sewn together but knitted. They soon discovered how much more comfortable they were without all the seams, especially the one under the heel that always rubbed. The new stockings clung to their legs without folds or wrinkles, and they were just as warm as the old ones made of silk, velvet or leather.

They were sitting with their legs stretched out, examining this latest invention, when their aunt came in. They quickly threw their skirts over their legs, leaped up and curtsied. She stood smiling at them and sent Johanna out. She had news of Hans.

After the long journey to Regensburg he had been busy receiving visiting electors, the bishop of Mainz and other notabilities from the German kingdom. Later he had pleaded his own and Denmark's cause before the great assembly at the imperial council, putting himself so handsomely that everyone present was impressed and all the electors had had tears in their eyes. It made a great impression on the girls, too, to hear how Hans had already made a mark for himself in the great world.

Late one night at the end of August at the palace in Brussels, Christina heard someone riding into the courtyard.

Filled with foreboding she sat up, listened and jumped out of bed. The two waiting-women sprang up from their chairs but Christina waved them back and opened the window on to the courtyard and the warm summer night. She saw the horse and the crowned double eagles on the saddle bag. It was the emperor's courier.

Back in bed she fell into a restless sleep filled with wild

dreams. She was out hunting elk with her father, in Sweden. But it was red everywhere. The earth was saturated with blood. The tree roots sucked it up and it stained the forest as red as the earth beneath. Her father stopped, leaped from his saddle and took bags of gold coins held out by little grey men with no heads. He pushed Christina towards the men as payment. She stared at their scarlet necks still pulsing with blood from severed arteries, and saw that in front of her they were already making off with Hans. He was being led towards a clearing where several headless men were standing with great axes at the ready; and she screamed and screamed and screamed . . .

Christina looked up into Johanna's ruddy face. By the door the woman stood terrified. She was given hot milk with herbs. After a while she fell into a peaceful sleep.

Next morning Christina and Dorothea were called to the regent. They saw their aunt standing by a window. She came to meet them, embraced them, while tears ran down her face into the black folds of her robe. Their brother Hans had caught a fever during the worst storm Regensburg could remember. After several days of battling against the disease his young body had given in, and he died with Jesu's name on his lips.

Hans was no more.

Christina prayed to God. Kneeling on the stone flags she begged the heavenly Father to explain to her why He took so many and so much.

After some time she was put to bed with a high fever. There she lay, wishing only to be taken where God kept her blessed mother and her beloved brother and aunt.

But on the fourth day she woke without fever. Cool autumn air blew in on her from open windows; there was the scent of fresh fruit, and she saw faces around her with tears of joy in their eyes.

Johanna threw her arms about her and stammered, 'Blessed be our Lady for my little Madame Chrétienne.'

She could say no more but ran out of the room, her apron to her eyes.

Christina lay in bed looking around her at the damask ceiling and bed curtains while the cooling air filled her nostrils and lungs and she was filled with a vehement desire to live her life as long as God willed.

Not until long after Christmas, when the new year had come and they were writing '1533', did the regent quietly tell Christina and Dorothea about their father's fate the previous summer. He had left Norway and sailed to Copenhagen trusting in his uncle's promise of safe-conduct. But it was broken, and he never set foot in the capital city. Instead, he was taken to prison, on an island called Als.

It had done nothing to change Christina's life; but it took hold of her imagination all the same. The faithful Norwegians up there in that long white country, and the townspeople and peasantry of Denmark. *They* had wanted her father restored, too. What was the truth? What were the real facts?

The regent's news nagged and worried at her. She wished she'd never heard it.

With the arrival of summer a bombshell of news exploded at the Netherlands court. At a ceremony in Barcelona on the 10th of June the emperor had signed a contract of marriage between his niece and Francesco Sforza, Duke of Milan. Christina, at eleven and a half years old, was to be married.

Count Massimiliano Stampa bent down to kiss Princess Christina's hand and began a conversation with her and her sister Princess Dorothea. But after five minutes the regent explained that the audience was at an end.

Stampa was annoyed, but the same evening he wrote a letter to the Duke of Milan giving his first impressions of the future duchess.

Like most of those at the Milanese court who were concerned with the marriage, Stampa regretted that it had not been possible to contract the elder sister. Now that the brother was dead it was she who had an hereditary claim to the Nordic kingdoms. But after his brief meeting with the royal princesses Stampa was pleased to inform his lord that the younger was far the better looking. She had also given the impression of being both lively and amenable.

Stampa had travelled from northern Italy to Ghent, where the court was staying at that time. After a journey of several weeks he had reached the Low Countries in the middle of September.

He had ridden through the flat countryside with growing astonishment. All of it was cultivated and in use. Fields abounded with crops; everywhere there were black and white cattle, and the houses and streets were clean. He had never seen such a fertile landscape. Most surprising of all, every woman and every man, high or low, could both read and write. Stampa had hastened hundreds of miles, with the object of reaching his destination as fast as possible. But from the moment he crossed the border he slackened the pace of his horse to a walk or a trot so that he could absorb his unexpected impressions to the full.

The harvest was finished, and well-fed peasantry were swarming in the fields ploughing and harrowing with newly painted implements, or, in many places, were sowing winter grain, while women accompanied by flocks of children brought them ale in pitchers.

Stampa knew the Low Countries were governed by a woman. Perhaps it was fanciful but it seemed as if everything here was guided by a thrifty, clean and orderly housewife's hand.

It could of course be the reverse, he philosophised, as his gaze roamed over mills and canals. Perhaps it was that the country and its inhabitants were of such a nature that they were suited to a lady's leadership.

In the inns he heard continual complaints about taxes and the wars against the French. But the peasant children he saw were well-nourished and he thought all too readily of the ragged skinny youngsters in the north Italian villages. In the Low Countries he saw hardship and black bread only in the back streets of the towns. Otherwise, all was prosperous, healthy and clean. On the other hand, Stampa had never seen such coarse and unattractive women, and their skirts were often indecently short.

However, it was not his commission to write reports on the Netherlands provinces. He was to fetch a bride, and accordingly the first thing he sought was an audience with the regent.

On his arrival in Ghent he was kept waiting for some time before finally being allotted those five minutes with the Lady Christina.

Rumours were circulating of a letter the regent had sent the emperor, protesting against so young a girl being given in marriage; and Stampa had to admit that the bride seemed younger for her age than her contemporaries in Milan. The strong sun of the South brought early maturity, but Princess Christina was a child of the North and had grown up in the hazy light of the Low Countries. Even in that short meeting Stampa had noticed at once that the breast above her bodice was still flat and the slightly lisping voice was that of a child.

The sight of the young princess caused him serious anxiety. Stampa was a Milanese and a patriot. His lord was the grandson of a man who had made himself duke through force of arms. There had once been a golden age when Italian princes rode with a train of thousands. But the turn of the century had brought warfare; and the present duke had grown up in exile until the emperor in his mercy had given him leave to return to his own land.

It was Stampa's lifelong aim to secure his country's independence; but that could only happen through an heir. The emperor had bestowed on the duke a bride of the noblest lineage. But he had imposed the condition that if the duke died childless the country would revert to himself. The duke was a sick man and the Lady Christina years away from childbearing age. It would be a race against time.

The contract expressly stated that the marriage must be consummated immediately; but Stampa realised that the clause was inserted purely for the purpose of preventing the French from contesting the validity of the marriage and thus the agreement as a whole. They must be excluded in order to introduce the Hapsburgs. A mere five minutes in the company of Christina of Denmark put Stampa clearly in the picture of the emperor's wily game.

Stampa had his orders: as the duke's deputy he was to marry the princess by proxy and take her to her rightful husband. But the regent produced new excuses not to speak to him. First a minor injury after falling from a horse; then council meetings and urgent business; and then without warning she left for Lille, taking her two nieces with her. Stampa followed her. In Milan the duke awaited his bride and the people the heir who was to preserve the dukedom's independence and save them from foreign rule. Despite Stampa's doubts of the ageing, almost crippled duke's capacity of carrying on the Sforza line, he intended to carry through his errand.

One day the imperial envoy, de Praet, arrived. Perhaps the emperor had sensed his sister's reluctance to allow the marriage contract to go through, for de Praet brought orders that he should be present at the ceremony.

Her Grace now became very obliging. She uttered effusive thanks for the horse sent by the duke as a gift; she arranged a supper party for Stampa; and she let him watch the two princesses dancing a *balla all'italiano* on their own.

The wedding took place on the afternoon of Sunday the 28th of September 1533. The dignified procession moved into the chapel of the castle in Lille. The bride was accompanied by the regent while Stampa, representing the duke, waited at the altar, clad in golden brocade. Violins and trumpets were playing, as the bishop of Tournai conducted the ceremony of marriage between Christina of Denmark and the duke of Milan in the person of another man; and Stampa thought he saw great joy in the bride's face as the bishop put the ring with its beautiful ruby on her finger.

After the festivities Stampa had a cordial conversation with the regent. She was gracious and jovial but no matter how he tried he could not get her to fix a firm date for departure. The regent's brown eyes regarded him archly, and she assumed an anxious expression, as she asked him to understand that she could not possibly send her beloved niece on such a dangerous journey at that time of year. Instead she invited him to go hunting next morning.

Count Stampa excused himself. He was obliged to return

home, and could only admit that Her Grace was the victor in this battle. In Milan the cannon would thunder, the church bells would ring and the people would rejoice that the wedding had taken place. But the bride did not come. Christina of Denmark remained with her aunt, who did not want to see her niece in the marriage bed until she was twelve years of age.

Even though Christina's departure had been postponed there were great preparations. Silks, damask and brocades, furs and pearls and jewels must be selected. She must have furnishings for her table and her chapel. Christina was the child of a man who had once ruled and who now rotted in a wretched prison, but the regent equipped her as a daughter of the house of Hapsburg. There must be livery for lackeys; escorts and waiting gentlemen were needed; and ladies and chambermaids must be appointed. All Christina's marriage expenses were to be met by the emperor, while she and her as yet unmarried sister went on happily living with their aunt.

Christina's twelfth birthday came and went. But as long as the winter lasted there could be no question of leaving. Instead she still shared the life of the castle, only with the rights now of a married lady. Once more she was able to laugh at the Shrovetide games, when cats and geese were tilted in barrels in the square, and to admire her sister's skills as an archer at the guild festivities.

Christina knew that marriage was the high point in a woman's life. She had a husband she had never seen. Now and again she had the feeling that the regent wished to talk to her about something. She noticed the usually merry eyes gazing at her, but thought no more of it. Besides, there was velvet to be measured up for her and her ladies' litters, along with countless other preparations.

One February day Christina was out riding with her aunt. The wide sky of Brabant was grey with winter clouds. There was no wind, and the windmills stood idle, while smoke rose straight up from cottages and farms. Snow still lay in exposed places and only a few cattle were outside.

They soon outpaced the rest of the court. The regent jumped her horse over a fence and Christina followed. It began to rain. Soon it was pouring, but the regent rode on, until she suddenly stopped in the middle of a field and burst out laughing.

Water ran down from her hat and rain cape; the bands of her headdress were crumpled, and her mare was slick with damp. She said, 'The others run for shelter. I prefer life.'

The storm increased and the sharp raindrops struck her cheeks as she turned her face to heaven to accept its fury. 'I have good news from Milan. You have married an honourable man, who wishes only for your happiness. But . . .'

She lowered her head for a moment and Christina felt she was about to hear something she already knew. Her aunt looked at her through the rain. Water dripped from her long nose. 'You must not worry if you don't have children straight away. God has not forgotten you; they will come.'

She patted her horse reassuringly three times. 'And you must not let the duke's poor health frighten you.'

She explained, smilingly: 'He is partly paralysed and can hardly walk unaided. But if you are a good, loving and obedient wife, which I am sure you will be, he will most probably regain his strength.'

Her aunt sent her a testing look but Christina was not frightened by what she had heard. She loved her husband as she knew she ought to, and naturally he too loved her, his wife.

As she turned her horse her aunt said casually, 'I seem to think there was something else I should have said. But never mind.'

She kicked her horse into a gallop. They jumped a narrow ditch, passed two canals and arrived home soaking wet.

Christina had felt nothing strange in this conversation; although she realised it must have been important, otherwise they would have gone on riding all day until darkness fell. She knew her aunt well by now. It took more than a downpour to make her turn back.

Later, as Christina sat in the big tub having her back scrubbed by Johanna, who knew how to wield a brush so you glowed, she thought over what it might have been that her aunt should have said, and why she seemed so merry when she talked about the duke's paralysis. But then the warmth and steam made her yawn with well being and she forgot all about it.

Christina set off for Milan on the 11th of March 1534. Only a day or two before had it really dawned on her what was about to happen. She had to leave her childhood home. She knew that the world awaiting her was utterly different. It was more beautiful, many said; but, for her, beauty was bound up with those things she had known for as long as she could remember. At that moment beauty was the great vault of the sky above Brussels, or the Shrovetide games in Brussels or Ghent. It was her happy years in Mechelen with the greyhound and the parrot and her sister, with her dead brother and aunt.

In farewell, Christina went running all about the castle in Brussels. She embraced Johanna; and she clasped her sister and her aunt almost feverishly, as if she could grab hold of them to take them with her to her new life.

But the bonds had to be broken, and on the day appointed, she duly climbed into her litter. After her came Madame de Souvastre, the head of her household, with six ladies-in-waiting, six chambermaids, four pages, ten gentlemen, six lackeys, twenty mules and three baggage wagons. Lastly there rode her escort of a hundred and thirty mounted horsemen. Her eyes filled with tears. But even as they did so she took in the richness of the velvet coverings. All this was in her honour.

For a brief moment her thoughts rested on her father. If he could see her now! But again she pushed her recollection of him away. She was a married lady, the duchess of Milan.

The great cortège began to move. Dorothea wept despairingly. Christina waved and waved to her family. The journey to Milan was under way.

Milan, 1534–1537

VI

Summer came early to northern Italy, but the air was still cool this May morning. It was scented with roses and myrtles. The shadows were long; there were rows of trees in tubs; and a steady murmur and plashing came from the fountains and waterfalls in the gardens of the Villa de Cussago. Christina stretched up her arm for the delight of picking a lemon from its branch. She ran on and picked another, thrilled with the magic of seeing them among the leaves instead of borne on a dish almost like something man-made.

Christina and her retinue were making their last stay here before their entry into Milan. Count Stampa had placed his property at her disposal, and this garden was one of the loveliest places she had seen.

She had already been charmed by the colourful splendour of the region; by its houses, gardens and landscape. One day, after almost two months of travelling through the spring rain along muddy roads, through snowstorms and over alpine passes, she first saw the beautiful green sunny kingdom for which they were destined. The valley of the Po lay at her feet, and their descent from the Alps began.

Christina knew that everything was being done to honour and please her. Everything revolved round her, whose smallest wish must be fulfilled. Everywhere she smiled back at people, in the street, on balconies and roofs, and enjoyed the feeling of knowing that in return she was able to brighten her surroundings with her smiles.

On this May morning, as Christina reached out for yet another golden fruit, held it to her face and breathed in its fragrance, she saw over her fingertips a distant dustcloud.

Horsemen were approaching, chance wayfarers perhaps. Or another distinguished Italian with his train, who wished to pay his respects before, in two days' time, she rode into the capital to meet her duke and bridegroom.

Her ladies wanted to pass the time in a game of croquet but Christina preferred to stroll in the gardens while it was still cool. She touched the leaves, breathed strange spicy scents, and picked a rosemary twig and tucked it in her waistband. It meant luck. It was good to have such a token when you were a young newly married lady going to meet the husband you knew you loved.

All around her were clipped trees and bushes in geometric forms or as fantastic figures or animal heads. There were mazes, too, and secret paths. Christina and her Netherlandish ladies ran about the gardens laughing. Leaving them behind, she found herself alone, and paused by a fountain. She bent down to see her reflection in the water. Her hair, which hung loose, fell forward. Laughing at herself, she straightened up to roam on.

Suddenly she noticed the heat. It was as if the sun rose higher in the sky with a great jerk and at the same time she heard a sound, like a rhythmical thumping or knocking.

Christina turned and looked around her but there was no one and nothing to be seen. Even the little birds seemed further away and silent. The air was hot and dry; the shadows were short and black now; and the sound steadily came nearer the fountain.

She gave a start when she saw the old man. He had to plant his crutch heavily on the paving stones to be able to move, and his hair and beard were grey. Alone, he approached her from under an arch of greenery. There was no one to present him; but his dress was distinguished, and it was clearly with a purpose that he limped out of the shadows of the maze and into the sunshine in front of her.

Christina was at a loss. Still clasping the lemons, she held them instinctively to her bodice. She must do something, but where were her ladies? The man came nearer. He had a big hooked nose, his skin was grey, and each thud of the crutch brought a twinge of pain to the left side of his face.

First the dull thud, then the twinge; thud, twinge, again and again.

The man stopped in front of her and looked into her face but did not bow. Did he not know who she was?

Christina stiffened. How dared he? She would tell Count Stampa. There would have to be punishment for this. All must bow to her. All except one. Only the duke ...

The lemons rolled along the ground, like golden balls, as she dropped them. In one horrified second she clapped her hands to her mouth. Then, controlling herself, she slowly lowered her arms and stretched out her right hand.

Christina looked into old, tired eyes. She felt cold fingers grasp her hand and lips like cracked leather against her skin. Voices came from around her, her ladies appeared and curt-sied to the ground. Christina stood facing Francesco Sforza, the duke of Milan. She had met her bridegroom.

The duke stayed only half an hour in Cussago in the com-pany of his bride. With his left hand resting on his crutch he stretched out his right to Christina, and accompanied by the ladies and Count Stampa the couple walked round the gardens.

The duke told Christina that Beatrice d'Este, his long-dead mother, used to come out here from Milan to hunt the plentiful game of the region. A deep violet-coloured climb-ing plant covered a wall. The duke let go Christina's hand, stretched out to break off a twig and held it up to her. 'A remarkable plant,' he said. 'It is the leaves that give it such splendid colour; the flower itself is but small and insignifi-cant ...'

He twisted it in his fingers so Christina could see it on all sides and continued, 'We must seek for the flower. It is the plant's soul.'

After a few steps further the duke stopped again and turned to Christina. She had the sun in her eyes, and was dazzled, so that she could hardly see as he expressed his joy and gratitude to the emperor for sending so distinguished a princess and so beautiful a bride. Christina must answer, not just stand dazzled and silent. The ladies around her were

65

waiting, and Count Stampa, and the duke. But the light made everything white, and she could hear nothing, as if the water of the fountains had frozen and all the birds were dead.

She sensed a movement in front of her. Something touched her cheek. It was his fingers, and then the whole hand; dry rough skin against hers. It felt like a cold insect. She took a step backwards and turned away with a cry. Just one word. 'Father. . .'

In an instant she came back to herself. She had no father. Why ever had she called to him? He was as good as dead and she was alone in the heat in a strange land, wife to an old sick man, and she had forgotten herself.

Christina turned slowly to the duke. She tried in vain to look into his eyes and see what they expressed. He bent down for a silent, formal leave-taking. Then he limped slowly and with difficulty towards the villa.

Later that afternoon Count Stampa requested an audience.

Christina received him on the terrace. He conveyed greetings from the duke, who had bade him tell her of the sincere devotion he felt for his young bride.

In answer Christina said that on her part she too felt the warmest affection for His Grace. She wanted to say more but came to a halt. She looked at the man she had married as representative of the duke. Once they had laughed at him, she and Dorothea; the correct Italian who always bowed a little too deeply, so that it looked as if he would lose his balance. He had waited for her at the altar, more than half a year ago, and she had been glad she did not have to marry such a tedious man. Down in Milan her real bridegroom awaited her, he to whom she was given in marriage; and marriage meant that God gave you a friend who would be the best one of all in your life.

Now Christina looked at Count Stampa, at his strong legs beneath the tunic, at his hair and beard that were still black, at his straight back and his skin golden from sun and wind and health, and listened while he told her about the duke's misfortune.

It had happened long ago. A madman had attacked the duke in the street and stabbed him with a poisoned knife. The citizens assembled to pray for his life in all the churches of Milan, and God heard their prayers. The duke's hair turned grey and his legs were partially paralysed, but his subjects venerated and loved their duke more than ever for his magnanimity and justice.

Therefore . . .

Stampa looked at her thoughtfully and said, 'That is why at this moment the people of Milan are erecting triumphal arches for the duke's young bride; why every man, woman and child is waiting to pay homage to their noble, beauteous princess. We are poor, we have been plundered, we know hunger. But nothing will be spared to please and honour Your Grace; for only thus can we honour and please the duke himself.'

When Count Stampa bent to take his farewell of her she saw nothing comical in his movement. She remained sitting there with the memory of the oath she had taken – to be a good and obedient wife. That was what the emperor expected of her, and her aunt, and her dead aunt, her dead mother, all those in the paintings in the twilit library in Mechelen. All who had gone before her and all who were living in her time.

Christina ordered her ladies to leave her in solitude. She sat on the terrace until the cool air of evening fell over the beautiful gardens of Cussago, and the mazes, the clipped shrubs and the citrus trees in great tubs again threw their long shadows.

When at last Christina rose she was a child no longer. With a single step she had entered the blurred borderland separating her from the world of adults.

Fireworks were exploding over Milan. Rockets burst with such brightness that they lit up not only the houses but the circle of ramparts outside the city wall. High up in the palace the spectators could see fireballs sending their white rain of stars down over the people. More rockets shot into the air, and made the night as noisy and festive as the day had been.

Christina was dazed, confused and exhausted by all that she had experienced. Everything had been multi-coloured: the houses, painted red, yellow and orange; crowds of lavishly dressed people, with the nobility clad in gold and silver; waving plumes, standards and banners. She had glimpsed great banners inscribed with the words, 'Today the wisest of princes weds the most beautiful of maidens and brings us the promise of lasting peace.'

Everything had been heavy with heat and blurred with the dust thrown up by the horses' hooves. She had cheerfully acknowledged the gaze of thousands, and smiled at children with dark eyes and women with painted faces and bleached yellow hair. She had inhaled the smells of dirt, garlic and damp plaster while chiming church bells and cannon's thunder blended with the crowd's shouts of 'Viva, viva . . .'

Christina was not a spectator on this day. She was at the centre of the stage, with all the world looking on, as a gilded canopy carried by professors of the university had shielded her from the sun. At the evening banquet, too, every eye was turned towards her.

A napkin folded into a crown was included in every place setting. As Christina put out her hand for hers, it seemed to move; and when she pulled the ends of the white damask, out flew a little live songbird. She shrieked with joy; and at once, to the delight of the guests, there came the rustle of hundreds of other small birds winging upwards. Circling about the ceiling, they made their way to freedom through the open doors and windows.

Wine from Tuscany was poured into glasses bearing the Sforza coat of arms in coloured enamel. Christina tasted fruits she had never heard of before. She was served with gilded peacock, and with trout glazed with silver and decorated with slices of a red vegetable from the new world, called tomato, which was now being cultivated in southern Italy.

In the chief place of honour at Christina's side sat the duke of Milan. He had received her outside the palace, where she had been given the keys of the city while still on horseback. When she dismounted, the crowd had surged forward and seized hold of the canopy, tearing it to pieces to keep the fragments as a memento of the day they received their duchess.

Serene and calm, she gave her hand to her elderly spouse and was led into the enormous castle. He took her through halls and state apartments. She heard kindliness in his voice as he presented the leading members of the court to her; and afterwards she noticed his smile when she showed her wonderment over the strange dishes and gasped with delight at each soaring rocket. When the last white rain of stars faded in the sky he led her again towards the most distinguished ladies and gentlemen of the court. They were waiting to escort the couple to the bridal chamber, where they would be undressed and laid in the marriage bed.

Fear suddenly returned. Christina knew marriage meant the sharing of bed and board, but she had never been alone with a man. There had always been ladies, servant girls, governesses around her. But there was no more time to think; for the duke was saying something in Italian which caused the court to exchange glances and the cardinal to utter a protest.

'But the French ...' came the churchman's querulous voice. His red silk rustled as he stepped towards his prince.

'The French?' he repeated. The duke stopped him with an imperious gesture.

Christina understood nothing of what was happening. She only knew a few words of Italian, so that she could get the meaning of 'Franchese'; also from the duke's reply it seemed he was saying something about a child. The cardinal wanted one thing, the duke another. Then the duke turned to her, drew her hand to his lips and wished her a blessed night.

Christina was taken to the bridal chamber. Chambermaids were waiting to unfasten her ribbons, brush her hair and bring bowls of water. She was exhausted, and longed to cry; but there was no one to weep with. From the town there rose shouting, noise, music and song. The girls curtsied to the floor and the ladies closed the bed curtains.

Christina went to sleep on her first night in Milan. She was alone. And all the while the town celebrated her arrival.

VII

Christina tried to concentrate on the letter she was writing. But the heat was enervating and constant chatter and noise rose from the servants and soldiers in the courtyard. Her ladies were sitting on their stools stiff and awkward in a strange new fashion that confined their waists into a tight corset. Stitching at their embroidery, they discussed the latest news from the court at Mantua, and Alexander of Medici's forthcoming marriage with the emperor's illegitimate daughter Margaret.

Christina had been in Milan for more than a year. But she could still wake up thinking she was breathing the scent of wet grass, even though there was nothing but dust, heat and din. The duke meanwhile had gone to Vigevano.

With the coming of summer his health had worsened, and the doctors had advised a spell in a healthier climate. Although he was ailing he always wrote to her, considerate letters full of affection. How long ago it was since she had dropped an armful of lemons in horror, at the sight of the aged man coming towards her by the fountain in the gardens of Cussago. Christina could barely recognise herself in the girl led alone to the bridal bed almost fourteen months ago.

She could remember clearly her first long talk with the duke. He had sat with her in the cool half-darkness of the Sala delle Asse, smiling as he explained that the whole of her retinue was to be sent back to the Low Countries. She was an Italian duchess now and should have an Italian court.

For Christina the prospect of parting from every familiar face was dulled by the new and unexpected experience of being asked for her opinion. The duke wanted to know what she thought about his proposal. But she knew that a wife must obey her husband in everything, be faithful and devoted; and she did not dream of making any objection.

The duke smiled again. Taking his stick, he pointed out walls and ceilings where painted tree-trunks and green foliage grew up the arched vaulting towards the arms of Sforza, at the very top. It was the work of Master Leonardo, he explained. He remembered in his childhood watching the artist crawling round on the scaffolding with all his apprentices. Master Leonardo had decorated la Saletta Negra as well, and had made an amazing plaster cast of the first Sforza. That had gone, however, destroyed by the French; and the bronze in which it should have been cast had been used for cannon.

Christina could hardly believe her ears as she heard the duke describing all the machines this master had designed; even a machine that was supposed to fly. He must have been very odd, even though his paintings were so beautiful and lifelike that she felt she could walk right into them.

When Christina took leave of her retinue she had only been in Milan a short time, so that she was still not familiar with the huge castle. She would run through one gigantic apartment to find another adjoining it, and then another. It was impossible to find her way. When she went outside there were rows of cannon everywhere. There were courtyards large and small; and from the rooftops she could look out over the biggest town she had ever seen. Several hundred thousand people lived down there; and she prayed fervently to the Holy Virgin that she might soon be with child, for that was what they wished for in her new country.

Now, however, that seemed an eternity ago, and Christina had stopped praying that prayer. Her thoughts returned to her letter. The duke had said that she must not exert herself by writing; instead she could dictate to her secretary. Christina replied that on that point she would not obey him.

The ladies were still discussing what was awaiting her cousin in her marriage with the dissolute Alexander, whose latest prank had been to ride through the streets of Florence in woman's dress, slicing the heads off as many ancient statues as he could. For a moment Christina considered hushing them, but knew it was useless. After five minutes they would start again, as if it were against nature for them to keep quiet.

She had never known people who could make such beautiful things with their hands. But neither had she encountered any who talked as much as the Italians. They talked from morning till night. The girls talked when they were arranging her clothes, the ladies when they were sewing. Even at Mass she could hear a hiss of voices. And they talked about everything.

Christina had soon learned Italian, faster than those around her had realised. Her linguistic talent had enabled her to discover that her marriage was no marriage as long as the duke only kissed her hand. She had listened, at first not understanding, then confused and frightened but curious as well; and before the year was out she had learned words in Italian that she had never heard in her native tongue. She understood why her aunt had called the duke an honourable man; and that it was with a Flemish servant girl that the emperor had had his 'accident', who was to marry the dreadful Alexander. The ladies, bare-faced, claimed that Alexander himself was the result of a love affair between Cardinal Giulio and a Moorish slave girl, which was why he bore such markedly negroid features.

She had listened to the malicious laughter aimed at the king of England when that whore Anne Boleyn gave birth to a daughter instead of a son. She learned that you had to count the days in order to be with child, but also to avoid it, and to douch yourself with alum to make quite sure.

A page announced that the courier was ready. Christina quickly ended her letter, signed it with 'Your ever humble wife', folded the letter and closed it with her seal. She had said so little to comfort and he suffered so sorely.

When, dazed and bewildered, she had been plunged into the whirl of wedding festivities, she had never imagined that the duke would be the only person in her new country to

73

whom she would feel attached; or that scarcely a year later she would dearly wish to see his bowed silhouette and hear the thud of his stick on the marble floor.

Christina could issue orders, and her every wish was fulfilled. But what she thought and felt must never be shown.

If she expressed an opinion on any but everyday matters, it was quoted, interpreted, expounded and finally twisted. She had learned as a part of general good behaviour to control her expression. But now she realised that, here, a smile or a coolness in her glance at the wrong moment could be interpreted as enthusiasm or displeasure, or perhaps a hostile attitude, towards the king of France, the duke of Mantua or the pope of Rome. Christina was a political personage, and a comment overheard by a chambermaid could easily find its way into a foreign envoy's report.

One person alone might hear her thoughts, answer questions or merely see a tired glance, and that was the duke himself. And as time went by she spent more and more hours in his company. He never touched her, other than carrying her right hand to his lips. He told her the history of Milan, of his father's tragic death in exile and of his gifted mother, who had died when he was very small. He guided Christina's first steps into the world of art, and told her about the cathedral the city had been building for a century and a half. He declared she had brought joy into his life and in time she felt he really meant it.

Christina discovered meanwhile that she had a will of her own.

The regent had had Christina's dresses made with wide seams. But when winter came she had grown so much that there was nothing more to let out in some of them. Fur, lace and gold braid were naturally unpicked to be used again. But when the fine materials were to be given away she broke the rules of the house, and passed them on to the most needy among her ladies instead of the most distinguished. It caused confusion, and at times sulky looks which she ignored and which therefore soon disappeared. Sometimes, too, she might advance a servant girl's dowry or have a doctor called to a sick lackey. If she was a wife in name only she was the lady of the castle in fact. But she still had to tolerate the general chatter about who was in bed with whom and all the details of how it had come about.

Now the ladies were gossiping about Catherine of Medici and her marriage with the king of France's son. Christina sighed. From the window she could see a cloud of dust hanging over the town, raised by horses and carts. Down there, people were moving about, leading everyday lives, talking freely together.

Everything was so different from her recollections of a year ago, on her arrival. When the banners and triumphal arches were taken down she saw ramshackle hovels, and when the people had doffed their glad rags there were often real rags underneath. But that winter, food prices had fallen and relieved the general hardship; and if peace was maintained prosperity would return.

When Christina walked through the streets with her ladies – when she passed the market place or the workshops with their glaziers, tapestry weavers, stone polishers and book binders – the people's eyes turned to her waist, in the hope that she was carrying the child who would continue the Sforza line and fulfil the promise of peace. But it was not until after the duke had gone to Vigevano, when she was in her fourteenth year, that her maids removed her sheet and bore it away like a trophy. It was in the heat of summer that amidst much chattering they measured her so that the tailor could let out the seams over her breast. They promised enthusiastically that if the duke returned in good health she could have a little prince by next spring, when the mimosa was in bloom.

But the duke remained in Vigevano. Christina looked out over the dusty rooftops. The page announced the arrival of the papal envoy; later on she was to receive a deputation from the clockmakers' guild; and after that there was a lesson in Italian literature. But whatever was happening around her, whatever duties or pleasures came along, her ladies were always with her. Christina was never alone.

Perhaps that was why she had so quickly grown used to

her old and sickly spouse. Little as she could imagine marital life with the duke, he had given her a sense of human companionship; and the sound of his crutch's dull thud seemed like meeting a loved relative in a distant country. Sometimes he had news, such as the course of the civil war in Denmark. At other times he brought her a rare flower or fruit so that she could admire its beauty or enjoy its taste.

One autumn day as they were returning from Mass he turned to her, and taking her hand between his, as was his custom, asked, 'What does the word "Faatha" mean?'

It was a cool morning, and Christina's thoughts were far away. The fresh air had brought back the memory of Mechelen; and she looked at him blankly.

'Faatha,' he repeated, holding her gaze, and slowly she remembered. It was the word she had cried out at their first meeting at Cussago, the only word she could remember in Danish.

'Padre,' she whispered. He must have been thinking of it for a long time. She was afraid he would be angry at the recollection of her horror at the sight of him. But the duke merely stood still, looking at her, until he said finally, 'A shame that children too should have sorrows.'

The summer went on, the heat went on. The main news of the year was the defeat of the Turks at Tunis, which was celebrated with a Te Deum in the cathedral.

For Christina the most exciting event was Dorothea's marriage, to Count Palatine Friederich. She did not know him, though she might perhaps have seen him as a guest at her aunt's court. The duke had gladly assented to his sister-in-law's marriage to the fifty-year-old German prince. But even though Dorothea sent happy letters describing how absolutely delighted she was with her new life, Christina was robbed of her dreams. When she imagined herself back at the palace in Brussels or in Mechelen, she still heard Johanna and her aunt's voice and footsteps, together with the other household sounds. But Dorothea's giggle had vanished. She was no longer there, swinging on the bed pole,

76

biting her lip with her sharp teeth to hold back a gale of laughter. Not even in imagination could Christina now encounter the one person in the world with whom she had dared completely to share her thoughts.

When the duke at last returned his health was still worse: the paralysis had spread. An anxious hush fell over the court. The autumn brought no improvement. He lay on his couch, pale and haggard as his fever rose. Christina watched beside him, and from time to time he took her hand and whispered, 'My beautiful child,' the same words her old aunt had spoken in farewell.

Early in the morning of All Souls Day 1535 Francesco Sforza, Christina's husband and Milan's last duke, passed away.

As many of the guests had long journeys to make, the date for the funeral had to be postponed.

For three weeks, from early morning to late evening, Christina sat in the mourning chamber with her ladies. All the daylight was shut out, all the walls enveloped in black. She heard nothing other than the music and singing of requiem masses in the chapel; nothing moved but the flames of the torches. Only now, in these November days, did she realise how lonely she had been. She recollected the duke through remembered sounds: the thud of his stick and his voice beneath the green foliage of the Sala delle Asse. The emaciated body, the tortured face, were gone.

The ladies were quiet now, and in the silence her longing to go home, to see living faces again, grew. But no one knew what was to happen.

The funeral took place on the 19th of November. Three days later Christina, a fourteen-year-old black-clad widow, received envoys from foreign lands, together with the city senators and delegates from all the towns of Lombardy, who came to express their sorrow.

That same day the ducal flag on the castle was lowered. In its place the imperial banner was raised and the crowned double eagles fluttered in the autumn wind. Christina had not borne the country an heir, and Milan's independence was at an end. It had become a part of the Hapsburg empire.

Winter came.

Christina was in Milan. She had received no instructions on where to go. The emperor kept silence and she stayed on, in mourning dress and with no real function, a symbol of sorrow who was yet a seed of hope to the people.

When the hoar frost painted the rooftops white, plans emerged to marry Christina again quickly. The emperor was interested and the pope and Venice glimpsed a possibility of preserving Milan's independence through her. She heard lists of names of prospective spouses, many mere boys and just as unknown to her as the duke had been.

When at length spring came, when the Po overflowed its banks again and the first shoots appeared on the vines, the French marched south to capture the duchy.

The peace was lost, and Milan's hopes were dashed. Christina could do nothing except write to the emperor begging for his orders. But letters often took months to reach their destination or failed altogether to arrive, because the courier was robbed or murdered by highwaymen. Meanwhile Christina took in relatives fleeing from the horrors of war. The emperor pushed into Provence, but the country behind him was laid waste. In Milan all that prevailed was fear and the clamour of Spanish officers and German mercenaries preparing for a siege.

In the midst of this pause the past came back to accost Christina. She had heard that there was war in Denmark, that citizens and peasants had risen to demand that her imprisoned father be restored to the throne. Dorothea was married now, and she had a husband who demanded his wife's inheritance. The count palatine was taking an active part in the war in Denmark.

It was Count Stampa who brought this information; and Dorothea, too, sent excited letters. Christina's imagination took fire. She saw herself arriving in Copenhagen to visit her sister Dorothea, queen of Denmark. A dream had come back, like smouldering ashes suddenly blazing again: the dream of a country to the far North. It was thirteen years since she had left it. She remembered nothing, except that the smell of tarred wood now and again brought a vague remembrance of being on board a great ship. Her father's treacherous uncle was dead, and his son now styled himself Christian the Third, king of Denmark. But Copenhagen had closed its gates to him and the Lübeckians were giving her father their support. The emperor promised help and her aunt was equipping a fleet; all this must advance Dorothea and her husband to the Nordic thrones. But gradually news filtered through of the sufferings of the beleaguered city. Christina's fellow-feeling for her countrymen returned, and at the same time her view of her father changed. Unconsciously she came to share his feeling that the townspeople and peasants were the sovereign's true and loyal supporters, and that the nobility were the faithless, power-hungry hereditary enemy.

The news late in summer of Copenhagen's surrender came both as disappointment and relief. They would not all have to die, the good folk up there. She had come to feel she knew them, and she rejoiced that they would still people her country.

Christina's time in Milan was drawing to a close. No longer was she an Italian. Instead, she was to return to the Hapsburg court in the Low Countries. Suddenly, though, she felt herself encumbered by the Hapsburg title as by a garment made to the wrong size. In a few short months during that last summer at the castle in Milan it had grown clear to her that her earliest childhood held more than memories of a tarred ship's decking. It contained her roots, her origins, something she could hold on to. Christina was fifteen.

In November the war between the emperor and France ended. The two monarchs signed yet another armistice, and Christina received a message to leave the city and go to Pavia for the winter. As a final function in her capacity of duchess of Milan she held a memorial ceremony for her deceased husband. Her departure brought farewells to faces with whom she had grown familiar and to a people who, she had discovered, could create so much that was beautiful. They stood there, fearful of the future under foreign rule. She had come to them when the blue Sforza banner flew over the country, and she left it in the daunting power of the double eagles. With a small train of Italian secretaries and ladies-in-waiting, she travelled to Pavia to await the imperial command.

But yet another north Italian winter, a spring and a hot summer were to pass before the order came to resume her journey.

It was pouring with rain when Christina left Pavia on the 15th of October, after a final farewell. Count Stampa was to return to Milan, being now under Spanish orders. It was a strange moment for Christina to part for ever from the man who had stood by her side at the altar in Lille. He had been her husband's main confidant, and her own informant, too, during her two years as a widow. She knew what high hopes he had entertained on her arrival. But they had gone unfulfilled, and his countrymen were no longer their own masters. Before he bowed for the last time she thought she saw sadness in his eyes, the first and only glimpse of emotion behind his façade of stiffness.

With a scanty escort she had reached the Brenner pass, when snow began to fall. The young captain responsible for her safety was nervous. They were short of money for the soldiers' pay and there were bandits about. Horses and mules were pushed hard and they were relieved when at last they heard cannon roar in a salute to the duchess. They had crossed into Austrian territory, where money would be available for the rest of the journey.

Earlier, they had met with two merchants from Genoa, who had travelled from the North through Germany. On their way they had seen the count palatine and his wife, the princess, with a great retinue, on their way to Heidelberg. As soon as she arrived in Innsbruck Christina wrote to the emperor, requesting permission to continue her journey by a route that would enable her to visit Dorothea.

*　　*　　*

On meeting, the two sisters threw themselves into each other's arms. Giggling, Dorothea described her new life: her travels, mountain climbing and the exciting fashion for enormous skirts. There was no end to the tokens of honour the count palatine showered on his sister-in-law, or to the delight he showed in the young bride he had received as a reward for his faithful service to the emperor.

In her brother-in-law Christina saw signs of what had once been a handsome man. But his fine features had become disfigured by flabbiness, and his liking for gold brocade emphasised the size of his belly. He showed great affection for his young wife amid uninhibited caresses, sliding his hand inside her bodice and being loud in his enthusiasm for the delights of the marriage bed. Again and again he described the New Year's night when the courier had arrived with the message from Spain, which he roared out with the full force of his lungs. 'I bring my lord a royal bride, the emperor's favour and an ample dowry.'

But as the days went by in Heidelberg that late November, Christina realised that however satisfied Friederich might be with his Dorothea, the emperor's favour was nothing but empty words, and the dowry, in the form of the Danish throne, was one that he would have to acquire for himself.

It had cost him dear to relieve beleaguered Copenhagen; and it was with a touch of irony that he mentioned the Netherlands fleet that in the event had never put to sea, and the imperial aid, which had failed to materialise.

But laughter broke through again. There must be celebrations; Christina was to stay over Christmas, and nothing was good enough, fine enough, costly enough; money was something that could be borrowed. The Nordic realms would not go away. It was only a question of time before they were king and queen of Denmark. In Christina's honour, yet another lavish banquet was held.

She had to travel on, however. Orders came again for her to leave. Her aunt awaited her in Brussels, and there could be no possibility of extending her stay at Heidelberg.

On her last day Christina managed to be alone with her sister. Dorothea described how blissfully happy she was. She laughed and laughed, but she no longer bit her lip with her pointed teeth to keep control. The once deep intimacy between the two sisters had gone. There were things now that could not be uttered.

When the parting came Dorothea did not weep as she had done in Brussels. She just stood silently beside her ageing husband, whose stomach protruded like a shiny yellow sun, looking strangely pale under her fair curly hair. The torches shone on the snow around the electoral castle in the early morning light, making Dorothea almost transparent despite her huge skirts.

From Heidelberg their journey proceeded along the Rhine to Cologne. From there they travelled overland to Aachen, Cleves, Maastricht and Loeven. On the 18th of December 1537 the regent stood in the wintry chill surrounded by her whole court and all the foreign envoys present, to receive the duchess of Milan as she rode into the palace courtyard in Brussels with her train.

Christina had come back.

The Low Countries, 1537–1541

VIII

John Hutton, the English envoy at the Netherlands court, was not a brave man. Many years' experience of the dangers inherent in words and opinions had taught him to keep silence. He contented himself with sharpening his pen, setting down his meticulous reports and sending them to London. Once, he had dreamed of a patent of nobility and the post in Paris; but that title had been presented to Anne Boleyn's father.

Hutton detested Anne, with her dark eyes, and the men she kept around her. But, as he had neglected to side for or against the new queen, he had never had a sight of the brilliant court of the king of France. Instead, he had to battle his way through rain and mud on the regent's insane hunting expeditions. It was even considered an honour, as it was an honour for him to hand her the little white freshly baked loaves with which she fed her white cockatoos.

'Here, my little ones,' she would whisper to her birds, putting the bread into the aviary. As she did so she would drop a casual-seeming remark really intended for his information, knowing full well that he would pass it on to London. As Her Grace threw him a smile or a friendly glance, whistled to her pets and gave her opinion on the latest news from the English court, he would feel a fool; for she was always up to date. Not only was Chapuy, the imperial envoy in London, quick at snapping up news and sending his couriers off with it, Her Grace also had a well-organised net of listeners, in market-places and wayside inns, where travellers were regaled with great tankards of ale to loosen their tongues.

Gossip hung like sweet incense in the air of the French court; but here the regent saw to it that news was for her ears and her ears alone. Only if it pleased her to let fall her own little comments was anyone else to share it.

It first happened when Anne Boleyn became pregnant. Hutton had known nothing of her condition. He was about to pick up a loaf from the tray held by one of the ladies when the regent said in her soft voice, 'I understand that Lady Anne has developed a strong desire for apples.'

At first he did not understand. She glanced at him again with her big brown eyes, and combed the long ribbons of her headdress with her thin fingers.

'The bread, Your Excellency,' she murmured, for Hutton had stopped in mid-stride. His deepest fears were confirmed. Anne Boleyn would take power.

It was thus to the chattering of cockatoos and observed by the eyes of women that he suffered the indignity of hearing news from home from Her Grace's mouth, several days before receiving the information directly.

'The king of England,' she said one spring day, 'has had the Lady Anne crowned queen, despite the fact that the king already has a crowned queen. Curious,' she breathed and closed the cage.

This was not news to Hutton, but he waited for her to continue.

And while her ladies brought a bowl of water and napkins, so that she could wash her fingers, Her Grace said merrily, 'The citizens of London refused to doff their caps when the procession passed by. It is also said that some dared to shout "Long live Queen Catherine ..." '

When she had finished drying her hands she added, 'I have the greatest respect for the English people ... and for the king of England.'

At that point the day's audience ended. But it was not the last of such revelations, and gradually Hutton's rage at his humiliation mounted to such an extent that he could gladly have stuck his fingers under their white feathers and wrung the neck of every one of her loathsome birds.

The summer passed and Anne's power waxed in tune with

her belly. The regent knew it, and so did he. The hunts continued, together with endless musical evenings. He had backache from sitting for hours on horseback, and all the while his thoughts whirled around the king he loved and admired, leaving him at a loss to understand how the king could lose his heart so completely to a chit worth no more than hundreds of other girls at the English court. The king had had his way. He had got his Anne. But now that the blow had been struck and the battle won, Anne would have to show she was worth fighting for. Hutton decided not to declare allegiance to Anne. He would wait to see what she was carrying under her heart.

'They say she is to be christened Elizabeth,' said the regent quietly that day in September. She said not a word more on the subject, but told her ladies the bread was too hard; they must fetch some fresh loaves.

Hutton was horrified. All the doctors had promised a son; all the astrologers had predicted it. England was shaken to its foundations. The king had fallen out with emperor and pope; he was excommunicated, and would burn in eternal hellfire. All this for the sake of casting off Catherine and marrying Anne. She had sworn to bear him a prince, for that was what she carried in her womb. And then it turned out – Hutton shuddered – a girl.

Hutton counted himself lucky suddenly to be listening to the chattering of cockatoos. He counted himself lucky to be anywhere else on earth than in the immediate neighbourhood of King Henry when he was told the news: 'a daughter'. He thanked God he had not expressed support for a woman who had just given birth to this Elizabeth, the most worthless, unwanted and unwished-for bastard in the whole kingdom of England.

When good pious Queen Catherine – or the dowager princess of Wales, as she was now to be titled – finally expired, released from further humiliations on this earth, Hutton was glad to be first with the news. But this had no effect on the regent, who could report that the king of England and 'that Lady Anne' had celebrated the occasion by going to a carnival in blazing yellow. It was only by the strictest self-control that Hutton concealed his horror over his lord's embarrassing behaviour. But as if to console him the regent said, 'I have heard that the king takes an increasing interest in Lady Jane Seymour, and that at times the Lady Anne's behaviour is somewhat . . .' She hesitated, and smiled faintly. 'Somewhat unrestrained.'

She caressed one of the birds, which she had allowed to come out and sit on her hand. She fondled it, scratched it under one wing and asked, as if speaking to the cockatoo, 'Is it true that Mistress Seymour is loyal to the emperor and a good Catholic?'

From the time when Anne Boleyn was imprisoned in the Tower until the day when the executioner from Calais severed her head from her slim neck, Hutton saw more white cockatoos than in the whole course of his life. But suddenly the strange audiences stopped. The regent felt no need to comment on the king's new marriage, for now the king had no other crowned queen living. Queen Jane was accorded the greatest respect.

Hutton knew the new queen. She had occupied a place at court for a long time. Jane, he considered, was quiet, mild and extremely boring. She would never expose the king to Anne's hysterical scenes, demands and tussles. She would yield to him in everything and be a good and obedient wife, and before long the king would be bored to death. Hutton failed to understand his master's choice.

The court waited and Hutton waited. When Queen Jane became pregnant the regent congratulated him in the presence of the whole court. The waiting continued.

When the news came the regent wept with undisguised joy. The miracle had finally occurred, and the king of England had a living son. But Queen Jane was granted a few days only to enjoy her life's triumph, before she died in childbed.

The regent could not have been more touched by the sorrow that had struck King Henry. She ordered a requiem for the dead queen and expressed her happiness that the king had granted his wife's last wish.

Hutton bit his lip; he understood the regent's feelings. For what Jane had wanted was for Henry to build a Benedictine monastery, a gesture undeniably odd for a man who had thrown out all the monks and nuns in his kingdom. And Hutton recalled all too clearly the time when the regent, during one of the cockatoo conversations, had expressed amazement at this new faith, which merely seemed to enable one 'to exchange one's wives as one pleased, plunder churches and monasteries and eat meat on Fridays'.

She, the regent, whose reformist leanings were well known, had had the nerve to say this to him, Hutton, a Catholic through and through.

For the present, meanwhile, the king of England's greatest wish had been granted, but there was no longer a wife in his bed. Like everyone else, Hutton knew that this could not go on for long.

Time passed, and Hutton grew bored, for nothing happened at the court of the Netherlands. In France King François had taken a mistress, as the new word had it. This had caused one faction to gather round her, against the queen, and another to favour the queen against her. Altogether it sounded a wonderful world, one made up of intrigues, gossip, betrayal and scandal.

But Hutton was in Brussels, and no matter how much he tried he could find no one in the regent's bed but the regent herself. There was no possibility of confidential chatter under the bedclothes, after the desires of the flesh had been satisfied and the urge to unburden oneself set free the scraps of news that invariably reached the ears of lackeys and chambermaids. Her Grace kept both her knowledge and her body to herself. It was frustrating to Hutton's talents, in sending his reports to London; and now and again he was seized with the claustrophobic sensation of being imprisoned in a nunnery.

One day at the beginning of December 1537 Hutton received a letter. It came from Cromwell, keeper of the Privy Seal. In it, Cromwell requested a list of possible subjects at the court of the Netherlands who might fill the vacant position at King Henry's side.

Hutton replied immediately that no person in this circle was suited to become queen of England.

He was all too familiar with the names of good men who had forfeited their lives for having supported Queen Catherine – and with the names of less good men who had died together with Anne Boleyn because they had believed she could procure them power. Hutton would do anything for his king, even outwardly suppress his Catholic faith. But he would never link his name to any wife his lord might choose. To be on the safe side he emphasised in his letter to Cromwell that he had in fact small understanding of women.

Hutton was well pleased with his reply when, on the 8th of December 1537, he waited, ranged with other envoys and the ladies and gentlemen of the court, to receive the regent's niece on her return from her stay in Milan. He had heard tell she was beautiful; but that was said of so many. Hutton took a guarded view of flattering descriptions, particularly where they concerned royal personages. His experience as a diplomat had shown that as a rule it was disparagements that were more apt to be accurate. It was thus purely as a duty that he stood there, his thighs freezing, because Christina of Denmark was on her way.

Hutton had never seen her before; she had left for Milan just before he arrived at the court of the Netherlands, and he was thus quite uninterested in her. Apart from the fact that Her Grace obviously set great store by her relative, Christina was of no importance whatever. Her mother was dead, and her father was in prison. The revolt to restore her father in Denmark had been suppressed, and the right of inheritance now fell to her elder sister. Hutton shook himself in his doublet and concealed a yawn.

But when his eye fell on the duchess he roused himself from his torpor, looked at her once more – and then again – and began to think.

That same evening he despatched a hasty note to Cromwell. Then he tried to recall the image of the young princess. She was very tall, and he remembered his king saying he was a big man who needed a big wife. Her face was narrow and beautiful, even lovelier than rumour had whispered, with brown eyes; and her mouth witnessed to her Hapsburg origins. Mixed with Northern blood, however, the underlip was only slightly prominent, and this gave her a touch of sensuality. He noticed three dimples, one in each cheek and one in the chin; and these made her even more delightful.

Hutton sighed over this unexpected turn of events. He ordered his servant to bring wine and throw more wood on the fire.

It was important to be frank. She had one fault, in that he found her complexion too sallow. It was not so white and pale as the late queen Jane's. He had safeguarded himself, and had carefully written down this fact, but could find nothing else about her to criticise. He ended by repeating what was being said at court: the duchess was both widow and virgin.

Hutton was determined not to be carried away by a momentary impression. He must find out more before writing to Cromwell again. Would the duchess's taste and manners come up to expectations? It would have to be looked into; perhaps she had a hoarse voice, bad breath or – worst of all – black teeth.

Hutton dogged the court for the next few days. All the while he tried to keep the young duchess in view. And as time went on he grew increasingly worried over the king's plans to marry one of the French princesses, and also about rumours of another match for the duchess of Milan.

But the clouds parted. The king of France would not comply with his English relative's demands, and send all the marriageable princesses to Calais to be looked over. 'This is not a mare market,' the gallant French king was said to have protested. King Henry had to forgo his unreasonable demand to see his bride before he married her; and the plans for the duchess seemed to have been shelved as well.

The third time Hutton saw the duchess he was certain. She was coming back from Mass in her mourning clothes, a simple long velvet dress and a black silk coat with wide sleeves and brown ermine lining. She did not wear a stiff white widow's headdress but a little black cap in the Italian manner. Hutton studied her gracious movements, her light step and her clear eyes; and when she smiled he saw not only dimples but beautiful healthy teeth.

Hutton tore up his list of possible failings. Christina of Denmark was the wife for King Henry. She was as high-born as Queen Catherine, far more beautiful than Anne Boleyn, more lively than Jane Seymour. She was tall enough to match the king and look fitting in royal processions; and she was clearly strong and healthy enough to bear a little Prince Arthur, and probably a little Prince Henry and a Prince William too.

The king had one son, and one son as often as not could be no son. They said the boy was sickly – his mother had never looked well – but Christina certainly did.

Hutton's dreams took him into a golden future. The king knew how to reward good service; and there was no doubt that the king's problems were all due to the fact that he had never had a proper wife. Christina was distinguished, she was peaceable, she was beautiful, she was strong. She had her three dimples; and Hutton sensed an earldom shining in the future. Now he came to think of it, on this January night in his house in Brussels, which the city merchants – with their eyes on wool prices – had so kindly allotted him, a ducal crown was perhaps not completely unattainable after the healthy little red-cheeked Prince Arthur had been brought into the world, successor to the delicate Prince Edward.

Christina of Denmark inspired Hutton to lay great plans.

One day a page from the duchess's Italian secretary presented himself. He inquired whether Hutton's courier might take some letters to London. Hutton, astonished, agreed immediately and the next day after Mass he attended on the duchess. She thanked him graciously and said she would never have requested him to take this trouble unless she had felt she could recompense him in some way.

Hutton was dizzy with happiness. He understood her. He savoured her slightly lisping voice, her sweet smile and friendly glance.

He was ecstatic after his meeting with this young woman, who was to bring his lord so much joy in the marriage bed and nursery, and himself a brilliant future. He determined to act.

First it was essential to gain Her Grace's favour. Hutton ordered the finest pack of hounds to be found in all England. Next he sent baskets of wine and peaches to the fat Johanna, who was said to be in the duchess's confidence. With the fruit, he put in a little leather bag containing twelve shining pearls, to assure himself of her goodwill. That proved a mistake, however. Johanna ate the peaches, drank the wine and sent the pearls back with the comment that it was not fitting for a simple woman to wear jewels.

He had better luck with Mme de Berghe, whose tongue was the busiest in the whole court. Perhaps it was because she had been born out of wedlock and so saw things as if from the outside. But she was useful and Hutton sought to win her friendship.

Mme de Berghe accepted pearls and fruit and wine and little boxes made of ivory and carved tortoiseshell, all of which he sent with casual spontaneity, regardless that it took toll of his purse. In response, she would smile at him with her big mouth in the flare of tapers and torches, during the concerts that took place at court against an unvarying backcloth.

While lutes and fiddles played a sarabande by Clément or a courante by Gombert, Her Grace sat with a red carnation in her right hand and eyes half closed with pleasure. The French envoy would gaze at the vaulted ceiling and the construction of its arches, trying to while the time away. And there beside Her Grace was the young duchess, gentle and beautiful in her splendid brocade gown trimmed with glittering diamonds. By day she was the widow, but in the evening . . . Hutton groaned at the sight of her and wished his lord could see the chosen one at that moment. Attentive and yet distant, she was there and yet not there. King Henry would never know whether she was enjoying the music or was preoccupied by something else, whether she was present in her thoughts or far away. He would never come to tire of Christina of Denmark, for he would never really know her. Christina of Denmark was possessed of the most essential of all feminine attributes. She was unfathomable.

One January evening after a game of cards, Mme de Berghe mentioned that she had received a promise of a portrait of the duchess of Milan. She told Hutton in a near-whisper, and then stood with her mouth slightly open, like a door ajar. Hutton bowed low, kissed the marquise's hand, straightened himself, bowed once again and next morning sent his servant off with a heavy gold chain.

An hour later the servant returned with the gold chain and a letter. Mme de Berghe expressed her regrets. She could not possibly accept so costly a gift, for the reason that she was unworthy. Should His Excellency indeed wish to give her something, nothing would please her more than to own a portrait of the king of England.

'Preferably a miniature,' she added in a brief postscript.

Hutton understood. He cursed himself for his stupidity and immediately sent orders to England.

Cromwell acted quickly. On the courier's return Hutton studied the miniature. There was his king's face, it was true; but he could see it must have been copied from one of the earlier pictures.

King Henry had put on weight in recent years, and his face and body were heavy with fat; but it was a problem that could be solved. In any case the duchess would not discover it until she had arrived at Whitehall. After all, the king of England was the king of England.

Hutton wrapped up the picture and the gold chain together and sent off the servant.

The marquise sent a touching acknowledgment. She expressed her admiration for King Henry's manliness and exceptional handsomeness. And this time she kept the gold chain, although without mention.

Three days later Hutton received a package from the marquise's secretary. It was a painting of Christina of Denmark, duchess of Milan.

Hutton was not satisfied. The picture was by the court painter, van Orley; and although it depicted the duchess's beauty well enough it lacked her almost evasive charm.

Hutton looked at the picture, considered, and finally sent it to Cromwell. At least it was better for his lord and master to be happily surprised than the opposite.

But less than twenty-four hours later a gentleman arrived from London, a certain Mr Hoby. He was a stranger to Hutton, but he was one of Cromwell's men; and he brought with him Master Hans Holbein.

Hutton fumed. He had sacrificed pearls and costly gifts on the marquise in order to get an indifferent portrait, and now here was an established painter, sent over by Cromwell himself. But he consoled himself with the thought that the great man must place confidence in his reports if Master Hans had been sent all the way from England.

Before long Hoby came to tell Hutton that the regent was so astonished at their request for permission to paint a portrait of the duchess that she had leapt out of her chair. But the duchess herself was extremely gracious and friendly, and the master was allotted three hours in which to draw a sketch.

It was not much. But when Holbein was back in England he would paint the portrait. He would then show it to Cromwell, who would take it to the king.

One day in March Hutton received a report describing how King Henry had studied the portrait of Christina of Denmark long and earnestly. He had stared at her face, and her tall figure, which, in her black costume and adorned only with a single ruby ring on her left hand, had seemed as if stepping to meet him against a background of turquoise.

Then Henry had summoned his musicians. It had been the first time since the death of Queen Jane that music had sounded in the palace of Whitehall. Hutton's diplomatic career was nearing its zenith.

That evening Hutton's servants had to put a querulous master to bed once again. Yet another hunt in fog and snow had meant that rheumatic pains racked his buttocks. His servants removed warming pans and wrapped him in hot blankets, while he thought of his remark about his deficient knowledge of women.

Hutton looked askance at his wife, lying beside him in the

huge damask-hung four-poster. Her sharp nose protruded from the mountain of bedclothes, and she snored and snorted so much that the ruffles and flounces of her nightcap fluttered around her sunken cheeks. She was a good and pious woman, and had borne him eleven children of whom five were living. For a moment he wondered why she had never had a desire to eat apples. Then his thoughts returned to Cromwell and what the great man would think if he were to remember Mrs Hutton's small gaunt figure.

Hutton gave his wife the usual dig in the ribs with his elbow. Grunting sleepily she turned on her side, and silence fell. Master Hans's picture was with the king; that was the decisive thing. Hutton closed his eyes happily. For one moment he boldly wished himself in Henry's place when the king should penetrate his new young queen for the first time; then hastily returned to his own future, in the glow of honour and earldom.

Hutton dozed off with three charming dimples hovering before his eyes. England would owe him everything.

IX

Christina could not understand why Mme de Berghe had such a burning desire for her portrait. But as the marquise was always up to date with the latest gossip, and as Christina could never help laughing at it even if half of it was lies, she had not the heart to refuse.

Not until Christina received the little portrait of King Henry did she notice how thick the marquise was with the English envoy. She began to study the gold-framed miniature more closely. '. . . to see for yourself how handsome and manly the king of England is . . .' said the marquise when she handed her the picture.

The king's face was heavy and square, and his reddish fair hair was cut short under the embroidered velvet cap with its single white ostrich feather. But there was something about his eyes, in his gaze, that filled her with a disquiet she had not felt before. He looked slightly to one side. What was it his expression held? Laughter? There was a smile on his narrow lips, but also something else she could not define.

Christina said nothing to her aunt about the painting, which was so small she could hold it hidden in her hand.

But when she lay in bed alone, shielded by the hangings, she pressed her hands to her breasts and dreamed they were his hands, and that she lay in his embrace in the four-poster at Whitehall.

She had been fond of her duke, but he was now no more than a pale ghost. King Henry was flesh, blood and strength. His eyes shone with power and spirit; he was lord, he was master. The duke shrank into a paralysed shell in her memory, for it was the king who had presence in her imagination. In just a few days Christina was whirled into her first infatuation; into primitive physical need for a man she had never set eyes on. She imagined she could feel his neck with her hands, his narrow lips against hers. She heard the sound of his laughter, felt the weight of his body and the smell of his skin.

Christina was aware meanwhile that something was going on at court. But she could not make out why her aunt did not mention the possibility of an English marriage.

Her eyes fell on Gian Battista. He was one of her Italian secretaries and had been in her train during the long winter in Pavia. She could rely on him, and he had once mentioned a childhood friend who now had a post in the royal mews in England.

An idea presented itself. Battista needed to see his friend again, and anyone over there would take an interest in her secretary if they were interested in her. Perhaps he might get an audience with Cromwell or – Christina hardly dared imagine it – with the king himself.

One spring day Christina and her aunt were to try out the new fashion in saddles, just arrived from Paris.

Up to now, ladies, when they rode on horseback in processions, had always sat in a sideways-facing seat. When hunting, or on journeys, they had ridden astride, for the sake of speed.

Now it was possible to ride at a gallop with both legs on one side of the horse, the right knee being supported by a crutch. To Christina the new saddle felt strange, but she soon learned to balance in it. The invention came from Catherine of Medici. 'To give a better view of her ankles,' said Christina's aunt. 'She has nothing good to show otherwise. Apart from her money, of course.'

In Italy Christina had heard a great deal about the unfortunate Catherine of Medici. There she was known as 'la Duchessina' and there was much talk of the colossal fortune she had taken to France from Florence. But at the Netherlandish court what they discussed was her round head, her prominent eyes, her inability to bear children, and

the humiliation she must suffer because her husband preferred a mistress who was more than double her age.

It was said that King François himself had been present
during the wedding night, while the pope waited till early
next morning before storming in to the young couple to
assure himself that the marriage had been consummated,
'for God and for man'.

The riders had left the city walls behind, and the conversation passed to other subjects than Catherine's barren
womb. Peasants in homespun trousers and motley-coloured
tunics were working in the fields, weeding vegetable crops.
Cabbages and carrots were shooting up and children played
by the wayside or ran around with dogs. As the two princesses rode by with their retinue, the peasants doffed their
caps, while the children gazed wide-eyed at the dashing
array of riders on horses bearing elaborate saddles.

On a hill to the east the execution ground could be
glimpsed. The wheels were empty, but black birds wheeled
above three grey corpses swaying in their ropes. To the
south the council hall and church towers of Brussels stood
out against the spring sky.

'How I should like to be alive in a hundred years' time,'
cried the regent. 'The young have never had such a good
education and upbringing, and we have never before been
able to do so much, know so much, read so much. What a
world we could create when we have learned from art and
science, when we can guide people away from evil. We are
only just starting.' She was breathing quickly, and her
cheeks bloomed in the fresh air.

Christina found it difficult to listen. Her thoughts
revolved around her secret of the little portrait, and why she
had been given it. Then there was the marquise's friendship
with the English envoy; and Christina also knew about the
peaches Johanna had eaten in the course of the winter, and
the wine she had drunk.

'Perhaps,' said her aunt, pointing towards the gallows,
'perhaps we'll be able to put an end to that as well. As long
as we catch only one robber out of a hundred and one
murderer out of two hundred it is necessary as a warning

and a source of terror. But one day we will take away the posts and plant fruit trees in their place.'

The regent went on to discuss her usual worries over tax burdens. Christina grew absorbed in her own plans. She had long since put the king's three dead wives out of her mind. Catherine had died of an illness, Jane in childbed. And Anne Boleyn?

So many people were executed. Anne had been a criminal. Everyone called her a whore, and she had been justly condemned for high treason. A king with eyes like that could pronounce only just sentences. Christina was convinced that she herself could give the handsome king the marital felicity he had never known.

Despite their unaccustomed design of saddle, and the feeling of sitting less firmly than usual, the two ladies soon succeeded in outpacing the rest of the company. They galloped across a meadow and into the forest.

After a quarter of an hour they halted. They listened, but there was no one following. A roe deer leapt up and vanished among the tree-trunks; pigeons fluttered in the foliage; and the sun flickered through branches and leaves still fresh with the green of spring. They rode on deeper into the forest.

'Can you hear something?' asked the regent.

Christina listened. From somewhere ahead came the murmur of water. They went on at a walk and after a few minutes came to a clearing.

They saw five mud huts with small shutters at the windows. One of them had a watermill, where the stream ran into a small lake. There were men sawing wood, and others fishing from a little boat. Women were washing clothes, and a group of children sat on a wooden bridge with their feet in the water.

The little community was isolated from the world, hemmed in by the forest on all sides. But no one seemed surprised to see the regent. Two men in red tunics went calmly towards them, bowed and took the horses. The children came running from the bridge, not taken aback but glad to see them; and the little girls among them curtsied instead of staring. This was evidently a place the regent visited often.

Seeing her, the men at once brought out a table and two chairs.

The air was fragrant with fresh-cut wood and wood sorrel. Water splashed from the mill wheel. Women in ankle-length skirts put blue glazed pitchers of wine on the table, curtsied and retired.

'A good place to be,' said the regent, reaching for a pitcher. She made a brief gesture, and men and women returned to their work. Only the children found it hard to keep their eyes from the table and the guests.

'The world is full of eyes and ears,' said the regent. 'But not here.'

She fiddled with her white ribbons as was her habit when thinking. Her eyes rested on the lake as if she were watching the fishermen; then she said, 'The king of England has asked for your hand in marriage. He desires you as his wife and his queen.'

The regent turned to Christina, let the ribbons alone and rested her hand on the table. 'As his fourth wife and queen.'

'It is a very great honour,' replied Christina, trying to sound surprised, and hiding her joy.

But the regent was suddenly distracted, by a boy who had caught a perch. She beckoned to him, asked to see the fish and gave him a coin that brought a broad smile to his sun-browned face. Patting him on the head, she sent him away. 'The harvest was good last year. The children are healthier.'

She reached for the jug again while Christina battled with impatience and with her violent urge to shout, 'Yes, yes, I will marry King Henry!'

'King Henry has three wives in the grave,' said the regent. 'Wicked tongues will have it that he killed them all. I personally do not believe them. If that were the case he would have had Queen Catherine put to death nine years earlier. And no one can blame him for Queen Jane's death.'

Christina felt her heart beating. Her aunt was in favour of the marriage. She exclaimed, 'And Anne was a whore who committed high treason.'

The regent did not reply at once. Instead she gave a brilliant smile in the direction of a little barefoot girl. 'As a woman I find it deplorable that a man can have his wife's head cut off because he is tired of her. It could well become a habit.'

Christina answered quickly, 'Just as it is a deplorable habit to deceive one's husband.'

The regent was still smiling. 'It is extremely doubtful whether Anne Boleyn deceived the king. But there is no doubt at all that she lost her head.'

'What does the emperor say?' asked Christina, determined not to give up.

'The emperor says nothing; the emperor is deliberating,' the regent said slowly. 'But ...' And as if she could read Christina's hopeful thoughts, 'You see, there are certain difficulties. As King Henry's first queen was related to you, the king cannot marry you without the pope's dispensation.'

Christina could not understand this. She said, 'But the pope always gives such dispensation to royal persons.'

The regent spoke slowly, her eyes following some sparrows. 'But it will doubtless be difficult for the king of England to ask the pope for dispensation, when the king does not acknowledge the pope's right to give that dispensation ... does not acknowledge the pope at all, for that matter.'

Christina felt trapped. She set down the pitcher heavily, trying to understand why her aunt was so obviously opposed to her finding such great good fortune. A solution occurred to her. But before she could utter it, the regent spoke. 'King Henry is a strange man. He demands to know what his bride looks like. He wishes to fall in love before he marries.'

Christina thought of the feel of his hands on her body. She thought too of the grey paralysed duke towards whom she now felt such coldness. 'That is not really so strange.'

Her aunt was unmoved. 'If he demands to be attracted to a woman in order to marry her, he may well demand to oust her when he is tired of her. One thing follows on from another, and where are we then?'

As they were remounting, the regent uttered her final comment. 'Besides, it is said that King Henry has grown fat in recent years. So fat that he probably will not let himself be painted again after having seen the latest pictures.'

Christina caught her breath. Did she know about the miniature?

But the regent merely looked down at the children, paid generously for the wine and spurred on her horse. As they rode away she took up the subject of the wars and her anxiety as to how long the people could go on paying the necessary taxes. 'They are impoverishing both France and ourselves.'

But Christina, her thoughts elsewhere, was not listening. She had been angered and wounded by her aunt's words. Would not the regent herself have accepted such a proposal? And had she never had the same feelings? Why in fact had she never married again?

To such questions Christina would never be vouchsafed an answer. But she was prepared to fight nonetheless for her place at King Henry's side.

She knew her aunt, with her light manner, and her apparently casual method of getting her way. King Henry had sent his painter, seen her portrait and wished to have her. Christina in turn had seen his picture, little though it was, and was willing to have him. There was Hutton, too; and the marquise and the English wool prices and, first and foremost, the emperor. Christina kept silence. But she had not given up.

The two ladies rode out of the forest and found their retinue; and when the regent set off at a gallop, Christina determined to achieve something she had never managed before. She would be first at the city gates of Brussels. She was young, her horse was as strong and swift as any, and she would show she dared and could do – just as there were other things she dared and could do.

Christina rode as she had never ridden before. She saw clods fly from under the horse's hooves, cows scattering and carts pulling in to the wayside. She cleared through the air in her new saddle, and after twenty minutes' wild riding she reached the northern gate of Brussels.

Christina straightened up. She had done it. Reining in her horse, she saw peasants making way for her with their baskets of vegetables, and guards standing to attention. But

– there in the sunlight on the other side of the gates, riding to meet her at an easy pace – the regent.

Her aunt smiled broadly, without the least breathlessness, and said, 'Let us wait for the others. They are rather cautious.'

Then she smoothed the ribbons on her headdress, which looked as if she had merely been walking through the palace. She showed neither pleasure, nor even knowledge, of her evident victory. Instead, she inquired after Christina's new saddle.

Christina was nonplussed. But she recovered herself, and uttered a few polite words. Turning her horse, she pretended to look for their retinue. And all the while she fought with her rage.

Gian Battista returned from England in high spirits. He was full of his new impressions and looked forward to telling his lady all about that wonderful country and its glorious king.

Battista had been attached to the 'English faction' at the court of the Netherlands for a long time. He was among those, led by Hutton and the marquise, who agreed it was the duchess who should by right become the queen of England. Before his journey Battista nourished no special feelings for the country over the sea, nor the slightest devotion to its king. His interest had been motivated solely by a selfless, almost religious affection for the duchess. Only a queenly crown was worthy of this exalted being.

Battista had met Christina of Denmark for the first time on a warm May day in Milan. He had been standing at a window waiting for the bride to arrive. When he saw the girl, pure and innocent and lovely, and still only a child, he was seized with feelings of chivalry. She had turned her face towards him, and in that short moment he seemed to see the face of the Holy Mother.

She rode into Milan like a last hope. They were impoverished and despoiled. The French had ravaged them, the Spanish humiliated them with their arrogance and power-lust. He had watched infants die because their mothers were too weak to give milk, and the old succumb because the meagre rations were allotted to those who could work and defend Lombardy.

And then she came, a shining Madonna of the North, tall, blonde, noble and virginal, daughter of a kingdom so far to the North that few had heard its name and fewer knew its whereabouts. Her smile fell upon high and low, children and old cripples, beggars as well as courtiers.

Battista felt for Christina of Denmark as for a saint. He spent nights in prayer for her, and when he crossed the courtyard before the castle he suffered fearful pangs at the thought of what might go on behind its closed windows. But the rumours in the town of the duchess's unscathed virginity made him feel that his prayers had been answered, and he swore to devote his life to her.

Battista entered the duchess's service. When the duke died he accompanied her to Pavia, where she was forced to petition to have a wooden ceiling put in her bed-chamber against the cold wind whistling through the shattered building. The more time he spent in her vicinity the more he admired her. The duchess was always kindly, always happy. She never mentioned her own sorrows, but occupied herself instead by caring for others. Battista was also present on the journey from Pavia to Innsbruck, from Innsbruck to Heidelberg and thence to Brussels, where they had arrived on that December day in 1537. Since then rumours of marriage had come thick and fast. There had been the duke of Cleves; the duke of Lorraine's son; the duke of Angoulême; and finally the king of England. All of them desired to marry his duchess; but for Battista there was only one possibility. It was thus with delight that he obeyed her wish for him to sail across the sea and take a look at England, where he had a friend, an old acquaintance from home.

Battista had nothing but praise for England. It resembled Italy in its beauty and the Netherlands in the fruitfulness of its verdant landscape. And he had met Cromwell. They called him England's evil spirit, the bane of the nobility and the church; all over Europe mention of his name evoked shudders of horror. But to Battista this fearful tyrant was courtesy itself. There had been no limits to his helpfulness

105

and it had been he who had paved the way to the high spot of Battista's visit: a meeting with the king.

Battista was shocked by the sight of King Henry. The king's huge bulk towered before him as Henry stood, legs apart and hands to his sides, as if preparing to do battle with some wild animal. Cromwell's malignant eyes had made an indelible impression on Battista despite all his cordial words. But in the case of the king himself, his initial shock over his monstrous size was soon allayed by the riveting charm of Henry's personality.

The king's resounding laughter boomed through the state rooms of Whitehall. He cracked jokes; his clap on the shoulder almost knocked Battista off his feet; and he questioned Battista about the duchess with such sincere interest that there could be no doubt. The king of England loved the duchess with all his heart.

Battista swayed slightly as he made his exit. He was ecstatic, delighted for his duchess. He wrote rapturous letters to his friends. This was the greatest and most illustrious prince in the world; and when he was home again his cheeks positively glowed as he recounted his adventures to his lady.

The duchess listened, smiling, and Battista noted the dimples that were to delight King Henry. His mind was in a turmoil. He was the god of love; he was besotted with them both. But even in these transports of delight he became aware of some slight change in his lady's manner.

Perhaps there was just a hint of remoteness in her eye. When he expressed his joy over what he had to tell her, there was no responding glow. Something was not quite right.

Battista was soon to find out what it was, for the news spread through halls and formal gardens like wildfire. There was someone else. Not the duke of Cleves nor the duke of Angoulême nor the duke of Lorraine's son; nor indeed any suitor from a far country.

It was young René de Châlon, the prince of Orange, hero of St Pol. Worst of all, the duchess was said to be in love.

They had known each other since childhood, and René had been a playmate of Prince Hans. But it was only this summer, while Battista was in England, that the unexpected had happened. The court was delighted, the regent was delighted; everyone was delighted except Hutton, the marquise and their English faction.

Battista had a long sleepless night. He recalled how his lady now looked. She was radiant, uplifted; her lovely hands fluttered like birds. Who could deny her life's happiness?

When the sun rose over the towers of Brussels he had come to a decision. The crown must be relinquished. He would support the Orange faction.

The duchess and the young prince were the handsomest pair at court and the object of all eyes. The more discreet spoke of the prince as a gallant knight when he fought in tournaments in the duchess's colours and for her honour, while the less discreet were already discussing a forthcoming wedding. For what hindrance could there be to the match?

It was true that the principality was quite small and situated in France a long way to the South. But René was a very rich man with great possessions in the Netherlands, and he was a loyal and brave officer of the emperor. The older members of court watched with pleasure and approval as the couple danced together. The ladies kept at a sufficient distance to allow the young people to talk intimately together; and it was a fact that such a break with etiquette could never have taken place without the full sanction of the regent.

But at the sight of the young couple the marquise twisted her big mouth into a grimace, and Battista could not fail to notice Hutton's pasty face. When in the autumn the Englishman fell ill Battista had to resort to a few white lies.

He went to sit with Hutton and told him that the affair was a cover-up for the duchess's real feelings towards the king of England. His lady was merely play-acting in order to confuse the French envoy. Such information brought a flicker of life and pleasure into the sick man's fever-glazed eyes. Seizing Battista's hands, he asked him again and again to repeat it.

Hutton grew worse. He developed violent attacks of

coughing, as his sorrowing little wife sobbed by his couch. While he became too weak to either write or dictate a letter Battista elaborated his descriptions of the duchess's longing for King Henry. The king had already equipped an army to go to war against Denmark in his bride's name. Secret letters were exchanged between him and the duchess, and before the trees came into leaf again she would be queen of England.

On a late afternoon in November 1538 John Hutton took his leave of this world. He died a happy man with faith in God and his own glorious efforts for the future of England.

The news of his death was heard with sincere sorrow. Everyone had liked the good little man. He was always pleasant, companionable, and ready with an amusing anecdote; and even if he had not been considered a great diplomat his well-liked and familiar face would be missed. Warm messages of condolence were despatched to his wife. Afterwards the court discussed who might be the replacement sent in the king's name by the odious Cromwell, before setting off on the usual hunting expedition.

Now Battista could freely express his joy over the duchess's radiant happiness. All that was needed was the emperor's assent for the duchess of Milan to go to the altar.

Christina had fallen in love at Breda, during the most glittering occasion of the summer.

She had known René since they were children. As one of Hans's friends, he had seemed as remote and almost as exalted as her brother. She could still remember how triumphant she had felt at the banquet where she had been seated at the high table while he was relegated to the company of the ladies-in-waiting.

Subsequently Christina had encountered him on her return from Milan. She had admired his courage in tournaments, and presented him with prizes and talked briefly to him as she did to any other young man. It had been with her thoughts on Battista, and his journey to England, that she had consented to be led in the dance at the Nassau castle by the son of the house. His hair was darker now; but he was tall, and confident in his bearing. When, later, he partnered her at board games she expected to hear about his heroic deeds at St Pol, or the usual courtesies to herself.

René talked of swans. Christina watched his dark blue eyes, while he described the swans at Bruges. On one occasion at the end of the last century Archduke Maximilian had been made prisoner by the dissatisfied citizens of the town. When they finally released him they were sentenced to an unusual penalty. From then until doomsday they were to care for the swans in the canals of Bruges. The birds would no longer be shot or eaten and in winter when the water froze they were to be fed and saved from starving.

René threw his die on the table without glancing at it. Instead he said, 'It is noble to punish by saving life.'

His gaze seemed to seek out every corner of her mind. She composed herself and asked, 'And do the citizens keep their promise?'

'From now until doomsday, yes. The swans in Bruges are protected.'

At last he looked down, he had thrown a five and passed her the die.

As always Christina was surrounded by members of the court who watched what she did and heard what she said. She picked up the die, 'And the swans?'

'They are bigger, whiter and more proud than any other swans in the world.'

He sent her a radiant smile. His eyes smiled too, until they narrowed. Christina looked at the veins in his hands. He wore a white shirt; and his doublet was dark blue, like his eyes. They played on, and the die rolled across the board. She followed it, then looked into his eyes again. She hadn't noticed before how they curved down slightly by the bridge of his nose. Light from tapers and torches was reflected in the courtiers' gold brocade. The room was hot from the crowd of people around her. René was silent. He had spoken last, and it was for her to say something. But she could not. She felt it would break an enchantment. The people surrounding them were transformed into flickers of gold; the only sound was the ivory die striking the marble table top.

She played, lost and thought of white swans on green water, swans that were tame because they were never shot at, swans that were so large because they did not starve in winter when the canals froze over. And she looked into his eyes curving a little at the bridge of his nose; laughing blue eyes the colour of his doublet. His nose was too short to be handsome but his mouth was neat and well-shaped, and told of his happiness. Christina was starting out on a journey into an enchanted world. She spoke to his eyes that contained everything, rapture without a word, humour without laughter, sorrow without tears. Without movement or speech, they were in accord. Christina was in a fairyland.

From then on Christina forgot the king of England. She felt embarrassment at the thought of her nightly imaginings and her ruse of sending Battista to England. When he returned, red-cheeked with excitement over his meeting with the king, she had found it hard to control her laughter. He had obviously not heard the latest news. But he would not have to wait long. Gossip travelled fast.

Christina did not hide her feelings. They were together, she and René, on hunting trips, at tournaments, at concerts. He led her in the dance. Autumn came, leaves fell to the ground like gold from the skies; winter came, the snow like white magic. She felt weightless when he danced with her. When he threw his lance, she gazed at his back and sensed every muscle beneath the armour; and she would cry out with fear when he fell. She loved the world because she loved him, and was aware of it only as it contained her and René.

The court kept its distance; her aunt's doe-brown eyes held a smile; approving messages came from Dorothea and Friederich; and Johanna excelled herself in dressing Christina and smoothing down her hair so that it did not curl too much. During the daytime it hung down her back without restraint; but in the evening it was put up, and fastened with pins decorated with flowers or pearls. She looked at her face in the mirror, seeing herself through René's dark blue eyes, and loved herself: her smile, her teeth, even – though it was slightly too dark – her skin. She didn't wash in asses' milk; René didn't like that. 'A woman should be natural,' he had once said to her that autumn, with sudden fierceness. 'She should be free. We live in the most wonderful of worlds; we are on the way to perfection, to the freedom to breathe, to live. And then one half of humanity starts to deny the colour of their own skin, their own body; to deny themselves.'

Christina was bewildered. She loved fashion and seeing herself in the latest style from Paris. She laughed at him in protest; but his eyes grew dark as he clasped her by the waist. Until this moment he had never been so close to her that she could feel his breath on her face. He said, 'And now you lace yourselves into corsets. It's idiotic. You make yourselves into dolls, into objects . . .'

His hands were still round her waist, trying to feel her body through the stays she wore. She saw censure in his eyes, but on his mouth she saw laughter. Christina looked at him, at the way his hair grew where it had been cut short around his temple. His eyes, no longer fierce, were blue once more. She caressed his arms, his shoulders, and his neck beneath the open shirt.

Christina kissed him, for the first time. Confused, she stepped back, staring up at the face that had brought about such a change in her, before her upbringing had brought her up short. Had they been seen?

'We are alone,' he said laughingly.

She relaxed, and laughed too, expecting him to bend down to her again. But he stood, looking at her, so still that she could see a vein pulsing in his neck. The wind beat against the window-panes; far away someone was shouting; somewhere a door slammed. She wanted to take his hands and guide them over her, beneath her neckline. But she did nothing. She sensed the warmth of his breath as slowly he raised his hand and caressed her hair.

'Christina . . . I love you.'

A fierce gust of wind whirled fallen leaves against the window. A fluttering sycamore leaf attached itself to one of the small panes and stuck there, as if someone outside had pressed a red hand against the glass.

X

Christina had kissed a man. Even though she and René had been alone they had been observed. Nothing ever happened in the palace without being seen and heard, by a gardener working in the grounds or a chambermaid behind a door; and everything in turn was reported back to the regent.

Days passed. Christina expected some reaction, but still the regent said nothing. Christina began to wonder how much freedom she was in fact permitted. All her life she had known what she could and might do; and now there were suddenly no rules any more. In Italy a young widow seemed to be permitted quite a lot, and if rumours spoke truth there were not many prohibitions at the French court either. It went without saying that Christina herself had listened and obeyed. Even after her introduction to a husband who was both elderly and sick, she had never asked herself 'Why?', or so much as thought the word 'no'. Only after seeing the portrait of King Henry had she tried to act on her own initiative; and only now did she really begin to assess her situation.

The days stretched into weeks. She walked with René under the pergolas in the palace garden, where trellis-work roofs shielded them from the sun. They met in remote forest places or sought privacy in the angle of a window. But always, as they kissed, aware of the closeness of each other's body, caressing beneath each other's clothes, they had a sense of stolen time. After five minutes or at most ten they would hear a horse whinny, the sound of steps on gravel or the rustle of a skirt – always some discreet warning sounds before someone or other happened to approach. Christina was not in Italy; she was not in France. She was at the Hapsburg court. She was aware of the tether confining her, and understood that no matter how smiling and silent the regent might be, it was her aunt who decided the precise length of the tether.

No limits meanwhile were put on the young people's conversations together. All through the winter they immersed themselves ecstatically in reading about the love of Dante and Beatrice, amused themselves over the *Heptameron*, and exchanged books and writings. They played with words, with expressions, with quotations, and suddenly grew serious: development grows fast, can we control it? The literature of the time was burgeoning, but was it a source of liberation or of menace? The Bible was now accessible to everyone; but in response various pedants had immediately pointed out that purgatory and indulgences and papacy had no mention in holy scripture; and the same heretics were even trying to destroy holy communion. The greatest works of literature were now translated and printed, and language and frontiers no longer presented a hindrance to learning; but in the wake of this there had followed a mass of political pamphleteering and lampoons. It was the hideous face of Satan misusing God's gifts to man, employing the word of God to breed hatred and poison souls with words when words should be used to express genius and strengthen the true faith.

But René and Christina were young meanwhile, and they were strong. They had a part to play in shaping their time and its glories; they would lead the people to make the most of the gifts with which God blessed them. All they need do was to avert evil, so as to maintain art, culture and science – all that was good and beautiful – under one church, in one Christian Europe united against the Turkish peril.

In anticipation they solved every problem. They were seized with the idea of universal monarchy, one world at peace in which the peasant could grow rich on his land without the burden of war taxes. Over again they read each other poetry and declared their love, the love of the soul as well as the love of the flesh, all the while awaiting the wonderful day when René should receive the emperor's permission to marry Christina, before God and man.

The emperor was expected; but when carnival time came round it was plain that he would remain in Toledo until after the birth of the empress's expected child. Meanwhile Christina and René were drawn into a whirl of festivities. There was cavalcade after cavalcade, men on stilts two yards high, fantastic costumes, painted clowns with tasselled bells, walking skeletons, bears, and tame wolves; and the people roared with laughter at screaming, mewing cats pulled along by their tails. They gaped at the jugglers' skills and at tightrope artists walking from church spire to church spire. You bade farewell to indulgence of the flesh by eating spit-roasted oxen and whole suckling pigs; and there was ale and cheap French wine for the people, while court and nobility grew merry on the noble grapes of the Rhine and Italy.

Night after night Christina was led in the dance by René. Her hand was in his, their fingertips met, and fire coursed through her body as their eyes held each other close. But wherever she was, whether on the balustrade by day or at the gaming tables by night, there was always one face watching her. It had a sober evaluating gaze, and it belonged to the new English envoy, Mr Wriothesley.

When Hutton had died that November Christina had been genuinely sad. Like everyone else she had been fond of him. He had played a part in her little intrigues concerning the marquise and the portrait that had been sent to England, and she had been glad when, at Hutton's deathbed, Battista had uttered his white lies. What did it matter if they were untrue, since they had eased Hutton's last hours? Drawing a sigh of relief from Battista, she had indicated that she fully approved of his action.

But now Wriothesley had stepped into Hutton's shoes, an influential man close to the king. In the past he had won his lord's favour by means of stripping holy Thomas à Becket's grave. That deed had brought King Henry seven full chests of treasures; and the Englishman made no secret of his ambition to consolidate his position by procuring yet another treasure.

The regent, continually pestered with his inquiries, responded amiably by saying it was merely a question of papal dispensation.

But Christina was no longer the unmarried girl. Although she had to have the emperor's permission to marry, she herself could now prevent wedlock with a man who was unacceptable to her. And Christina no longer loved a fat old man who already had three wives in the grave.

Her ladies and her secretaries were questioned, and her maids were presented with little gifts by the intolerable Englishman, anxious to assess her inclinations. One evening, however, she gaily let drop to a group of courtiers that she would be glad to marry King Henry if she had an extra head to spare.

That was imprudent, and she knew it. Her remark, which produced roars of laughter, was bound to be repeated. But Christina just shrugged and resumed her part in the festivities. Dicing, dancing and laughing, she breathed the very essence of life, savouring it a hundred times over with each hour that passed.

The carnival ended, and everyone's diet returned to fish and vegetables. Public high spirits calmed down; but for Christina and René's love went on growing throughout the damp March days. It unfolded like an enchanted flower that could live without sunshine, without proper nourishment. But still no news came from Spain, and the regent showed signs of mounting disquiet. Her brown eyes still held their subtle smile, but she cut down on hunting and concerts. She also spent much of her time travelling around the country. The provinces of the Netherlands were impoverished by taxes and political informers reported rising anger among the inhabitants.

With the green leaves of May came bad news. The empress had been delivered of a son, but he had died soon after birth and a few days later she herself was no more. Now there was only one eight-year-old son, 'Don Philip', as the sole male heir of the enormous realm, and the emperor, a stricken widower, had retired to a monastery far away down in sun-parched Spain.

The blow was a double one for Christina and René. Christina listened to her aunt's anxieties. She watched her pacing the floor wringing her thin hands, dark circles under her eyes. The emperor was likely to remain in Spain. He would not come to ease the burdensome taxes, nor to give René the word of assent that he and Christina longed so desperately to hear – the one short word that would offer them a lifetime of joy. One other chance: Dorothea and Friederich were down there, having travelled the long road to Spain to seek the emperor's support for the conquest of Denmark. Perhaps, Christina hoped, they would put forward her case as well.

Christina and René waited, passively at first. But nothing could keep the wild optimism of their love from flaming up. They began again, briefly, and in secret, to meet and talk together, and at the end of June, on the brightest night of the year, René came to Christina's bed for the first time.

Christina awoke. She heard a nightingale and felt René's kiss and his breath. For a moment she lay still; then her hands moved over his shoulders and down his body. She smelled his hair, his skin; and she uttered a brief cry of pain and joy as she felt the earth open.

Afterwards the nightingale was silent. They lay side by side quiet and exhausted. When René rose she was about to say something. But he hushed her, pressed his lips to hers, smoothed her hair with his hand and vanished through the curtains.

The next night he came again and the next and the next. Each evening she lay waiting, hearing the nightingale in the palace gardens and giving not a thought to how René might come to her room unseen. She caressed his shoulders, feeling every muscle beneath the skin. His arms were used to holding a lance; now they held her naked body. Night after night she and René made love and forgot the rest of the world.

But one week later there came a reminder of that world.

It was morning, and the regent was receiving in her bedroom where, leaning back against a pile of pillows, she was surrounded by her dogs. Her ladies sat on stools at their embroidery; at the end of the bed a little greyhound scratched for fleas. The Portuguese envoy had just left, and conversation turned on the subject of modern moral laxity. Stories about the queen of Navarre were mentioned, as an example of what could degrade public morals, 'but then she is French'.

The regent listened with interest, and now and again with a glint of ironical surprise. Folding her hands, she said, 'Morals and morals . . .?'

She looked at Christina. 'I prefer to say: if not chaste, then at least hushed.'

A servant brought wine and passed it round. No more was said; but Christina saw deadly earnest in the regent's eyes, and understood.

She and René grew careful. He came to her later in the night, when they could be more certain that everyone was asleep. Or they took advantage of the warm summer nights, and of festivities when wine flowed and the court drank deep, and crept out into the gardens. They lit candles and paid for indulgence; receiving forgiveness for their sins, they sinned again. But they were hushed, and the regent made no further comment.

When the regent did converse with her niece she discussed politics. France, she said, was wholly to blame, crying out that it was surrounded by Hapsburg power but ruining both the Low Countries and itself with destructive wars.

Christina came to realise how isolated her aunt was from other human beings, lacking both husband and children. She ruled, in her brother's name; but her power deprived her of trust in those around her. She was remote on her lonely peak, her name illustrious but she herself denied human regard.

Christina and René dallied their way through the summer, totally absorbed in the intoxication of their love. The regent's problem was not theirs.

In August the court moved to The Hague. Dorothea and

Friederich arrived from Spain, and in honour of her niece and the count palatine the regent gave a banquet.

There, while guests were being served with a dish of wild cranes, Mr Wriothesley begged leave to communicate some news. The regent graciously assented. After briefly glancing at Christina he announced that his lord, the king of England, intended to marry, with the Princess Anne of Cleves.

Christina stiffened. She saw horror on the faces around her, for this was dangerous news. The duke of Cleves was the richest and most powerful prince in North Germany. He had earlier proposed to Christina; but now he was demanding Guelderland, offering a serious threat to the Netherlands. Marriage between his sister and King Henry, together with political alliance between the two countries, could prove catastrophic.

There was complete silence. The Englishman was clearly enjoying this moment.

Suddenly came a burst of uncontrolled merriment.

The regent was laughing, doubled up. Her widow's veil quivered.

All the guests looked at each other, and the Englishman grew confused. 'It's perfectly true,' he muttered. The regent, handkerchief to her eyes, said she did not doubt it. At length she reached for her goblet, and raised it to propose a toast. Mr Wriothesley decided to play his trump card. 'They say the princess of Cleves is a very elegant lady.'

That was too much for the regent. She slammed her goblet down on the table and rose, red in the face with repressed laughter. Followed by the count palatine and her two nieces, she left the hall and retired.

'Anne of Cleves is . . .' She gesticulated as if there were no words to express what she wanted to say. 'She is *frightful*.'

Dorothea guffawed. Everyone else laughed, and the regent had to dry her eyes again.

'The king of England, who loves wit, elegance, fine manners, accomplishments, art and music, to marry a great north German cow who can do nothing except embroider and speak Low German. He'll get a shock when he sees her.'

The evening and most of the night was spent in discussing the new English–north German alliance, which was assured of a sticky end. They laughed on, served with wine and small delicacies, and made varied guesses about the course of the wedding night and how long King Henry would endure her. In a voice that resounded with glee the regent said, 'If all the women in the world conspired to wreak revenge on him for what he has done to our sex, they could not find a worse punishment than to put Anne of Cleves in his bed.'

But that was the last time Christina saw her aunt in high good humour.

The relationship between Friederich and the regent soon grew strained. She tried to restrain his financial extravagance, together with the horde of German retainers who ate their way through five meals a day; and it was with great relief that she agreed that Dorothea should stay at court, while Friederich himself went to Antwerp to borrow money for the journey home.

The two sisters were able to enjoy each other's company for less than a week. They went riding together, visiting places well known to them from the carefree world of childhood, and teased Johanna, who grew ruddy-cheeked with confusion. But one day it was over.

It was nine o'clock in the morning. The sisters had gone out riding after Mass. When they returned to the palace, a strange silence reigned.

The small black figure of the regent stood at a window, her back towards them. The autumn sunshine shone through her starched headdress, making a halo round her head. At length she turned, and hissed at Dorothea, 'What is your esteemed spouse doing in England?'

Dorothea turned white. Her mouth opened, but she said nothing. The regent took a step nearer. 'The count palatine is in London, not Antwerp. He was here, in this room, laughing at the king of England's idiocies. And now he is eating off gold plate at Windsor Castle at the table of the English king.'

Dorothea uttered a plaintive little cry. But the regent

screamed at her, 'We are on the brink of war with England and until the king realises he has married a Rhineland cud-chewer we shall continue to be so. His accursed agents are running around my cities rousing unrest, and your spouse has gone over there . . .'

She pointed into the air as if her thin index finger could reach across the sea to England itself, and hooked it. 'What is the intention?'

'Denmark,' stammered Dorothea.

'Denmark,' repeated the regent in amazement. 'Denmark . . .?' Her lower lip dropped. It hung like a fold of skin as she stared at her terrified niece. She said wearily, 'He must be mad.'

The regent turned slowly round to face the window. Standing with her back to the room again she spoke as if to a stupid child. 'King Henry has concluded an alliance with the north German princes. They are in league with the new heretical government in Denmark. And then the count palatine, married to the emperor's niece, believes he can . . .' She stopped, turned her head and asked over her shoulder, 'What did he actually think King Henry might do?'

'Send a fleet against Denmark,' came faintly from Dorothea.

'No . . . no . . .' gasped the regent. 'Of all crazed ideas this is the most lunatic. It is not possible, it . . .'

She stopped and looked at Dorothea, who stood with her round eyes wide beneath her fair curly hair. Twisting the white ribbons of her headdress in a gesture of impotence, the regent spun round and walked out of the room. Her ladies-in-waiting followed her in silence in single file.

A month later count palatine Friederich returned from England, crestfallen. He had been given a hearty welcome, eaten marvellous food, listened to beautiful music – the choral singing in St Paul's had been absolutely magnificent – and been met with great understanding regarding his demands on Denmark. But his case was one in which the king of England did not intend to hoist a single sail or fire one shot. Friederich fetched his little wife and hurried back to Heidelberg.

                    *   *   *

The regent's uneasy suspicions of civil unrest increased. Ghent refused to pay any more taxes, and the town was in open revolt. Couriers were despatched to Spain. It took three weeks to get there, but this time the emperor acted swiftly. Only six weeks later the regent was able to announce that the emperor was on his way and that his route lay through France. King François was another ruler who did not care for unruly citizens who refused to pay taxes. There was as much danger for him as for the emperor.

On the 14th of February 1540 the emperor rode into Ghent at the head of his court, his nobility and his army. On his entry into the city the regent rode on his right, Christina on his left. After them, carried in litters, came the ladies of the imperial family, followed by the chief courtiers, foreign envoys, princes and knights of the Order of the Golden Fleece, Cardinal Farnese, the viceroy of Sicily, the prince of Orange, the duke of Alba, the counts Egmont and Buren and a host of Netherlandish aristocracy.

Then came the troops. One thousand archers, five thousand mercenaries, artillery, cavalry, infantry. A total of sixty thousand men and fifteen thousand horse marched in an endless file behind the emperor as, with his sister and niece, he made his way towards the Prinzenhof. Six hours passed before the last soldiers entered the city gates and marched through the fine streets, and everywhere the citizens looked on trembling at this demonstration of imperial, ecclesiastical and military power. They stood, at windows and on roofs, powerless and afraid. It was an unforgivable thing that they had dared to do, in setting themselves up against their prince, against the authority of the state. And whereas there had been no limit to the promises they had received from foreign agents, in fact no help had come.

The emperor's long chin was on Christina's right. It protruded from his face as if this deformity were itself the source of his enormous power. Behind them came the ringing sounds of harness, of thousands of hooves and hundreds of wagon wheels on the cobblestones. Ahead was nothing but silence. Christina's eyes roved over the crowds of people. Among them, suddenly one stood out as somebody she recognised.

Kiki was perched on some scaffolding. The dwarf's short legs swung to and fro under green skirts and her hair hung down over the wooden boarding like a curtain. Her wrinkled face wore a broad grin. Christina shuddered at the huge red tongue in the wide red jaw, and realised there were rich pickings to be had just now in the town of Ghent for one who knew how to listen, and how to report on each rebellious word.

The dwarf rose. For a moment she tottered on her plank. Regaining her balance, she picked up her green silk skirts and bounced like a ball on a roof. She crawled up on all fours until she was sitting astride a steep gable top. Christina looked down and away. She herself was riding on the side of power; but seeing the tool of that power disgusted her.

Twenty-three leaders of the revolt were brought to trial and condemned. Nine of them were executed in the market square. The citizens were compelled to pay the four hundred thousand florins that had caused the rebellion. The town lost all its rights and privileges, and confiscations and heavy fines were imposed.

On the 3rd of May the emperor took his seat on a tribune in front of the Prinzenhof. The corps of archers were positioned in a semicircle around their prince, who was bearing the crown and sceptre of the realm. The senators and leading citizens of the town approached him, bareheaded, barefoot, and clad in black. Kneeling in the dust at the emperor's feet, they begged him for mercy.

Thousands looked on from roofs and windows. The black figures lay on the ground; but the emperor did not speak.

There was a faint rustle of skirts. The regent rose and began to speak. She reminded the emperor that this was his birthplace; and she begged for compassion on its citizens who so humbly craved mercy.

Finally the emperor responded. He would restore their

property to the citizens 'out of brotherly love for his sister and compassion for the rebels'. But they were not to regain their privileges; the taxes must be paid; and a citadel would be built to prevent further revolt. At one blow Ghent had lost its standing as the richest and most powerful city in the Low Countries. Its hour of greatness had passed.

The court moved to Bruges. One evening, Christina and René were watching the swans that were sailing along one of the city's canals. A weeping willow trailed its branches in the moss-green water, and grey cygnets swam in and out among its leaves. The sun picked out crinkles on the water and sparkled on the mirror of its surface. The white head-dresses of the lay sisters swayed from side to side over the bridge to the herb garden of the Béguinage Convent.

This was to be their place, the city of their happiness. It was here, so the emperor had promised, that René would be granted an audience. They would be betrothed here, in the town of the swans, where the light from the sea made the heavens so vast and so vaulted. In the last two years they had come to know each other's laughter, each other's thoughts, anger and joys. They had talked of childhood, their family; and of hunting, of the world, of faith and of death.

But in this hour, when the church bells were ringing the sun down, they were silent. They were united in another sphere, they hovered in a daze above marsh and meadow and out over the sea, where they moved with the pale light of the summer night beyond the horizon.

XI

It was dark; all the world was asleep. In the narrow streets of Brussels only the watchmen's cry was now and then to be heard.

Christina stood looking out of the window. René had just left her bed, after the last night they would spend together. The emperor had said no.

She had had to stay up. René had gone, and yet he was still there, not until the sun rose would she lose him finally. She could still feel his lips, and hear the last words he had spoken. 'Now I am only my skeleton; I am skin and flesh and blood no more. I am as dead as if I were already in my tomb and the worms had devoured me.'

His voice had rung out against the walls. She had felt his skin against hers as the darkness pressed him to her, holding him fast.

The watchman called; it was half-past twelve. How many hours were left to her? The summer night was short; if it had been January she could have kept him during Mass: three or four hours, maybe five.

The emperor's word was law as firmly as God's will. That it should be so was ingrained in both of them, so that it had left them struck down, undone, as if they had undergone one another's death.

A promise made long ago to the duke of Lorraine: his daughter Anne was to marry René. Just that. There was nothing else. A word that must be kept. So absurd, so meaningless. Her beloved René was to be sent off to a woman he had never seen, as she had once been sent to the duke of Milan. He protested, fighting for his cause. But the emperor refused: never would he give his assent to the marriage of Christina and René.

But while René was still here she clung to him, caressed him, responded to him. The daylight must not come; they would live together in the dark, in eternal frost; in the name of love they would go down with torches and break holes in the ice to let the swans find food. The world could go under, but not she, René and the white birds. They would fly with them towards the light, to find a place on earth where the sun was always in the west, where the shadows were always long and the evenings cool. They would live in citrus groves, and her children would be born under the blossoming branches, small girls and boys who grew tall and stretched out for the golden fruit as she had done that day in the garden of Cussago, the last day of her childhood.

When the rosy dawn light outlined church towers and the roofs of houses, when the first smoke rose from chimneys and the first lighters pushed out from the canal sides, she awakened to agonising reality. She wished with René that she could feel herself dead and gone, her flesh eaten by worms. But she was alive, and suffering the pain of the living.

The night watchmen had gone home. Sounds came from the streets, shutters were flung open, bells called to Mass; and when a pair of swans left their nest on the bank and slid down into the water, followed by five grey young ones, Christina stood with her head against the window-frame and wept.

She did not hear the door open before steps sounded close by. She turned, and saw the regent standing before her alone.

Under her eyes Christina noticed the dark circles that had been there ever since the revolt in Ghent. But she sensed something else as well, something that had nothing to do with problems of government. It was a hint of pain, of something within her that had its roots far back in time. Christina had never seen it before, but it was like a reflection of her own sorrow.

'Come,' the regent said softly.

Christina did not answer. But her aunt spoke again. 'Come ...'

It was not the same as the 'Come along . . .', that time at Mechelen when she was taken to see the portraits of her father and mother. It was terse and unechoing, as if cut off. And yet it had the same tone, as of a woman's longing to pour out her love on the child she did not have.

'Come . . .' her aunt repeated in the same quiet voice, and added, 'We will go to Mass. It helps . . .' She stood, occupied with her own thoughts, and added, as if doubting her own words, 'A little, anyway . . .'

Bruges now lay bright beneath the summer sunshine. Christina, glancing, saw that the glazed tiles of the house-tops sparkled. The miracle had not happened. The world had not come to an end. It lived on, and she would have to live. Amid the pain and the longing, she was to suffer the unkindest fate of all, to remain on this earth alive.

Christina tore herself away from her thoughts. With a defiant lift of her head she straightened herself, as if pos-sessed of the strength to free herself from all emotion, all life and all dreams. She stood in the centre of the room and said, 'Yes. I am coming.'

For a moment she thought she had heard the singing of swans' wings, and felt herself borne aloft by the white birds. But that was a fantasy. The swans lived in the real world. Within the waterways of the city they looked after their young, and lived out their lives in a way that she never could.

René married Anne of Lorraine in Nancy, and some months later he brought his bride to the Low Countries. There, the regent had arranged a celebration for the newly married couple.

Christina looked at herself in the mirror as her hair was being parted in the middle and swept up at the temples. She felt the need for something physical that she could seize.

She was going to see René again, this time with another woman at his side. What could she find to support her, what could hold her up, help her through this evening and give meaning to the days and years to come?

The stays of her corset were closed around her waist; her dress was fastened; golden chains were hung around her neck. It was a long time since she had wept. But she often felt the urge to do so, rather than to feel emptiness, like the sensations of a hand reaching out to find nothing.

Christina's eyes swept the festive company gathered in the great hall. They were celebrating a marriage, his marriage; and she had joined in receiving the bride and groom. She looked into his blue eyes. It was like looking at coloured wax. His look communicated nothing; was he dead to the world or just to her? He presented his bride, neat and comely with a big wide nose, who smiled, apparently happy. Didn't she know, or was she merely being polite? Or had René forgotten everything?

She glanced around, seeing faces, diamonds, coiffures, burning torches, brocade, gold and tapestries. She heard laughter and talk, her own voice, her own words.

Friederich's skin hung down from his chin, flopping like cloth, as he conversed with the regent, the centre of the assembled company. She was a hub, on which all the room's colours were mingled, concentrated and turned into a diminutive black central point.

Count Egmont gesticulated. Christina knew what he was describing. It was the best story of the summer, the lightning duration of King Henry's marriage, the divorce, and what Anne of Cleves had received as a consolation. What would they all do if they did not have his private life to gossip about, and their speculations on wife number five? Christina felt the English envoy's gaze resting on her. No, she would not be discarded with a couple of castles as an apology and the ridiculous title of 'the king's adopted sister'.

Dorothea was wearing a gown of red velvet with magnificent gold embroidery, her sleeves so wide that they hung down to the floor. Suddenly it struck Christina how long her sister had been married. Four years; and her waist was still slim; they had no children.

Christina had not thought about it; no one had talked of it or even mentioned it. While the musicians struck up and the bridal pair began the dance, thoughts raced through Christina's head quicker than they could have been formulated in words. She retraced them, repeated them to herself: Dorothea and Friederich had the hereditary claim, Denmark had been their affair, not hers. She was merely a little sister. But if they did not have children; if there were no one to hand it down to . . .

Friederich left the dance and went over to a corner alone. Christina followed him. She seated herself beside him and was about to say something, when the bridal pair danced past. René and Anne were smiling at each other; she thought she might scream. She felt her brother-in-law's hand on hers. He gave it a fatherly pat. 'Believe me, I know how it hurts.'

His eyes were bloodshot from much wine. He shook his head as if trying to rid himself of unwelcome memories, and snorted, 'Look at your sister, poor child. She's saddled with an old wreck like me, with a fat stomach, spindly thighs and indigestion.'

He emptied his goblet and held it out to a servant to have it refilled. 'I don't trouble her in the summer; there has to be no light. I don't want her to see me naked. It's enough for her to bear with my belly when it's unseen.'

He tossed off the goblet at one gulp. 'Why by all the fiends of hell couldn't she have had a better husband? A young man who could beget children with her, so that all her affections wouldn't have to be poured out on puppies? It's a confounded shame. She's only nineteen; and I'm thirty-seven years older and could be her grandfather.'

Christina hushed him. He said slowly, 'You were luckier. He died. God was really good about that. He took the old duke to Him and you were spared a feeble dotard's efforts. There are limits now to what they can offer you. You lost René; but there'll be someone else. Someone young. Someone you can make love to on light summer nights without having to hide your disgust.'

Friederich's head drooped; but he suddenly pulled himself together and straightened, as if he had not realised that he'd fallen asleep. 'Poor girl. She's too good for this.'

The servant poured him more wine. He took a gulp and swilled his teeth with it. 'You'll be happy one day. You'll have children. And, one day, you'll be queen of Denmark.'

Christina jumped. He had expressed, out loud, what had merely skimmed the surface of her mind. She, Christina, as queen of Denmark.

It was as if something was awakening in her, to snatch her away from the dancing and talking. All around her, other people, in satin and silk, gold and silver, were celebrating. They drank sweet wine and ate fruit. Friederich was snoring now. His heavy stomach hung down between his thin straddled thighs.

The trumpets sounded a fanfare. The sound was familiar to Christina; but it had never seemed so beautiful. She saw the standard with the imperial crowned double eagles. It was a symbol; an expression of power. Something, long awaited by her, had been formulated in words, and her inner self stretched forth both hands to seize it.

Christina was well informed on the political situation. But on personalities and division of forces she had no particular opinions. Now, with the coming of autumn, she began to hold long conversations with her aunt. The Danes were on the point of signing a treaty with France. But the regent considered that it would not be of much use to those heretics in the North – for how could the French get an army up there if the emperor did attack?

The regent was more worried, in the event of new war negotiations, about access for shipping in the Sound. 'If they cut off grain imports from the Baltic the Low Countries will starve.'

She described to her niece the human being behind Gustav Vasa, the self-made king of Sweden: gifted, a brilliant orator; 'and he knows from his own experience how easy it is to bring the Swedes into revolt, and fears they will do it again'.

But though she thought there was little prospect of regaining Sweden, Denmark–Norway was another matter. The burghers and peasantry had not forgotten, they were still opposed to Christian the Third. The nobles too were outraged, over the Holsteiners being granted fiefs in payment for the costly civil war. Meanwhile Christian was a weak man on a wavering throne and in fact could only look to the north German states for support. In a confusion of military alliances and political intrigues and enmities the emperor was the solution. He wanted the rightful ruler in Denmark, and he had the means to carry it through. But first he had to rid himself of his other enemies.

Christina drowned her lost love under a welter of political ambitions. She wanted to crowd out her memories, and relieved the pain by seizing again on her anger over being robbed of her birthright. She substituted her place at René's side with her own position in the European arena. As she rode out from the city gates that winter in the first swirl of snow, it was with no feeling of happiness. But at least she could feel satisfaction over her own importance; and the yellow December sky and wintry cold suited her mood.

Christina was informed of the emperor's desire for her to marry Franz, eldest son and heir to the duke of Lorraine.

She was in no doubt of the value of the match. Lorraine was a borderland between the imperial German states and France. For far too long now, it had been dominated by the French. The duke's daughter was married to René, the emperor's faithful officer and subject. If the son were now to marry the emperor's niece this important region would change sides.

Christina deliberated. She did so soberly and swiftly. She knew Franz. He was young, only four years older than herself; albeit his steady gaze always had a look of melancholy. For three years René had commanded all her senses. Now she tried to assess Franz. Like something that had been lying at the bottom of a cupboard, she now took him out, dusted him off and began to consider him.

His face was long and gaunt and there were deep lines around his mouth as if the whole of life was one long sad thought. He would never laugh like René; he had not his smile; and she would never be moved with desire at the sight of his neck. But he was cultivated, not a comical pompous object like the duke of Cleves. Franz was well read, interested in music and art, and not bad to look at; but the laughter and the white birds were not his.

On the other hand it would be a distinguished alliance. His family was ancient; the duc de Guise was his cousin and one of the most powerful men in France, and a cousin of his was married to the king of Scotland.

Coolly and calmly, Christina came to the conclusion that, of the young princes who courted her, Franz was the best. He was not comical or old, not foolish or ugly. Time and married life would tell how much he could offer on the positive side. Christina had absolutely no expectations. Romantic love was a thing of the past; she had known it and she had lost it. Physical love would be a ritual, but a ritual that could bring her what her brother died too young to gain and what Friederich was clearly too old to give Dorothea.

Christina wanted heirs, for the sake of the Danish throne – for otherwise she would be unable to get it for herself. As a wife she would discharge her duties at table and in bed, and she would serve the emperor in being his faithful niece who had rescued Lorraine from French domination. And one day, when she should demand them, the emperor would then repay her, by rewarding her with her throne, her kingdom, her right.

The festivities at Christina's wedding were coloured by news from elsewhere. The duke of Cleves was to have married Jeanne of Navarre. But, although only twelve years old, the young lady had her own ideas on the matter. She would neither own nor have the German prince, and on entering the chapel on the arm of her uncle the king of France she threw herself on the floor and screamed.

There had been total confusion. There lay the bride, in her beautiful gown adorned with precious jewels – diamonds were everywhere – wailing like a two-year-old. King François, visualising an important political alliance vanishing to the accompaniment of the girl's howls, ordered that she be dragged to the altar. But there could be no doubt about the outcome. The marriage had had to be declared invalid. It was impossible to declare that it had been entered upon with the partners' consent. It was one thing to force two people to live together, but to carry this out before the eyes of all the guests and clerics by dragging an unwilling bride was another, and the slight little girl had realised this and made use of it.

The incident provided Christina with food for thought. It *was* feasible to get your own way – if all possible means were used. As she danced with her melancholy future duke of Lorraine she wondered why she and René had not employed such methods, why they had not had the courage and violence of twelve-year-old Jeanne. Christina noticed her aunt's smile of satisfaction at the forthcoming marriage. But she also observed the sad eyes of her betrothed, and felt worn out at the thought of all that learning. For where was he; where was the man, the lover? What kind of being was she about to live with?

Christina was married in high summer. On the 10th of July 1541 she embarked on her second marriage, in the town where her mother had once accepted the proposal of the king of Denmark's representative. Guests had come from far and near; the hall where the celebrations took place was a splendid sight; and at Christina's side was a bridegroom for whom she felt nothing. Christina accepted Franz of Lorraine, with gladness in her smile, common sense in her head, and coldness in her heart.

Lorraine, 1541–1552

XII

Wherever in this world Anders Brygger happened to find himself there was always someone who asked how things were in Denmark. True, there weren't many ways to pass the time at inns and lodging houses, other than in telling stories and reporting the news from home until you fell asleep. Anders was a source of wonder and incredulity everywhere. Cattle dealers and Lübeck merchants would always have something to tell; but it was good to have general rumour confirmed by one who knew.

Where it concerned the kings of Denmark, Anders could boast knowledge at first hand, for he had himself been in the harbour at Copenhagen when the fleet of King Frederik had been out in the Sound. The ships had saluted so that the whole town could hear. All, that is, except the one with Christian the Second on board.

It had been that hot July day in 1532. Round about him people had tears in their eyes. Many wept to remember the time nine years earlier when they had seen King Christian's sails disappear round Skovshoved point. The poor queen, beloved of them all, was dead. But was King Christian bringing the children home with him? And anyway, what was going to happen to the people, standing as they now did, between two kings? Frederik in the city, behind the thick walls of his castle, and Christian the Second, to whom he had promised safe conduct, out at sea.

But the oath of safe conduct had been broken. What the burghers and peasants, and the people of Norway, thought was of no consequence; now it was the nobles and the Holsteiners who made the decisions. The ship had sailed past the city and taken the returning king to Sønderborg Castle. He was a prisoner, even though he was their king.

Anders was a man who had had an education. He could talk well, and had a good knowledge of both German and Latin. As the son of a burgher, he was in no doubt as to where his heart was. The nobility were a rabble. All that concerned them was grabbing for themselves. Whatever the trade in question they were after it: hides, cattle, corn, fish – if they could sell the very flies, they would.

Anders was the only son of Mads Brygger. Mads had known how to hold on to money; and when Anders duly inherited he set off to see the world. At home, he would have had no idea what to do with himself.

It was not only the business of the wrong king. Anders had studied theology, and there had been a time when he had wished to dedicate his life to the church. But he had hardly started on the introductory subjects of rhetoric and dialectics before there were people on street corners bawling that there was nothing in the Bible about indulgences and saints and the worship of Mary, that Christ had never mentioned purgatory and that you could not buy your way to salvation. He heard the hue and cry at the town hall on Gammeltorv, listened to the insults hurled at Bishop Rønnov and saw Hans Tausen dragged before the court.

One of the kings died in Gottorp Castle, where he had hidden himself, because he could not make out the Danes. Now his son was demanding the crown, and still the other king lived on in his Sønderborg prison.

Anders made a decision. It was in books that he would find the word of God. As strife harassed the land, he studied day and night. Throughout the siege of Copenhagen he was gnawed by hunger. Rats fed on the corpses lying in the gutters and lanes of the Snaren Rodemål where he had rented a little room; and the rats themselves were eaten by those who still had the strength to catch them.

Anders paid eight farthings for a dead crow and three farthings for a live frog, and went on reading the Bible line by line, word by word. He buried himself in Luther and Erasmus. And when Copenhagen surrendered and the king that some called Joker rode into town, Anders stood and stared, lean as a skeleton, and was not one jot closer to true knowledge. Erasmus's measured common sense and faith in humanity appealed to him, but it solved no problems. Was the Church of Rome right or was Luther?

There was nothing in the Bible about purgatory, indulgences or Mariolatry. But had not Jesus said to St Peter that he would give him the keys of heaven? What you keep bound on earth will be kept bound in heaven, what you set free on earth will be set free in heaven? And was not Saint Peter the first bishop of Rome and the popes his successors as God's representatives here on earth who could interpret and explain the words of the Bible?

Anders saw the Catholic Church in Denmark collapse, to be replaced by the new faith. But people around him were only prepared to complain about the Roman Church grabbing everything for itself; hardly ever did they talk of holy communion. If bread and wine really were transformed into the body and blood of Jesus, it was much less interesting than the pleasure of seeing the rich fat bishops thrown out of their posts.

It was a small and bitter congregation who maintained the old ritual. Another small faction claimed to understand the deeper significance of the new Church. But the rest of the population merely thought it good that they were no longer controlled by Rome.

The new king was kindly. He did not penalise the town and its inhabitants and he made the break with the Church of Rome, as they wanted. Supplies arrived, and people could eat again. It was all satisfactory enough, but they would still have preferred the return of Christian the Second. He was Danish; he was theirs; and he was opposed to the hated nobility.

On his travels Anders heard much to interest a man like him. In the Low Countries he met the Mennonites, pious humble folk willing to go to the stake for their convictions. In Germany the horrors of the peasant rising had not been forgotten; nonetheless people there were glad to sacrifice their lives for their faith, be it Lutheran or Catholic. They knew why either one belief or the other was the truth; and they responded with horror to Anders's account of how Danish bishops had accepted gifts of land from the king in return for forgetting their oath to the Church.

When Anders was journeying through Denmark he had spent a night at a parsonage, in Funen. The same priest had stayed on, merely conducting divine service in the new form, even though he did not really understand it. The local peasants had thought at first that they could take over the bishops' property, until it had been given to the Holsteiners. To start with, too, they had believed that now everyone could be buried within the church, not just the rich. But they began to think again, as time passed and the house of God became a fetid graveyard where you had to jump over the holes in the floor. Rain poured in through the church roof, and there were cracks in the walls. But there was no one to carry out repairs, for there was no one who could pay. That evening, talking to Anders, the priest wept. He missed all his saints, in particular the Virgin Mary. She was so beautiful and she had always been with him. Why did she have to be cast out in this way?

But when Anders mentioned this incident in countries to the South, people looked askance. They thought the Danes were heathens. Horrified, he wondered whether he too was a heathen as he could so easily decide which king he wanted, but not which faith held the truth.

Anders saw beauty on his travels, and he saw splendour. There were towns with cathedrals, with palaces, fountains and statues. Once, especially, his way was brightened by a splendid spectacle.

He was on his way through Germany. Beyond the flat fields a distant cloud of dust rose up from a company of travellers on horseback. They were evidently people of importance, for the dust cloud was huge. Anders reckoned a royal company was approaching.

He stood, marvelling at the brilliance of the cavalcade. At the head, in magnificent green riding habits with golden edging, rode an elderly man and a blonde young woman. The harness of their steeds was adorned with gold, and glittered in the morning sun. Next came hundreds of horsemen; but, as they passed, gradually the gold changed to silver, silver to iron. Velvet became cloth, and cloth, homespun, which turned into rags. Royalty was followed by nobles who in turn preceded servants. Then came the soldiers, and asses bearing loads of chests and pans, and rattling carts drawn by mules. At the tail end came a rabble of beggars, hags, loud-voiced wenches and vagrant mercenaries – all those who hoped to steal, beg or whore in return for the pickings always to be had from so huge a display of wealth and power.

Only later did Anders learn that he had seen the count palatine on one of his constant journeys, together with his wife, Princess Dorothea. He regretted having stared so hard at their display of wealth when instead he might have studied their faces more closely. Christian the Second's eldest daughter had gone riding past him, so close that he might have touched her horse. He felt a surge of joy, to think how near he had been to her, the daughter of his beloved king – and to her husband the count palatine, who had tried to relieve the wretched Copenhageners during the siege of their city. That was something neither they nor Anders had ever forgotten.

'Hadn't the count, through his wife, the best right to the throne?' went the whisper through the workshops and small houses of Copenhagen. When Christian the Second came to die, the count palatine was the man they wanted, especially if his wife could bear him and Denmark an heir.

But although Anders had caught only a glimpse of the princess he had noted the narrowness of her waist. Was Christian the Third indeed to have the satisfaction of seeing the prisoner king's line dying out? And could the rumour be true that the Holsteiners had sent agents to Regensburg, to poison the little Prince Hans?

Anders continued on his wanderings in search of a meaning to his life, and a true faith. Time passed, and the wolfskin lining of his coat lost its fur. Europe was being ravaged by warfare. In France, during the cold winter of 1543, the front pushed him eastwards; and one January day he found himself crossing the border, into the neutral dukedom of Lorraine.

In the couple of years he had been journeying, it was the worst weather Anders had seen. The timbers of the little inn creaked in the gale; and snow drifted down through the smoke-hole in the roof as Anders gnawed a dry ham bone that he was trying to wash down with sour wine.

He was only an hour away from Nancy, but this was the fourth day he had been snowbound. The inn was not much more than one room, containing scullery, kitchen, a few scrubbed tables and benches and a pile of hay where the serving wench slept. The walls were bare and blotched with damp, and rats ran like shadows in the rafters. Now and then one of them lost its balance, fell to the floor, and scurried off before anyone could hit it with the shovel.

The innkeeper sat nodding in a corner with her hands in her apron. She was a surly creature with drooping corners to her mouth and breasts of the same inclination. She resembled a plant that had shot up too fast and not had time to put out leaves; and she obviously thought that others could live on the same meagre diet that supported her.

Two Franciscan monks slept, their heads on a table. Their grey-brown cowls hid their faces. A silk dealer from Nice leaned against the wall, snoring. He was an elderly man with a bony face. Judging from his clothes and the absence of a servant he was not having much success with his business. Lastly there was a young woman. She was plump, with a pleasant face and big bold eyes; but Anders had no difficulty in guessing her occupation. A respectable woman did not travel alone. Anders cast her one more sideways look, and saw her mouth curve in a smile of invitation. But he decided against it. She was the type who passed on the French disease.

Another rat fell from the rafters and vanished under one of the benches. Anders's thoughts were far away. He was depressed and tired and slightly drunk and was wondering what all this travelling around foreign countries had brought him. At that moment the door was opened.

A rush of air and snow burst into the inn before Anders could take in the two strangers. Only when they had finished shaking the snow off themselves did he gather that here was a distinguished-looking man, with his servant. The sullen innkeeper woke up.

In a trice she had hauled the servant girl out of the hay. They curtsied deep to the new guest. The gentleman and his servant merely moved to the fireplace, where soon a fresh pile of logs was blazing.

The monks awoke, and three grey-brown cowls were raised from the oak planking of the table. Out of them peered one lean and two fat faces, as three pairs of eyes observed the strangers. The woman beamed at the sight of them. Only the silk dealer went on sleeping, oblivious.

Anders, after years of travelling, knew all about the kind of inns that were open to everyone, and those that were reserved for the highborn. So he was all the more curious about the man now warming his hands at the fire. Only atrocious weather could bring a man of rank and position to a place such as this.

The man was short of stature and dark-complexioned. Hair and beard were black, and his eyes were darker than Anders had seen even on his journeying in France. His voice, as he sat down and gave his order to the woman, was not quite audible. Did he speak German, or the impossible French that was also the language of this region?

The woman brought wine, goblets and a jug. Nothing lacked when it was a matter of serving the gentry. But the man seemed nervous. He grasped the goblet, emptied it, put it down; but he kept hold of it even though he clearly wanted no more to drink.

What was it he expected to happen; or perhaps feared? Anders could not take his eyes off him. He pictured robbers pursuing him, enemies lurking, or . . . Anders was lost for ideas. The mere sight of the man's costly clothes excluded his imagination from so distant a world. He sat, staring as if at a mathematical puzzle impossible to solve. What earthly thing could you fear when you were rich?

But now Anders could hear something. It came like a faint

booming through the roar of the storm. What was it? He turned his head but it was gone. Then he heard it again, and noticed that the distinguished stranger had also straightened himself to listen.

It could not be thunder at this time of year unless the Devil had taken possession of both heaven and earth and was about to destroy God's kingdom. And again . . . Anders thought he felt the floor vibrating slightly. Was it war? Not in this weather. What did it mean? The skinny ale-wife sat quite still, listening too, holding her apron with her red swollen hands.

Suddenly the fine gentleman threw himself at the door, tore it open and went to stand right outside. Snow came hurling in. For a moment he stood, listening, and then began to do something strange. He was counting on his fingers, like a child who has just learned to reckon.

Anders saw the woman doing the same thing, and then the three monks. All of them were counting on their fingers. A drift was forming around the man as he stood in the doorway, and Anders shivered. The others went on with their counting. How much had they calculated? Confused, he looked at the monks, at the woman, the nobleman and his servant. Nineteen, twenty, twenty-one, twenty-two . . . they all looked at each other . . . twenty-three . . . a cry rang out from them. The sound from outside continued, but the nobleman slammed the door. He, the woman and his servant began to dance around, shouting at each other: A prince, a little prince, Her Grace has borne a prince!

Anders felt he was in a madhouse. Suddenly he understood. He was in the dukedom of Lorraine; and the duchess must have had a son. But the duchess was also the daughter of Christian the Second.

Christian the Second had had his first grandchild, and it was a boy. This was an historic moment. Christian the Second's only son was dead; but now, at this moment, his grandson had been born. The Copenhageners' beloved king had a male heir again.

Anders was trembling with emotion. He wanted to weep, he wanted to laugh. He, the brewer's son from Copenhagen, to be in the midst of this, to be the first Dane to know that the line of Christian the Second would not die out with his children, but would live on through his youngest daughter. At this moment he was possessed of knowledge which Christian the Third would not have for several weeks, and it was news that would bring fear to the self-appointed king. Now he could say as often as he liked that no woman had been chosen to govern Denmark – but had not Queen Margrethe acted as regent for her under-age son?

Anders felt uplifted, dizzy, he raised his goblet, held it with his arm outstretched and shouted, 'Long live the future king of Denmark!'

The distinguished gentleman broke off his dance and stared at Anders. The others followed suit.

Anders went on holding up his mug as he added, 'I am Danish; and we Danes want to see the duchess and her son on the Danish throne.'

Silence. It seemed as if the storm itself quietened in the face of his sudden strength. The nobleman approached him. Standing before Anders, small and dark, he bowed as to an equal, and introduced himself. 'Gian Battista. I come from Milan.'

'Anders Brygger,' replied Anders, attempting to imitate the elegant gesture.

'Her Grace's secretary,' Battista said.

'Graduate in theology,' responded Anders, promoting himself slightly.

'And you come from Denmark? All the way from Denmark?' asked the Italian incredulously. Anders nodded, noting the other's astonishment, as if his fatherland were a patent of nobility in itself.

The Italian's look of pleasure vanished, and a shadow of anxiety crossed his fine features. 'Is there an altar nearby that we can visit? We must pray for Her Grace's life.'

Anders felt himself invincibly optimistic. With a wave of the hand he said, 'Her Grace will live.'

The Italian looked at him as at a saint. They cavorted with joy as the last of the salute sounded from the battlements of Nancy. A hundred and one reports.

The duchess had borne a son. It was the 15th of February 1543; and the ale-wife and her servant lass, three Franciscan monks, a merchant from Nice, who had woken up at last, a loose woman, an Italian nobleman and his servant and Anders Brygger from Copenhagen were bawling and singing in the flickering light. In the hostelry known as the Golden Lion they danced and drank the night away. Despite its high-sounding name, the shoddy shelter had never before welcomed so distinguished a guest to celebrate so princely an event.

They laid the child in Christina's arms. A small creature with reddish skin, with arms, legs, hands, feet, ten tiny fingers. His hand closed around her finger. He cried, and she lifted him to her cheek and felt him against her skin. It was an incomprehensible miracle.

Voices were speaking around her. 'Her Grace is a strong woman . . . an easy birth . . .' There was the howling of the gale, and torches, and flames from the fire; and his little body against hers, his little head on her naked shoulder, his warmth against hers. She held him with both hands, his screams changed to little whimpers and as he slept she thought how painful it must be to be born. She swore a holy oath that nothing human should ever take him from her.

There were sounds again; she opened her eyes; Franz stood there. He was hearing the witnesses' assurances that the child had been born of her body. She had been married to him for nineteen months, during which time her coldness had slowly abated. It changed, though into something less than love. What was it? Tenderness? Yes, and pleasure in seeing him coming towards her, in hearing his step, in talking with him of architecture and art. Christina had come to know him, this wistful, inquiring man.

When Franz took the child in his arms she saw tears of joy run down his cheeks; and at that moment she loved him. It came in a brief flash and she found herself hoping that she would finally be able to force her feelings away from what was lost, that this moment could be lasting.

She heard a booming sound. The cannon were saluting

146

from the battlements out into the snowstorm, while the midwife massaged her breasts with crushed snowdrop bulbs to ease the tension and release the milk. She had given the dukedom an heir. But it was the child, her little boy, who slept in her arms.

Not only were all her pains forgotten. They had given her love; different, more selfless and perhaps even stronger than the love that had once given her pain.

Christina had seen her new capital city for the first time in the September of 1541. She had dismounted from her horse at the Porte de la Craffe. Young peasant girls dressed all in white stood before the massive round towers of the gate to present the bride with baskets of fresh fruit. With Franz at her side she had walked through the gateway and along narrow rue St Georges, where people were crowded against the walls to see her. She had seen banners and flags, and rose leaves were strewn before her feet. People were pressed against every window. The town's two-storeyed houses were built in the southern style, with their long side facing the street. They lacked the fine gables and stepped silhouettes of Netherland streets, nor did they own the lively colours of Milan. Everything she looked at was grey and dull. But the beautiful statue of Duke Anton, above the main entrance of the ducal palace was graceful enough. Christina entered her new home.

The great Deer Hall was renowned throughout Europe. It was a hundred and fifty feet long, and furnished with stools and chairs covered in gilded leather. Its beautiful wall paintings represented scenes from the life of Christ, depicted allegorically as the life of the deer from a small calf grazing on the banks of a stream up to its death in the chase. This indeed was splendour.

But when Christina stood on one of the semicircular balconies of the palace, she felt a sudden movement of anger. They shouted up to her from the street, 'Hoch!', 'Hoch!', and occasionally, 'Vive!'. Franz's gaze rested on her, enamoured. But everything she saw was grey and outdated. A mere seven thousand people lived here, crammed inside the city walls. It was a capital city without palaces or fountains, without air. The new Italian style had not yet arrived here; the only things worth seeing were the equestrian statue, the Deer Hall and the spire of St Evre's church. She felt as if she were relegated a century back in time. She smiled at Franz and she smiled at the people and all the while resentment grew in her. Here was she, a king's daughter, and the emperor's niece, in a wretched dukedom with a wretched capital.

She waved to the people below. It was not their fault and it was not Franz's, nor the emperor's nor anyone else's – except the treacherous Danish nobles who had betrayed her father, and bereft him of his power and her of her rights.

The crowd milled beneath her, as they started to throw flowers up to her. She saw white lilies whirling through the air, and bunches of three red carnations, symbolising the three nails in Christ's cross. She saw a glint of happiness in Franz's face and recovered herself. Her indignation faded, and she looked at the faces, broad heavy faces below, faithful just as the citizens of Copenhagen had been faithful to her father. They stood in the dark street, under the sandstone demons that jutted from the eaves of the steep slate roofs.

From the high second-storey balcony, Christina leaned out to catch the flowers. A bouquet fell into her hands, thrown by an old woman.

It was not flowers, merely some twigs bound together with a scrap of string. Rosemary, signifying fidelity.

Christina untied the string. There were nine twigs. She took one of them and put it into her bodice as she had done once before long ago. The others she threw back one by one. The poor woman's simple gift to her became her gift to them, and a shriek of joy rose from the street. Hands stretched up to catch eight little green twigs while the ninth nestled in her bodice like a jewel.

Christina returned to the hall, and the many people awaiting her there. As Franz presented them to her, they were each smiling, but their eyes were nonetheless appraising. The balcony doors were closed, and the noise from the street lessened. Christina found herself in conversation with her

148

husband's brother Nicholai, a young man of twenty with prominent eyes and a soft, weak mouth, whose office was bishop of Metz. He was courtesy itself; but Christina had caught a glimpse of him whispering with the acknowledged leader of the nobility, Count Salm, who now stood only a few steps away.

Salm's eyes met hers. He was dressed in brown velvet and stood rubbing his hands, on which gold rings dug deep into the fat of each finger. Politically, he adhered to the French whereas Christina was the emperor's representative. The two of them exchanged friendly words, while on the wall behind him the young fawn suckled from the doe. Count Salm was the most dangerous man in Lorraine.

Also present was Louise de Batonville, who had been chosen as Christina's principal lady-in-waiting. She was a dignified, youngish Frenchwoman, with a glimpse of brown hair under her widow's veil and considerable beauty in the severe lines of her face. Looking at the fullness of her mouth, Christina pictured her lover also as someone young.

The slanting rays of the morning sun fell through the windows. Christina moved around the room, speaking briefly to each person there, trying to get a first impression of everyone who would be around her from now on. They included her husband's closest relatives, the mighty duc de Guise and his family, all of them wholeheartedly French and opposed to the emperor and his policies.

Christina felt hostility. Not openly expressed, but in the air that was encompassed by those exquisitely decorated walls. There was more whispering than talking, and looks were exchanged far more than words. Outside, clouds were building up. Franz was at her side; nonetheless she felt herself alone. Her hand strayed to her bodice. She cast a long look at the crowd of de Guises. They had their castles, their armies, power and great fortunes, intrigues and ambitions, the cardinal's hat and a sister on the throne in Scotland. Christina's fingers played with the narrow leaves on the little twig thrown by a poor woman in the rue St Georges.

Where both people and speech were concerned, Christina

had come to a borderland. Some inhabitants spoke German, others French, throughout the dukedoms of Bar and Lorraine. West of Maas the French insisted on legal sovereignty, and here the duke was the vassal of the king of France.

The region had great military importance. Once before Christina had been a pawn in this game, when the Hapsburgs had taken Milan to close the circle around their arch-enemy France; and she knew exactly what her task was here.

As long as her father-in-law was alive she was prepared to be silent politically. But there would come a day when she would use her position in Lorraine; a day when she would be of use to the emperor again; for she had not forgotten what it was she wanted him to do for her.

She had devoted herself to Franz. She tried to believe it was René, his body, his love, that she was receiving with her body and her love. The swans would not vanish from her life. During the day, she dreamed about Denmark. She would bear an heir for Lorraine; but that signified little compared with the Nordic thrones.

Franz slowly grew closer to her. He was there in the flesh, after all, and he was always thoughtful and considerate. He brought her gifts: a chess set from Augsburg in black and gold, a globe showing the newest countries, and a silver clock in the form of a death's head. When she opened the clock she saw that the dial lay behind the teeth of the lower jaw. Around it ran the words, 'Ex his una tibi'. A black enamelled cross adorned the inside of the skull.

It was the latest fashion, and she had been delighted with it. It was beautifully made, a work of art in fact. You could see each join in the cranium, and each tooth, despite the fact that it was no bigger than a dove's egg. The hand moved round; time passed. She was living this, the only life on earth. And while she felt another life coming into being and growing in her womb she had watched the hand imperceptibly moving. 'Ex his una tibi.' 'One of these hours will be yours.' The heavenly life awaited her; it was inevitable, and the earthly life was but transitory. Each time she looked at the hand of the clock it had come a little closer to that moment the Almighty had determined should be hers.

Christina had no fear of childbirth. She was already big and heavy with the onset of winter. From the palace she could see the low mountains around Nancy turn white under snow. Franz would put his hand on her belly and feel the life moving there, to be born when the day, the hour, the moment had come.

Christina's son, a healthy well-formed child, was given the name of Carl. She had fulfilled her first, elementary duty to her new country and this altered her status at court. Visibly favoured by her husband's love, and with a son in the cradle to whom the astrologists promised a long and brilliant life, she was a person to be reckoned with.

As long as Duke Anton lived, Lorraine was his concern, just as Denmark was still the count palatine's. But Christina's interest in both was not diminished by motherhood, even though she stood on the outside of events and only received information at second hand.

Shortly after Carl's birth Battista reported to her regarding the encounter he had had at an inn outside Nancy. He had had to find shelter from the storm and among the other stranded travellers had been a Dane from Copenhagen, who was now in Nancy.

At first Christina was delighted. What Battista had to say about the man from the North sounded promising. She laughed at the description of how they had celebrated the prince's birth. It was hard to picture the dapper Italian leaping and singing in such company. When he repeated the Dane's words about her little Carl as the future king of Denmark her cheeks glowed.

But then she grew suspicious. The man might be a spy. After so many years Christina had absolute confidence in her secretary. But was he being naïve in his assessment of the stranger when he said that the Dane seemed to be a reliable and honourable man?

A citizen's son, apparently, from Copenhagen and with a degree in theology. Christina asked, 'And in holy orders?'

'Not as far as I gathered,' replied Battista.

But after talking to Franz, she came to the conclusion that there could hardly be any risk in merely receiving the Dane.

Christina was excited and curious. She was the second in line to the throne of a country not one of whose inhabitants she had ever seen.

The Dane was announced, and Christina stared at him, much as she stared at every new fruit and plant that had arrived from the new world. The first thing she noticed was his clothes.

They bore the mark of Battista's hand, for he could not possibly have looked like that after tramping around Europe for several years. The man seemed utterly ill at ease in his short modern doublet, and his big hands clutched at it as if to pull it further down over his thighs.

He was tall, his hair fair and wiry, and there was something ram-like about him. His skin was blotched. Christina would have to find out later where it was that Battista had had him scrubbed so thoroughly. The man bowed – and kept on bowing. He had clearly never talked to a royal personage before. She enquired kindly about his travels. Once he had lost some of his awkwardness, and begun to speak, he expressed himself in excellent German. He was also fulsome in his interpolations of Latin sentences, chiefly quotations from the Bible. Christina understood, and questioned him on his studies.

The Dane bowed yet again, while his fingers felt once more for the edges of the doublet. He obviously felt extremely indecent. He launched into a long theological exposition, and described what was taught at the University of Copenhagen which 'Your Grace's great-grandfather, blessed King Christian the First, in his inexpressible wisdom, and thanks to the blessing of the Holy Father of Rome, had bestowed on the land and its citizens, for the benefit of its more gifted sons'.

Christina made haste to compliment him on his great learning. The man beamed with pleasure, so that the scrubbing marks on his face shone red; and she asked if he had made his promise to the church.

'It is no longer permitted,' he said evasively and added, 'And besides . . .', then stopped. There was something he did

152

not wish to reveal. She pretended not to have heard the little aside but realised nonetheless that the man was not a practising Catholic. It was a serious defect; on the other hand he could hardly be a spy, or he would not have uttered such a foolish remark.

Christina thanked him heartily for coming, saying it had been a great pleasure for her to meet someone born and bred in the town where she herself had been born and from the country where her father was king.

The man launched into an enthusiastic encomium of Christian the Second. But she quickly stopped him; he could regale Battista with that. It was the best way to go about things. Anything else would be both dangerous and undignified.

Although the Dane's faith was not as it should be, his education was superior to his manners, and his knowledge better than his appearance. In brief, a plain man; but not stupid, not dishonest, not useless.

Battista was to offer the Dane employment. He would have direct authority over the Dane, and talk to him as much as possible in order to get an impression of the man and what he knew of conditions in Denmark.

Christina needed to know how much support she could reckon on from the inhabitants in the event of military invasion. She did not need, meanwhile, to remind Battista that all the information he gained should be reported direct to her and to no one else.

All the Dane's letters were to be examined – without his own knowledge Anders had entered employment as a spy. He was given a post in Battista's secretariat, a minor position but reasonably well paid. Meanwhile every letter that passed in and out of his lodgings was read and copied by Battista in person. The adroit Battista had warned Anders to write his letters in German and to ask his friends to do likewise, as letters were often opened in transit and an incomprehensible language could arouse suspicion.

In the course of four months Christina had received much information on the state of dissatisfaction among the Danes.

It was there, in and between all those lines of more or less halting German. Deep within her she bitterly regretted that she had forgotten the Danish language, the only thing her father had asked her not to do.

In May 1544 Christian the Third's envoy went to Speyer, to sign a treaty with the emperor. In it, the emperor acknowledged Christian the Third's right to the Danish throne.

The count palatine raged, and Christina protested. But 'We must have grain from the Baltic or we shall starve,' the regent had once said. The right to import food took precedence over a dynastic claim and religious disputes. Christina took note; and perhaps one day she would still have control over this vital sea route. For although the emperor had rejected the father's right he had not denied the daughter's claim to the throne after Christian the Second's death.

Meanwhile he sat triumphantly on the throne up there, the man who called himself the Danish king. It was his claim that he had won approval by ordering better conditions of captivity for his cousin and permitting him to go out hunting.

But he was still unsure of his position, as he revealed when he offered Christina and Dorothea substantial dowries. A hundred thousand dalers was promised to each of them in return for relinquishing their rights. The count palatine refused, however. 'Now, if they were to make it a million,' Dorothea's husband had said, thinking with Christina that no one would dream of offering a hundred thousand for something that was not worth much more.

The sisters' rights remained intact. Rights that Danish envoys maintained did not exist – but were nevertheless willing to buy.

XIII

Christina was delivered of her second child on the 20th of April 1544. It was a daughter, and she was to be christened Renata after her paternal grandmother.

When Franz came into her bedchamber he had fourteen-month-old Carl in his arms. The little boy pointed down at where his mother held the newborn baby. He looked at his father inquiringly, and laughed. Now they were four.

In a flash Christina remembered her aunt's satisfied look at the wedding. Had the regent foreseen this? Had she known already that Christina would be happy?

She loved Franz. It was not just for that moment after Carl had been born. She did not need to struggle to maintain her feeling for him. It had grown by itself, nourished and sustained by the sight of Franz's happiness.

It was Carl who had brought this joy. For the first time the ducal palace had rung with laughter, a father's delight at his small son. He carried him, played with him, gave him rattles of gold, and coloured wooden beads on a string. He held him on his first rocking-horse. Franz was not interested in power; what he needed for nourishment was art, and a love that would be reciprocated. And he was given it twice over. From Carl and from Christina.

On summer evenings they went out in a boat together, and had themselves punted down the Moselle with the infant Carl between them. His hair was already fair and curly and his eyes brown. Christina wore light muslin, Carl was in an open-necked shirt. They leaned over the child looking at him. His eyes were Christina's and his mouth like Franz's; but they couldn't agree about his forehead. The child laughed up at them and they laughed down at him. There was no other sound except the croaking of frogs and the soft purling of water against the bow.

Franz constantly thought of surprises for them. Once he had a complete pleasure house built, covered with fresh grass and newly picked marguerites. It appeared from out of a mild veil of mist as if it was sailing to meet them across the water. Another time an artificial garden with shrubs and small trees was planted in pots on a wooden raft, or an orchestra was placed among the rushes and the notes went dancing like elves among the green stalks. The sun went down, but the blue canopy on the boat still gave them the blue of the heavens above their heads.

Christina and Franz made love in the gleam of floating torches, and under trees where hundreds of little cages with yellow canaries and blue budgerigars were hung. Renata was conceived on cushions in a Moorish silk tent, where turban-clad servants stood guard by the river bank against non-existent enemies.

Christina and Franz sported all through those summer nights, and in winter they went skating. They were a happy family, the three of them, then four. But outside their frontiers was the war, and within them an unreliable aristocracy and agents of the French. Franz dreaded the day when he would have to shoulder responsibility for government.

'You are more suited to it,' he would say to Christina. It was as if he wished she could take the burden from him, so that he could spend his time and talents in beautifying the town and furthering the cause of art, instead of speculating on what his younger brother was plotting during his frequent hours with Count Salm.

Now and again Christina found herself wondering what marriage to René would have been like. Would she have been as happy as she was with Franz? Their love had been an intoxication; but now she asked herself whether its demands would not have been too great. She had given a cold assent to Franz and expected nothing, and yet she had found joy in all that had indeed been given her. She had learned to love the one who had come to her when she had been unable to have the one she loved. It was quieter, it was different; and it lacked the challenges she and René would have posed each other. This was more love than passion. She had found a practicable love, where the wilder realms of passion might have craved what was impossible, total bliss.

There had been a time when she had wished the world would perish, because it was too painful to live in. But the fields turned green again, the forest put on its leaves in April, and she saw the beauty of nature once more, as she rode with Franz over the mountains and heard streams murmur among the trees.

One hot July day Christina was sitting in the shade under the arcades of the ducal palace. At moments she could imagine she was back in her childhood at the palace in Mechelen; but the columns were wider and the arcade longer and the sun shone from a different angle. Its rays fell on the sandstone flags where Carl was playing with a hoop and Renata slept in a plaited basket.

She sat leaning back in her chair, filled with the deep peace of harmonious family life. She had two healthy children. Franz was out hunting but would soon be back. Madame Louise sat beside her, chattering of who was sleeping with whom, but as usual not saying a word about who was in her own bed; and her other ladies were playing shuttlecock on the lawn. Their laughter reached her shady seat. A gust of wind ruffled the leaves on the newly planted young trees. One was a magnolia recently sent by the regent who wrote that when it flowered it was like seeing tulips blossoming on the branches. The scene was one of beauty and peace when the courier arrived.

The letter was for Franz. She sat with it in her hands, looking at it and at the imperial seal with strange foreboding, and wished she need never know its contents. Carl played on, and Renata slept. But the ladies' laughter seemed distant, as did the lawns and the little magnolia tree which might have tulips on its branches next spring.

The coolness of late afternoon had fallen on the garden

when Franz returned, took the letter, broke the seal and read the contents. He raised his eyes and said, 'René is dead.'

He passed the letter to her without looking at her, as if there were something he did not want to see.

She had known it, was not even surprised. Franz bent over Carl and lifted him up. She said quietly, 'Poor Anne. They were happy together.'

His long back was towards her. He clasped the boy to him as if in fear; and she read the letter.

It had happened during the siege of Saint Dizier. René was struck by a splinter from a cannon ball, which had torn into his shoulder. Three days had passed before he died, in the emperor's tent. The rest of the letter was about his will. Anne was to have the income from his estates. The ownership of them, and the title of Prince of Orange, went to his eleven-year-old cousin Wilhelm.

Christina rose. She went slowly over to Franz and put a hand on his arm. 'We must write to Anne. We must help her. She is having a hard time.'

At last Franz turned to face her. She saw tears running down his cheeks and such sadness in his eyes as she had never seen before. Was it on account of his brother-in-law's death? Or was it a doubt about her feelings that had stayed with him all this time? She neither knew nor asked. She was sure she would never get an answer.

Franz said nothing. He looked at her for only a moment to seek the answer she in her turn could never give. He kept Carl in his arms, mumbled that it was getting cold, carried his son indoors and left Christina there.

Two weeks later Christina was in the Deer Hall when a letter arrived from Anne. She was in despair. But who was not? thought Christina.

Anne requested permission to carry out René's last wish. He wanted to be buried in Breda. But his heart was to be laid to rest at Bar, in Lorraine. His monument was to be his dead body carved in marble, as he would look . . .

Christina stopped reading.

This could not be true . . . but the words were plain enough.

As he would look . . . four years after his death.

She was hurled back in time, to Bruges. Again she felt his breath, as he whispered, 'Now I am only my skeleton, no more skin and flesh and blood. I am as dead as if I were already in my tomb and the worms had devoured me.'

He was breathing on her again, but with the cold breath of mortality. He had been one of the living dead, since that night four years ago.

Christina had betrayed him, whereas he had never failed her. The worms had been devouring his skin, his flesh, his blood. Only his bones, his dry skeleton, remained; and she alone knew it, and why.

She wanted to die. She seized her silver clock, opened the little skull, and stared at the hand. 'Una tibi'. Bruges would never come back; the future only held the moment of death.

She touched the little clockface. The hand moved on around the numerals. Would it be that hour? Or this? She spoke to it aloud. The hand must hurry, go faster; she longed for the scythe-bearer to come, riding on his blood-red horse. Fools and jesters tried to hide or flee; but it was release that he brought when he swung his curved blade. Dead bodies brought sorrow only to the living, who still had to wait awhile for the final goal.

Christina rose. She did not notice she was trembling. The deer on the walls were moving; higher they leapt, and higher, as if she saw the resurrection itself. Her eyes dimmed, and everything went black.

When Christina came to herself again the doctor had bled her. She lay in bed looking up at the green damask sky. Her ladies-in-waiting were standing about her, and her corset had been loosened. Death had not come for her. He had spurred his red horse towards others, whose turn was first.

Christina fell asleep and woke again to hot soup. The steam warmed her face and the nourishing liquid gave inner warmth; but she was still looking up at her green roof when a page ran in with a message. Franz had fallen from his horse.

Christina leapt from her bed as they carried him in. Franz

turned his pale face to her. He stretched out his hand for hers and she gave it him.

He was not hurt, just not well, he explained. But it was not the first time it had happened. He would suddenly collapse and be unable to breathe – only for a moment – it soon passed. The doctors reassured her; they thought it nothing serious. But what was it?

Death had brought René back. Now anxiety had given Franz to her again. She stood there, disorientated and wretched, looking at her sick husband.

The sun went down behind the towers and roofs of Nancy. The citizens made their way home and, another day gone, locked their doors for the night. Christina looked over at St Evre's church. A red shadow tinged its spire, rising like gauzy lace in the dim light. Could there, she wondered, ever be any true union between two human beings other than that generated by hope, by fear or by death?

The war with France continued. The imperial armies advanced, while Lorraine remained neutral.

Duke Anton, wanting to negotiate between the disputing nations, had started for Paris. But before he had gone further than Bar he was taken fatally ill.

Franz and Christina hurried to his deathbed. The duke left this world with a plea to his son to avoid war to spare the citizens from impoverishment by taxation.

On the 14th of June 1544 Franz became duke of Lorraine.

Lorraine's greatest problem was one of foreign policy, notably in her relationship with France. Christina had met King François in the very first year of her marriage. The king of France had then considered it a matter of urgency to honour her husband with the distinguished order of Saint Michael; and although the ducal family had had their suspicions about the invitation, a refusal would have been a gross insult, as well as an unforgivable diplomatic blunder.

As she travelled to the meeting, in her litter, it was not without excitement that Christina looked forward to encountering a man who was so much talked about. In the

Low Countries he was accused of every kind of fraud, swindle and infamy. But the ladies of the ducal court looked more ambiguous at the mention of his name. He had elegance and fine manners, courage and a knightly bearing; and they quoted his verses delightedly.

Christina was not going to let herself be charmed, however, and the first thing she noticed about King François was his feet. She had never seen anyone with such flat feet. They were like two runners, rolled out in front of a pair of thin, far too long legs winding up themselves in turn towards a body swathed in heavenly-blue satin.

The king lifted her hand to his shapely lips and uttered an exquisite compliment. During the subsequent banquet his eyes lit up each time he glanced at her sidelong. She dined amid a profusion of witty remarks; he clearly relished her laughter without the least idea that what really amused her were his lower extremities, to the exclusion of anything else at his court.

The king showed them his cabinet of curios. There were Roman cameos, gigantic stuffed insects, Persian coins, illuminated manuscripts and Greek statues. So as not merely to surpass other royal collections in extent but also in choice of objects he had had thirteen thousand six hundred and fifty gold buttons struck, which could be worn on one and the same costume.

There were also splendours such as were not to be found anywhere else in the world. There were Clouet, and Raphael; and Christina again felt resentment at having been sent to live in such an insignificant little country as Lorraine.

But the queen of France was not to be envied. Heavy and melancholy, Queen Eleonora had to endure being eclipsed by the star of the court, Madame d'Estampe. This was the king's mistress, a delicious lady with a face like an affectionate cat, who could boast of being the first woman ever to have had her place in the king's bed promoted to an official position.

The heir to the throne, Henri, received them with less elegance. He was dark and gloomy, lacking his father's sparkle and lightness of touch. About him hung the shadows of years of imprisonment in Spain as a sacrifice for his father's lost battles. He showed not the least interest in his wife, round-headed, pop-eyed Catherine of Medici, who resembled an excuse for herself more than anything else. She was said to be intelligent. But that was of little use to her, when she was constantly humiliated by her husband's infatuation for the ageing Diane de Poitiers, whose fishy eyes now and again swept over her rival Mme d'Estampe with an expression that seemed to say Soon-it-will-be-my-turn.

Christina witnessed her husband being presented with the order of Saint Michael by the king, amid effusive cordiality. And on the following day François demanded the fortress of Stenay. It was an ultimatum. They could relinquish the fortress voluntarily; or he would move in with his troops and take it by force. The emperor was in Algiers; and rumour had it that his fleet had been sunk. There was no help to be had.

They travelled home shaken and indignant. One of their most vital bastions was lost to them, and every ill opinion Christina had heard of the king of France was confirmed.

Their journey took them over potholed muddy roads. The litter tilted dangerously as the horses plunged about in the slush. Carts stuck fast and the rain poured down. Christina forgot her amusement over the flattest feet ever seen, or the magical brilliance of the court and her astonishment that an old woman could rule over the young heir to the throne. There was only bitterness left. They had discovered that as long as this man possessed the French throne he would plague Europe.

They pushed on, each night stopping in a state of exhaustion, and starting off every morning at dawn. Eventually they arrived back in Nancy sad and silent.

Their impression of that visit remained with them. And during the years that led up to the death of old Duke Anton nothing happened to change their opinion.

Madame Louise could go on as long and enthusiastically as she liked about her early days at the French court. It changed nothing.

Christina thought Madame Louise the most inquisitive person she had ever met. Her stories were amusing enough; but Christina had quickly made it clear that as duchess it was not for her to laugh at individually named persons, much less to express a point of view. Madame Louise had apparently understood this, and had restricted herself to more innocuous reports. In any case, Christina was not particularly interested in the garrulous lady herself, rather, she was concerned to discover what had caused her ineffectual brother-in-law to be on such intimate terms with the Francophile, Count Salm. What were they scheming for?

France alone was to blame for the current state of war. Without this glittering gilded tumour on the map of Europe the emperor could rule the world, master the Turks, keep the English quiet, put a stop to heresy and install the rightful ruler in Scandinavia.

The world might have been at peace, and lived in plenty under God's favour. But by the time Franz succeeded to his throne war had been raging so long that both sides were on the brink of ruin. With the coming of autumn another truce was declared.

Franz had determined that when he assumed power his country and its towns should enjoy a burgeoning of creative art. He and Christina spent the winter laying plans for the adornment of Nancy; for building churches, and designing squares and fountains. Towns would be catapulted into the present. The people would no longer be sharply divided into nobility and peasantry; there would be a citizenry to strengthen both land and princely power, and the towns would be large and beautiful. The court painters, Crock and Chappin, were sent off to Italy to buy works of art.

Christina was expecting her third child. Her pregnancy, and her joy over her first two healthy children, restored her happiness in family life. She retained the memory of René, but as it were she embalmed it. Carl took his first lessons and Renata her first steps, and the child was moving in her womb, when Franz fell ill again.

The doctors advised a trip to Blamont, in the hope that the

air would benefit his health. But the fainting spells grew more frequent. In despair Christina sent for the best doctors in Strasbourg and Freiburg; also her aunt provided a specialist from Brussels. But none afforded help.

At the end of May Franz was taken by litter to his hunting lodge at Remiremont. The forest slopes were greening and the mountain air clear. He dictated his last will and testament to his notary. The care of their children was to be in Christina's hands, and he appointed her regent for his son until Carl should reach the age of majority.

With the coming of summer Franz's strength was clearly failing, and those around him knew the end was near. He received the last sacrament; and Christina stayed at his bedside, with a few of his servants gathered around.

Franz was still conscious, but his face bore the yellow tinge of death as he opened his mouth and whispered, 'Love the children.'

He fought for breath. 'And rule Lorraine in peace and beauty.'

His head fell back against the pillows as he struggled to breathe; his chest rose and fell in jerks. The servants wept as they kneeled in prayer by his bed. Christina saw his eyes open again. He wanted in vain to say more. His dim eyes were fixed upon her.

Christina took his hand, and pressed it to her so that he could feel for one last time the unborn life in her womb. She saw the smile on his lips, the happiest perhaps since that winter's day when he had held his new-born son in his arms. He went on smiling while his eyes slowly closed and his hand fell from hers.

Now, while he was still alive but unconscious, came the dangerous moment when the Devil might steal his soul. Christina rubbed his hand. It must have the strength to hold the Bible and drive the evil one away. She looked at Franz in despair. He said nothing; but he must make the sign, and show his faith.

'*Oh, Lord, help us!*' said the servants.

She leaned over him and pressed the Bible firmly in his hand, while the priest started to intone. 'NUNC DIMITTIS

SERVUM TUUM DOMINE, SECUNDUM VERBUM TUUM IN PACE.'

Franz's eyelids moved. She felt a stirring of strength in his fingers. He parted his lips. She prayed fervently, and heard his whispered 'Yes'.

The servants sang. 'The Lord is my shepherd, I shall not want, he leadeth me in green pastures . . .'

The priest resumed. 'QUIA VIDERUNT OCULI MEI SALUTARE TUUM.'

Christina fell on her knees. She begged the almighty Father to take to himself this noble soul, to shield him from the tortures of purgatory. He had said 'Yes'; he had uttered the word, made the sign; he was constant in his faith, the faith that gave him salvation from the devil and the flames of hell.

'QUOD PARASTI ANTE FACIEM OMNIUM POPULORUM.'

The shutters were closed against the night. Torches were lit along the walls, and the servants sang. '. . . he leadeth me in the paths of righteousness for his name's sake . . .'

Christina was still absorbed in prayer, when the door was thrown open.

It was Count Salm. He stood in the doorway and threw a glance at her and at the servants, lifting an eyebrow in his heavy face. Behind him was her brother-in-law Nicholai, the bishop of Metz. The count avoided her gaze, screwed up his weak mouth and walked in, followed by a dark-suited notary bearing paper and writing materials.

Christina rose from her husband's deathbed. She looked at the men aghast. The servants fell back to the wall, still singing. '. . . though I walk in the shadow of death . . .'

Christina spread out her arms protectively to shield the dying man, and cried, 'No . . .'

Count Salm pushed her aside. He beckoned Nicholai and the notary closer to the bed, and they gathered around the sick man.

'NO!' said Christina again. The servants sang louder, 'I will fear no evil, for thou art with me.'

The count leaned over Franz.

165

His fingers seized hold of Franz's shirt, his rings sinking still deeper into his plump knuckles. He shouted into Franz's dying face, 'My lord, if it should please God to call you to him, do you desire Monseigneur de Metz, your brother, to have his share in governing the state and in the guardianship of your children without regard to what you have already agreed in word and writing with your gracious consort, the duchess?'

Franz's lips parted very slightly. The count laid his ear close to them. All that could be heard was the servants' singing. '. . . thy rod and thy staff shall comfort me . . .'

The count straightened himself again and looked triumphantly at Christina. 'He said, "Yes".'

Nicholai smiled happily across his dying brother. 'He said "Yes".'

'LUMEN AD REVELATIONEM GENTIUM; ET GLORIAM . . .' cried the priest.

The notary standing at the foot of the bed nodded ceremoniously, held up his pen and said, 'The duke said "Yes".'

'PLEBIS TUAE ISRAEL.'

A rattle came from Franz's throat. The notary's quill scratched across the paper, the flames from the torches flickered restlessly and Christina sank down beside the bed. Franz was dead.

Christina made the sign of the cross. The count snapped his fingers at the notary, folded his hands so that the gold rings ground against each other and ordered, 'READ!'

The notary was chattering something; but Christina could not understand it. The words were like insects dancing over the corpse. She could only stare at the man spitting out these sounds. He stopped, and passed the document to Count Salm who put his signature to it and then gave it to Nicholai.

The young man ran his eyes hastily down the lines, folded the paper and said to Christina, 'Where are the children?'

This was not possible. What did they want? She took two steps towards Nicholai, placed herself in front of him, looked straight into his wavering eyes and said, 'The two eldest are in my care and will remain there. The third is in my womb where it will stay until it pleases God for it to be born.'

She took a deep breath, summoned all her strength and screamed, 'GET OUT!'

Nicholai shot a sideways glance at the count behind her. He nodded curtly and the three men left the room. She saw the door close behind them. They were gone; but when would they strike again? In the morning? Or after the funeral?

Franz was dead. The heavenly Father had taken his soul to Him.

The black gown fell over Christina's swelling stomach as she tied the white ribbons of the widow's veil under her chin. It felt cool against her skin, and she needed to think coolly. The regency of Lorraine and the guardianship of the children was to be shared equally between her and her brother-in-law. But behind Nicholai there was Salm; and whereas there was not one person she could rely on, Salm himself had friends, family, and connections in high places. With such a balance against her she had no chance of asserting herself.

Christina wrote to the emperor. And this time he was not in Algiers. He was in Worms, he was within reach; moreover France's strength had been lessened. Christina, soon to be confined, regarded herself in her widow's weeds and awaited a reply.

The emperor acted quickly. Monseigneur Bonvalot, the abbot of Luxeuil, arrived at Deneuvre, Christina's dower house.

The little abbot uttered a stream of courtesies in a dry voice, expressed his sympathy for the heavy sorrow that had befallen the duchess, and voiced the anger of his lord, the emperor, at the treatment that had been allotted her.

'We must find a compromise,' he said thoughtfully.

'Not with the children,' replied Christina sharply.

'No, not with the children,' responded the abbot with a smile. '– Duke Carl, the Princess Renata and . . .' He threw a paternal glance at Christina's belly. 'Their guardianship remains absolutely and entirely in Your Grace's hands. But in regard to the regency it is unfortunately the general opinion in this country that it runs counter to custom to have a woman in power.'

And, as if it were something he had just realised, 'But customs can be changed. If not, the world would be at a standstill; so-o-o . . . in any case, the king of France will not be opposed to a reasonable arrangement . . . he has not the means or any possibility of that now . . . So-o-o . . .'

The abbot smiled artfully at Christina and Christina smiled back.

On the 6th of August a document was signed at Deneuvre. Christina had sole guardianship of the children; but all documents of state were to bear both her and her brother-in-law's name and seal. Where appointments were concerned Nicholai was to have power, but to appoint only one for each two of Christina's.

Representatives of the nobility appended their signatures with stony faces; and Christina requested their attention.

She expressed her gratitude to her brother-in-law for his extremely kind and tactful conduct during her time of trial; and she extended her thanks to him for his willingness to support her in the difficult task of governing Lorraine on behalf of her son.

When Christina saw the delighted smile on Nicholai's face she knew she had won. Salm had been knocked out of the game, and Nicholai was easy to handle.

The late summer beauty of the forest was dark and heavy outside her windows. Autumn was here. Christina had come to love this land that had once seemed so alien.

She was twenty-four years old, a widow for the second time. Her third child would be born any day now, and she felt heavy and clumsy in her body. But she was clear in her mind. There were people who might betray her at any moment. But they would have to learn. She had the emperor behind her, and the people on her side; and ahead lay a yet greater goal than the one achieved already. By day was the battle for power; by night, sorrow over Franz's death. But she knew his memory would fade. They had had so few years together; not long enough. Only time could have given her feelings proper fullness and driven René from her consciousness; and time had not been granted them. Christina was at one and the same time filled with purpose and in despair.

Her pains began. If it was a son he was to be called Franz after his father; if a daughter, she would name her Dorothea after her sister.

A girl was delivered, a strong, vociferously crying child. But ... Christina wept when she saw her. One of her feet was misshapen; the child could not move it. Was it a punishment from heaven for having loved another?

XIV

A surge of fear and loathing surged over Louise de Batonville that day in the Deer Hall when she saw Christina of Denmark standing on the little semicircular balcony above the rue St Georges. She stared at the long slender back, saw the rosemary twigs being thrown down and heard the cries of jubilation from the crowd below. Louise hated everything German, and with it everything to do with the empire; and she despised the people with her whole heart.

Louise was French. Her family was as distinguished as it was poor, and she had grown up on the furthest sandy lands of Normandy to the accompaniment of her mother's whining, her father's tales of the crusades, and the braying of sheep.

When she was eight she came home beaten black and blue by a lad from the village. Her father took no steps to find the culprit, but explained to his little daughter that a long line of noble ancestors was no consolation for the regrettable lack of francs when it came to avoiding the injustices of this life. She would have to fend for herself.

Louise learned how to jump on to a horse at speed, to shoot with a bow, to throw a spear. She ran like an arrow and climbed like a cat; but, most important of all, she was soon adept in the art of self-defence, which her father had acquired during his stay in Venice.

Next time the boy went for her she twisted his arm and sent him flying. He ran off terrified, howling that she must be a witch. After that she could go where she liked in safety.

When Louise was ten her father went off to the north Italian wars. At Pavia the king cried that all was lost except honour and life. Louise's father had to rest content with less than that, for when the dust cloud subsided after the battle he was found on a branch stuck through with a spear.

Louise's mother was reduced to a sobbing wreck. But in a moment of clarity she wrote a plea to the king's mother. This moved the queen mother sufficiently for her to send for the noble young lady, a year later, and to allow her to continue her education at court, in the company of other daughters of noble families.

Louise soon made good her lack of academic knowledge; and she learned to carry herself gracefully and speak with discretion. Each morning she prayed for her dead father's soul, never gave her mother a thought, and knew all about counting days when she had her first love affair, with her music master under a cedar tree beside the Loire's green banks.

The brilliance of the court intoxicated her. She idolised the king, even though, since he was still in prison down in Spain, she had never seen him. But she did not forget her childhood accomplishments; moreover she was destined to make use of them. Louise had grown into a strong, lithe girl with hair as shining and brown as chestnuts in September. Her skin was fair and fine and her eyes big and astonishingly innocent. When she was fourteen her benefactress brought her a suitor. Or rather a letter from him for her to read.

He was a German baron, and a landowner from Lorraine. A wealthy man, he was the last in line of a family that could trace its forebears right back to the emperor Hadrian. He had served as an officer when the peasant rising was put down in Germany. Now he needed a bride, to bear him an heir. For a moment Louise wondered why she, a poor fatherless girl, should have been chosen. But she thought little more about it and set off, happily enough, eastwards towards her future husband and future home.

The baron received her on the main steps of his castle. He was a tubby, bald man of about fifty. His bloodshot eyes looked coldly past Louise while he questioned her about her digestion and her teeth.

Louise's portrait was hung in the gallery, and her coat of arms carved in sandstone over the main entrance door; but that was the end of the honours shown her. Chickens ran around in the castle's damp rooms, which swarmed with retainers who had served as mercenaries. Clad in shabby livery, they went sloppily through the motions of service and, as the effects of drink waxed with the evening hours, shared both their lord's table and his bed.

Louise was allotted a room on the second floor of the castle, together with a single scared girl as servant who could neither mend embroidery nor set a modern coiffure. The baron visited her bed only occasionally and left it with every sign of nausea. She experienced something unknown to her before: idleness.

She had tried to take over the running of the house, but the keys were not given her, and all her orders were received with coarse laughter or scornful glances. She was met with rude stares and derisive grins. She put a cloth on the table and they blew their noses on it. The servant girl was raped five times in one night and ran away. Roars of laughter from the baron and his lackeys and the shattering of glasses on the stone floors and walls were the sounds accompanying Louise's existence. No one spoke to her, except when the baron bawled that he needed a son from her cesspit of a womb.

Louise had not expected love from her marriage. She had merely intended it to save her from the prospect of a tedious existence in one of the poorer nunneries. She was thus not especially put out by the baron's infidelity, or by the fact that he deceived her with his own sex. She had discovered at the French court that there were men who preferred other men, although she could not imagine why and was not in the least interested in how. But to be humiliated by the servants made her furious. She had never thought it possible that she would be neither respected as lady of the house nor treated according to her rank.

Gradually her rage burned itself out into impotence, which again smouldered into a glowing hatred of the men who dared to conduct themselves in this way. She was dis-

173

gusted by their ugly German speech, which could not be pronounced without spitting; and she realised now to the full why the baron had had to find a poor bride outside the boundaries of his own country.

Neighbours ostracised them; he had no relations; and when she rose in the morning she went down to a house stinking of vomit after the night's orgies. She put out bowls and buckets but they still used the floor, and one day she fetched a cloth, threw it at one of the lackeys and ordered him to clear up.

He looked at her, cocked his head and replied languidly, 'Do it yourself.'

Louise bent down. She collected up some of the stinking matter in the cloth, straightened up and in one jump was upon him. She grabbed hold of the man's hair, pulled his head back and stuffed the cloth and its contents into his open mouth.

When the baron came home Louise had bolted her door. She listened to his hammering and shouting, waited for a while, then answered in a soft voice that she was with child. Silence followed. Then came his cry of jubilation and she wondered what pleased him most, the idea of having an heir or the knowledge that he would not have to sleep with her again.

The baron and his lackeys celebrated the event with revels that surpassed anything she had previously seen. They used the hens for targets to shoot at. Her husband shouted that she was the holster protecting his son's life. As the night hours passed Louise considered what to do when he discovered her lie. When day dawned over the castle all the glass and porcelain had been smashed, the furniture floated around in the moat, the wind howled through the broken lead panes and the baron was collapsed senseless on the floor.

He did not come out of his stupor for two days. Then he sat bolt upright in bed, swung his feet to the floor and walked stiffly towards Louise, who had been dutifully sitting at his bedside. The light of transfiguration gleamed in his eyes and he whispered that he must go to Jerusalem, for he had had a revelation. The Holy Virgin had urged him to liberate the city from the heathen. Louise was surprised. To her the whole thing seemed more like a miracle. She was heartfelt in encouraging him to follow his calling, and he nodded so hard that the tasselled end of his nightcap swung to and fro above his naked fat shoulders.

Three days later he rode out of the courtyard with a little band of followers. Louise watched them go from the doorway where she stood in her voluminous riding habit. She waited until they were out of sight and then looked around her.

She was surrounded by them, all his remaining servants and lackeys and grooms. Up until now they had not dared to lay hands on her for fear of their lord, who insisted the child was his. But now that he had gone she would have to act.

Her glance fell on a hulking straw-haired stable-boy. He had always ill-treated the horses and was one of those who had raped the servant girl. Louise walked slowly towards him. She saw his taunting grin, lifted her riding crop and hit him full in the face.

He put his hand to the red mark, more in astonishment than pain. Louise was aware of every one of them: on the steps, in the courtyard, beside the stable wall. She was fifteen years old and she was alone, surrounded by more than fifty coarse men with instincts lower than the beasts'. The stable-boy took his hand from his face. When he straightened up and rushed at her she was prepared for him.

He struck the stable door with a crash, but Louise stayed where she was and waited until he got up again. His lips drew back in a snarl that revealed all his black teeth, and she sent him reeling at the stable door again.

This time his head struck first and he sprawled on the cobbles like a bundle of rags. Louise sensed glances being exchanged. Around her there was total silence. She walked slowly towards the unconscious man.

To make quite sure they understood her intentions she set her heel squarely on the man's nose and trod down hard until she heard the sound of cracking bone.

As Louise walked back to the house with light steps she

175

felt the horror in their eyes. She realised the value of her harsh upbringing, and let the men around her go on believing in her witch's arts. From that day forward they obeyed her.

In the course of the next month the house was set in order. The chickens were thrown out, window-panes were repaired, the floors were scrubbed. Louise sent for decent furniture, damask and linen. She kept a check on each sausage and the weight of every ham in the larder; the horses were fed and cared for; and she knew the name of every puppy in the kennels and kept the key to every room in the castle. The lackeys were set to work until they dropped. She took to receiving visitors, and three times she took a French nobleman into her bed.

Twelve and a half months after the baron's departure Louise gave birth to a healthy boy, and while she pondered over which of the three might be his father she sent for the priest.

When Louise announced that she would present the church with new bells tears of joy ran down the priest's face. He refrained from making any comment on the astonishing length of her pregnancy and instead leaned over the child in Louise's arms and expressed his pleasure in seeing that her son was the perfect image of his gracious father.

Louise agreed with him wholeheartedly, all the while expressing her anxiety over the child's frailty. The priest, bewildered, looked for a long time at the healthy newborn child. Finally an understanding smile came over his face.

An immediate christening was arranged and the little boy was given the baron's name. There were no guests, and Louise thanked heaven for the lack of relatives with rights of inheritance.

But she was still slightly nervous at the thought of her husband's homecoming. When one day a message came that the baron had fallen overboard twenty sea miles from Malta she turned all the Germans out of the house, ordered twelve yards of black material and heaved a sigh of relief.

She looked at herself in the mirror, wearing black. She found the white veil becoming. Smiling, she played with the keys on her table. With a live heir in the cradle and a husband at the bottom of the Mediterranean, the world was hers. She was young, she was beautiful, she was rich, she was free. From now on she could act exactly as she pleased.

And that was what she decided to do, as, to the joy of the priest, the parish and its inhabitants, the new bronze bells rang the day to its close.

All Louise knew about was hate and love. She hated the people. They had once shown their true nature and what they were like when they were not kept down. She hated Germans and the emperor and everything connected with him. But she loved her dogs and horses and idolised her small son. She discovered that there were advantages in not being sure of his paternal origins. He took after only her own family, being a good-looking, intelligent boy; and, pleasingly, it seemed as if he had been created by her and her alone.

Louise was preoccupied by her rank, her standing and her sex; and she never forgot the land of her birth. France was God's gift to Christian humanity. It was Europe's most beautiful kingdom. New trends might come from Italy, but it was in France that they were brought to perfection.

No other country had castles like Chambord or Chenonceaux; no court could match her king's court; no language had so elegant a ring. There was an abundance of people, and of land to feed them. Here they enjoyed the delicate intoxication of wine without drinking themselves senseless. France was the jewel of Europe that sparkled on surrounding countries and showed up all their mediocrity.

But an imperial spear had killed her father; and for as long as she could remember the emperor had encircled France with iron. She was surrounded by enemies on all sides: Germany, the Low Countries, Spain; and northern Italy, which the emperor had also seized. Ferociously, he coveted the wealth of France; but the French had fought, and had held their position. Louise was proud of that, and had brought up her son to think and feel like a Frenchman.

When the boy was seven she decided, for the sake of his

education, to take up residence in Nancy. She soon made contact with the court and became friends with the powerful Count Salm. She shared his anxiety over the old duke's tendency towards more amicable relations with the empire. Anne of Lorraine's marriage to René of Orange was something she viewed with mistrust. Count Salm was exerting all his influence meanwhile to win over Prince Nicholai to the French cause. However, the young man vacillated. He talked, and made promises; but he would still not set himself up against his father's policy. Louise offered the count her help.

While out hunting one day she made a point of riding ahead of the princely young bishop. She contrived to fall off her horse; and when he gallantly sprang to her aid she let her hand as if by chance slide between his legs. Louise saw at once that despite his ecclesiastical office he could be salvaged for her cause. Minutes later, when the rest of the hunt had galloped away over the hill, behind a woodpile at the edge of a coppice the two bodies joined.

It did not take long for Louise to convince the uncertain young man of his great political mission. Nicholai now listened compliantly to Salm. Louise had got herself a lover who was both fumbling and uninventive; but she also had the consolation of knowing that she had won over an important personage to the cause of France. She would often remind herself of this, while accepting his wet lips and sweating body; for she was not blind to the fact that his elder brother Franz, heir to the ducal throne, had a tendency to faint and was only able to sleep sitting up.

When Louise was offered the post of lady-in-waiting to Franz's future bride she accepted it with delight. Not only was it an honour; it also gave her the opportunity to observe at close quarters yet another whim of the emperor, Christina of Denmark.

Everything she had imagined, everything she had feared, was confirmed when she saw the bride on the balcony playing up to the mob down in the street. She was soon to discover that Christina of Denmark also had the brains to rule over her dreamy husband, to the point that her will became his will, and her viewpoint, his.

The duchess brought a staff of foreigners with her: Netherlanders and Italians. Even a stray Dane appeared, whatever he was there for, with his broad peasant face and all his theological rubbish. They followed the duchess like faithful hounds – but they were the only ones who did. True, the people in the street yelled for joy when she showed herself; and the peasants out in the country loved her, as did poor widows generously aided, and old servants given unreasonably large pensions. But not the nobility; and for Louise it was only the nobility that counted.

At heart Louise supported the aristocratic republic. She saw no sense in having kings and dukes at all. Countries were best governed by aristocrats, who had many good brains while the princely ruler had only one – and not always a very good one. The king of France was the only ruler who could rightly call his position a throne.

When the king took Stenay, Louise rejoiced. She could not endure her lady. She regaled her with all sorts of amusing gossip – as opposed to real news – but she could never really get near her. She relished her knowledge that the young duchess, in reality, loved René of Orange; and it was a point on which she understood her. The prince was the hand-somest man Louise had ever seen. But he too was com-pletely impregnable – until his sudden death.

Louise hid her pleasure, and her annoyance when, as an onlooker at the birth of the duchess's first child, she saw the child was both living and a boy. That pushed Nicholai down a place in the line of succession; but he was still wax in her hands. Though he continued to be just as boring as a lover he was just as easy to rule over, so when Duke Franz lay dying in his hunting lodge Salm knew exactly how to make use of Nicholai.

It had been easy, Louise said to herself later. And she should have realised that it was too easy. She had to acknowledge bitterly that the duchess had too much imperial power behind her and too many brains in her head to let herself be overthrown, and that in reality Nicholai was more vain than ambitious. For six months the nobility tried to regain their foothold after the agreement at Deneuvre; but they lost, and had to submit to being ruled by a woman, a foreigner and a traitor.

They seethed with resentment and so did Louise. Her lady spoke gently, smiled sweetly and asked no questions of anyone at all except the imperial envoy Bonvalot. More foreigners came swarming in to fill important posts; and positions that had always belonged to the old families were given to plain citizens. The duchess could be ludicrously mild over heresy or what she called the weak elements in society; but she disregarded the views and opinions of the nobility as if they did not exist.

Life had taught Louise patience. She knew that if you waited long enough the right opportunity would present itself. She pensioned off Nicholai now he had proved himself worthless, and took a more knightly lover into her bed. But she was determined not to lose her freedom and power by going to the altar with anyone. She saw no sense in being bored before the reckoning came. She flattered the duchess and followed her every step. Meanwhile time was working for her and Salm, and the nobility and the cause of France.

Louise considered Christina as a Hapsburg, yet another of that family's many power-hungry women, and brought up by the Netherlands regent, of whom it was said that her heart was as big as it was hard. But her father, as king of Denmark, had lost his throne because he believed he could rule with the help of citizens and peasants. The nobles had deposed him; and the day would come when the duchess would find to her cost that the nobles here were of the same mind as those in Denmark, that they had the same intentions and sought the same power.

Louise brought up her son, and held her conversations with Salm. Every day, she spent three hours in the saddle, preferring to ride astride, in the old style, to preserve the correct curves of her stomach. Meanwhile she stayed on the alert, ready to strike her prey.

The plague came. With the first signs the authorities took the usual precautions. The towns were closed off, and red crosses were scrawled on the doors of houses where people had fallen ill, and doors and windows were nailed up. Only food supplies were allowed along the infected streets. The rich had long since fled to their country houses. While they survived, the poor remained behind and died.

Nancy too was afflicted; but by Christmas it was safe for Christina to return to the capital. The city was free of infection now; and in country districts the disease slowly burned itself out, although there were still towns with empty streets, and without priests, judges and other officials.

Burials and reorganisation went on, and Christina embarked on her task as regent. She was twenty-five that autumn. The States General had produced as many objections to the Deneuvre agreement as they could find, but she had stood firmly by her rights and with the emperor's support had carried through her intentions. But the feeling that she was surrounded by the aristocrats' hostility was confirmed. It was a case of her or them. Christina was determined it should be her.

Rebuilding the capital's fortifications was a priority, for rapid developments in the power and mobility of artillery had rendered the ancient walls obsolete. Christina called in Italian experts to advise on the works, and new defences were constructed further from the town centre. This gave more space within the city, which had contained only three open spaces, none of them large enough for tournaments or tilting at the ring.

Meanwhile the peace treaty of 1544 had given Stenay back to Lorraine. Even though the fortress lay on the approach road to Luxembourg, and the regent had asked for it to be rebuilt, Christina here forebore to do so, in order not to provoke the enemy to her west. No matter how much she desired to support imperial policy it was imperative to avoid unnecessary confrontations with the king of France.

Christina went round Nancy inspecting the works. She also gave money to those in dire need, favouring religious orders that cared for the sick and destitute. The grey sisters of Elizabeth received an annual grant. She made donations, too, towards the cost of church-building. All her free moments were taken by the children. Carl, blond as his mother, could write his first alphabet now, and Renata, who had her father's dark colouring, was clearly going to be good-looking. But none of the specialists she called upon could bring any movement to Dorothea's afflicted foot, and through sleepless nights Christina would find herself wondering if her daughter would ever be able to walk.

The duc de Guise presented himself as a suitor. He was Franz's cousin, and had shown courage at the siege of Boulogne, when a spear in his forehead had stuck so fast that the doctor had had to brace his foot against the duke's head to pull it out.

But beneath the scar on his brow the duke's eyes were icy. Christina could not stand him. She knew exactly why he wanted to marry her. He was after the regency of Lorraine, together with control over Carl and the opportunity to carry out the policies of the French.

The mere idea of this man having any say over her son made Christina tremble with rage. She answered that, having once been married to the head of the family, she could never contemplate an alliance with a member of a collateral branch.

In the heat of the moment she enjoyed her impudent response. Afterwards, though, she realised that if the duke ever had the chance of revenge he would take it. He was not a man who could forget.

The beginning of 1547 saw the death of two of Europe's mightiest men. King Henry had achieved six marriages. After Anne of Cleves he had chosen yet another English lady. Before long he had sent her to the scaffold; and rumour alleged that the sixth wife had also come close to losing her life.

His private life had been chaotic. Now, although the man had gone, his shadow remained; and it began to loom from across the frequently stormy sea over Europe.

According to reports his successor the boy king was sickly; and apart from him there were only the daughters: the sad spinsterish Mary, and Elizabeth the bastard, a red-haired girl no one took seriously. Yet she, Christina, could have borne the healthy son, the healthy heir. She was a king's daughter, and the emperor's niece; and no one would have dared send her to any scaffold, or so much as think of displacing her.

Three months later news came of the death of the king of France. Christina's ladies grieved, quoting his poems to each other with tears running down their cheeks. She herself gave more consideration to the fact that now Catherine of Medici would be able to wear the crown as queen – she had eventually borne children – although she was no more than a Florentine merchant's daughter.

Yet another queen was a topic of conversation just then. The king of Scotland had died, after losing the battle of Solway Moss; and the throne had passed to his daughter, Mary. The little queen was now four years old, and Christina was worried at the rumour of a betrothal to the three-year-old French heir to the throne, knowing that such a union would give yet more power to the covetous de Guise family.

Each day Christina worked late. She had piles of documents to see to. There were dozens of pleas for mercy, chiefly from persons condemned for murder and other violence. She made clear distinctions in such cases. A crime committed without premeditation, in self-defence, or to save another person's honour, could be forgiven. But no mercy could be shown for a premeditated offence.

Heresy had increased to a dangerous extent, and during the last year of Franz's life yet another culprit had been tried and burned for spreading the evil teaching. Nevertheless Christina abolished the death penalty for Lutherans and Calvinists. She replaced it with fines and with confiscation of half of the accused person's property. Only violence should be punished with violence; not words and ideas. Was it that she was influenced by her aunt's sympathies? Or was it because according to rumour her mother had died in the Lutheran faith? She did not know. To Christina there was only one true faith. She could not understand how so many could adhere to the coarse monk Luther, with his contempt for women. Certainly there were reforms to be discussed, and bishops and pope might do well to live differently. But heresy was a brutalisation of humanity, and an act of treachery to the rules that had been built up over fifteen hundred years. It was merely a matter of ideas and opinions even so, rather than of murder and robbery. Christina refrained from passing judgement; she preferred to leave their final punishment to God.

The town of Bar had once been the capital of Lorraine. Now it led a quieter life. The Benedictine monastery and the church of Notre Dame lay down in the eastern end of the town. On the west side of the river, low reddish brown houses climbed up the mountainside towards the castle that stood at its top. The castle was more a fortress than a dwelling house, and Christina had long had the idea of replacing it with another, more comfortable residence. But the present state of her finances would not permit it, and she had had to content herself with making do. A few rooms had been improved by the addition of tapestries; and modern furniture, in walnut and exotic woods sent her from Antwerp, had replaced the crude oak benches and tables. The windows had had to remain sparse and hopelessly small, many of them only with wooden shutters and no glass.

On this occasion Christina had not come to Bar to dream of building. New cases and stacks of documents awaited her; but there was something else she wanted to see.

The sculptor Ricier had long been in the service of the ducal family and had been commissioned to create the monument to the Prince of Orange. It had now been completed, and placed in la Collégiale Saint-Max, in the old castle.

Christina told her ladies to wait, and entered the silent half-darkness of the church.

The upright skeleton stood before her. It was carved in stone, but it was him. Dry bones, but him. It was René. His skin was threaded with worm holes, and hollow spaces lay between his ribs, but his left arm still held its sinews. It was raised high in the air, his skull proudly thrown back. The empty eyes were gazing up at the heart that he clutched in his bony fist.

Christina fell on her knees. It was René. Her beloved René, with his ermine cloak painted on the wall behind him. He stood before her beneath shield and helmet, dead and eternally alive, so proud, so manly; just as he had been in flesh and blood when she lay in his arms and felt the warmth of his body.

The silence was broken by church bells ringing for Mass. But Christina still kneeled, weeping. Life was so short. Why? Why had she not been allowed to keep him? Why be born if one could not live?

The bells were still ringing. She hardly noticed them, or the passing of time or the cold creeping into her from the floor. Quiet steps sounded behind her. She started, dried her eyes hastily and stood up.

It was Madame Louise. The lady-in-waiting stood in the dim light, smiling under her widow's veil, and asked softly if anything was wrong. Christina shook her head briefly, and raised her eyes to the heart in the bony hand held up near the Orange coat of arms, the heart that broke long ago one summer's night in Bruges.

With a slight gesture, Christina dismissed Madame Louise. She did not trust her; did not trust anyone. She walked with quick steps towards the door, out to the light, the sun, to trees in leaf, to the life that was still hers, and that she would have to go on bearing until the hour should come.

She looked out for a moment over the town, down on the roofs, on children playing and running around and people working in gardens and workshops. Christina went back to the land of the living.

XV

Augsburg was cloaked in darkness and rain on the day in November 1547 when Christina and other members of the imperial family arrived to stay at the magnificent house of the banker Anton Fugger. He was one of the richest men in the world, with a fortune that outdid even that of the Medicis, and in its time his family had played a leading part in electing the emperor, by lending money for the requisite bribery of the German princes.

Christina was glad to see her relatives again. The regent was there and King Ferdinand of Austria; and Dorothea and Friederich, in favour once more after having supported the cause of the north German Protestants. Problems and loneliness were forgotten; there was music and dancing, and people she could rely on; and there was also Margrave Albrecht of Brandenburg.

Albrecht was beloved of women and of his soldiers alike. Although a Protestant by upbringing he was for the present in the emperor's service. Wherever he appeared with his army he aroused terror. Now he sat at her side fair and handsome as a young god. His eyes were bold and restless and revealed who and what he was, a princely mercenary.

While they were eating trout he told Christina she was lovely; while lemon sorbet to take away the taste of fish was being served he glanced with interest at her breasts and asked whether they were still firm; and when pies were brought round he slid his right hand down between the stiffeners in her skirt and gripped her thigh.

The emperor was sitting only four places away. There were several hundred people around them and Christina asked him to take his hand away. But he merely went on eating deftly with his left hand. She didn't know quite what to do about it. Albrecht sat in morose silence all through the following course but kept his hold on her thigh until he threw a chunk of meat down on his plate and said, 'You have a fine figure.'

He emptied his goblet and added, 'When you come to look at a battlefield most of them have ugly bones. They are bent and crooked. Bow-legged and knock-kneed, the lot of them, as they lie cluttering up the ground, fingers crossed over each other, but . . .'

His goblet was filled again and he added thoughtfully, 'But that probably has something to do with the diet.'

'Move that hand,' Christina repeated, irritated.

'Come to my bed tonight,' he replied.

Christina said nothing and he announced, 'It is the experience of a lifetime.'

The carver dextrously swung his knife high in the air and slices of lamb fell on to the dish. When Christina still made no reply Albrecht asked sombrely, 'I doubt if I am the first to make the offer?'

'No,' said Christina, 'but seldom before the tart.'

He laughed noisily but then grew serious again. 'I haven't time to wait for the tart. Who knows, one might be dead tomorrow.'

In the end he had to withdraw his hand, when a toast was raised; but he continued his importunate courtship for the rest of the evening and throughout the days that followed. He passed by her in the dance and just managed to tell her to name the time; and sitting next to her at table another evening he assured her that women's chastity existed only in the troubadour ballads.

'Just before Mühlberg we stopped for the night at a mansion. The lady of the house was on her own. She was a slight little thing, her husband either dead or away at the wars, so I thought I would cheer her up a little since I was there. But she fetched me one with the poker and said her ancestors went two centuries further back than mine and I could take myself off. But in fact she was keen on one of the stable-boys and went creeping down to him that night. I couldn't help knowing about it for I was bedded in the straw next door. The rooms were so low you could hear the scratch of her long aristocratic toenails on the ceiling.'

Christina stifled a laugh and asked what this story had to do with her?

'So much for ancestors and chastity,' he replied thoughtfully. 'And for women,' he added, chewing noisily, and asked if she had more time to spare that night.

Albrecht persisted. He handed her bouquets of flowers on the tip of his sabre; he stuck to her side in the chase; he sang serenades under her window, completely indifferent to making a fool of himself, and cheerfully admitted he was half-crazed. But he loved her unto death, and all the sieges he had known were as nothing compared to the dream of capturing her fortress. Christina laughed till the tears ran down her cheeks. She laughed at his stories and at his unrestrained adoration and after a month she gave in and whispered the hour when he could come to her.

Spent, they lay side by side in the darkness behind the curtains and she listened to his heavy breathing. After a long time he stretched out a hand, let it slide down her body and come to rest on her stomach, and spoke, muffled in his pillow. 'Too bad we cannot get married . . .'

She had not dreamed of marrying him. But she had expected him to propose and had already formed an elegant refusal in response. His hand moved up her body again and squeezed her nipple. Then he turned on his back and said, 'I am as poor as a rat and have nothing to offer. It makes no difference, anyway; you can't take it with you.'

Christina stayed in Augsburg for three months. She continued to amuse herself with Albrecht in the daytime, and slept with him at night except on the 'dangerous' days. But she found it too hard to take him seriously and grow deeply involved. There were no gossiping tongues around; Madame Louise and all the French-minded ladies had been left behind in Nancy. There was no hostile curiosity, and Albrecht was not in the habit of boasting about his conquests. But he was no René, nor yet a Franz. She would forget him as he would forget her, and she did not think he had ever nourished a really deep thought. Or was it that she was no longer capable of being in love?

Christina could enjoy the delights of love, weep tears of laughter, dance herself into enchantment, and hunt until she felt she could reach the moon; but there were bonds between her and her children that were unbreakable. There was a little boy proud of his first cap with its ostrich feather, a small girl with dark hair who could already wear a dress with a train gracefully, and a little girl who did not realise yet that she might never be able to walk.

They owned her. She was theirs, and they were her wealth; but unending anxiety for them was the curse of her wealth. There was room for a man in her bed, but she doubted if there was room for a man in her heart.

The end of her stay in Augsburg drew near. The emperor was going on to the Low Countries, and a mood of departure spread through the numerous visitors. Chests and boxes were packed, military escorts made ready, horses crowded the streets. One after another the royal guests set off on their journeys.

When Christina said goodbye to Albrecht she saw something she had not expected – tears in his normally merry eyes. He bowed to her in farewell but said not a word. She was confused, surprised. Was he something other and more than the audacious mercenary? Perhaps. She could not be sure; but as she rode away it made no difference. She hoped to see him again and would doubtless allow him to come to her bed, but there could be nothing more lasting and deep between them.

The winter chill nipped her cheeks and a whirl of thoughts filled her mind. She pondered on the Fuggers, those rich people who could buy all the world's beauty, as the Medicis had bought themselves the queen's throne of France.

Her thoughts turned to the luxury of the Augsburg house. In Nancy she had open fires, as was still the custom in the French-speaking countries. Of course the French knew about stoves with glazed tiles. They gave much more heat, but on the other hand they smoked so much you couldn't breathe. There was no smoke in the Fugger's house; instead they had stoves which gave plenty of heat, and you could go about indoors without fur-lined clothes. They had organised that as well – like everything else you could buy for yourself as long as you had the money.

She would soon have to make a stop for the night. The feeling of being in familiar surroundings brought her back to the present moment. The longing to see her children had increased with every day. They were waiting for her, blocking the way for others, cutting her off from ridding herself of the solitary life.

When Christina reached Nancy and saw two of the children come running towards her and a third on the governess's arm all her dark thoughts evaporated. She spread out her arms, embraced them, hugged them to her, felt their soft hands round her neck, and heard their squeals of joy. She lifted them up one by one. They were her joy, they were her life.

In the spring of 1549 Christina revisited the Netherlands. Her presence there was occasioned by a visit from Don Philip to the provinces that one day he was to rule.

Philip was the emperor's only son, heir to a vast kingdom – Spain, Naples, parts of Italy, the Netherlands and the colonies in the new world. He was destined to be the world's mightiest ruler. Don Philip was twenty-two years old and had lived in Spain all his life. But rumours about him had already gone the rounds all over Europe.

Philip was Spanish, and he was very Spanish. People from the Low Countries who had been in Spain had a great deal to tell. His smile resembled a grimace and no one had ever heard him laugh. Philip equated life with work and spent all his time on it, except for the inordinate amount he spent on his prayers. He did not know the meaning of the word festivity, was ignorant of the idea of joy, and never indulged in the flowing bowl. More spiteful tongues maintained that all this industry merely covered a sheer terror of making decisions.

'They say,' one of Christina's ladies remarked, 'that he considers the details of a case thirty times when others manage with two, and when he has to decide something he gets diarrhoea from panic. It positively gushes out of him . . .' she added, nostrils wide with malicious delight.

That had been too much for Christina, who uttered a sharp reprimand. There were limits.

Philip was a blond young man who wore violet-coloured velvet and rode a magnificent blood horse. Christina gazed curiously at him. He had his father's prominent chin and heavy underlip, and deep serious eyes whose glance wandered around the crowds as if he felt extremely insecure in these unaccustomed surroundings and at the same time was trying to please everyone. It was only when he dismounted that Christina noticed how small he was. He had narrow little hands and feet and walked with mouse-like steps. Don Philip lacked body.

The Spanish heir to the throne had taken six months over his journey. He had passed through all the Italian parts of the empire, and through most of Germany, whose princes had held festivities in his honour, sometimes from noon, until midnight. They had tried to make him jolly with drink, but had only succeeded in making him ill. They told him jokes that were met with icy silence and had tried to elicit witticisms from a mind blank of such things. Slowly but surely the prospect of the imperial crown had slipped from his hand and head. When the time came they would never elect this man emperor.

But he would have the Netherlands. They had sworn their oath that the country was Don Philip's rightful inheritance, and in every town he came to triumphal arches were raised to honour him and festivities were held to please him. He sat, stiff and expressionless, staring at lion and bull fights, and listening to performances by local committees of rhetoric. Courtly romances were played in the courtyards of ancient castles. And Don Philip continued to look on at all this as if it had nothing whatever to do with him.

At a banquet in Brussels the dancing had to be set back to allow the guests to recover from the huge quantities of wine they had drunk. Lackeys helped silk-clad ladies and gentlemen out into the fresh air. Don Philip rose and addressed Christina. 'Is this always the custom here?' he asked in horror.

'It is seldom we have such an occasion to celebrate,' she replied.

She saw one corner of his mouth twitch and could not be sure whether she had said something right or something wrong. After a pause he bowed deeply and asked her to dance. Christina was surprised. Until now no one had seen the prince dancing. He was six years younger than she and several inches shorter, and every one of the princes present would be happy to see his daughter married to Don Philip.

Next day when they were out hunting he rode up beside her and began to talk to her as if she were an intimate friend. 'Is what they say true, that five hundred ships come into Antwerp harbour every day?'

'I think so,' she answered, looking into his joyless eyes and wondering what his childhood had been like.

'And there are a hundred and fifty schools in the town?'

'Well, it has a large population.'

This reply left him deep in thought. She heard him breathe deeply; not because he was tired by the hunting, which had hardly begun, but more as if someone had laid a heavy weight of problems on his shoulders and presented him with ideas he had never dreamed existed. The hounds ran around in confusion looking for scent. His eyes were troubled and remote when he finally asked, 'How can you rule a country with seventeen provinces that each wants to be governed in a different manner?'

Christina wondered why he did not talk to his father or his staff of advisers about such things, and he lapsed into gloom again.

They neared the forest. It was an April morning like those she remembered from childhood. The trees wore fresh new foliage, moist and sappy, so that you felt you could bite into the leaves for nourishment; and there was an abundance of game. Christina led the cavalcade, as she had been used to do when as a young widow she rode out with her aunt. Although many today were above her in rank she rode in front. All gave way to the Spanish prince, and he had chosen her as his partner in the chase as well as in the dance. She enjoyed it but she felt an army of eyes behind her, noticing everything. Also she was at a loss to understand why she should be the only recipient of the only mild intimacy the prince had shown anyone. Perhaps, with all the people surrounding him, he was never accustomed to getting a sensible answer to a sensible question. He was oppressed and subdued when he ought to be assured and masterful. They whispered that he was arrogant, but what she saw was a little man fumbling his way to answer a shower of questions, filled with horror at the thought of making even one single mistake.

Christina had arrived in Brussels ahead of Don Philip. She was greeted by the emperor, her aunt, sister and brother-in-law and all the old well-known faces. Albrecht was there as well and he soon succeeded in arousing her desire again. But she asked him not to sing under her window any more; that would be too much. He came to her at night, and in the daytime he introduced her to his best friend and comrade-in-arms, Adolf of Gottorp.

The thought of meeting Adolf caused her pain. Should she be cold or friendly? Adolf had been at Mühlberg as well, but he was also the younger brother of the man who called himself Christian the Third, king of Denmark. He was 'one of them'. But when she saw his heavy but quite pleasant face she felt it wisest to give a good impression.

She smiled and dropped a few witticisms, which had an immediate effect. In a day or two he declared his love for her. To the question as to his betrothal to Princess Kunigunde he replied that betrothals were made to be broken, and went on to his favourite topic, the Ditmarshes.

He was obsessed with it. The other imperial officers plagued him continually with humiliating remarks on the situation of his uncle King Hans, and the king's campaign against the fierce peasants of the marshes. Had they spiked the Danish cannon with their pitchforks? Or had they used dung forks? What had actually happened there to produce such a result?

'Those oafs think a country can be ruled without a prince,' said Adolf darkly. Then his face lightened into an adoring smile, as he invited her to be duchess of both Gottorp and the Ditmarshes. Wouldn't she like that? Christina was amused. She took neither of these cavaliers seriously. But the third, Don Philip, was another matter.

The Spanish prince was lord of the future. He invited her to dine with him *à deux*. At dinner, he handed her some small brown loaves. Christina found the taste soft and strange. He told her they were made with some new beans recently discovered, called cocoa.

He repeated the word several times. It sounded like three short glottal stops. Then she saw what none other had seen, Don Philip's smile.

It came suddenly and without reason. She looked up from her plate and it was on his lips, a thousand restraints falling away in one moment. It expressed no joy or humour, but a limitless admiration; and she suddenly realised it was time to go home.

She was getting too involved, going too far. There had been grumbling at court for a long time. She was stealing Don Philip's time and attention, to which other more important people had a right. Whatever Philip's own feelings might be, the emperor would choose his bride, and it would never be Christina.

Meanwhile Albrecht, who had some grievance against the emperor, had asked to be released from his duties. He was offered an honourable post in the royal mint, but he responded sourly that as he had never been able to keep hold of any money himself he did not want the responsibility of others'. Adolf merely went on talking about the Ditmarshes, and complaining that he had been given far too small a portion of the dukedoms and that Christina did not realise the depth of his love for her.

It was all getting too difficult. The atmosphere was

deteriorating; she noticed the regent's reproachful glances and Philip was becoming a bore. Besides, her interest in him rested solely on his future power. Ahead of him lay a journey to the northern provinces with their lakes and dams. Christina did not belong here, and she determined to pack and be the first to leave.

When Christina and her train rode out of the gates of Brussels the Spanish prince accompanied her for mile after mile. He rode at her side, silent and reserved, his crescent-shaped profile etched against the green May landscape. Dust whirled up from the hooves of their escort's horses. When he finally stopped to bid her farewell it was with an air of suffering.

Christina rode on. There was a long journey ahead of her. As the distance from Brussels grew, one single face stood out in her memory. It was that of Wilhelm of Orange.

He was an attractive blond boy of fifteen, who had inherited René's great possessions and his position as the most eminent member of his country's nobility. There had been moments when his face reminded her of René's; not so much in its features as in its intrepid expression. How different he was from his Spanish counterpart, the duke of Alba and the inscrutable, arrogant Spanish aristocrats in Don Philip's train. What a difference, indeed, there must be between Spain itself and the Netherlands.

What would be the outcome of his rule? Would this man find the solution that her aunt had once envisaged, and that she and René had dreamed of? The enlightenment, edification and unity of the whole Christian community of mankind?

It was as if something had come to a stop and was hesitating at a crossroads. Would it go onwards or backwards? Was there any way at all? A rude strength prevailed among the three old rulers. Each in their own way must fight their way forward. They knew about storms and were prepared for them. But how would it be with the new ones?

After her homecoming Christina decided to go to la Mothe.

She had held back for a long time from complying with the emperor's desire to strengthen the garrison, in order not to provoke France unnecessarily. Now she did not intend to hesitate longer.

Without informing Nicholai or anyone else, Christina set off to get the increased fortifications under way herself. It was time for Lorraine to offer full support to the emperor.

XVI

In February 1552 alarming news reached Christina. A certain Michael Müller, a dealer in silver from Augsburg who brought silks and fashionable goods back with him from France, was accustomed to call in at the palace in Nancy. There he passed on what he had heard of happenings great and small, gossip and news, and received small sums in return. Up to now all his information had proved correct, as could be expected from a good listener and a good reporter. People with bad memories or who gave their imagination rein in the hope of extra reward soon gave themselves away. But Müller was not like that.

Müller was from south Germany. He had black hair and eyes, and a skin that was grey and unhealthy. A thickset man approaching sixty, he was both well-covered and well-heeled.

Müller was acquainted with the cupbearer at Chambord, and this was the key to his present knowledge. The cupbearer had officiated at a secret meeting with the king of France at the castle on the 15th of January. Also present had been representatives of the north German Protestant rulers, with whom an alliance had been formed and an agreement reached. The rulers acknowledged the king as the German–Roman emperor's substitute. France would support the north Germans in their battle against the emperor, and their right was acknowledged to occupy the non-German-speaking towns of Lorraine, Metz, Toul and Verdun, Lorraine being the nearest and most dangerous road for the new allies.

Christina was shocked. She studied the man's open face and felt sure he was not a double agent.

This meant war. Christina rewarded the man handsomely – no doubt the cupbearer had something owing to him – and began to think.

She said goodnight to the children. Carl was growing into a little gentleman. He was still very blond, and a sweet boy with a soft mouth and a gentle mind, and was not too big to put his arms round his mother's neck and give her a hug at bedtime as if she and only she protected him against the powers of darkness. Renata was already a little lady. She was a southern type, with her black eyes and dark hair, and had a more headstrong nature. Little Dorothea, Nordic like her brother, had at last begun to walk. She was six now and limped along on her bad foot. It was massaged every day with ointments, but grew slowly and had hardly any feeling in it. Nonetheless Christina had never seen a child so happy as she was.

Christina wrote a short report to her aunt: 'Secret agreement between German princes and the king of F. King given the right to Toul, Metz and Verdun.'

The contents of the letter were for her aunt's eyes only and Christina decided to send it in code. Each month had its code word, its code letter and its code number, which only she and the regent knew. Naturally she knew it by heart but was obliged to write it down while she worked on it. The code word for January was ROMANUS, and she set up an alphabet which began with the word and continued as the normal alphabet minus the letters used. ROMANUSBCDEFGHIJKLPQTVWXYZ. The month's code letter was L. So she wrote an alphabet which began with L: LMNOPQRSTUVWXYZABCDEFGHIJK.

Christina took her report letter by letter. 'H' was the fourth last in the lower alphabet and she took the fourth from last letter in the upper one: 'W'. 'E' in the lower alphabet was seventh last letter and was replaced by the corresponding one in the upper alphabet: 'Q'. She wrote 'M' as 'O' and continued. 'Secret' was transcribed as 'BQLSQC'. 'Agreement' became 'JVSQQOQMC'.

She soon finished transcribing and read through the text: BQLSQC JVSQQOQMC KQCFQQM VQSOJM NSXMLQB

JMD CWQ ZXMV AT T. ZXMV VXEQM CWQ SXVWC CA
CADR OQCI JMP EQSPDM.

Christina checked the code once more for mistakes and
immediately burned the alphabets and her original message.
She did not want to use code numbers; the intention was to
use the altered letters in an apparently innocent message.
But that was complicated, it took time, and she had every
right to send secret messages. She folded the letter and
sealed it.

She gave orders for the defences to be strengthened; and at
dawn the swiftest courier rode off to the regent. The
emperor must be informed at once of what was happening.
She had to have help.

Quivering with nerves, Christina waited for an answer,
but a letter from the king of France arrived first. He wrote to
her and Nicholai from Rheims.

The king demanded free passage through Lorraine for
himself and his troops on their way to Germany. He referred
to the friendly sentiments he had always cherished for the
ducal house and assured them that his army's passage would
not impose any burden on the populace.

This was monstrous. Once they had entered the country
she would never get them out again. The regent's reply
offered scant hope. True, the electoral princes of the Rhineland offered to oppose the French if the emperor would send
troops. But the emperor had neither money nor soldiers
enough and the French king was approaching.

Christina and Nicholai decided to ride to meet him at
Joinville and if possible come to a compromise.

King Henri the Second was not noted for brilliance. He was
said to be ill-educated despite his flair for languages, and in
many ways downright childish. He preferred old-fashioned
knightly ideals, and romantic plays like *Adamis of Gaul*. He
banned the works of Rabelais, and left Machiavelli to his
wife. The king's ideas of honour tended towards respectable;
there were no other women in his life apart from the boring
queen who worshipped him and the wrinkled mistress who
ruled him.

His beard was kept trimmed, and contributed to make his flat face seem even more broad, and his eyebrows hung down. But the gloomy, repressed expression Christina had noticed earlier had vanished when she met him at Joinville.

The king put forward his demands, which were the same as in his letter. Christina requested him to respect Lorraine's neutrality but his response was a firm and flat refusal. It was his intention to go to Nancy, he said with a gentle smile, and to talk to the nobility there. In addition he wished for agreement on a future marriage between the young duke and his own second eldest daughter, Claude.

Christina made no reply. She and she alone would decide her son's marriage, and she had no plans whatever for it to be on the French side.

The king responded to her silence by affably explaining to her what an honourable match it was for her son to marry so distinguished a king's daughter.

He stood firm on his demands, sure of himself. It was a despairing Christina who rode home through the spring rain to Nancy. She felt indignant at his words about the distinguished king's daughter. Was not she herself daughter to a king, of far nobler birth? No merchant's blood ran in her veins. But war was inevitable and Lorraine would be the first country to suffer.

Metz fell and Toul was taken after scattered resistance. Christina was desperate but she received a message from the emperor to play for time. She would have to try further negotiations with the French king.

On the 14th of April at two o'clock in the afternoon the French army was at the gates of Nancy. After a hasty consultation with Nicholai they agreed to allow the French king and his personal retinue to enter. The army should remain outside the town, and the king arrived at the ducal palace as a guest.

The king was in great good humour as he and his courtiers entered. They were received with ceremonial honours by Christina, Nicholai and representatives of the nobility of Lorraine, in the Deer Hall on the upper floor of the palace. It was the day before Good Friday; outside, the sun shone and trees had come into leaf in the gardens. The king spoke.

He repeated his demand for a betrothal between his daughter Claude and the young duke and again emphasised that the princess was an exceptionally brilliant match.

Christina had expected this. Already she had considered it and decided to give her consent. She could always break her word later and explain that the agreement had been extracted under duress. She smiled at the king. A fresh breeze blew through the open windows as the king expressed the desire to add a further request.

The king proposed to take Duke Carl with him to the French court, to enable him to continue his education and upbringing there under his personal direction and with no contact with and influence from his mother, the duchess of Lorraine.

The breeze wafted in through the windows again and there was silence in the hall. She must not faint; she must go on standing erect. The king spoke again; he said something about regency. But she was somewhere else. She held a little child in her arms, so infinitely little; and she held him close, felt his warmth and thought of the pains he must have known at birth. She had sworn then that nothing human should take him from her; and now there stood the king of France before her, a mere man, and she screamed.

Her 'No!' hung in the hall, in the silence, it diminished and was lost out through the open windows. She wanted to scream it again; she wanted to hit out. Through the left-hand window she glimpsed the magnolia. But when she turned her head and looked over the rooftops and defences she could see the tents and fires of the French army and their arrays of cannon as far as the eye could reach. To fight was an impossibility.

Christina took a step towards the king and began to speak. She would relinquish all rights, promise him fealty and loyalty; but begged only to keep Carl. She was a woman, she was alone, she was a mother. Carl was her only son. Was not the Holy Virgin, the noblest of all the saints, the symbol of motherhood, of all mothers and their love for the children they had borne? Had not the king himself suffered greatly during years of imprisonment, separated from all affection, when he was a hostage in Spain, so that his father could regain his freedom after the lost battle of Pavia? Could he of all people on earth wish the same cruel fate for a child as that which he had so bitterly endured? Carl was only nine. Might she not keep him for two years, or just one more? Did not the king recall his own loss and his longing for his dead mother? He loved his children. What would he feel if someone were to do anything so cruel as to take them away from him and the queen? She had no husband to protect her. All she could do was humbly to beg him not to take her beloved son. Not that; only not that.

Christina was at a loss for words. She saw tears in the French courtiers' eyes, and even the king wept. Had he understood? Did he remember what they had done to him so long ago? Was he a human being after all, and unable to do this to her?

The king bent down and took her hand. He carried it to his lips, which were still wet, and said softly, 'Madame, Duke Carl shall have all the love a child can have.' Then he straightened himself, looked into her eyes and added, 'He will have it from the queen and myself.'

His own eyes were still moist, and several of the Frenchmen were weeping openly. But Christina saw only cold, dry glances from her own nobles. She had lost everything. They knew it, and they relished it.

She struggled to behave naturally when she came to say goodnight to the children. They must not notice anything yet; and perhaps there was still a scrap of hope – perhaps. Nicholai would try to plead her case, though she had not expected that from him. But there were no others. Well, there were the people in the street, the artisans, needy citizens' wives, the country peasants, but what say did they have? It had been her father's fate, and now it was hers. To want to help the weak meant that no one helped you yourself when you were in need; for the help of the weak meant nothing. They had no cannon, nor tents filled with infantry like those outside the walls now.

She lay awake at night tossing from side to side. Carl was still in the same house as she was; meanwhile she wept and wept and clutched at a desperate hope. They could make him French, they could teach him Turkish, they could forbid him to ride; but she would never let him out of her sight. She could go with them to France; or perhaps the king might still be moved. Had he not been moved to tears when she spoke and reminded him of his own sad fate? After all, he was a human being and only a human being. But outside the day began to dawn. The sun rose over Lorraine with cold inevitability, as if it were a purely ordinary day.

The king held a meeting with the nobles. Christina did not know what it was about and she made no attempt to find out. She went into the garden with the children. She hardly noticed the girls, but hugged Carl close. He was a big boy, always sensible and calm, who loved to talk of animals and birds.

The boy stopped to look up at a flock of starlings in the trees. They stood watching them for a long time. The sky was high and blue, the weather vanes quiet, and the birds flew around busily.

'Where do you think they go in the winter?' Carl asked.

'If only I knew,' replied Christina. She kept her arm around him as if to make him an inseparable part of herself.

'They fly south or west,' he said, 'but they always come back.'

He lowered his head and looked at the wall. 'I shall come back too.'

Christina started. Did he know? Had someone said something? But she had no time to speak before he turned to her with a serious gaze. 'You must not be upset, Mother.'

They looked at each other. How grown-up he sounded, she thought, as if it were she who was the child. But his eyes filled with tears, and they wept and wept.

Christina threw herself at the king's feet. She pleaded, she begged to keep Carl. She repeated her promises of eternal fealty and loyalty. He must not think of her but of the child. It was a child he was wounding, it was . . .

But the king stopped her torrent of words and bade her rise. 'Consider, Madame,' he said, 'the young duke is in the best of health. If he should fall ill I have the best physicians. Consider that he is a clever child and I will see to it that he has the best possible education. Duke Carl will be brought up as our son, he will have my son for a brother and there are many kind relatives at my court.'

'Kind relatives', the king said. They were the de Guises. Was this the revenge of the rejected suitor? Or was it the price of fortifying la Mothe?

Christina saw a trace of something humane in the king's eyes. But now at last she understood that nothing could make him alter his decision.

Each footstep on the stair was a step nearer their parting. Christina held Carl's hand. He had recovered his courage, comforted his sisters, and walked now with a calm step. She wanted to go to the door with him. Nicholai was on her other side. One step and then another. For a moment she thought her legs would give way under her. But she managed to go on. She felt the boy's hand in hers, and the last step, the last space covered between the horse, and the final brief embrace before he was lifted into the saddle.

Christina fought with herself. Carl was so handsome, he sat so upright; the most beautiful boy on earth. The gates were opened and the horses made their way out towards the rue St Georges.

Carl turned round in his saddle; they gazed at each other. A last glimpse of his fair face under the silk beret, and he was gone.

But then came a cry, a child's cry for help. 'Mother . . .!'

Christina made to run out. She wanted to catch up with him, to take him to her again. But Nicholai held her to him, pressing her face to his shoulder. She heard no more; the sound of horses' hooves on the cobbles grew faint; and she looked up.

Through the still-open gateway was a wall of people. Eleven years ago they had acclaimed her; now their mute, powerless sympathy reached out to her. They had to fight hard for their living and many of them had buried children. Christina stood there for a while, responding to their glances, until the gates were pulled shut and she walked silently into the castle.

The emperor would come to their aid. Christina was sure that despite everything he would not tolerate the French occupation of anywhere militarily as important as western Lorraine.

After three sleepless nights of weeping, will-power returned. Christina was going to get Carl back.

She had the little girls made ready for the journey, and set out for Deneuvre. It was her dower house, something of her own; and even if the property was small and comprised merely a few villages she would find the feeling of her own worth there and the ability to fight back.

Christina's court was more or less intact and to a certain extent it was also her intelligence service. By night she would wake with a start at the sound of Carl's scream; she heard it again and again, echoing in her mind until she thought it would tear her apart. But during the day she was calm and purposeful, holding low-voiced conversations with Battista, who brought news from travellers and traders come through the enemy lines. She gathered information about positions, the strength and placing of artillery, and weak points in the defences. Reports filtered through from the Netherlands that the armies of the emperor and the south Germans were on the move.

She caught herself whispering, 'I'm coming, Carl, I'm coming ...,' and she rose from bed in the light summer nights to write her messages in code to the regent. She could almost feel his small hand in hers, as she sent off courier after courier. She felt Madame Louise's sympathy; she too was a mother and understood her feelings, and had asked to retain her position, a request that had surprised and moved Christina. The emperor's troops were on their way and Christina received intelligence about Metz that might well be decisive.

The French army in the town was much larger than

expected but the reports held some uncertainty. Christina pondered for a long time, got up in the night and began to write. She tried to express herself briefly, in the same way as she had written to accede to the emperor's entrance into Nancy.

It was May; the code word was LUCAS, the code letter S. Christina had composed her report; but she could not despatch it as it was, because she had promised loyalty to the French king. Using the second code, she transcribed her letter. Each letter of the code had to function as the second letter after each comma and full stop in an apparently innocent missive. It required imagination, and was heavy and trying work that went on all night, until she could hear the rattle of carts carrying meat and vegetables to be sold at the kitchen entrance.

Christina was at a loss. Her best courier was out already on another errand and she had need of someone she could rely on completely.

Battista agreed without hesitation. He thought it wisest to dress as a merchant. His servants were ordered to announce that their master was ill, in order to cover up his absence for as long as possible and give him the greatest possible start. At four o'clock in the morning, on one of the last days in May, Christina handed him the letter.

Battista kneeled down and carried her hand to his lips. She was moved at the sight of this man, who had been so faithful to her for so many years, and she asked God's blessing on him, and His protection on this dangerous journey. She caught a last glimpse of deep earnestness in his black eyes. His disguise was good; but had he too great an air of nobility for it to convince? It could not be changed now. He stole through the fortress to the moat and the servant waiting on the other side with a saddled horse.

The next afternoon a lace pedlar arrived. Christina knew him well. She asked him the price of a particularly fine piece of black lace.

The man fumbled in his purse for a moment. He mumbled that he could not remember, then pulled out a scrap of paper and handed it to her. The price was there but so was something else: 'Twenty thousand in Metz'.

Christina bought the black lace, paying an excessive price for it, and sent the man away.

So it was right. That night she again got up. She lit a candle and began work on the codes. It was still May and she wrote:

LUCASBDEFGHIJKMNOPQRTVWYZ
STUVWXYZABCDEFGHIJKLMNOPQR

Christina decided to send only the one word TRUE, which became UZCJ; but then followed the tedious task of transferring it into code number two: 'Must I go on living without Carl? Azure skies delight me no more. Ache tears my heart apart. Ajudge for yourself what is right.'

Christina started to go through the draft carefully, to make sure there were no errors. But the letters grew jumbled before her eyes.

It was lack of sleep. She had noticed her tired face in the mirror for a long time now, with the swelling round her eyes. No one must know she worked at night; meanwhile there were only a couple of hours left for rest.

She rose, went to the window, opened the shutters and went out on to the balcony for air.

It was a mild night. The sky was cloudless and somewhere in France Carl lay asleep under the same sky. If only she could send him a word of greeting through the stars, tell the moon to embrace him for her or ask the planets to look upon him with love. Might the Almighty Father bring them together again? Inwardly she invoked the aid of the Holy Virgin.

'Carl,' she whispered again and again, hoping her voice travelled through the stillness of the night into his dreams, wherever he was, his eyelids dark in sleep.

There was no sound except for the steps of the guards. The night air made her forget time and place.

Christina came back to herself with a start. What had she sensed? What sound had her ears caught? She leaned outwards, searching, and saw nothing. But there *was* something or other down below.

Suddenly it came. The sound of hooves at a gallop across the courtyard. Christina caught a glimpse of the rider's outline silhouetted in the moonlight. It was somebody riding astride but in skirts. She clapped her hands to her face: Madame Louise. The sound changed as the hooves met wood; the drawbridge must be down.

Christina ran in and saw. The code on her table was gone. She checked the door lock, but it was open; someone must have unlocked it with a key from outside. She screamed. People came running. 'Follow her!' she cried.

At once all was confusion. Horses were brought from their stalls and saddled, candles and torches blazed, questioning eyes surrounded her; and at last the soldiers rode off.

But in her heart she knew it. Someone was waiting out there for Madame Louise. It was too late.

Days passed and she heard nothing. The soldiers' mission had been unsuccessful. It had been impossible to discover why the drawbridge had been let down in the middle of the night. No one knew anything; everyone covered up for each other. She gave the officer in charge his discharge.

On the 4th of June a gentleman announced himself. He was a certain Monsieur Rastaing and he brought a message from the king of France. Christina stood before him and read it through quickly.

The king authorised Monsieur Rastaing to express what he himself wished to say. Christina threw a questioning glance at the Frenchman. He stated that his lord the king of France required her to leave Lorraine immediately.

'By what right can I be asked to leave my own property?' she asked coldly.

'Our troops,' the man replied, 'have arrested a certain Monsieur Battista, who was in possession of a letter written by Your Grace and addressed to the regent.'

'And why should I be prohibited from sending a greeting to my gracious aunt?' asked Christina, fear creeping over her.

'The letter was not entirely harmless,' answered the man, his mouth twisting in a triumphant smile as he handed Christina the paper.

She had only to throw a glance at it to see what it was. A transcript of the coded message. Why? she asked herself. Why should it have gone wrong? Why that inattentiveness that particular time? But outwardly she composed herself and asked curtly, 'Where is Monsieur Battista?'

The smile vanished from the man's face and he answered, 'I regret . . .'

'Regret?' . . . cried Christina, her self-control slipping.

'Monsieur Battista was treated as what he was. A spy in disguise.'

She fumbled behind her with her hands, she had to find strength, her fingers touched the wall panelling while she said, 'Was . . .?'

She read the answer in the man's eyes. He looked hard at her. 'The king of France can no longer guarantee Madame's safety.'

'I am perfectly capable of looking after my own safety on my own ground,' replied Christina. But she doubted her own words even as she asked him to leave.

Battista? Why? Why had she failed him? She was to blame. She had killed Battista by her carelessness. Why hadn't she taken the code with her when she went outside? How could she have done it? Faithful, faithful Battista, who had paid with his life. She cursed herself, hated herself. What was she doing to the people around her?

Had she been too self-willed in the seven years during which she had ruled? The idea had not occurred to her before. But now it was gnawing into her consciousness; it smarted and bit into her, a painfully growing awareness of her own guilt. Carl had paid, and now Battista . . .

'No,' she cried, and began pacing restlessly up and down. No, treachery was to blame.

But she knew better. She had failed; and Madame Louise, whom she had regarded merely as a gossip, must have been on the watch through all the years she had known her.

Through all those eleven years she had waited for Christina to commit that one slip. She had had a duplicate key cut, and Christina's servants or bribed guards must have been on the watch for a line of light between her shutters and reported at once if she went outside. With fiendish patience Madame Louise had been prepared every hour, every day. Christina had never given herself away to her, had never expressed an opinion on people or views. Madame Louise had never been given an opportunity to discover her secrets until that night.

That one night, that one instance of negligence, had been the one time she had been unequal to her task; and Battista had died for it. Christina clenched her hands in despair, and in rage against the world and against herself. She wanted to call back that night. She wanted to change its course. The hand on the death's-head clock must go into reverse. She would never ask for it again, only this one time must it go backwards, and she would pick up the code and burn it as she had always previously burned it. Then the French could seize Battista and find merely a casual greeting to her aunt. They would have to let him go, for he had done nothing wrong; and he would soon return, pure faithful soul as he was.

Christina squeezed the silver timepiece as if to confer magical powers on it. She opened it carefully, but the hand registered the correct time. It was half-past nine in the morning, outside was day, not night, it was the 4th of June 1552 and Battista was dead.

Christina sent letters of protest to the king of France. She pointed out that she had never interfered in anything but trifling matters, and according to Lorraine custom a widow kept custody of her children as long as she remained unmarried. But she knew it was pointless. The king was furious and repeated his order for her to leave.

Tired and broken, Christina gave in. She set off at the end of June with hardly a thought of where she would go, and stayed for the time in Strasbourg. She did not know what to reply when Renata and Dorothea asked why they were not going home soon and when Carl would come.

The imperial armies were on the move and Christina received a summons to the camp at Landau.

She was shocked on meeting the emperor. He was racked by rheumatism and cast down by the humiliating recollection of having to be carried across the Brenner pass in May in pouring rain fleeing from the enemy. They had pursued him so closely that they were able to steal his baggage. He had escaped nonetheless; and he promised her a permanent home in Brussels. In the meantime he recommended her to go to Heidelberg.

Friederich spread wide his arms and embraced her. The old man planted a fatherly kiss on her brow, and she saw a broad smile on his face as he held her before him. 'The duke of Alba's troops are ready to besiege and occupy Metz,' he said, as if handing her a precious gift.

'Metz!' she cried incredulously. 'If . . .'

At last, at last . . . Wild joy flooded through her. If the French were beaten at Metz, then . . . Christina gave a cry of happiness.

Days passed in celebration as they waited for news. Ecstatic rejoicings continued in Heidelberg throughout the last days of summer. In October came a report that the imperial troops had surrounded the town with a rampart.

Albrecht came whirling in with an army. For a time he had been on the French side, and no one knew whom he would now support. To everyone's surprise he attached himself to the emperor. Within the besieged city it was the duc de Guise who led the surrounded forces: Christina's lover and her suitor faced each other.

But as time went on and winter advanced all the news from Metz was concerned with frostbite and sickness among the soldiers, both inside and outside the town. Typhus raged, while in Heidelberg they waited in vain for the report of a French surrender. Courage dwindled, and hope froze like the waters of the Rhine. Alba and Brandenburg kept up the siege; but de Guise still resisted. In December Christina decided to go on to Brussels.

Once again she was returning to the land of her childhood. Once again the regent and all her court and the foreign envoys lined up to receive her. Then, she had been sixteen. Now, she was thirty-one years old, robbed of her son and cast out of her home. She saw pity in the faces around her but did not want it; it merely humiliated her and emphasised her downfall.

Christina held up her head, took her daughters on each hand and accepted every gesture of respect as if she were the victor. No one should see her sorrow; no one should pity her. She managed to whisper a questioning 'Metz?' to her aunt, received a headshake in reply, and sensed defeat. There was no more to hear, nothing more to say. Christina smiled proudly when the regent held the two small girls in her arms. Christmas was approaching, and would be celebrated no matter what happened. She was with people she cared for; her aunt's face also beamed with pleasure at the reunion.

She was Christina of Denmark; no one could alter that, and she had nothing to add.

The Low Countries, 1552–1559

XVII

That February the emperor was in Brussels, and on the 13th he spoke to the States General. When he described how the treacherous French had taken away the little duke of Lorraine by force and thrown his mother out of the country there was a roar of anger from the assembly.

Christina was back in the Netherlands of her childhood. She was loved here. Her thoughts were cooler, too, her judgements clearer, in these well-known surroundings. The regent put at her disposal the same suite of rooms she had had before her second marriage. The bed was the same, as was the sound of the sentries' steps at night and the smell of juniper twigs from the fire. A reassuring cloak of security encompassed her. But at night she woke weeping for her son. She whispered his name, spoke words of comfort into her pillow, tossed from side to side under the covers, until at last the maidservant brought her fresh fruit juice and called her for morning Mass. When she left the chapel and took her two daughters to the first meal of the day she was again calm and self-controlled. Carl was alive and she would get to him if she had to cross over a thousand fronts and a thousand frontiers.

The attack on Metz was a catastrophe. The duke of Alba relinquished the siege on the 2nd of January 1552, after the bloodiest battle in modern history, leaving the duc de Guise as victor.

Old Johanna fell ill. At the beginning of February death was near. Johanna smiled happily at Christina. At last, at last God would take her to Him. She had been waiting so many years for His will to be done and now the moment had come when she was to see her dear ones again up there with the heavenly Father. Her last wish was to be buried in the churchyard of the little village in southern Brabant where she came from, so that God would be quite certain where she belonged. For he had so many people to take care of every single day.

It was a good death; but Christina felt the gaps around her. So many were gone who once had been near her. The frailty of life, earthly life, that ended with a breath not drawn. It could be stamped out at any moment, and Christina felt as if pieces of herself were flaked and chipped away with each vanishing face.

Christina had brought some of her court with her. Even the ponderous Dane was there. At first she was not sure what to do with him now Battista was dead, and set him desultory tasks. Denmark had suddenly grown remote; but one day in early spring during a conversation with the regent the old dream returned.

Her aunt thought it was time to find suitable matches for Renata and Dorothea. They were now eight and seven years old respectively, too young of course to be married but at an age when it seemed reasonable to look around. Christina had given the subject some thought, but the regent's proposal took her completely by surprise.

The name of the Danish king's eldest son, Frederik, was brought up. Christina was dismayed. The idea of a member of that hated family as her daughter's bridegroom was repugnant. But the regent was obviously prepared for her reaction for she said with a little smile, 'It is always better to take what you can get than to aim too high.'

The regent said no more but sent Christina a long, cool look and changed the subject. No doubt Christina would bide her time, and calculate what would be most advantageous. There was no hurry.

But the incident renewed Christina's interest in Anders. Battista was no longer there to open his letters, and for a time she pondered whether to appoint someone else to the task. Instead, she herself drew Anders into closer contact.

Talking to the Dane, Christina noticed how he had changed since their first conversation in Nancy. Naturally she had seen and observed him; he was a member of her staff. But only now did she see how assured and aware he had become. It was as if a burden had been lifted from him.

Christina asked what he thought of conditions in Denmark. He responded by describing the apathetic atmosphere of Copenhagen. It was true that peaceful times had come and there was money to be made through trade. But wounds had not completely healed and the people were indifferent towards both king and prince.

Now and again Anders came out with strange remarks. 'Not the right faith,' he said of the Danes – but he did not think much of the Catholic church either. Christina disregarded this, and instead listened to descriptions of councillors and mayors, of bookbinders and cobblers; small details that might one day be of use. She soon came to feel that she knew every street, and every other person, in the city of Copenhagen.

Albrecht turned up at the emperor's court, airily unconcerned over his changes of side, and soon found his way to her bed again. Adolf of Gottorp threw himself at her feet, and no matter what she did or said he merely grew more ardent.

He wept, he entreated, he wrote her ridiculous poems; he would not be shaken off. In her heart Christina enjoyed seeing him, a son of the man who had stolen her father's land and throne, abjectly begging for her love. What would his revered father feel if he could see his son now? She was conscious of her own lower instincts when she could not forbear to send him an encouraging smile in the dance or did not remove her hand quickly enough from the backgammon board to evade his attempts at caresses.

They had a lot to pay for, that branch of the family; and playing off brother against brother was merely an unobtrusive beginning. Albrecht, too, now proposed. Friederich was all in favour of the match, but Christina refused. She questioned herself as to why.

A wife's duty of obedience to her husband was fundamental and obvious. There could be only one head of a family. But the idea of subjection to a man and lover like Albrecht seemed impossible to her. Perhaps it was that she felt superior to him. Or it may have come down to practical considerations: as a widow, a free woman, she had everything; there was no earthly account rendered for the joys of the bed – but there would be if she gave her promise at the altar.

There were times when she longed for a man's protection. But he could never have understood when she was weak and when she was strong, when she was in need of shelter and when she was seized with the urge to ride out into the storm, feel its brute strength and enjoy her own powers of resistance.

Her intercourse at night with Albrecht was sinful, it would have to be paid for after this life. Christina knew that; but having ruled for seven years she was now unable to contemplate being ruled by anyone else.

The boy king of England died in July 1553. The event brought recollections of all that King Henry had subjected England to in order to get this one and only son. He had been obsessed with male inheritance; and now the throne was going to his eldest daughter, Mary.

Christina still remembered her first banquet, when her aunt had mentioned the king's young daughter to the cardinal. She knew the humiliations the princess had suffered. The repudiation of her mother; her own degradation to the title of mere Lady Mary; and Anne Boleyn ordering her to become lady-in-waiting to the little Elizabeth. She had borne all this with the dignity to be expected from the granddaughter of Ferdinand and Isabella. She was never resigned to having been forced to renounce her faith, even though it had been under threat of execution that she had kneeled at her father's feet and acknowledged him as head of the church.

For all these years the regent's court had felt sympathy for this girl, who was no longer a girl but now an ageing woman.

They had felt for her adversities and suffering, and for the fact that she had never had a husband. And now at one stroke Mary was queen of England. She was thirty-seven years old. It was her intention to lead her country back to the embrace of the mother church; and it was the intention of her cousin the emperor that she should have a husband.

Talk soon circulated at the Netherlands court – of how Don Philip was struggling to escape so old a bride, but also of how he would be bound to concur with his father's wish in the end. Philip married Queen Mary.

Strange news filtered through from England. Like all Catholic monarchs, the queen was obliged to wash the feet of the poor at Easter time. But the like of such scrubbing and scouring had never been seen. It was also said that the queen laid a healing hand on ailing shoulders; reports that she had pressed her lips down into their suppurating wounds made the regent swallow with disgust.

Despite attempted revolt Mary ascended the throne, carried by a wave of sympathy from almost every class and denomination. But before the prince had crossed the Channel to meet his bride emotions had cooled. The serious threat of a coup had to be put down, with executions in the Tower. Even Mary's little second cousin, the sixteen-year-old Lady Jane Grey, lost her head, albeit to general regret, in that many believed the intelligent girl was innocent and merely misused.

In the Low Countries the court anxiously awaited news from England on the progress of the marriage, and the announcement of Queen Mary's pregnancy was received with joy. The queen's belly grew visibly larger, and by Christmas she felt the child kicking. But there was anxiety over her age, and doubt as to a happy outcome.

Christina often spent the evening in the palace of Wilhelm of Orange in Brussels. The prince's gatherings were renowned, not least because he had acquired the best chef in Europe. The food alone was enough to bring all the princes in the world to his house.

He greeted them, young, blond, handsome and erect. Not

221

only was he rich; he enjoyed his wealth. Money was meant to be spent and life to be lived.

At table, Wilhelm emptied his goblet with zest. It was there to be emptied, just as the goblet of life should be emptied. With stomach filled and blood intoxicated, he was entirely happy. Everyone joined him as he raised a toast to the emperor, to the regent, to Don Philip and to the Netherlands and, late in the evening, to Spain and England as well.

Wilhelm was Orange, not René; yet he was René all the same, with the easy gaiety Christina had noted in his manner even when he had been fifteen. He had the spirit and power she recollected from her own childhood when she rode out of the palace in Mechelen one bright autumn day. Christina wished he and she were both twenty years younger, so that she could love him as she had not loved since June nights in Bruges so infinitely long ago.

She listened, entranced, to what he had to say. 'What do we want with all that talk of heretics and papists? We are all Christians after all; let us practise our faith whichever way we like.' Egmont and Hoorn applauded, with a loud 'Bravo, bravo', and such conversations often ended with her, Christina, being hailed as the future regent, the guests clapping in time to show their agreement.

Day dawned over Brussels. The drunks were carried out; the more sober went on to Mass; the torches were extinguished and the goblets emptied. The party was over.

Christina enjoyed those evenings, just as she enjoyed the feeling of being at home in Brussels and living in the company of people she knew and cared for. But when the hangings closed around her bed and she was alone, childhood nightmares returned.

She saw a horse, a beautiful young creature, galloping through a forest of magnolia trees with large leaves. The leaves changed, grew lobed, altered their colour to red, and turned into bloody red hands that stretched out and seized hold of the horse and cut its throat. But it went on without a head, dripping blood. She could see its ribs through the skin, and they sat a boy on the horse's back, a small fair-haired boy, and he turned his face towards her. It was Carl, and she heard him scream: 'Mother . . .!'

Christina woke up sweating. The scream faded; it had been a bad dream. But it kept coming back. Again and again she saw the bloody, headless horse and heard Carl's cry.

By day there were thoughts, worries, a more controlled fear. Was he getting enough to eat and sufficient fresh air? Who comforted him when he was miserable and who helped him when he fell off his pony or found his sums difficult? She made little marks on the wall. How big was he now? Was he as tall as this, or that? Renata and Dorothea took part in the guessing like a game. Christina, looking at herself in the mirror, saw an expression that at first seemed strange. When she smiled at herself it vanished; but when the muscles slackened it was there again: bitterness was creeping up on her. It became a part of her personality, and as time passed she knew and acknowledged what the mirror told her.

Then there was idleness. Christina had no other function in this country than to administer her staff. Every attempt to comment on the government was sharply rebuked by the regent. She would tolerate no discussion, and so Christina never heard any answer to the question raging inside her. She could not see the necessity for the cruel persecution of heretics, and least of all why her aunt, who was herself not hostile to the new teachings, could act so harshly. It was the emperor's will: the regent was merely carrying out his orders. But was it really impossible to refuse? Could it not have been avoided, the bloodbath that had gone on in the mid-forties? Christina's own Catholic faith was still unwavering; but she sometimes felt like hurling at her aunt Wilhelm of Orange's words that we are all Christians, after all.

New days and new events came along. In May a bulletin announced that Queen Mary had been delivered of a living son. In England, church bells chimed, and cannon fired a salute in Antwerp harbour.

It was a miracle. A ruler was born, coming into the world,

like an Isaac, from an old woman's womb. Everywhere, in the streets of London as well as in the market squares of Brussels, the populace came running out to light bonfires to celebrate the birth of the prince.

But when the couriers arrived with messages of congratulations from Spain the tankards were empty and the wild boar bones thrown to the dogs. The feasting was halted, for there was no child – not yet, anyhow. Instead it would be born at midsummer for, as everyone knew, the queen was as round as a barrel.

In July the regent was heard to remark that one of her bitches had once suffered a false pregnancy. She sent Christina a telling glance as she did so, and made no further comment. But it was not long before everyone realised that the queen's stomach had shrunk; there had never been a child. It was tragic; it was absurd; it was madness. Everyone felt for the poor woman, who had suffered so much wrong throughout her life. But it was hard to keep a straight face or to control the outbursts of ill-controlled speculation on what actually there had been in that great belly.

Queen Mary was inconsolable. She persecuted the Protestants with more zeal than ever before. They would have to pay for her tribulations, brought about by God's anger at her betrayal of her faith and her church.

But there was one person Mary dared not put to death. It was she whom she hated above all others, her half-sister Elizabeth. Meanwhile Elizabeth had been imprisoned in the Tower. All her life she had been unwanted. She was an official bastard; her mother had been executed; and she herself had been rejected by her father because she was the wrong sex.

No one had ever accounted her of any significance. A mere red-haired chit, come into the world as haphazardly as an unfortunate remark. Christina had been in Milan when the child was born, and she remembered the malicious laughter at the time. Elizabeth had been the king's punishment for breaking with the papacy for a common whore's sake. Her life had hung by a thread, and still did so. On the other hand, no one could blame her for the revolt against the Catholic

Queen Mary, and even Philip had contributed to save his wife's little half-sister.

Soon curiosity awoke in the courts of Europe. What was she really like? And what did she look like? The envoys in London suddenly grew busy sending reports, page after page, describing the unknown girl. 'Not beautiful, but ...' followed by praise of her charm, shapely hands and dark expressive eyes. It was also claimed that she had a good brain.

Christina had her own ideas on why Philip wanted to save Elizabeth's life. Queen Mary was unlikely to live very long. It was no bad thing to be married to the throne of England. But if the queen, in addition, had dark eyes, beautiful hands, a talented mind, and a youthful body for bearing children, it would be still better. What nobody had thought could happen might perhaps become reality. Who could tell? More questions went off to England about the girl who languished in partial imprisonment at Hatfield, north of London, to be answered with 'She is not beautiful, but ...' Or, 'She is cautious, and she has time to wait ...'

In August 1555 Philip left England and an unhappy wife behind. He was unpopular there. All the blame for the religious persecutions was laid at his door. He himself was embittered, because the English parliament had refused him the title of king.

Philip had the best of excuses for his departure. The emperor wished to abdicate.

The emperor was fifty-five years old and a sick man. He wanted only to find peace for his remaining years, in a monastery in Spain.

As long as Christina could remember, the emperor had been an idea rather than a human being. He was power, raised above all questions. It was unthinkable to doubt the rectitude of his decisions or hesitate to obey his orders. When she had stood, a little girl, outside the council chamber in Mechelen and watched her uncle coming to meet her for the first time, she had regarded him as standing somewhere between God and man. Nothing had changed when, on the 25th of October that year, dressed in black and with the Order of the Golden Fleece around his neck, he entered the great hall of the palace in Brussels to pass on his ruling power over the Netherlands to his son. The nobility and over a thousand deputies looked on as the emperor bade the assembled company obey and serve his son with the same loyalty with which they had obeyed and served him, and asked their pardon for any wrongs he had unwittingly inflicted on them. His cheeks were sunken, his skin sallow; his voice broke as he addressed them, and tears ran down his cheeks on to the tip of his long chin.

It had been as a matter of course that the emperor had seemed to be everywhere. He had discussions with Luther in Worms; went into battle with his fleet against the Turks at Algiers; and shared the fortunes of his troops in various camps throughout Europe, in heat, frost and rain, under attack or in retreat. And all the while he had been constantly followed by couriers presenting endless cases for decisions, tax demands, marriage contracts or peace treaties. His wife had died, and he had ignored his children's development. Now, at this moment when he was relinquishing power, he was more than ever an idea, and a symbol, set apart from all human norms. It seemed as a symbol that he wept; the husky voice addressing the crowded hall was that of a symbol; it was as a symbol that he was tired, in pain and exhausted and wished to end his days in the garden of a Spanish monastery.

Don Philip kneeled at his father's feet to receive the regalia of the kingdom. He rose again as Philip the Second, ruler of the Netherlands and soon to be king of Spain and large parts of Italy. But he was not to have the imperial crown; that was to go to his uncle, Ferdinand of Austria. The mighty Hapsburg empire was to be split lengthwise and with it the dream of one united Christian kingdom.

Peace reigned in the land. But food prices had risen sharply – many considered because of the huge imports of silver and gold from America. What did the future hold? Christina knew that that was the question in the minds of that crowd of over a thousand before her, as their eyes tried to penetrate the façade of their new ruler, seeking not the symbol but the person.

The regent, too, did not wish to remain in her post any longer. Like her brother she wanted to go south to the sun. She excused herself by saying that she was fifty and no longer had the strength for such a demanding task.

Christina did not know what she was to do with herself now that both the emperor and her aunt were quitting the country for good. Would she be able to return to Lorraine?

Negotiations were under way for yet another peace treaty. She dared not believe it, hardly dared to hope. Four years had gone by since she had last seen Carl; four years in which she had made her little marks on the wall of her bedroom and had heard of him only through indirect reports from the French court.

But when the subject of the boy's release was brought up during the negotiations, the French threatened to walk out unless the demand was removed. And so it had to be.

Christina wept out her sorrow in solitude, revealed nothing outwardly and considered whether to go to her dower house at Tortona in Milan. But during more solitary dinners with Philip he asked her to stay in the Netherlands. He sat opposite her, sad and sorrowful. He was bewildered by the world he found himself in, and unable to understand why everything was so different from his beloved Spain. He listened to Christina; but she felt it was often the sound of her voice rather than what she was actually saying that so clearly appealed to him. He looked at her adoringly, but at the same time he spoke of his wife with the greatest respect and admiration. Philip was faithful and loyal to Queen Mary. Even so he asked Christina to visit him after he had returned to England.

A relative arrived at the Netherlands court: Christina's cousin Margaret, who had journeyed from Italy. The 'accident' had returned.

After her short-lived marriage to Alexander of Medici, who was murdered, and mourned by not one single person, least of all his wife, she had been forced into marriage with Ottavio Farnese. It was said that the letters concerning their marital battles took up shelves in the imperial archives.

Margaret was now duchess of Parma. She was exactly the same, merely twice as large in every direction. She strode across the room like a man, pearls and gold chains clinking about her. Her generous figure sparkled and glittered. The sound of her coarse voice and jovial witticisms caused raised eyebrows among her courtiers, who had placed bets on whether she was a man disguised as a woman or a woman who was merely half a man. They had come to favour the second solution, however, when a son was undeniably proven to have been born of her womb.

Philip the Second was delighted to see his half-sister. While everyone else regarded her as the Flemish maid-servant's offspring, Philip chose to see her as the emperor's daughter, a person so close to him that with her he dared to drop his habitual suspicions. It was of no importance to him that she still could not keep her big feet under the hem of her dress; the only thing that mattered was that she was a member of the family. Meanwhile if Margaret had not learned graceful deportment, she at least knew how to advance herself. She clearly basked in her half-brother's favour, never forgetting to point out that she was the woman who stood closest to him at the Netherlands court. The question arose of whether there was something she was out to get. Perhaps favours for her son in the distant future? Surely that was it; what else?

In February 1556 Friederich died, at the age of seventy-three. Christina hurried off to help and console her sister.

Dorothea lay in bed sobbing, surrounded by her ladies and her dogs. Again and again she repeated the same phrase. 'He was so good to me . . . always so good to me . . .'

It took two days for Christina to get her calm enough to hold a normal conversation. Friederich had begged her to marry again, but she would not hear of it. 'I should never find anyone who would be so good to me,' she sniffed, holding a puppy in her arms. 'And besides, with a younger man I could get pregnant. I'm thirty-six. It's much too dangerous to have one's first child so late, even if . . .' She started to cry again.

Christina raised the Danish question.

Dorothea snapped that she wanted nothing to do with it. She did not understand that sort of thing. It had always been Friederich who arranged what had to be arranged. She was a mere nothing, with no husband and no children. What would she do with all that in the North? 'I am nothing but an amputated arm, no more; and besides Friederich said that we have been in a much weaker position since the armistice. In any case, the Danish and Swedish kings have agreed to stand together against us, even if they can agree on nothing else.'

Christina set off for home deep in thought. Dorothea's hopeless despair pained her; but she was also slightly irritated by her sister's helplessness. Again the idea of Renata's marriage to the Danish prince occurred to her. It was not what Christina would have wished for, but as matters stood it was better than nothing and certainly worth looking into. There had been no advances from the Danish side; but then her own unyielding attitude had not invited them.

Adolf of Gottorp was waiting in Brussels. There, a friend had come to visit him. This was the powerful Holsteiner Henrik Rantzau, who was close to the Danish court. When Christina rode into Brussels she had long since come to a decision. All the engineering of the hereditary claim now rested with her; and she had determined, as a start, to show herself agreeable.

Adolf of Gottorp sparkled with joy when she greeted him with her warmest smile. And he could hardly control himself when she casually let drop that she and her sister felt that a reconciliation with the existing government in Copenhagen was not out of the question. Adolf could not rush off quickly enough to Rantzau to tell him the great news.

Christina waited. As usual she was aware through Anders of many little details of life in Copenhagen. The royal castle had been rebuilt and modernised, but more in Saxon taste than Italian. This Lord Christian spent most of his time gazing at his southern border in fear of attack from herself.

His free time was spent in the reading of theological treatises and in studying maps. She had heard from many sources that young Frederik showed no sign of interest in the task that awaited him. Instead he preferred hunting, and making love to various well-born maidens.

This was news to delight Christina, given that she was prepared to see her daughter as wedded queen instead of herself as reigning queen – though Christina did not want her daughter to live in 'French conditions' with official mistresses or a Dyveka at her husband's side. However, there was plenty of time to think about that. Meanwhile Christina sought aid from Philip the Second.

After lengthy consideration King Philip found the idea of such a marriage extremely suitable. He suggested that a reliable and not too eminent person should be found to investigate the mood in Denmark. Christina in the meantime could reveal her intentions to this Rantzau.

She made the offer as attractive as possible. Naturally, though, she refrained from any official announcement. Rantzau was given to understand that she herself, her sister and her son Duke Carl of Lorraine would make no claims on Denmark, Norway and Sweden. Renata would remain heir to Lorraine after her brother in the case of his dying without heirs. Also Renata should have the sum still under offer from the Danish king as dowry to go to Christina and her sister, and when the time came she would inherit the largest portion of the two ladies' fortunes.

It was a generous offer. At one stroke Christina had made her daughter an exceptionally good match. Renata would bring all her Hapsburg connections with her; she would bring peace to the question of the Danish succession; and she would have a sumptuous bridal dowry, to which would be added further wealth in the form of inheritance from mother and aunt. Christian the Third could sleep secure, and he would acquire a daughter-in-law who would contribute to his coffers.

Christina settled back, however, to await developments until a suitable envoy was found. She was not absolutely sure she meant it.

The man chosen was Gerhard von Buckholt. He had been in the service of the emperor for a long time. Loyal and reliable, he had proved on his other missions to both France and northern Italy that he had a good memory for reporting clearly and accurately. He had grizzled hair and beard and a calm expression. His appearance indicated that he had no desire to rise very high – a useful quality when one wanted truthful accounts, free from wild exaggeration.

Buckholt was not being sent to Denmark to weave intrigues, merely to compile a sober report. But King Philip suggested, as justification for sending an envoy there, that he should take with him a letter from Christina, a message expressing a daughter's love and tenderness for her old father in all his tribulations.

Christina stood on the shore watching the ship that was carrying the regent away from the Netherlands. The emperor had already left. Christina had bidden farewell to the man who had ruled over her life, and now came this parting with the woman who had been a mother to her since her tenth year.

A light easterly breeze blew from the land. It pulled at her own widow's veil and filled the sails at sea. Her aunt's hair was grey now, her body thickened and heavy; but she had the same spirit as the young woman in black who had galloped out on those wild rides, and had shouldered the government of the Low Countries and the upbringing of three small children one spring day long ago in Mechelen.

As the ship set its course southwards the last ties with the safe world of childhood were severed. There was no longer a place called 'home', nor anywhere to go back to. The walls that had always sheltered Christina had been torn down. Storms might rage, but there would be no emperor to write to and no aunt to offer shelter. Now she acted as the wall, the outermost one, and the only protector of the two children in her care.

She must set about composing a letter to her father, whom she remembered only from the sound of household possessions being smashed, and from his desire for her to remember the Danish tongue. But her language was forgotten as he himself now was. Once she had hated him. Later, though she still waged war against his spirit, deep within her there had been the realisation that she resembled him much more than she did her Hapsburg mother. Through all, she had kept a sense of their common destiny, the similarity of their political aims and crushing defeats.

She, his daughter, must write to her father. She tried to picture him in his present surroundings and was shocked to recall that he had been a prisoner for twenty-four years.

She had grown used to the knowledge that he was in prison. But for so long, and why? Since the peace of Speyer he had been permitted to go hunting; and even so ... Twenty-four years? And how could she write a mere note of greeting to someone who had undergone that?

The effort would be worthwhile, for the sake of the children. Christina began to formulate a new letter. Feelings of falseness still held her back; but she pushed them away, and after hours of work it was finished and ready for Herr von Buckholt, about to set off for Denmark.

XVIII

Gerhard von Buckholt was worried. As an official he liked order in public affairs and peace in the land. All his adult life had been spent in the emperor's service. Imagination had no place in his working method, and dissident thoughts were as remote from his mind as the planet Jupiter from Mars. But he was so accustomed to testing political currents and sensing out what the future might bring that the change of monarch had engraved deeper lines in his already ageing face.

The people of the Low Countries did not care for King Philip. He was stiff, arrogant and rude. He was not like a ruler so much as an adversary. The mere sight of the king threw a shadow of silent fear over the populace; and Buckholt knew how little was needed to turn apprehension into anger. He feared for the loss of yet more souls.

When King Philip received the crown from his father's hand heresy had been more or less wiped out. Two thousand people had been put to death. That fact alone had quelled rebellious natures and religious anarchy, and Buckholt felt, like most people, that the punishments had been reasonable, right and absolutely necessary.

But there was a different and more serious problem in the provinces of the Low Countries. Not only had the emperor's wars cost enormous sums – and general opinion held that it was the Netherlands that had paid for Spanish conquests – but the price of food was still rising, at an alarming rate. The country was not self-supporting in foodstuffs. Usually a quarter of the corn supply had to be imported, and recently there had been hard winters and crop failures. Large areas of land in the North were depopulated because the peasants had been starving and had moved into the towns in the hope of survival. The tally of destitution rose steeply; famine threatened; and where there was nothing to lose revolt soon acquired currency.

But peace reigned for the time being. Buckholt stayed loyal to his new master, and when he was commissioned to go to Denmark he prepared himself carefully for such a difficult expedition. He was not enthusiastic about having to travel to the North in winter. He was also slightly uneasy at the idea of visiting a country with an incomprehensible tongue. But he was happy nevertheless to work for Christina of Denmark.

Buckholt had known the duchess since she was a small girl. She was their Princess Christina, and everything King Philip was to prove not to be. She spoke their language and shared their joys. Indignation in the country almost rose to boiling point over the way she had been treated by the French; and it was generally felt that she should never have been sent to that piffling dukedom.

Buckholt's official brief was to deliver a letter to the imprisoned king from his daughter; but it was openly being said that the real purpose of his journey was to ascertain the mood in Denmark and collect as much information as possible about the king, the queen and in particular the prince.

Buckholt appreciated the position at once. Little Princess Renata would soon reach marriageable age and this would be an ideal match.

But as usual Buckholt kept his opinions and his knowledge to himself. He had no one to talk to anyway. His wife had died eight years earlier and he had never considered marrying again. The four children had married well and had long ago stopped trying to get anything out of him, and he regarded his colleagues with the deepest suspicion.

Buckholt's silence was no hard-won virtue. It gave him a secret satisfaction to be in possession of knowledge nobody else had. He liked to walk along the street and find himself laughing at the sight of some haughty Herr this or that, all the while thinking 'If he only knew ...' That was his treasure, his property. He relished the joy of ownership, and it pleased him hugely to be hugging the knowledge of marriage plans of which many a high-placed notable had not the least inkling.

Buckholt received the letter from the duchess in person, together with her prayers for God to hold a protective hand over him. Christina was no longer young; her face was marked by sorrow and adversity. But she was still erect and beautiful. Anyone could have uttered the words she said, but her own way of saying them was granted to but few. There was something in the duchess's manner that was both noble and direct. Her voice had a gentleness and her gaze a sincerity that he could not remember having noticed in any other woman. No one treated their servants with such kindness and care, and no one was more suited to be the next regent. Egmont, Hoorn and Orange all desired it, for she knew the mind of the people, and understood them.

Servants and baggage were made ready. Nothing must look too splendid, for the journey was to be undertaken without an armed escort. Nonetheless Buckholt had to take suitable attire in which to stand before a king, even when that king was a prisoner. A white frost clothed Brussels. Buckholt rode off northwards.

He had gone no farther than a tavern in north Germany before he heard talk of the Danish prince. The prince's penchant for crossing swords exceeded his intellectual ability; also, though he could drink every one of his nobles under the table, he had trouble in writing a legible letter. And there were murmurs of his love for a certain Anna Hardenberg, lady-in-waiting to the queen. The rumours were vague, however, and Buckholt waited to hear more details when he should have arrived in Denmark.

Buckholt took note of everything he heard, from sober as well as merry mouths; from merchants as well as from educated travellers. Naturally he did not write anything down. That would have been risky – and quite unnecessary since he had an excellent memory, as indeed was essential for a man in his position. Crossing the frontier between the dukedoms and Denmark itself, he arrived in Kolding. There, he observed Koldinghus.

Lady Anna was there. She sat in that house at her embroidery, the object of the prince's love even though she was betrothed to a certain Herr Oluf Mouritzen Krognos. The queen was devoted to Lady Anna, for the girl knew perfectly well where the rights of her station began and where they ended. Though Anna declined to break her oath to Herr Oluf, the prince was able nonetheless to prevent her marriage to her betrothed. Most people thought that, though the prince's affections were all very fine and noble, they showed how immature and unfitted he was to undertake the calling of a king.

Everywhere Buckholt went there was a particular name he overheard each time the talk centred on Denmark or its government. At first he thought it had something to do with cattle breeding, because in this foreign tongue he caught only the sound, without its context. But gradually he became aware that it referred to an aristocratic Danish family, and to one of its members in particular. The subject of discussion was Herr Peder Oxe.

Peder Oxe was the most powerful man in the kingdom. At the sound of his name Buckholt listened, knowing that this was important information to take back to King Philip and the duchess – far more important, probably, than the extent to which the prince loved Lady Anna or not, for that kind of folly faded away when a man took a suitable bride.

Peder Oxe was a state councillor and the man who in actual fact possessed the keys to the kingdom. Also, he had offended the queen. There were innumerable explanations for this, varying from a rumour that he had been unwilling to allocate enough money for the royal household to his having uttered something derogatory. The topic was a favourite both among Germans and among those Danes who spoke German. The mightiest lord in the kingdom had made an enemy of the kingdom's mightiest lady, and the reason this was so freely discussed was because everyone foresaw the end of the battle.

Buckholt had to wait a long time for the ice to break up in

the Great Belt. But when he finally reached Kalundborg his thoughts were elsewhere than with the man who was to be overthrown. He was about to meet with a former ruler. Behind the red walls of the castle Christian the Second was waiting.

His hair and beard were white. Two mild eyes met Buckholt's.

'Does she really remember me, my little daughter?' His voice was moved as he took the letter. He went over to the window. Holding the letter away from him with shaking hands, he read it. Buckholt gazed at him in disbelief.

This was a king. A prisoner, to be sure, but still a king. Yet there stood a shrunken and humble old man whose posture indicated that he would thank his guards for every kindly word. This was the man who had once had the nobility of Sweden beheaded on the great square of Stockholm and who had plundered and ravaged the Netherlands. For a moment Buckholt thought he must be confronting the wrong man. But with his back to the window the prisoner said, 'Has my daughter, the duchess, quite forgotten the Danish language?'

Buckholt sensed that this referred to something that had occurred between father and daughter. He was not sure what to say, and ventured, 'The duchess speaks so many languages.'

'But not Danish, then,' the old man mumbled at no one, as if he were in the habit of talking to himself. He turned round and gazed out at the snow-covered fields.

The sun was shining. A sharp light fell on the old man's shoulders, bent and subdued under the weight of twenty-four years' confinement. Holding the letter, he mumbled something inaudible, and slipped it under his doublet. Suddenly he grew aware of his guest once more. 'I should like to have taken you out hunting. But it is late now.'

And suddenly, as if on impulse, he said, 'I can sing a hymn. It is beautiful. It was written by Herr Knud, who was guard in charge here.'

He burst into song with his hoarse voice: 'Oh, God, Father eternal . . .'

The voice rustled round the walls like oak leaves, until it came to a halt, the words forgotten. Buckholt felt it was time to leave.

'Thank my daughter, the duchess,' said the king. The last thing Buckholt saw was his hand reaching for the letter under his doublet. Buckholt went away deeply shocked.

The official mission was fulfilled and the letter delivered, given on behalf of the daughter to her father. But for the first time in his career Buckholt determined to erase an impression from his memory, so that later he could make a report without wrapping it in a cloak of lies.

There were plenty of other things to remember. Denmark was blanketed in snow. But the people felt the advantage of the high corn prices that had cast such shadows over the Netherlands. By now Buckholt had acquired an impression of the country. It seemed much more sparsely populated than his own, and the towns were small and unadorned. But game teemed in the forests, and there had been a good harvest after the failure the previous year. He found the people attractive; the girls especially were good looking. But most were uneducated and ignorant, and he had never met a nation that ate and drank like this one. Women in their cups beat each other with roasting irons; and the executioner was so drunk at his work that he could not chop properly, and was hooted by the mob.

Buckholt was horrified to find that they all seemed to have accepted the heretical faith as easily as if they had merely swallowed it down with yet another tankard of their undrinkable ale. What comes easily cannot go deep, he thought; Princess Renata's Catholic belief would not prove as great an impediment to the marriage as expected.

In Copenhagen Buckholt took lodgings in an exclusive inn in Kannike Street. The town was beautifully sited beside the Sound; but it was without splendour. He found the church of Our Lady dull and the royal palace frightful. It was old, but it had been adorned subsequently with copper and spires, and stood there beside the canal like a painted dotard.

Piles of rubbish were everywhere; the place smelt of pigs,

decay, wet wool and furs. The rain soaked the muck down with it into the earth so that the ground water was pure poison. He went for a walk in the palace courtyard, which was always open to all. Here stable-boys could buy draff for the animals, and servants gossiped with washerwomen, while paupers begged for what they could get. There was life there, and talk, as there was when wine was served in the town hall vaults and the taproom at the inn, where you could also get good Rostocker beer instead of the revolting local brew.

Many people there could speak some German, and whenever Buckholt revealed his origins he was always questioned about the duchess. A man from Copenhagen was known to be in her service; and rumours abounded.

Was she really so beautiful? And so noble? Buckholt nodded quietly. He saw glances being exchanged, and knew what people were thinking, and hoping for. Only royal employees behaved as if they were not aware of her existence, and behind this lack of knowledge he sensed orders. The duchess represented a danger. The king was in constant terror of attack from the South. Lorraine was a foreign country and could be made into an enemy, and although officially the king feared Lorraine, not the duchess, she was Danish and could all too easily become the gathering point for dissidents. She would have to be eliminated, using the weapon of silence.

Denmark was a dark country and Buckholt grew cold in its small capital as he worked at gathering information. Poor students who had some knowledge of German told him that aristocrats no longer studied at the university because there was no money to be earned in ecclesiastical posts. Merchants were sure that there would be a rift between Denmark and Sweden, for even though Christian the Third was a man of peace he was old. The prince on the other hand had been born during a time of discord – a fact that had left its mark. He desired war and battle and nothing else. The Swedish prince Erik had been born with a caul, and with a red cross on his breast. When those two became kings the worst could be expected. Meanwhile the outcome remained to be seen. Although the nobles had taken an oath of allegiance to the prince, you never knew what might happen with them.

Many people tried to convince Buckholt of the beauty of the country, when the snow should at last have melted with the late spring, and the nights grew short and light. He still could not comprehend how any Christian soul could willingly live in this god-forsaken place. It was with a light heart that he went off to Elsinore to find a ship's passage home.

At the harbour the cold salt breeze swept away all human stench. Buckholt clearly recalled what it had meant to the Low Countries when, in the early forties, the Danes had blocked this seaway and now he saw with his own eyes what power Denmark could wield over the access to the Baltic. Cannon frowned above the narrow channel, forcing every ship in the harbour to pay Sound Dues. He saw how easily the Netherlands could be cut off from all their Baltic sources of supply. In Denmark the authorities trembled with fear of what the duchess and King Philip might be planning; but King Philip had far more reason to worry about what was happening here, at the entrance to the Sound.

Buckholt took a last look at the cannon which decided whether the Netherlands populace lived or died of hunger. He shook himself and went on board a Netherlands ship laden with the vital grain. The sails were hoisted; the ropes creaked; shouts and whistles came from the sailors up on the masts; and the ship heeled before the wind. Krogen was left behind astern, Kaernen to starboard; and Buckholt had time at last to set down his impressions.

At Christmas, in 1556, King Philip decided to return to his wife. To please her he had invited Margaret; but he quickly found a reason for taking Christina as well. Although previously Philip had shown interest in Elizabeth, he now thought it might be wise to dispose of her, to the duke of Savoy, the temporary regent of the Netherlands. Christina was to help him in this enterprise.

King Philip sailed first, while Christina and her cousin

Margaret followed a few days later, crossing the Channel in a heavy sea.

The deck rolling under her feet, the smell of tarred wood, the feel of the salt spray falling on the ship – all this awoke something in Christina. It was no more than a vague memory; perhaps merely a mood echoed in her past experience.

Ahead, the white cliffs of Dover rose out of the sea mist. This was England. And it was a kingdom, she said to herself, the old ambitions rising up like the sea around her. It might have been her son who ruled it; everything could have been different. It was like a curse, that at each crossroads she was sent the wrong way. She went to the right when she should have gone to the left and to the left when she should have gone to the right.

The ship was in smooth waters now, and Christina gazed at the coastline. What star had she been born under, that doomed everything to failure; and how long would things continue so? She looked around her as she journeyed from Dover to London. Huge oak forests alternated with great stretches of grassland for thousands and thousands of sheep. They were everywhere in their thick winter fleeces that would be shorn when warm weather came. Long ago the wool had been sent to the Netherlands for manufacture, but now the English had established their own industry.

Queen Mary had sent splendidly equipped litters to Dover to take the two duchesses and their retinues to London. Christina had to keep pulling the hangings aside to be able to see everything better. The climate was damp, but the wide expanses of the rolling countryside, with its numerous isolated trees, attracted her. It had been summer when Battista came here. He had been delighted with both the king and the country, and she hoped she would stay long enough to see it as he had seen it, green and flourishing and scented with roses and honeysuckle on the beautifully decorated timbered houses in the small towns.

King Philip received them on the steps of the palace of Whitehall. He seemed tired; but a rare flash of happiness lit his eyes at the sight of his close relations in this strange land. He led them in to the queen, who was waiting on the first floor.

Christina saw a thin little woman dressed in a brown velvet gown over silver brocade. She noticed a stringy neck above the high collar. Mary's hair and eyes were the colour of the velvet. There was a glance of forced friendliness; but what Christina was most aware of in the queen's sharp-featured face was her mouth.

It was narrow, with the upper lip almost invisible but pressed inwards; and it told of the countless years through which she had suffered and battled with her urge to shriek aloud at her sorrows. To give utterance was to die, to be silent gave a chance of life. Twenty years of humiliation and injustice had pushed her voice down into her gullet, and had turned her mouth into a stiff line that expressed nothing but bitterness and fanaticism.

But when her eyes fell on Philip they at once grew soft and her movements took on a hint of feminine grace. He in turn treated his wife with the greatest devotion.

Whitehall Palace lay beside the Thames, and from the eastward-facing windows Christina could see the city walls with their eight gates. The old stone bridge spanned the river to the low buildings, workshops and Southwark Cathedral on the south bank, and the water thronged with life. Ferries carrying those who lived far from the bridge were plying up and down. Barges passed by, laden with goods. Hammering and clanging sounded from the other side, while the houses of great families on the north side had splendidly laid-out gardens with private landing-places.

Christina enjoyed studying this town. The smoke from thousands of chimneys rose up and in quiet weather veiled the ponderous tower of St Paul's and the spire of the Guild-hall. She liked watching the fishing boats and the added surge of life and movement when noisy and excited citizens sailed off for the theatre, situated to the south because the city merchants would not allow that sort of performance within the walls. When the wind blew from the east Christina caught the smell of smoke, fish and wet wood that drifted into the palace.

242

In his time King Henry had commissioned Holbein to decorate the interior of the palace. Christina was reminded of another picture. She calculated that it must be eighteen years ago that Master Hans had come to her in Brussels to make the sketch that had later become a portrait for the king of England. She remembered her happiness then and the master himself with his fringe, square face and wise eyes.

Christina had seen only the sketch; the final painting had been finished in England. But she was unable to find it anywhere. It seemed strange, almost impolite, of Queen Mary not to have it on display. Perhaps what some people said was true, that it had been given away to the earl of Arundel.

Christina was reluctant to ask. On the other hand she was distressed at the idea of the portrait having been given to a mere noble as a gift. However, other things occurred to occupy her mind. The queen was to receive an envoy from the tsar of Russia.

This strange man from the faraway land no one knew much about arrived in a coat sweeping to the floor. His form of greeting was to prostrate himself full length. He presented the queen with priceless sable furs as a gift from his prince. But the real purpose of the visit was a mutual interest in the exchange of goods that had been started when a couple of English ships had discovered the route to the White Sea a few years earlier.

As the weeks went by, Christina came to realise that there would be no opportunity of meeting King Henry's younger daughter. Elizabeth was still kept in isolation at Hatfield House. Once Christina mentioned her name to the queen, but all the reply she had was a flash of hatred from Mary's eyes. She did learn a little, however, from people at court.

Elizabeth was proud, they said, and she lied like a trooper when she maintained that she was a good Catholic. But the people loved her and that was probably what had kept her alive. She was English on both maternal and paternal sides and proud of it. Christina soon found out that the English loathed anything foreign. When Philip's envoys first went to London, people in the streets had thrown snowballs at them; and as a whole the people here took liberties that would be unthinkable in other countries. Many of them did not doff their caps when King Philip rode by. Sometimes they even turned their backs on him; or surly mumbling was heard from the crowds without any action being taken against them.

It was during her stay in London that Christina received the news of Albrecht's death. She stood a long time at a window, looking at the boats passing on the Thames. He had left Brussels, restless and impressionable, unable to understand her refusal. Perhaps she had wounded him more deeply than she had thought was possible. He rampaged around Europe ravaging and plundering; the emperor banned him; he saw his family home burned to the ground and travelled root- lessly from one lesser court to another in search of shelter, protection, funds or whatever it was he happened to be in need of. On the 8th of January he had died, at his brother-in- law's home, ruined, without a country and without know- ing the old age he could not have endured.

Albrecht had been just one of many princely mercenaries and condottieri who ranged through countries and king- doms offering their services to a ruler one day and the next attaching themselves to his enemy. They were on the side that offered gain, and in whatever beds where there were women to be had.

Christina knew it had been so. He would not have settled down in any marriage, not even with her. But his impudent charm had affected her more than she had realised. She felt deep sorrow and a tempestuous longing for him. Perhaps he had been capable of deep feelings after all, provoking thoughts that drove him onwards in ceaseless flight, cease- less chase, further and further. But what was it he had seen in her? Had he loved her not only with his body but with his heart? Might he have been able to come to a stop, to deal with other than immediate, superficial concerns?

She did not believe it, did not want to believe it. It was too painful to bring that train of thought to a conclusion, to try to see what might have been if she had dared to take the step that would have led her out of her self and all her claims.

Albrecht of Brandenburg had been thirty-five. An adventurer who had died before the adventure started.

Christina celebrated Easter with her friends, and saw England in its green spring dress, the landscape she had once imagined through Battista's description long ago. She liked the country and she liked the people. Here she felt at home, and old ideas reawakened as she watched the queen zealously set about washing the feet of the poor. But although she felt for this woman and her tragic life, Christina failed to touch Mary's heart.

Philip did not hide his pleasure at Christina's company. Again Christina suffered the feeling of being unwanted. She had once seen the queen on the verge of rage because Philip had led her in the dance at Greenwich; and once was enough. She took her departure of this country that might have been hers, with its oak forests like ships growing up out of the earth to become a mighty fleet. She said farewell to a queen who showed much warmth and sympathy towards her nearest subordinates but did nothing for the many she never set eyes on. And a farewell to a lively, enterprising people who maintained their trust in their queen's barren womb and unhealthy complexion while stealing glances towards Hatfield. Christina journeyed back to the Netherlands.

In Brussels Buckholt's report awaited her. She read it thoroughly, over and over, concentrating in particular on the Danes' casual attitude to religion. A Catholic queen was not inconceivable – it might even be herself. The perpetual terror of attack from her side strengthened her conviction that Christian would receive her offer with enthusiasm on behalf of his son. But would it be the right thing? The armistice with France was broken; a French defeat would upset the balance. In Denmark they saw shadows in corners, in a way that indicated uncertainty about their own stability.

Besides, the young prince was obviously not an ideal husband. He needed to mature; the whole thing needed to mature. And the prince's demand to see his bride before deciding shocked Christina.

He must be out of his mind. Were the envoys' descriptions of Renata's beauty and virtue not enough? And if not, then a painting should surely suffice. Her daughter should not be made a spectacle of, to be either rejected or accepted. It was unheard-of.

On the 10th of August the French forces suffered a swingeing defeat at Saint Quentin. Christina's heart lifted. At the same time new visitors were announced from Sweden. They shared a characteristic that perhaps was peculiar to their nation. Their front teeth were too big and their noses too short. Christina gave Herr Olav Magnus and Herr Marcus Klingensten a hearty welcome; and on hearing what they had to say, she grew increasingly interested.

The Swedes were dissatisfied with King Gustav. The peasants' revolt in favour of the Catholic Church might have been stamped out, but it still smouldered; and Lübeck and Hamburg, which had once prepared the way to the throne for Gustav Vasa in order to acquire ancient privileges and freedom of trade, felt cheated. They were ready now to take arms against him.

The tall toothy Swedes made it plain that all bad feeling against Christian the Second was gone. True, some still called him 'the Tyrant', but after having suffered new and far harder tyranny they preferred the old.

Christina listened with a warm heart. Her offer of marriage between Renata and the Danish prince had been sent to Christian the Third, but that did not prevent her from taking an interest in Sweden.

Why get mixed up in this? But then why not? Sweden was quite a nice titbit, even though it naturally could not match up to Denmark–Norway. A man called Herbert von Langen was an intermediary for the Hanseatic League; and he too mentioned support against Denmark from the Ditmarshes. For the time being, however, Christina chose to look at the possibilities of an attack on Sweden, especially if the campaign could be funded by others.

The prospect of a rich bride and an amicable settlement would probably keep the Danes quiet – besides, they had no great love for each other up there in the North – and she gave the Danish envoys to understand that there would soon be a legation arriving in Copenhagen to pursue the marriage negotiations.

The resistance of the French had broken meanwhile, with the result that they were willing to agree finally to the peace that Europe had desired for so long as Christina could remember. Christina was reminded that that peace would bring Carl back to her.

He was nearly fifteen now and Christina had given up marking his growth on the wall. Was he small or tall? The nightmares diminished and with them the image of the bloody headless horse with her boy on its back. More and more rarely did she hear the sound of his cries and see his pale face turned towards her. Carl was big now, almost grown-up. Sleep revealed her subconscious acceptance that years changed everything. She would sleep the night through, hardly ever disturbed by those dreams that previously had tortured her mind.

Christina's thoughts shifted continually between the North and France. Nothing seemed to come of the call to arms in the Hanseatic League; while the prospect of peace was shaken when de Guise took Calais from the English and three months later celebrated his family's political triumph with the marriage between the dauphin and his niece Mary Stuart.

Philip gave Christina a small task. Her sister had finally embraced the Lutheran faith. It was a scandal, and she ought to come to Brussels to live there until she thought better of it.

Dorothea was all smiles as she received her sister in Heidelberg. Thereafter, though, she grew cross and sullen. She could not manage her hair in the latest fashion; many people did not treat her in accordance with her rank; and to make things worse she was having trouble with her digestion, nor did she want to discuss the papists and all their black magic. Her servants were cheating her. Denmark could go to hell; she would rather have a wig; but if they were kind enough to send her portion that would be all right. It was remarkable how respectful many people were if you were rich enough.

That last came at just the right moment, from the point of view of negotiations with Denmark. Christina wanted to keep the game going. Messages were sent off from the two sisters to Copenhagen indicating that both were interested in reconciliation. The word marriage was not mentioned; Christina wanted to know the military situation first. Meanwhile Dorothea flatly refused to go to Brussels; the mere idea of all those Spaniards made her feel sick. She grimaced as if she had already caught sight of a grandee. Christina gave up and went back.

There she heard from von Langen that after all Lübeck did not dare join the enterprise against Sweden; and now Magnus was dead they ought perhaps to wait a while. There were rumours, albeit vague, that the Danish prince was seeking the hand of Emperor Ferdinand's daughter. Accordingly von Langen was thinking of going to Denmark himself to investigate.

Christina felt that this presented no problems. Nothing would come of such a courtship. Besides, she had another son-in-law in mind. He had just been widowed; he was rich; he had everything. She glanced at her daughter, and watched her black hair being brushed till it crackled, then being put up with white pearls. The girl smiled confidently at herself in the mirror as the ruff closed around her slim neck.

Christina had every reason to feel satisfied with Renata. But a voice within her whispered, 'If only it were me'. As Renata's husband she had singled out Wilhelm of Orange. She caught herself, in his presence, feeling as skittish as a young girl.

But suddenly all was forgotten: Sweden, Denmark, Renata and Wilhelm; every plan and idea; the whole round world with all its realms. Christina was to see Carl again. After six years of torment, longing and waiting.

The king of France would permit her to enter his country. In April 1558, trembling with anticipation, she left the Netherlands with her two daughters and a splendid retinue, for her reunion with Carl.

XIX

Christina was dressing up for a celebration. She had her hair brushed until it shone, and decided on pale green silk, as the finest background for rubies and drop pearls, together with her biggest lace-edged ruff. She had been in black when Carl went away to the French court. But now he should see that his mother could outshine all the French ladies in taste and elegance. Renata and Dorothea looked at her delightedly – but they must hurry; they too must look their best. Carl was on his way.

Christina appraised her daughters. Renata's hair was drawn back too tightly. It should be looser, otherwise she looked too small. And Dorothea must wear another cap, the one with grey pearls that suited her fair colouring so well.

Suddenly the occasion overcame her and she fought against tears. What had he suffered, how many nights of longing had he undergone? How often had he cried himself to sleep? They had robbed him of the most precious thing in the world, his mother. *He* had suffered, not she, just as he had felt much greater pain in being born than she had done in giving him birth.

At last the moment came. Christina, her daughters and her whole court were assembled in anticipation. The sound of hooves approached, as it had once died out. She could not control herself, and wrung her hands in expectation. Now, now it had come.

She saw the riders. Her gaze travelled over them. Where was he, her fair boy? She had no idea what he looked like now. In a flash she understood. Only his position in the procession indicated that the straight-backed young man on a brown mare was Carl. He dismounted and came towards her, a self-confident stranger. Her hands slackened and fell, like those of a beggar who abandons hope of alms.

As he knelt she saw her little Carl had gone. Instead here was a young man of nearly sixteen, betrothed to a French princess. He was an adult almost, brought up and forced in a foreign hothouse, with ideas that were not hers, with feelings directed towards others, and implanted with ideals remote from her. She knew it from that first moment. 'Men are not born, but educated,' Erasmus had said; and Carl had been educated into something other than her son.

Christina allowed the young man to kiss her hand, and permitted him to put his arm around her. She swayed and tottered as she had not done even when she had stood before the king of France in the Deer Hall in Nancy.

She had wanted to talk to him of the migrant birds who returned, as if it were only a season from leaf-fall to spring green that he had been away from her. Instead she was looking into an abyss.

Someone supported her and helped her indoors. Slowly she fought to regain her self-control. She had hardly looked at him, only noticing what was missing. This was not a continuation but a beginning.

Carl was tall. He had grown darker and resembled his father more. His hair was combed up and back; and his eyes? Yes, his eyes were hers; but his nose was growing large and prominent. And there was something about his smile she recognised. After all, there was some bond or other still reaching back. She must have time, get hold of herself properly. And he was speaking to her. It was her he was looking at; the almost mature voice was directed at her, not at all the others. He was telling her how well he had been looked after, about the love he had received from the king and queen, and how nothing had been spared to give him a happy upbringing. Christina felt pain but forced herself to listen. Of course he had to say that, to make her happy, so that she did not suffer from the loss he had suffered.

It was for her sake. He did it to assuage her pain; he was her own boy still. Although he was so French in dress and manners, it was merely a habit, on the surface; what did it matter? He kissed his sisters affectionately. He had not forgotten, she said to herself – and went on saying it, as she observed her son's charm and assured adult bearing with increasing pride. Not until all were seated at *déjeuner* had she recovered sufficiently to be able to express in words her joy at their reunion.

It was the 15th of May, spring was in full flower, and she thought she could feel a glow of happiness.

They had three days together. Everything had to be fitted into three days. She watched him ride, he described his teachers and friends, and she heard him happily talking about his coming marriage with Claude of France. It was purely good, purely wise, she thought now. If only he was happy, everyone would be happy. She saw warmth in his eyes and felt his hands on hers. She hid the longing to take him in her arms and weep, and he listened kindly as she explained the question of the Nordic thrones.

Three days, after six years. There were moments when her voice broke. She heard her own nervous laughter and felt the awkwardness of her movements. She was invited to his wedding, and that hurt. Ought she to be invited at all, rather than just be there? Was *she* a guest?

At moments she was as if distracted with joy, at others overcome with longing to hear him just once talk about the time before that cursed Easter. But naturally he would not do that. He knew it would be equally painful for both of them and tactfully refrained from it.

On the 18th of May he swung himself on to the brown mare. He sat as erect as ever. The escort moved off, and she heard the hooves on the cobblestones as once again he spurred on his horse, bound for the French court. Turning his face to her, he sent her a brilliant smile and lifted his hand in farewell. Christina was left behind.

She had seen him, touched his hands, looked into his eyes, heard his voice. On the journey home Christina rid herself of any thoughts that could mar her happiness. She struggled free of the first shock of the reunion that was no reunion, and fought off the bitterness against the French king and queen, who had seized her Carl for themselves. He was still very young and she would win back her place in his heart. She had carried him in her womb and brought him into the world, and all the world's great powers and armies could not take that from her.

What had this Claude to give him of wisdom, prudence and experience? They said she was the least attractive of the three French princesses and clearly quite insignificant. Carl would soon be coming back to Nancy to take charge of his country. But most important of all, Christina had a memory of her son.

It would not be long before they met again. Next time it would be a real reunion, a continuation of these three days they had spent together. Now there could be a 'Do you remember?', a 'That was how he moved his hand last time.' They would doubtless laugh at the stiff way they had behaved; or was it only she who had lost control of herself?

None of that mattered. She had seen him. Seen his sympathetic glance at Dorothea and heard the laughter when he teased Renata. And his elegant reply to Egmont, and didn't he put his feet in the same position as his father had done? Now she remembered he had talked about hawking. She would send him the best bird that could be bought. Even if it was necessary to search the world over, she would find one better than any they had at the French court.

The memory of a little boy and his hoop and his first pony and first cap with an ostrich feather alternated with the sound of a young man's voice, words and laughter; and she returned to Brussels with a wealth of new memories.

Summer brought the cessation of hostilities. Now efforts would be made to find a lasting peace. King Philip asked Christina to preside over the negotiations.

Naturally she was flattered. The road to the Netherlands regency lay open and a great deal more as well. The dark years were gone; she saw the whole horizon bathed in light. But the conference had barely begun before there came bulletins of deaths.

On the 21st of September the emperor breathed his last.

Silence fell as the news spread through Europe. A symbol had gone. To her amazement and horror Christina felt no grief.

But when the regent died a few months later Christina wept. The ship had borne the old lady towards the South and the sun of Spain. Her going had been a farewell then; it was a deep sorrow now.

There was no time for brooding, however. The negotiations went on.

Calais was one of the greatest problems. The duc de Guise had won it from the English and would not relinquish his prize. But Queen Mary's envoys clung on to it, as the last English territory on the continent. Philip supported his wife's point of view. He was obliged to do so, of course, having himself drawn her country into the war. Talks had reached stagnation when the French with their sharp hearing reported to the English envoys in triumph that Queen Mary was dead.

At last, Elizabeth emerged from the shadows. The silence that followed her accession was not that of grief but that of a pause for thought. Again the question sounded: What is she like?

Once, a whore's brat. The most unwanted, worthless and useless being in the whole realm of England. Her mother had danced herself higher and higher, until she had danced without a head and became 'Anne-sans-tête'. Elizabeth, old King Henry's daughter, was laughed at when she declared herself to be married to the English people. But what did the people have to say?

'Queen-for-a-year', they called her. She would reign for so long and no more; for who wanted her? She had been asked to keep England in the old faith; but she responded merely by offering the Catholic Church friendship. She would just sit and twiddle her thumbs until she fell; and France could then pull out Mary Stuart as their trump card. Mary was legitimate; she was the rightful successor; she was queen of Scotland, and the future queen of France. There were not two but three royal coats of arms on her shield.

King Philip used other methods. He offered discreet bribes

to the appropriate minister – and an annual sable fur was no mean protection against the damp English winter. But Elizabeth had the Spanish envoy summoned, and told him amiably that she valued this manner of rewarding her people, since it saved her from spending the money herself.

What more was she than an inexperienced chit, the insolent, guileless head of a mediocre kingdom? Nonetheless, King Philip now made a munificent offer. A husband could help her; he could rescue her, and govern for her. He offered the greatest, the mightiest, the noblest of all princes: himself.

Elizabeth thanked him for the offer without any great show of enthusiasm, and promised to consider it.

Most people shook their heads despairingly, but not Christina. She had been in England, and had her own impressions of a people who lived sufficient to themselves. She had never met Elizabeth, but she knew the hardships she had endured. Elizabeth had survived up to now, and that alone indicated that she would survive a good while longer.

England was not easily accessible; and there were the forests, like ships, growing up out of the English soil, their green crowns transformed into white sails. Her mother had danced and danced until her head fell off; but Elizabeth let her suitors dance. Envoys and informers and spies, they all danced. Al the devils in hell might have possessed her body, but her head was still in place.

Death had taken the emperor, the regent and Queen Mary Tudor; and at the turn of the year he harvested two Danish kings at almost one stroke. Christian the Third died in Kolding and Christina's father, Christian the Second, in his prison in Kalundborg Castle. The old enemies had taken a meal together: now they went together into another and higher life.

For Christina it was a conclusion, a full stop. Sometimes she felt conscience-stricken at not having kept in touch with her father. If she had, she could now have felt sorrow. The emperor had taken over her father's rôle but had not filled his place in her heart. And neither of their deaths now left a void.

One card in the pack had been turned over and now a new one was uppermost: Christina wrote to the queen of Denmark, Sweden and Norway; the rightful heir to the Danish throne after Christian the Second was her sister Dorothea.

But in Denmark an immature and pugnacious young man was calling himself Frederik the Second – and felt that he should rule over England as well. Elizabeth received his proposal with friendly indifference. The Swedish Prince Erik, offered to present himself in person and kneel at the young woman's feet, likewise asking to help her with the heavy burden of power.

Those hotheads would surely get their fingers burned. Something in herself helped Christina to understand what Elizabeth wanted and why.

But she had her 'eyes' out far and wide. Buckholt, for one, had told her what could happen in the Nordic lands when Frederik came to power and when Sweden had Erik, born with a red cross on his breast.

A war between those two countries would be excellent, while a peace down in Europe would suit her equally well. The negotiations were to be resumed. She was appointed president of the conference at Cateau Cambrésis and sent staff to arrange suitable furnishings of the castle. Pleasing surroundings often had a good effect on mutual understanding. Before leaving, she also managed to get the latest news from Denmark.

The most powerful man in the country, this Peder Oxe whom Buckholt had mentioned, had apparently taken himself off. The Swedes were furious meanwhile that the Danish king was using the three crowns on his coat of arms; and in Copenhagen rumours were circulating again about Christina being on her way with an army.

Where did they think she could get the money from? But they were welcome to go on believing it; and with a successful outcome to the conference in view, idle gossip could soon become deadly earnest. Philip would allocate forces to her, and they could march in her name against the North.

*   *   *

There was also time for Christina to receive an unexpected visitor. Kiki announced herself and begged an audience.

The dwarf looked the same as ever. She curtsied respectfully and humbly thanked Her Grace for the great honour of receiving her.

The red tongue slid over her lips, and Christina listened to a flood of subservient words before the dwarf came to the point. 'A person in Your Grace's service is frequently taking part in secret meetings at night,' said Kiki, clapping her mouth shut like a frog that has just caught a fly.

Christina made no reply. The old disgust at the sight of Kiki came over her, but it was necessary for her to know.

'They meet to hear sermons preached by a heretic,' said Kiki, smoothing her skirts. 'One of Calvin's priests,' she added slowly, eyes wide with evil excitement.

Kiki had come for money – and for payment twice over, since she planned to report to the authorities immediately after her meeting with Christina.

Christina nodded pleasantly. Kiki could come back tomorrow.

'Does not Your Grace wish to know who it is?' asked Kiki, disappointed.

'I have not time to get such an accusation confirmed. You will be rewarded at four o'clock tomorrow.'

Kiki's mouth widened in a smile at the mention of payment, but there was a spark of suspicion in her eyes as she said, 'It is one of the priests trained in Geneva who are sent across the border to overthrow the king.'

Christina knew all about them, and their punishment in the form of the burnings that had started again.

Kiki left. It had started to rain, and Christina sent for Anders. He came in, straight and assured in his plain black coat, and she asked him directly if he had any contact with the Calvinists.

'Yes,' he replied in a loud voice.

His eyes were bright. His face still revealed his modest origins, but there was now an air of emancipation in his expression and bearing. What was it he had found in this teaching? How could he stand there, saying Yes to certain death? When they took him he would repeat that Yes, and go straight to the stake.

Christina was silent. The raindrops beat against the window-panes. The silence must have given him the impression that he had not expressed himself clearly enough, for he said, 'I have seen the face of Almighty Gód. That is what matters. The only thing.'

The words fell like a hammer on the anvil. Christina knew it was hopeless, but still she said, 'It is treason.'

There was no answer and she added, 'And will that lead to salvation?'

'There are no earthly rulers to obey if they do not obey God. My salvation is of no consequence. The sacredness of God is all-important.'

Christina gave up in despair. Was not salvation important? What was of consequence, then? What was any of it? She had heard of the new rebellious teachings and the anger in society that they expressed. As if he could read her thoughts the Dane said in a deep voice, 'I have met God.'

There was no more to add. She could not understand this movement, and never had done.

Christina handed him a bag of gold coins and bade him leave the town at once this evening.

Anders knelt, took her hand and kissed it. He rose slowly in the twilight. His expression remained transfigured, unshakeable and steady. He said, 'I bowed, not to a ruler of blood, but to a ruler of the soul.'

The rain fell more heavily; it was winter and turned dark early. She was suddenly aware of the situation. The ponderous Dane stood there in his shabby coat. What he said was an honour but at the same time an outrage. The lashing of the rain filled the silence. She asked where he intended to go.

'Northwards,' he said.

'To Denmark?'

'No,' came the reply. 'We have no foothold there. I shall go to Friesland.'

The rain stopped and both turned to look at the small panes, now transparent and blue again. Christina knew the gold would be spent on anything but himself. She begged him to hurry away and never show himself again. But she wished him Godspeed nonetheless.

Christina was left feeling confused and unhappy. She sensed no anger, however – nor any real understanding of what had happened. It was just that something had shaken her to the core. The evening grew still darker. Noise from the street faded, and people took shelter behind closed doors.

She herself was indoors; the storm had passed; and yet she was outside, somewhere without any sheltering walls or roof. She had no idea where it was. The last light had gone, and she was forgotten and outside the world as once before, in the library at Mechelen, when church bells rang for death all over the country. She was fumbling her way onwards as she had then, unable to comprehend either past or future. Is man educated? she asked herself in her impotence. Is he born? Does he merely exist? Could he create his own salvation? What was it Anders had said, that that was not the most important thing, the only thing? It was God's face. The meeting with God the Almighty.

Had the Dane seen something she had not seen? Where would she find the Creator's face? How could earthly beings find the truth? She stretched out her arms to receive it but she knew that the light had not been granted her.

The first hourly cry of the watchman rose from the street. Then silence. Christina slowly bowed her head.

Next day Kiki was told that the duchess was engaged. She would have to wait longer. Not until the fourth day did the authorities make enquiries about the Dane, but by then he had long since vanished, and Kiki had to be satisfied with only one bag of Judas money.

On the 6th of January 1559 Christina saw her son. The emperor's death made it impossible for her to join in the festivities at the wedding in Paris, but they were able to spend two days together, at Trier.

Christina knew now whom she would see in Carl. They

could gather up threads, resume topics of conversation. There was this 'can you remember?'; but still the threads were flimsy, and when she expressed her love for him, and her years of longing, there was a nervous twitch around his mouth, and she switched to a humorous tone.

She told him stories and they laughed together, while for his part he was tactful enough not to mention his attachment to the king and queen of France. He admired her newest golden dress; they had laughter in common, and taste, and an interest in art. Christina was proud of him. It was suitable to show that, but she had to battle nonetheless with her own impatience as to when he would reciprocate her love – if ever. And she was filled with despondency as she returned to prepare for her weighty duty at Cateau Cambrésis.

Christina was not Spanish. She was not French. But she had a foot in both camps and was acknowledged by all parties as the right leader for the conference, which was to open on the 6th of February. The bishop of Arras, Granvella, the duke of Alba and Wilhelm of Orange, who remembered to bring his chef, represented King Philip. Lord William Howard was the chief English negotiator. Christina received Lord Howard heartily and asked kindly after the young queen. She also tried to put in a good word for Philip as the right husband for Elizabeth, but was met with an evasive reply.

The French sent Montmorency, and the cardinal of Lorraine, a member of the de Guise family, who wanted anything but peace. Hectic days were under way.

The French tried to get Spain to relinquish its support of England, and maintained their demands for Calais. On his side Philip would not dream of giving up his rule in Italy; and the duke of Savoy wanted his land back. There were disagreements, meetings were broken off and the cardinal shouted at Lord Howard that his queen was a bastard.

Christina had to work hard at damping down fiery tempers and keeping the negotiations going. There was no longer any room for aversion for the French. What counted was peace. But Granvella, in a moment of fury, shouted that there were too many women present; they would be more use if they kept away.

When Howard's composure cracked and he left the meeting chamber in a rage, Granvella said drily that the French were better defenders of a bad cause than the English were of a good one. A breakdown of the talks seemed to be impending; and the French representatives were preparing to leave, when Christina forced them into a conversation in the garden. She suggested that they should hold Calais for eight years, in return for an annual disbursement to Queen Elizabeth as a guarantee of its eventual transfer. Philip was in despair over the lack of results. His coffers were empty, he had cancelled all payments, and in Paris Diane de Poitiers was urging the king to abandon the de Guise cause. It was agreed to try out Christina's suggestion. Meanwhile she put on some entertainments.

She arranged hunting parties and banquets for the delegates; she called for her daughters; and to her surprise Carl arrived, with his bride.

Christina welcomed her daughter-in-law affectionately, and at the same time studied her closely. Claude wore the latest French coiffure, with the hair on her brow cut short and in tiny curls above a face that unfortunately resembled her mother's; but apart from that as a whole she was quite passable. Very fair, slightly shy, she gazed continually at Carl with big adoring eyes. She seemed transparent, almost frail. Christina would probably have chosen a different type for Carl; but she comforted herself with the thought that at least Claude was not likely to cause any trouble.

Granvella hissed that the time was being spent on pleasure instead of work; and Elizabeth announced from England that she obviously could not marry King Philip as she was now a heretic, and that would not do for him. Christina saw to it that enemies came together in a friendly atmosphere on hunts and during pleasant evenings, and roped in furious Spaniards about to break the meetings up.

Her suggestion regarding Calais was the solution. That question settled, they could at last see the emergence of peace; and the appropriate marriages should seal it. The duke of Savoy was offered Marguerite, sister of the king of France. She was middle-aged, having been difficult to dispose of; but she was the condition on which the duke would get back his land. He squirmed like a worm before accepting; but he sent his future wife a kindly message, saying he would make every effort to please her.

Elizabeth's rejection of Philip turned his eyes in another direction, to look at another Elizabeth. She was not red-haired but dark, not English but French. After Christina had tirelessly calmed down the squabbling delegates and urged them back to the conference table there was agreement on Philip's marriage to this Elizabeth, eldest daughter of the king of France. At the same time Philip retained his power in Italy.

At Easter 1559 the Peace of Cateau Cambrésis was signed. It was the decisive agreement between the Hapsburgs and France that generations had longed for. Everyone was exhausted; everyone was relieved, too, and went to church to join in the Te Deum. In the evening the little town was illuminated by fireworks, and Montmorency yelled flippantly, God be praised, we are at peace and Madame Marguerite disposed of.

Seven years had passed since the ill-fated Easter when Christina had lost her son. Now, she could be triumphant.

She had regained her son; she had her daughters; now too she had a daughter-in-law. As a splendid gesture she presented Claude with the jewelled necklace she had received long ago from the emperor on the occasion of her marriage to the duke of Milan. The girl beamed her gratitude. 'Dear little soul,' thought Christina and hoped Claude's children would be healthier than she appeared to be.

Christina had used all possible means to bring about peace. She had threatened, flattered, wept, begged, and put forward suggestions, alternatives and compromises in order to keep the different factions together. If they could not talk to each other they had to ride together or celebrate together. She had arranged it all, and it had worked: the war was over.

In the Netherlands triumphal arches were raised in her honour in town after town. People streamed to her, rejoicing. She had brought them the peace for which they had been hoping for as long as anyone could remember.

King Philip rode to meet her with his train, and poured a stream of gratitude into her ears. He rode beside her for the final stretch of the journey to Brussels, and saw for himself how the people loved her. It was she they called for, her name that was written in flowers alongside roads and streets; it was she they wanted.

This was what she had been waiting for; this showed her greatness – and there was more to come. Carl wanted to return to Lorraine. Renata was to marry the most wonderful man alive, Wilhelm of Orange; and she would rule the Netherlands provinces herself when the king returned to Spain.

True, a few people, Granvella and the duke of Alba and their flock of Spaniards, were disgruntled; but this was not Spain. They knew it and they would have to swallow it.

Following the treaty the prison doors were opened. French captives came streaming out and set off for their homeland, while others were set free in France to go back to their families in Ghent, Mechelen, Brussels, Antwerp and Bruges. Everywhere church bells were chiming for peace and celebration. Beasts were slaughtered and goblets filled. The event was celebrated in the streets, in whole towns, whole provinces; for now, instead of cannon fire and death, it was a time of prosperity and ordinary daily life.

Christina lived her triumph to the full. She was borne on by it, uplifted by it. Years of darkness were over. She was not in second, or third or fourth place, as she had been all her life. She was first; and that was where she belonged.

The thought of her father haunted her. If only he could see her now, at this zenith of her life and on her way to further triumph. She hoped he could see her, looking down from his heavenly home.

At Whitsun the peace treaty was ratified. King Philip put his hand on the crucifix and took a holy oath not to break its terms. At the banquet that followed, Christina sat in the seat of honour. Carl and Renata and Dorothea were present, too, and shared in her moment of greatness.

Christina returned Carl's smile. Now he could see that whatever they might have said about her at the French court, the truth was another thing. His mother was sitting here beside the most Christian of monarchs. Carl could watch her, in this exalted hour, with no nervous quiver in her voice, no awkward laughter. His admiration was unmistakeable.

The ducal crown of Lorraine was Carl's, and the regency of the Netherlands would be hers. The announcement was expected at any moment; Wilhelm of Orange was already preparing a banquet. She and Carl would be equals.

Christina was tired, and she had lost her youth. But she looked at the torches and candles and silver and porcelain in the light summer night, and experienced perfect happiness.

A few days later silence fell over Brussels. Smiths put down their hammers, women took pans off the fire, busy hands fell from looms and lace cushions. People went out to gather in the squares and at street corners, and the silence turned into murmuring.

Philip the Second had nominated the new regent of the Netherlands. He had chosen his half-sister. It was to be Margaret of Parma.

XX

Egmont was shocked. Usually he was a good-natured, ideal-istic, perhaps slightly naïve paterfamilias. Now Christina saw him almost speechless with rage. 'That's precisely why,' he burst out when Christina, herself furious, pointed out that it was she the people acclaimed, and she they wan-ted as regent.

'Precisely why.' That was precisely why this 'Madama' had been selected to obey orders, even if to do so she had to chop the heads off little children. Now we are in for an inquisition, for hatred and violence, Christina thought. King Philip does not want someone with ideas of their own, only a machine.

The lost regency was not the only shock for Christina. King Philip had also put a stop to Wilhelm of Orange's mar-riage to Renata. Egmont had his own views on that matter too. 'Wilhelm is too young to understand. The marriage would have made him not only strong but too strong for the king to tolerate.'

Christina had had enemies, and she had felt the effects of malice and coldness. But this was her first encounter with direct deceit and faithlessness. She had spent her life actively serving the Hapsburgs, and paid dear for it. And now she was left high and dry, ruined and cast aside like a piece of wreckage, and plagued by screaming creditors. She had done her duty; now she could go.

But Philip would not get away with it so easily. He should at least hear about it. Christina was not going to stay here. She sat down to write a letter.

She demanded the dukedom of Bari in Calabria. It was independent and had once belonged to the Sforzas. She did not forbear to mention that the whole of her next year's income had been pledged to cover the huge expenses of travelling to both England and France in Philip's service. She was constantly dunned by creditors, and she alone had borne the cost of the education and upbringing of her two daughters during the past seven years.

She gave free voice to her indignation. King Philip was cheating both her and the people of the Netherlands by giving the regency to Margaret of Parma. No one wanted her in that position, neither the nobility, nor the common people, who had not forgotten her mother's origins. They no longer hid their feelings: none of them wanted to be ruled by that female Margaret.

Christina signed her 'Chrétienne' in large impetuous characters and folded the letter. She thought with inward satisfaction that the king could hardly have read a letter like this before, and that it was about time he did.

The reply came through Granvella, that long-faced intriguing cleric who had doubtless played his own part in the calumny against her. Her demand for Bari was abruptly refused. Her appanage would be raised, so that she could pledge this as well if necessary; meanwhile the king wanted no more of her comments on the regency. It was as unworthy of her character as it was detrimental to his interests. Finally he suggested that she should reside at her dower house in Lorraine, where she could be of assistance to her son.

'And of assistance to Philip,' she thought. Well, there was no hurry. If that was how it was there was something else she wished to do first. Margaret of Parma was expected in the Netherlands, and Christina was looking forward to observing her reception.

The duke of Alba journeyed to Paris, to marry the French king's eldest daughter by proxy for King Philip. The event was celebrated with pomp and ceremony, and with tournaments. It was during one of these that the French King Henri charged at a young knight whose lance struck his visor. The visor cracked, and the lance penetrated the king's eye.

For ten days Europe held its breath as they tried to save the king's life. The prohibition against dissection was broken. Some condemned prisoners were hastily beheaded to investigate which part of the brain had been damaged. But on the 10th of July the king of France died, after horrific suffering. His eldest son and his Scottish queen ascended the throne. Catherine of Medici was a widow, and on behalf of the under-age king the de Guises seized power in France.

The news reached Christina as she was on her way to Ghent. She hastened to write to Catherine of Medici, to express her deep grief and sympathy.

Christina received a final guest before setting off on her journey, an English gentleman on his way to Italy. He brought with him an invitation from Queen Elizabeth to come to England. Although Christina had not the means to accept, the invitation pleased her and bolstered her up. There were some at least who appreciated her worth.

King Philip received Christina in Ghent, to a chorus of demonstrative acclaim by the citizens that pleased her greatly. She revealed nothing of her feelings to him, and on his part there was no mention of her angry letter. As usual he invited her to his select dinners, where she demonstrated her charm with assured grace.

But Christina knew it was useless. She had come to realise that Philip's personal feelings were never allowed to influence him. He was a man of principles. Principles ruled his life and principles determined his decisions when they were finally made. She would not allow him to see her defeated. But he should experience to the full the difference between the person he had chosen and the one he had rejected.

Margaret arrived. There was no rejoicing and no cheering. She was presented to the States General, who raised cries of protest against her appointment. The States also refused to grant the monies that had been requested by the king.

The king was furious. Margaret walked around helplessly

and Christina looked on with a little smile. The king blamed Wilhelm of Orange. 'Hardly,' thought Christina. She enjoyed all the more receiving the French envoy who came from the French court to praise her for her efforts at Cateau Cambrésis. It all helped. She ate a final dinner with King Philip, before he left for the Spain he understood and which understood him.

Christina and Margaret of Parma remained behind. Many of the noble families demonstrated disaffection by retiring to their country estates. But the court was obliged to stay. Christina, borrowing yet more money, offered magnificent hospitality. Ladies and gentlemen flocked to her apartments and the regent was left to herself. Christina found this amusing. She entertained her guests with stories, including even the little tale of how she and her sister had once called the duchess of Parma a 'misfortune'. The laughter echoed long and the title of 'misfortune' was uttered so often and so loudly that the new regent can hardly have failed to hear it.

It failed to affect her, however, unless it increased her arrogance. She would begin every other sentence with, 'My brother, the king of Spain, considers . . .' or, 'My brother the king thinks . . .' and everyone about her would groan. The stable-boys made faces at her behind her back, as she rode out of the courtyard with her great behind in the air like any man, while the chambermaids described with relish how hard it was to lace her into her corset in order to produce something that even resembled a waist.

Christina chuckled at the ridicule to which her rival was subjected, and was deft in luring all the courtiers over to her own camp. But Margaret of Parma was still regent, and King Philip's calumny still had its effect on Wilhelm of Orange.

In public Wilhelm was all charm. But in private he avoided Christina. She tried to ascribe this to the vast debts he had inherited from his thriftless dead father, and was shocked when he began to court Anne of Saxony.

How could he? Anne was rolling in money, but she was also a hunchback and as bad-tempered as the Devil himself. There were those who hinted that the prince set more store on keeping his precious chef than on a wife's beauty. He could always hide her away somewhere; but he had to like what the cook produced, several times a day. Moreover Anne of Saxony was a Lutheran, and a stubborn one; and it would be a counterblow to King Philip's underhand dealings to install a heretic as the most distinguished Netherlands princess.

But harsh realities remained. 'Misfortune' or no, Margaret was regent, and Renata was still not betrothed.

Christina enjoyed her playful successes. But behind her pleasure there was anxiety, and fear for the future of the people, who had always been as her own. They were enterprising and they were honest. They seemed to have something in common with the English people, whom she liked so much and who gave her the feeling of being at home over there on the other side of the Channel.

The situation was precarious. She might laugh when Renata walked up and down giving a talented imitation of Margaret of Parma's voice and movements and saying, 'My brother the king says . . .' Renata could make everyone laugh at her performance; the girl had quite a sense of humour, and a touch of devilry as well. But though Christina, her daughters and her courtiers could laugh as much as they liked, Margaret was the figure in the foreground. And behind her was Granvella.

Christina had noted his observant glance. He knew very well what was going on, and did not want the regent made a laughing-stock. That would damage the king. Granvella disapproved of the constantly repeated words 'bastard' and 'misfortune'. He was displeased, too, that the king's official deputy in the Netherlands had to appear without a proper retinue because that retinue attached itself to the duchess of Lorraine.

Christina saw the stormclouds gathering and decided to leave.

Von Langen, who had once offered to raise an army against Sweden and who later went to Denmark to sniff out the ground, had instead taken service with the Danes. Christina was not especially surprised at this – she knew his type – but the Danes would hardly have 'bought' him if they had had nothing to fear. Just before she set off she summoned Buckholt.

The old man gave dry, brief answers to her questions. After the change of monarch he doubted whether peace would be maintained in the North; and now that Peder Oxe had gone the aristocracy had lost their only powerful leader. Things were taking the course he expected. Frederik the Second still had no wife at his side, and went on with his hunting and drinking, and with working off his aggression in his campaign against the Ditmarshes.

She questioned Buckholt through a whole long afternoon. She wanted more detailed information about certain points in his report, together with a clearer idea of the financial situation, military conditions, popular moods and opinions, the nobles, burghers and church; and also where this Herr Peder Oxe might be.

Buckholt could not give an answer to this last question. There were so many rumours; but it appeared that at least Peder Oxe had managed to save his skin.

There was one question Christina omitted to ask; instead she contented herself with pondering it. What was Herr Peder Oxe's relationship to the Torben Oxe her father had long ago executed on account of Dyveka? Just as names were inherited, it could happen that feelings of hatred were. The desire to revenge a possible wrong could remain through generations.

Christina took her leave of the old man and thanked and rewarded him. Her thoughts moved to all those mercenary armies who were more or less available for hire in Germany. Then she recalled England's Elizabeth, who would have none of the Danish king, nor of the Swedish prince. And she thought of the man who was more emperor in name than in fact. There were so many details, so many possibilities, so many ways.

It would be good to get away from the Netherlands and Granvella's long sight and sharp hearing. What she did was none of his business any more than it was that of Margaret of Parma or the king of Spain.

Christina gave orders to pack. September was an ideal time to travel, before the autumn rains made the roads soggy. With Nancy as her goal she left Brussels.

In France the de Guise brothers were governing in the name of the young king. They had plans for Renata's marriage of which Christina did not approve. France had already decided on Carl's bride, and that was enough. They must not be allowed to interfere with the girls' future too. In order to avoid such unacceptable meddling Christina felt obliged to leave her daughters behind, in Brussels.

The parting was hard, harder than she had expected. Renata and Dorothea had always been with her. She had watched over their education diligently. Nothing had been spared on teachers, dress or equipment, and she had searched tirelessly for new doctors and specialists to instil more life in Dorothea's bad foot. Nonetheless her heart had always been with Carl. All her nights of weeping and longing, all the aims and hopes of her days, had been directed at the reunion with her son, with her lost child; and now at the moment of parting with her two girls she felt she had failed them.

They were big, fifteen and fourteen. One dark, the other fair; one temperamental, the other gentle and affectionate.

She wondered if they had felt how far away her thoughts were. And how much did she know about their own most secret feelings? What went on in their girlish minds?

They were both of marriageable age. It was not a good thing to wait too long. Their roots in childhood must not go too deep. Wherever they were to be sent they should accustom themselves as quickly as possible to new customs, new manners and perhaps a new language as well, and the sooner this happened the easier it would be to adapt their characters to their surroundings.

But Christina had no plans for her girls. She would have liked to have brought about the Orange marriage, but that had had to be abandoned, and naturally she never discussed her ideas with Renata. Perhaps the girl had her own notions. There were brides of her age, and sometimes she seemed moody and reserved.

273

But there could be no question of any of the several matches put forward by the French. Meanwhile separation was necessary for a time, until she had consolidated her position in Lorraine.

In Bar Christina met Carl and the whole French court and was drawn into a whirl of hunting and festivity. The young king of France was there. He was just a great child, who lacked character, and seemed slightly frail as well. But his devotion to Carl was like that for an elder brother.

Catherine of Medici was also there. At their first meeting in 1541 Catherine had not actually said a word, and all the renown she had had then was for a considerable knowledge of herbs and medicines. She could bring the dying back to life – even if evil tongues maintained that she sometimes intended the opposite. Her head was still just as round and her eyes as prominent. But in the intervening time she had borne the Valois family four sons. The woman riding now at Christina's side through the golden woods of autumn was of quite another calibre.

There was something purposeful about her and something too with which she burned inwardly. She had put on weight and was almost ugly; but that was as nothing beside her wise, far-reaching glance. Catherine was no longer down-trodden by any Diane de Poitiers; but her complex over not being distinguished enough, which had always tortured her, could still sometimes be glimpsed. It had been under cover of darkness that her coronation procession once rode into Lyons. That kind of thing made a lasting impression; it ate into one. So too could her mass of other humiliations; and from such wounds came either a permanently disfigured personality, or one that understood everything because it had been through the fire.

She yielded to the de Guise brothers, who had built the whole of their power and influence on their relationship with the young queen. There was so much about her that Christina liked. Catherine had been a good mother to Carl, and that too affected her feelings throughout the fine autumn days as they rode out together through the falling leaves.

This stay brought her first meeting with Mary Stuart. The deceased king had once said that she was the most beautiful child he had ever seen. But Catherine's astrologer Nostradamus had declared that at the sight of the little girl he had seen blood.

Mary was a woman now, tall and graceful, with eyes and hair the colour of amber. Surrounded by her courtiers, she resembled a young roe-deer among heavy tree-trunks. She was the star, the hub of everything and everyone; there was a whole kingdom in her person. Sweet, mild and beautiful, she hovered above intrigues, gossip and malice. Such things were no concern of hers; they never touched her. Mary Stuart possessed all the natural nobility Catherine of Medici lacked and was unlikely ever to acquire. No rival woman had ever humiliated Mary. There was an opposition that she had never met, there were battles she had never fought, and a reality of which she knew nothing.

She was so graceful, this French-married and Scottish-born queen, who also believed herself entitled to the throne of England. It was all so simple and natural to her. She shone with self-confidence like the deer in the wood who one summer evening forgot that both the fox and wolf were abroad.

Christina took Mary Stuart round the orangery. She showed her the little birds who had been patiently trained by the gardener to feed out of one's hand. The young queen held out her lovely hands and sparrows and titmice flew up to her to take grains of corn from this most beautiful of princesses. She bent her head towards the birds in a halo of gold, framed by the orange fruits and dark-green foliage.

Christina turned from her guest for a moment and suddenly there came a subdued little cry.

Mary Stuart still stood there in all her beauty, but at her feet in a sprinkling of corn a bluetit lay flapping a broken wing.

The queen met Christina's eyes. She gave a little start and straightened herself, as if expecting a reproach too harsh for her sensitive mind. She wanted to go now, to see her dogs, she said. She left the orangery, her mouth set in an injured line.

Christina's eyes followed her. How old was she? Sixteen.

And since her birth she had worn the crown of half the kingdom across the sea, while the other half fell to that Elizabeth who in childhood was said to have had hardly a rag to her back. So strange was the way of things.

Christina picked up the wounded bird. She held it, and felt the warmth of its feathery body.

'May I, Madame?'

It was a gentleman's voice, slightly hoarse. Christina looked up into the eyes of a priestly member of the retinue, an abbot. He stretched out his hands for the bluetit, put it on a branch of one of the orange trees and said,

'It will go on living. There are no predators here, no cats, no danger . . .'

There was a little smile on the thin face, 'Everything is somewhat artificial in a hothouse.'

The bird sat on a branch. Its wing hung down, but it began to hop away. It would be fed, it would be cared for; it would live on, in its protected world.

Christina had not seen whether the abbot had observed the incident with Mary Stuart. It was possible; but what he said could also have been coincidence. The abbot quietly drew her attention to a young couple walking at the far end of the orangery and a spark of delighted curiosity lit his eyes. 'The count and Madame have not been seen together since that fatal night at the fireside on the second floor at Chambord . . . It was all most unfortunate . . .'

The abbot was twisting a golden chain on which hung a cross of rubies. He took his eyes from the pair. 'It was the briefest of love affairs, lasting only five minutes. Madame tried to explain that it was on account of the cold, while the count . . .' The abbot chuckled as the cross spiralled in the air. 'The count has quite a different explanation, which everyone knows. So . . .'

The chain fell, the cross came to rest on the black cassock. 'But perhaps it is a sign of reconciliation, which will produce some more little stories.'

Christina did not know the couple behind the orange trees and was not interested in their private life. An official in Catherine of Medici's retinue approached. He was a quaint man, with a pointed nose, a high arched forehead and a heart-shaped mouth. She did not at once recall his name; but she had talked to him before, and had found his conversation sometimes striking and wise. On one occasion he had expressed his concern about the exaggerated amount of knowledge that was crammed into children. Children should not only learn, he had said; they must learn to understand. Otherwise knowledge does not lead to intellectual wealth.

The courtiers smiled a little at the sight of this odd man, with his peculiar opinions. But Christina was more interested in talking to him than to the gossiping abbot.

She returned to the subject of education, and asked whether knowledge was not the prerequisite of understanding.

'Children must have knowledge,' he said in his high voice. 'Not as much as possible, but the best possible. To give a child the desire to learn is more important than the learning itself. And desire can only come through deep understanding.'

They walked through corridors of dark shining foliage. The air was damp and scented. Christina listened to the small gentleman's numerous criticisms of current schooling, and was surprised. Was not knowledge always spoken of as the road to wisdom?

'Quantity of knowledge is the way to nothing but itself. It does not lead to wisdom. Nor to what is most important of all: learning to know oneself; learning to live.'

Christina stopped and turned to him, and asked if he were a philosopher.

'No, Madame,' – with a slight smile – 'I live.'

As they walked on, they talked of punishment, and of virtue, which he said lived in a blossoming meadow, not on top of a barren, inaccessible cliff. He compared learned people with an ear of corn. As long as they were empty they proudly lifted their heads; but when they were full they bowed their necks in humility. They went on to speak of pleasure, of intoxication. Christina asked him about life – and the gentleman answered by talking about death. 'Suppose it were taken from us? Suppose it could be? It would be the cruellest punishment if people could not die. It would rob us of life.'

'You ought to write,' said Christina. 'And I should read a few lines every morning and think about them for the rest of the day.'

'Madame, I am a public servant; time will not permit me. Besides, I have no great opinion of myself. It is egotistical to be an author. How can anyone believe their thoughts are wiser than anyone else's, that they should be worth printing in many copies? The written word is too revealing.'

Darkness was falling. Reluctantly Christina ended her conversation with the Frenchman. His observations made her see the world from another angle. She had meant it when she said that every sentence provided matter for a whole day's reflection.

The visit of the French court to Bar was drawing to a close and Christina was due to travel on to Nancy. It had been wonderful to meet Carl again even though they had had little opportunity for talking alone; and little Claude seemed to be proving a loving wife.

Christina continued her journey, living over in her mind her happy time with the Valois court. The greatly changed Catherine of Medici was moving towards something or other; but what was it? Mary Stuart, and that glimpse of cruelty she had revealed behind her gracious charm, disturbed Christina. Meanwhile she treasured the brief comments spoken in that tropically humid air by a public servant who, the queen dowager had later informed her, was a certain Monsieur de Montaigne.

The trees still wore their golden crowns. There was no wind. The vines drew red lines across the hillsides and the grapes were being harvested. Everywhere she passed, work came to a stop, the peasants putting down their baskets and gazing at Christina and her train as they rode by and Christina smiled back at them.

She had asked about life and received an answer about death. It kept recurring to her, until she saw the palace and the towers of St Evre's church rising up in the distance behind the walls of Nancy. This was the sight she had been waiting for, for more than seven years.

Lorraine, 1559–1568

XXI

Peder Oxe was in Basel. It was the dullest town he had ever lived in, and he knew most places worth seeing. From the age of twelve till he had returned to Denmark as an eighteen-year-old he had travelled and studied under the direction of Master Morsing, whose knowledgeable hand and considerable learning had guided him through Europe and various universities. It had once irked him to have to leave such splendours, and go back to a country where even the wealthiest lord's house contained little more than damp rooms, fortifications and one strong-room for storing gold coins, letters of debit and deeds of ownership.

As the days crawled past in the Swiss town crowded with its population of hysterical Calvinists, he discovered emotions in himself he had not thought existed.

Peder Oxe was sentimental. He was homesick; not merely for power and wealth, but for the country, for the land and its forests. He dreamed he was riding over the commons and the rye and barley fields of south Sealand in the pale light of a summer night. He dreamed of the cuckoo's call echoing among the beech trunks on a May evening around his beloved Gisselfeld.

There it was he had built a house worthy of a nobleman. A gateway had been erected. It had not been necessary, given that the house had only one wing; but the idea was to extend it, so as to do down Johan Frijs, who had stolen a march on him by building the splendid Hasselagergard, in east Funen.

Now all that was in the past. Lost, like the nocturnal rides and the enticing notes of the cuckoo. When only twenty he had won Gisselfeld, in a legal action against his maternal grandfather, Mogens Gøje; and he lost it again through one man's malicious tale-bearing, the man he had always despised and looked down on: Herr Herluf Trolle.

When Peder brought his successful action his contemporary Herluf Trolle had only just left Our Lady's school. That fact alone revealed how they differed. Herluf was ponderous; he was slow. The only thing he did that showed any sense was to marry Peder's rich aunt, Birgitte Gøje.

Peder Oxe rose higher and higher in the king's favour, and he acquired more and more landed estates. He laid an impressive document in front of an uncle who was too stupid to read it properly, and by heaven if he didn't put his signature to it, thus making Peder Oxe sole heir to Gunderslevholm. He swept his contemporary Uncle Herluf's complaints and litigation off the table, regarded him with the deepest contempt and laughed his head off over Herluf's pompous absurdity. 'Wherefore bear we golden chains,' said Herluf Trolle, self-important, complacent, self-satisfied; and more high-flown twaddle followed, the product of his feeble understanding.

Peder Oxe was a Danish nobleman and he never forgot it. But he was also a man of the world, with a knowledge of what lay beyond his immediate circle. He felt the limitations of his family surroundings, often sought company outside his own associates. A talented theologian, a knowledgeable alchemist or a learned lawyer made for more profitable friendships than any oaf of a cousin.

In public life, too, Peder advanced; and one day he entered the portal of Copenhagen Castle, to take over the administration of the city in the king's absence. As he did so, one thought crossed his mind: his uncle Torben Oxe had trodden the same path. He had entered as governor; and years later he had gone out by the same portal with his hands tied behind him, sentenced to death because of that whore Dyveka. Christian the Third was king now; but when Peder Oxe was summoned to court he remembered the thoughts that had come to him when first he had walked across the stone bridge to the castle. That was the way of it; you were in and you were out. History was a good teacher.

282

Peder had his own opinion on royal favour and its duration, and was all the more unenthusiastic about the element of repetition.

For a while he had thought his own danger was over. He was well aware of Mistress Birgitte Gøje's poisonous tongue, and how she disgorged her venom to the queen. He knew all her slanderous tales: the lampoons, the accusations of his calumny of the most distinguished lady in the land.

But when the king tried to catch him out, using the old trick of demanding statements of accounts for taxes collected in both Denmark and Norway, Peder Oxe came out on top, ordering his servants to bring in sacks of coins. He was required to deliver eighty-two thousand dalers; and eighty-two thousand there were, delivered as found, and ready for counting. He had even been ordered to present these accounts while he was in the middle of entertaining the electoral prince and princess of Saxony on behalf of the king, with swan shooting at Gedser and roe-deer hunting at Guldborgsund. They thought they could spike him, but they failed – on that occasion anyway.

But Herluf was stubborn as only fools can be, and his wife was clever, and they persisted. One fine day Peder Oxe was called before the king. He refused to comply and instead went south to Gedser. From there he sent the king a petition begging him to withdraw wrongful accusations made against him.

Peder Oxe was interested in land, and in land he had invested. The crops might fail, as they had done in 'fifty-six, when there was hardly any corn to be seen; but a new spring always came, and a new seed-time followed by a new harvest. It was merely a question of keeping something in reserve. Some people hoarded gold; but the trouble with gold was that there could suddenly be a glut – as indeed there had been in recent years – when it fell in value. With land it was different. There could not be more or less of that. Seven fat years could follow seven lean ones and vice versa, but it still stayed there, unchangeable and sure; and how he had loved the feel of his feet sinking into the good, heavy, rain-soaked soil of Sealand and Lolland.

But you couldn't take it with you, as he was finding to his cost as he languished in exile pondering the accusations levelled against him. There were those who claimed that he had exploited the peasants. Sheer balderdash; it was his simple duty to see they worked and did not lie about in the corn poisoned with alcohol. And he was supposed to have over-felled the forest. It was easy to accuse anyone of that; in fact he had cut neither more nor less than any other high sheriff.

There was one further unknown charge; something obscure to do with some other sort of criminal deed. But he could get no explanation of what it was.

Had he offended the queen? Gossip maintained that he had laughed when she sang out of tune. It was perfectly true that she sang out of tune, to the point of stridency indeed. But he had not laughed; he certainly could resist doing that.

No, it was entirely a question of money. Not the money he had unlawfully acquired, but sums that he had retained in the state coffers, rather than allowing them to dribble away into the queen's household expenses. When he took over the treasury there had been a deficit; but when he surrendered it there was a surplus. Ingratitude was all the reward he got; for Birgitte Gøje had the ear of the queen, who in turn was furious at having to be niggardly when she would rather have entertained visiting princes in style.

Peder Oxe was thus not impressed at the news of the Danes' victory over the Ditmarshes. His knowledge of finance told him clearly enough that the expense of the campaign would never be offset by any additional income from their land. Young Frederik might enjoy being hailed as conqueror; with his mercenary's mind he had long dreamed of it. But he had hardly given a thought to how extremely costly it was to wage a war. Meanwhile another day would come – many days, indeed, when as a king Frederik would have to show favour by being open-handed. And it would be awkward if there was nothing to be open-handed with. The honour and glory of conquest soon faded when money was short. Nothing strengthened a ruler's arm so much as a full coffer, and nothing could make it waver like the hollow sound of emptiness.

Peder Oxe had no idea where to go. He thought of Saxony. But the gratitude of princes was often as brief as their favour, and he had a feeling that they would agree to a demand for extradition. He had already discovered that the court at Lüneberg would safeguard him only against violence and not against law, and he had quickly taken to his heels.

Down in continental Europe he heard the news of Christian the Third's death. It did not improve his position. At least the old king had been favourably inclined; but now that his hothead of a son Frederik had succeeded him it aggravated the situation. Peder Oxe had left Denmark with only eight men and a single lad, and his means were slowly dwindling. He was unable to find out what he was actually accused of at home; he knew only that they wished to rob him of land and property. If that happened, a stranger would take possession of his beloved Gisselfeld. So now he was obliged to listen to endless sermons by fanatical Calvinists condemning earthly joys – no religious movement could have been further from his own sympathies than this – while soon the sound of the hunting horn would be ringing in the ears of other huntsmen in the woods around his mansions.

Peder Oxe longed for what he would never have believed he would miss, the countryside itself. Nakskov fjord and the level acres around Halsted monastery – what could they offer compared to the riches of France? But they led across the chasm dividing the present from his childhood years at Nielstrup, where he had run around free as a bird and where every year had brought a new little brother or little sister, until they were a round dozen and he had been sent out on his grand tour.

Peder thought he had taken everything into consideration on his way to the summit of the realm. But he had over-looked the pettiness that took its strength not from one but from many. Resentment and malice and envy grew so freely among the majority, who lacked the intelligence to suppress such things in themselves. That was why he was kicking his heels in safety and solitude here in Basel with far too much time for thinking.

When news of Christian the Second's death had reached

him it had brought him up short. There was something pathetic about the old man's demise after so many years. He had been reduced to a skeletal monument to the ideas of his time. Peder remembered nothing of the era his family had talked about so much. But he knew they had been bad times for Denmark. Christian had called himself the peasants' king, but no peasant grew richer under his rule, notwithstanding the diminished power of the nobility. He called himself the townspeople's king; but only those merchants who were already wealthy profited from his actions. The rest lived in even greater poverty than before. It had been a lie, one of those myths created to keep a ghost of the past alive.

If Peder Oxe had been in doubt about conditions in Denmark, much was made clear to him when he returned at the age of eighteen. He found a country wasted by conflict. The peasants had ravaged and burned. His fellow landowners had hidden in attics and cellars, and many of them, once found, were killed after the most brutal tortures. His own father was dead. This was what happened when the people took power; and it was not what Peder Oxe wished for Denmark.

He might look down on his own class, and despise his cousins and uncles and aunts; and his lip might curl at their ignorance. But replacing them with the common herd was out of the question. Its roughcast arrogance and cruelty were even worse, once it had first tasted power.

Peder Oxe felt glad that Christian the Second, that shadow of the past, had passed to another, more heavenly existence. If, that was, the old king had not had to pay the penalty for his deeds and was burning in hellfire now and for all eternity. He had wanted to make the Danish state resemble the Netherlands. But Denmark was not the Netherlands, nor could he rule his kingdom without the best brains. And those, in spite of all, were to be found in the heads of the nobility and not in that of an old hag picked up in a Bergen market because her daughter had talent between the sheets.

Peder Oxe did not mourn the royal dotard's death. But his

passing opened up exciting perspectives. It might mean that there was something to be gained, given news that had reached him of the definitive peace treaty signed in Cateau Cambrésis. He had an idea.

Christian the Second had been a prisoner and was now dead. But his daughters were still alive. By all accounts the elder had little character worth considering, and was childless anyway. But stories about the younger one were on everybody's lips. There was her beauty; there was her intelligence; and there was her demand for the Danish throne. Peder Oxe knew all about the king's terror of this lady.

Even though she was exiled in Brussels and had small means to draw upon, the rumble of war seemed constantly to have sounded from her direction. At home it was officially known as Lorraine's war against Denmark — even though everybody knew that it was not Lorrainians who would rule the Danes, being merely citizens of a remote little dukedom. It was Madame herself who wanted to rule in place of Christian the Third, and many influential burghers as well as a number of the nobility found the idea of interest.

Since the duchess of Lorraine was Christian the Second's daughter, by rights Peder Oxe, with his feelings about his own family, ought to hate her. But that kind of idea was foreign to him. His thinking was practical; and with peace assured between France and the Hapsburgs the duchess was in a stronger position. She could return to the dukedom, there to join her son; and he in turn stood close to the French court through his marriage. She had friends and relations in both camps, and both the great powers were with her; and that completely overshadowed an execution that had taken place by St Gertrude's churchyard even before Peder Oxe was born.

The burghers had rejoiced to see Torben Oxe go to his death, whereas the nobles were enraged, and still spoke of it. But at this moment Peder Oxe did not give a jot for past events. He had glimpsed a path to follow, a place in which to act.

*   *   *

In September Peder Oxe heard that the duchess was on her way to Lorraine. As he made preparations to set off he found himself wondering what she might be like, this daughter of the old tyrant.

Peder's relations with women had always taken the form of chance attachments with females of the lower classes. He had not married, because as a rule beautiful women were too poor and rich ones too ugly; also he could not stand women's chatter; and finally he had no time for anything as complicated as getting married.

Naturally Christina, a king's daughter, was far above him. But all the same he was increasingly curious about her as a woman. What was it about her that had made Adolf of Gottorp lose his head so completely? Peder Oxe remembered all too well Christian the Third's indignation over his younger brother's courtship of the arch-enemy's daughter.

Peder Oxe knew that she was highly educated, and that she possessed all the accomplishments with which the new king of Denmark was not exactly over-endowed. She was said to speak several languages, having a mastery of Latin as well as of Spanish, Italian, High German, French and the local Dutch. But it could not be only this together with her beauty, her feeling for art and conversation, for graceful movement and elegant riding. There must be more than formal accomplishment, something not covered by the usual descriptions.

Christina the Second was a dead myth, but the duchess was a living legend. Adolf was not the only one to have thrown himself at her feet. They said that King Philip himself enjoyed her company.

The legend of the duchess had caused Christian the Third many a sleepless night. True, the danger had been exaggerated; but as matters stood it might easily turn into reality, now that the great powers – with bankruptcy as an alternative – were living in a state of friendly tolerance.

Peder Oxe set off for Lorraine.

It was as Peder Oxe reached Nancy that it first occurred to him that the gracious lady might well feel the same resentment towards his family as his family nourished for hers. The Oxes had not wasted time in allying themselves with the younger branch of the Oldenburgs, whom she so obviously refused to acknowledge; and it had been Torben Oxe's cousin who had subjected her father to the final humiliation, by tearing off his distinguished Order of the Golden Fleece before the key turned in his prison door at Sønderborg.

He wondered if she was petty-minded. The father had had a vengeful nature. What about his daughter?

Peder Oxe sought an audience at the ducal palace in Nancy with mixed feelings. It seemed strange to be about to meet her, the detested man's admired daughter. So many years had gone by since she had been carried aboard the *Lion* as a small child and had left her own country.

Peder Oxe was conducted into an ante-room with walls of green silk. It led into the renowned Deer Hall. As he entered he stiffened.

He saw a living stone column draped in black without a single ornament, with an ageing face and heavy, bitter eyes.

She stood facing him at the far end of the apartment. For a moment he hesitated to approach this sombre monument of a woman. A shudder of fear ran through him as if it were Medea herself he was about to meet. Was it revenge she sought for his family's broken oath, or was he looking at the scars of life's wounds? She had been deprived of her son for many years. He had never given a moment's thought to how much that could mark a woman. He walked slowly forward, kneeled and kissed her hand. The duchess bade him rise, and she smiled.

At once he understood everything. Adolf's adoration, all men's enchantment. In a flash her smile swept away from her face all bitterness, all suffering, all sign of age, as when spring brings light and colour to the winter landscape. The dimples appeared, one in each cheek and one in her chin, her cheeks glowed. She talked and bade him welcome to both her land and her house and expressed her pleasure in receiving a gentleman from Denmark.

Peder Oxe was spellbound. This was a princess. Not a

sharp-tongued female like the dowager queen at home, or the over-dressed objects he had come across in Germany. He had to take a hold on himself when thanking her for the great honour it was to be received by Her Grace.

He saw her smile again. It was more fleeting but held a touch of humour as if something amused her, something she did not need to say. Her father had killed his uncle, his family had broken their oath to her father; but now they had an aim in common and speech was superfluous. This princess perceived everything, understood everything; even those small facets of the vicissitudes of fortune which can be strange, sometimes entertaining, and valuable into the bargain. She emphasised once more that he was most heartily welcome, and the audience was at an end.

Peder Oxe needed time to collect his thoughts after the meeting. He pondered deeply over what had happened. She grieved, naturally. A number of her relatives had died in the past year; but she did not grieve for them. It was for her dead father. He had seen that at once and the duchess had clearly been amused at his initial fright. It was beautifully done; she had intended that little slap. He went over every word she had said – but in fact she had said little apart from bidding him welcome. The rest, everything else, he had read in her expressive eyes. They were a valuable asset, for eye-language cannot be quoted.

Peder had found sanctuary. He had found the means of action and he had found someone he could partner. With the duchess he would not encounter resentment and envy. The danger threatened from the other direction, and here he must play well and play for high stakes or she would win the tricks. Peder Oxe dared not think what would happen if she so much as set one foot on Danish soil. Burghers and peasants would flock around her, and not a few of his own class too.

But for the present he was here and she was here. They both aimed at the same end: to regain their lost places in the Danish kingdom. Peder Oxe rejoiced at meeting the first partner and opponent worthy of him. Here was a use for all his talents. The duchess had put down her hand and taken the first trick.

Christina had seen no fear in Peder Oxe's eyes as he entered. But she had noticed his hesitation, his sudden pause; and it had amused her. The rightful king of Denmark was dead. He just needed to be reminded of that and she was glad to have succeeded.

Christina had chosen to make it a short meeting. She wanted time to think over her immediate impression of the man before talking to him at greater length.

Peder Oxe cut no elegant figure. His neck was as short and thick as the beast of his family name. His beard was cut in a trim point resting on his chest and as a whole you would take him rather for a theological scholar or influential mayor than the foremost nobleman of his country. There was no finery or boastfulness about him, no attempt to display himself. His manner was controlled and his expression worldly and expectant. What was he seeking?

And what had she found?

Christina was informed about his life. It seemed to be interesting, and his outward appearance was calm and attractive. This was a gentleman who took everything into consideration – almost everything. Once the most powerful in the land, now fallen; but still self-assured. He wanted to be at the top again, but would be unlikely to beg in order to get there. He intended to win back what he had lost, and that would take time.

Christina had seldom come across someone who could be so useful. No one could inform as he could. She decided he should have Schaumburg in fief, so that the loss of his lands in Denmark did not pain him too much and soften him into servility. An apple of purest gold had fallen into Christina's lap and she did not want to see it roll off again.

Christina had left Lorraine humiliated and broken. But she knew how to come back in style, as the victor of Cateau Cambrésis. She accepted homage graciously, as a matter of course, as if those seven years had never existed. Meanwhile the French were still in Metz, Toul and Verdun; that was the price Lorraine had had to pay for stopping the war in Europe.

Christina met several people from the past. If they were

fearful over her return it was unnecessary. She would exact no revenge, no tit for tat; her eyes were on the future, not the past, for all was well again. Feelings of resentment and revenge were such heavy burdens to bear; they bound you to a time that was over and done with and blurred your vision when you needed to look clearly at present and future alike. Christina confronted the past with peace in her heart.

She had never formally abdicated from the regency of Lorraine. Carl himself elected to stay on at the French court for a time. After all, he was very young and should be allowed to amuse himself. So it was as regent that Christina found herself again in the Deer Hall, where she had once been received as a bride and had later heard the king of France demand that she should relinquish her son.

The magnolia tree in the garden had grown; but it was autumn and it had lost its leaves. Salm was his old self, and Nicholai seemed to have matured. But Madame Louise stood before her, thin and old, in shabby widow's weeds with a limp veil.

The passage of time had helped Christina to understand that Madame Louise had acted according to her views and ideals. Her anger had faded; but the change was so great that Christina felt she must know what had brought it about.

It had all begun with a duel. A German nobleman had offended Madame Louise's son, young Baron Étienne. Naturally Étienne challenged the German and killed him with his foil, which put an end to that matter.

But Étienne behaved strangely in the days that followed. He disappeared for a while, then started asking odd questions; and one day sounds of strife came from Madame Louise's rooms.

The noises swelled. Mother and son were quarrelling so violently that it could be heard on the staircase and out in the gardens. More and more curious folk gathered to listen for this was quite unheard-of. Up to now there had been no more loving mother than Madame Louise; and no more devoted son than Étienne, who allowed her to manage his estate and choose the right bride for him.

Rows were common enough, but not in that family. And

now it all came out. The dead German, when in his cups, had accused Étienne of being the son of a downright whore. It was not enough for the young man just to avenge his mother's honour. He wanted the truth; and he found it, by questioning those servants who remained from the time of his birth.

'Twelve and a half months!' he screamed, while courtiers on the stairs and in the garden stood in tense silence so as not to miss any of this exciting scene. Madame Lousie shouted back that the servants were lying hounds. She had not brought up her only son to listen to rabble. She screamed louder and louder, and worked herself up more and more and lost control of herself to such an extent that she let things drop that gave her away. It was then that Étienne started in.

Words like 'harlot' and 'whore' cut through the air, and in an effective conclusion the young man said that he had been looking more closely at the baron's will. It was correct that Madame Louise was to manage the estate until he came of age; but she was not entitled to the sums she had spent on hunting and festivities and clothes, on Italian furniture and Turkish horses and saddles from Paris. No, merely a modest pension had been her due. It was so small that it was a pittance; but it was with that that she would have to content herself from now on.

The affair ended with Étienne going to the estate he had inherited from a father who was not his – for on that point he did not deny his origins – and leaving the mother who *was* his to a humble existence at the court's mercy.

It was the general opinion that Baron Étienne had behaved disgracefully. But then on the whole modern youth was intolerable, with all its strange ideas about morals. Life would not be worth living if people all went on like that.

Christina felt sorry for Madame Louise. She decided to grant her a small pension, to enable her to live at least moderately in accordance with her rank – and accepted in return her old enemy's servile and tear-choked gratitude.

Christina had longed for this moment. It was to have made amends for her life's humiliation. She had returned; but she had not come home after all. Everything was as it had been then: walls hung with green silk, the duke's statue over the gateway, the people in the streets, the steps where she had once taken those agonising paces with Carl; and the Deer Hall in red and gold with the nobles waiting to receive her. It had all been lived through before, heard before, felt before.

There were eighteen years between the first entrance and the second, seven years between her departure and the present. It was so similar; and yet somehow different. The colour of the green silk seemed paler, the statue smaller and the deer less beautiful. She did not notice change in the faces, for each in its way had gone along with her.

Christina was no longer the bride who had thrown rosemary twigs to the people in the rue St Georges from one of the little round balconies. She was no longer nineteen. It was past, it was gone. She stood there in the hour of victory; she had fought for this. But, as in a single autumn storm, her leaves had been torn from her. The hand on the clock moved one way, and one way only. She walked into the shadows of her own youth and was bereft of her years.

But she turned her mind from deeper reflection. The news of Peder Oxe's arrival in Nancy presented fresh food for thought; and she enjoyed her anticipation for several days before the meeting took place.

The first meeting was followed by others. Christina asked after old Rikke and her bad leg and whether she was still living in her little house in Mag Street. She saw the surprise on Peder Oxe's face. Rikke had been his wet nurse; but Christina saw no reason to tell him how she had discovered that.

Peder Oxe soon recovered himself. In his deep voice, with a merry glint in his eye, he asked if what they said was true, that as a young girl she had told the English envoy, 'Tell the king of England I would gladly marry him if I had a spare head.'

Oh, so that was common knowledge now, thought Christina. A mere aside to some courtiers turned into a reply to an official envoy; and she gave him the correct version.

The introductory small talk was soon over and they came to the real topic of discussion. First a casual remark, uttered as if in passing, which the hearer pretended not to hear. After a time the answers came; and before long they were immersed in their mutual interest, their common aim: Denmark.

Peder Oxe had a suggestion, in the form of Wernher von Grumbach. Christina had often heard this gentleman mentioned. He was an officer in the German forces of the French army, when not otherwise occupied with his own affairs, and no very pleasant character. Peder Oxe suggested giving him help and support in his efforts to stir up every kind of unrest and trouble in and around Saxony. Grumbach had put the idea into Duke Johan Henrik's head that he ought to have Saxony. He saw princely crowns before his eyes and the angels spoke to him, and Johan Henrik was a fool who swallowed it whole. Saxony was Denmark's strongest ally in Germany. The electoral princess was Frederik the Second's sister, and it would be a good thing if the electoral prince had something to do other than supporting his brother-in-law. Denmark would be cut off from her allies and left a prey for the taking.

Excellent, thought Christina and closed the conversation by asking Peder Oxe to make contact with Grumbach and offer him money for the enterprise. In November Peder Oxe was in possession of his Schaumburg fief and castle.

Christina received other petitions. Von Langen appeared. He had a fine new plan concerning an attack on Sweden. The Danish king, he maintained, would applaud such an action. Christina, however, did not put much faith in this verbose gentleman.

From Sweden came tentative hints concerning a separate peace between Sweden and Lorraine. That possibility seemed somewhat flimsy as well. But a Danish proposal to Renata was another matter.

It was presented in the Netherlands through Henrik Rantzau. Frederik wanted Renata for his bride. Christina asked Peder Oxe for his opinion and more long conversations ensued.

On the one hand there was the possibility of isolating and conquering Denmark. By cutting off Saxony through Grumbach much ground would be won. The Ditmarshes would support her, and the Hanseatic League. A weakened, isolated and divided Denmark should not be hard to beat. But it would cost money.

The alternative was marriage. It would not provide any position for her up there, or Carl, only Renata; and the thought of that Lady Hardenberg was not enjoyable.

Snow was falling. The view was familiar. She had seen it when she was carrying her children. She had ridden through the countryside both with Franz and alone, after his death. It was unchanged out there. She was feeling her age, and could see it in the mirror; but her will for action was still the same.

Christina was approaching forty. She had lived for longer than most. But she had not achieved what she desired. She was no longer at home here. Nor was she any longer at home in the Netherlands. A circle must be completed. She wanted to go back to her tender years. A return to her origins would unite her with an abiding place and mend cracks and heal scars.

She saw a light towards the North. All Buckholt's descriptions of dirty towns, darkness and foul smells were pushed aside and she breathed in the scent of the Seal and beech woods on a summer evening as Peder Oxe had described them. The country was green. She had said that to her father one night by the fire. She had been only four years old then, but the country was still green and her father's dreams and ambitions were more than ever her dreams and her ambitions.

But which way to go? Through Renata? To go there merely as mother-in-law? Or should the nobles who had once deserted their king be given the opportunity to desert again and allow her her inheritance and her right?

Christina hesitated to give an answer to the easier but less attractive solution: the proposal to her elder daughter.

Peder Oxe regularly received letters from Denmark,

which he showed her. Most of them came from one Jorgen Skriver, who went around ravaging and pillaging in southern Sealand. Skriver kept in touch with angry mayors and burghers and provided information about the nobles' increasing dissatisfaction.

She would keep Peder Oxe. She plied him with lands and heaped him with honours. She listened to his information and his ideas and picked out those that suited her. He was a cool, cunning player; and she liked his methods and his manner of reasoning. It was logical, it was all of it pure common sense; and he had at his fingertips a constant stream of names of nobles who were for sale, if only they had not already sold themselves up there.

Christina thought about the Danish nobility and its history. That was the way of it; that was how an oath was taken so that the crown went to another.

Christina glimpsed the possibility of a repetition of history, and the idea delighted her.

XXII

Christina was too old for the joys of youth; but she was still too young for the passivity of old age. She held her meetings with the bull-necked Dane, looked forward to them and found herself a place in the world of Machiavelli.

Peder Oxe's proposal was clear and simple: what was needed was money for 10–12,000 infantry and 5–6,000 mounted troops. The recruitment should be carried out quietly, in various areas, so as not to arouse attention. It would thus leave the king of Denmark unprepared, with only his own unwilling populace to support him. The army would strike by pushing up through Jutland. The whole campaign was estimated to cover six weeks – and Christina could well afford that.

She went over the plan, trying to see how Peder Oxe could profit by giving false information. She perceived nothing; and in February 1560 she came to a decision.

Christina would acquire the necessary monies, recruit troops and start an invasion. Denmark was to be conquered by force of arms.

Peder Oxe spent the winter planning a new meeting with this Grumbach. But there was one thing lacking before Christina could take action. She could not by right call herself queen of Denmark as long as Dorothea was alive, unless Dorothea renounced her rights.

In the middle of the cold month of March Christina visited her sister at Germersheim in the Palatinate.

'Well,' said Dorothea pensively. She grumbled though, over Christina's dealings with this Herr Oxe; from what she had heard he was a bad character. She ought to show him the door without further ado. Christina began again. It was a matter of the Danish rights. Dorothea responded with a long list of complaints about how costly everything had become. She could neither live nor die on the miserable means she had at her disposal.

Dorothea sat there, stolid, querulous and limp-haired. Christina sighed and asked curtly, 'How much?'

Dorothea explained that she loved Christina and her children, and that she would gladly relinquish everything for them: she herself asked only for peace in the remaining years God would allow her on this earth. But she had to live, and prices rose steadily; and it was not easy to be a widow on your own. So 6,000 dalers a year would relieve her hardship until the kingdoms were conquered.

'And then?' asked Christina.

'Then it must be increased to 25,000 ...' Dorothea hesitated a moment. '25,000 dalers; or, if you prefer, 500,000 once and for all. Remember, Sweden is included.'

Christina groaned inwardly but said nothing. It was a monstrous sum. Dorothea was unlikely to budge, however, and added quietly, 'You see, you are so dear to me, my dear; my only family. It is you I'm thinking of. It cost Friederich 300,000 to try to relieve Copenhagen, and I must have that covered as well ...'

Christina had not the least idea how to get hold of that amount. But she must and would have those rights. A document was prepared and Dorothea renounced her rights. Christina promised to pay, and hurried back to Nancy.

That evening Christina sat alone and very still. Everything had gone so fast. There were papers, the signature, and family affection; money, pensions and compensation. But the document lay before her. She looked at it, went on looking, ran her finger down its words and letters in the light from the tapers. It had happened. It had come. It was hers. She heard a rushing sound. The people cheered; cannon thundered in salute; church bells rang all over Denmark, all over Norway and soon all over Sweden. Her father's inherited kingdoms were her inherited kingdoms, from Holstein to the North Cape, from Iceland to the Russian border.

An appointment required Christina's signature. She bent to write her 'Chrétienne,' waited a moment to fully enjoy the act of writing, then added, 'By God's mercy Queen of Denmark, Sweden and Norway, of the Wends and Goths and Slavs, duchess of Slesvig-Holstein and the Ditmarshes, Lorraine, Bar and Milan, countess of Oldenburg and Blamont and lady of Tortona.'

Christina slowly laid down her quill and regarded the hand that had guided it. She saw veins beneath the skin, the scar of a small gash, and lines on the palm; fingers, nails. She turned it round to observe it, held it up still higher. Everything about it was so strange and new, like something she had never seen before. This was the hand of the Northern queen.

The Nordic kingdoms had been assigned to Christina and now the rest of the world must acknowledge it. She sent off a messenger to Emperor Ferdinand but received the reply that it was not his concern. What else could be expected of him? Many years ago Christina's mother in her poverty had begged his aid and received humiliation in return. Imperial power was no longer what it once had been. Christina took his lack of support calmly and went on with her plans.

It had been in Jutland that her father's uncle had instigated the revolt and stolen the crown. It was from Jutland that she intended to conquer Denmark. Ahead waited the Copenhagen she could rely on with certainty, and further north was faithful Norway.

She would come. They were waiting for her: burghers, peasants and many dissatisfied nobles; she, their queen, was on her way. It was her right and also her duty.

From Peder Oxe she learned more and more names of towns, estates and people. She felt she could reach them, with her whispered 'I am coming, I am coming,' as she had once felt she could stretch across hundreds of miles and reach Carl in France. Recruitment would be under way with the thaw; when spring came she would set off for the North, cross frontiers and like a bride of high summer enter in to wed her people in the far countries.

Everything was prepared, everything was ready. Christina was counting the days; she felt youthful again as she watched the first water trickling from the snow-covered river banks. Then Peder Oxe came to her with letters from home. Denmark had sounded the alarm.

Rumours had gone around that Peder Oxe had sent troops up there with the salt fleet. Herluf Trolle had received orders to arm the men-of-war. Messengers had been sent to the commanders of all the coastal castles as far north as Trondheim.

The country was no longer unprepared. Christina felt searing disappointment.

What now? Should she set off as planned or wait? A prepared Denmark was different from a Denmark taken by surprise. Now she would have to anticipate a lengthy campaign, and for that she lacked the means.

'Wait,' said Peder Oxe, reckoning how much it would cost the Danish treasury to keep the fleet in readiness with arms and powder. 'Wait,' he said, 'Gustav Vasa is a sick man, perhaps a dying man, and his eldest son a warlike fellow like his Danish cousin.' 'Just wait,' came again after Peder Oxe's men were arrested in a thoroughgoing slaughter all over Sealand. And now there were long intervals between the letters.

When summer came and she should have been in the Copenhagen she had left so long ago, she recovered her optimism. Perhaps she could recruit next year. Her thoughts turned to the document that had been signed at the peace of Speyer.

The emperor had acknowledged Christian the Third, but also her own claim to inheritance. That committed Philip, who also had every possible reason for wishing to see his loyal and Catholic cousin gain control over the Sound. It behoved her merely to make the request at the right moment and give him time to think.

*　　*　　*

Christina enjoyed every meeting she had with Peder Oxe. He carried no pomp but he was cultivated and knowledge-able. There was an undercurrent of something insatiable in him; but it seldom penetrated the cultured façade, and merely showed itself in a tireless capacity to find new avenues.

When he sat facing her and talked, when she saw the face that was somehow screwed down between his shoulders, when his round clever eyes rested on her, she let herself be captivated by ideas and thoughts to such an extent that she always had to spend a long time collecting herself in order to see what was for his benefit and his alone and what she herself could gain by.

Peder Oxe was dangerous, but he was also courageous. One of his trusted men was murdered that summer in the Netherlands. Frederik's people were behind it. They thought they would find something among the papers on the body, but they were wrong. There was nothing.

Next time it could be Peder Oxe himself. He showed no sign of worry. He never mentioned fearing for his life and merely took care always to ride with a sizeable armed escort. 'The invulnerable' he called them and put about a rumour that they were in league with the Devil and could make themselves invisible. That may have deterred a few people from attempting an attack. But according to Grum-bach some person in Lorraine had nevertheless told the Danish king that he would murder Peder Oxe, in return for 2,000 dalers. Grumbach had passed the information on because he would regret it so deeply if anything happened to Herr Oxe.

The friendly relations that had grown up between the Danes and the Hanseatic League also put a spoke in Christina's wheel. Peder Oxe had not in fact been voyaging with salt boats along the coast of Sealand, but the rumour alone frightened the life out of Frederik, and that in itself was interesting.

Sweden was still there, and reports filtered down of a possible revolt. But Christina preferred to leave the Swedes to start that themselves. Besides, the route there lay through

Denmark, and that would cause problems. Grumbach was kept in reserve. She must scrutinise and sift through Peder Oxe's ideas and allow things to develop in their own time. So much was in ferment, smouldering and bubbling. All that was needed was the final shovel-load of fuel to bring the pot to the boil.

Christina stopped to listen. A messenger had arrived. The young king of France was dead. An ear infection had spread to his brain and put an end to his brief life.

The throne passed to the eleven-year-old second eldest son of Catherine of Medici, who filled the post of regent.

A woman again, thought Christina. They ruled Scotland, England, the Netherlands, several smaller states and now France. She wondered if it had ever happened before, that her sex had held so much official power. Wives had always taken over the management of farms and castles when their husbands were at war or died, but this went a step further. Women rulers were no longer an exception; it had become a normal occurrence.

But when the mighty kingdom of France came under the rule of Catherine of Medici people began asking themselves if it would bring changes – if between them so many women rulers had in mind to govern their territories and kingdoms in a different manner.

Catherine of Medici started out by working for peace among the disputing religious factions. She held that the variant ways of believing in God were less worrying than the sums the disturbances had cost the treasury. Were women less open-handed than men? Did they think more of money than of honour and glory?

They ruled most of Europe now. Was Denmark really to be an exception? There had indeed once been a queen, Margrethe. She had been known as 'The nation's lady and head of the house', not the queen of Denmark. But Christina would have had no objection to that. All she wanted was to be there.

Mary Stuart threatened danger meanwhile. She was to return to her land of fishermen, shepherds and rebellious lairds. She would need a new husband. Might she decide to marry one of the Nordic kings? That would be unfortunate; it would create an undesirable international alliance. Christina did not like the idea but she comforted herself with the knowledge that the de Guise family were distanced from French politics. In the meantime she threw herself into the immediate concern of getting her daughters back from Brussels.

Christina had not seen them for eighteen months. But she had enjoyed their letters, which were filled with charming chatter about life in Brussels, and about Margaret of Parma whom they invariably called 'The lady with the moustache'.

A fanciful imaginativeness ran through the letters, particularly Renata's. Her coming reunion with the girls led Christina to reflect on how different young people were now.

Neither of them would dream of riding astride; that was not thought seemly for ladies. They would rather ride gracefully than boldly. They decked themselves out, tight-laced and powdered, and passed their time in a world of artifice, tending stuffed birds and porcelain flowers. Renata and Dorothea were young, but their lives were not young; they did not throb with vigour and enjoyment. Where were the visions? Where the pulse-beat? Had they ever had the feeling of stretching out their arms to embrace the whole round world?

Christina's happiness over the reunion emphasised, all the more clearly, the difference between then and now. They had had the same education as herself. They were influenced by her as she had been influenced by her aunts. But at the same time they were affected by the trends of the time and could be severe and censorious. They spoke of the new attitude of the Church as the salvation of the world. Of course it was good that popes and bishops no longer had all those children. But that did not make it necessary for the rest of humanity to live as if the whole lot of them were to be canonised.

Christina could not understand the young. It was all so

taken-for-granted, so clear-cut. No one would draw flying machines any more – for what was the use of such fantasies when everything had already been invented, everything there was to be discovered had been, and every idea obviously thought of?

But nothing overshadowed her joy at Renata and Dorothea's return, to the town where they were born but which they could hardly remember. Their merry laughter echoed through halls and apartments, and they flirted and smiled their way around accompanied by courtiers, dwarves and little black boys wearing turbans of shiny brocade.

They would be married in the most distinguished and dignified manner possible. The noblest blood ran in their veins. Several suitors had already sought Renata's hand, and yet another prospective husband's representative was even now on his way.

It was a certain Count Günther von Schwarzburg, and he came on behalf of his master, the king of Denmark. Frederik was once more soliciting Renata's hand.

Christina had frequently heard mention of the count. He had married the sister of Wilhelm of Orange, an alliance that had in no way diminished his feelings of grandeur. Boastfulness, drunkenness and murder were his standard-bearers; they were also the very qualities that had won favour with the Copenhagen court. He was apt to reel off endless stories of his brave feats in the war against France, liberally sprinkled with the names of his grand acquaintances around Europe. Two emperors had lavished favours on him; the highest nobility in the Netherlands were his very best friends; and his accounts quickly passed over those courts where, because they considered his lies and boastfulness intolerable, he was persona non grata.

But Peder Oxe was enthusiastic. He recommended Christina to accept the proposal – if he could go to Denmark to negotiate the marriage, for then he could return to his estates in all honour. But Christina had other ideas.

The jabberings of this count, this Schwarzburg, had long since come to her ears. He was to bring about what Rantzau had failed to achieve in the Netherlands: to mediate familial peace between Lorraine and the Danish houses. A great task had been laid on his shoulders, but there was no doubt that he was man enough for it, not least because the duchess was so eager to clinch the contract.

This roused Christina to indignation. Was she supposed to be eager to have anything at all to do with that upstart in Scandinavia? Had she ever shown any interest in such a marriage?

Well . . . there had been a single feeler while she was still in the Netherlands; but it had not been very serious nor had it been repeated or confirmed. What did he really think he was doing, this loud-voiced ridiculous clown of an envoy, starting a courtship by insulting her in so coarse a manner?

He must be taught a lesson. He would hear about it, this Schwarzburg. There were plenty of counts; but only one queen of Denmark, Sweden and Norway.

Christina received Schwarzburg in the old castle at Bar. In black velvet and her finest veil she gave him her hand and an icy glance. But Schwarzburg's conduct was even worse than rumour had painted it.

The hulking German behaved as if everything was in fact signed and sealed. All she had to do was state her conditions. This was too much for Christina's self-control.

She was, she announced to the man, queen of the kingdoms that his master, this Lord Frederik, claimed as his. Frederik was self-appointed; he had occupied foreign property. It was a unique honour, an undeserved favour and entirely out of the goodness of her heart that she received his envoy, and if there should be anything at all to negotiate, about anything whatsoever, the offer could be put forward for her consideration and not vice versa.

That helped. The count turned pale, grew subdued, and then suddenly burst out with proposals for bridal treasure for herself, for wedding gift and indenture for Renata. Her daughter would even be permitted to retain her Catholic faith, if another conflicted with her conscience.

Christina answered coolly that she required a delegation from Denmark with full legal authority if the conditions were worth discussing at all.

But after Schwarzburg had gone Christina pondered long

and deeply. There had been that comment about a Catholic queen in Denmark. God knows if she had been meant to hear that. God knows if Schwarzburg had not revealed a good deal more than he had been instructed to tell her. Denmark would need to safeguard herself on all sides when war with Sweden came. The enemy would be isolated, and that explained why the bride would be secured the right to practise her own religion. A bride . . . or a reigning queen.

Schwarzburg journeyed on but the echo of his gossip came back to Christina. He had forced her to yield; he had in the most brilliant manner introduced an idea which no other could do: a happy and peaceful union of the two branches of the House of Oldenburg.

But Christina found yet another reason for taking her time. It was true that Renata was sixteen, but what was the hurry? There was no longer any danger of Mary Stuart marrying a Scandinavian king. She was far too much influenced by her fanatical Catholic uncles for that.

Renata was the most attractive bride Frederik could find. Christina relaxed. Time was on her side and held far greater possibilities than the role of mother-in-law.

Peder Oxe was becoming pressing. If he showed no fear for his own life, the thought of that von Dohna with his hands on Peder's beloved Gisselfeld robbed him of all self-control. He would strangle him with his own hands. He would plunge his knife into him himself. Despite all the honours, glory and land Christina heaped on him, the Dane's longing for home was draining him of strength, and as autumn drew on she increased her promises of financial support. He could quietly approach Grumbach again, promise him money and announce that Christina was willing to undertake a campaign next spring.

In May Schwarzburg again presented himself. Christina grew irritated. Were they out of their minds to come running to her again with no news at all? Schwarzburg was a braggart and he was happy to betray his master's confidence by talking about the expected conflicts between Denmark and Sweden; they would bring fame to men like himself.

Christina listened to the war rumours with interest and read the few letters that reached Peder Oxe eagerly. Up in Denmark they had begun cutting off the heads of his men. One day a messenger arrived from Sealand, which was really just a huge camp of mercenaries. Frederik was proposing a meeting at Oldenburg or Munster, with the condition that it take place before Morten's Evening. But by now Christina had decided that her daughter was not to be used to prop up a failing king. She replied forcefully that it was most inconsiderate of him to choose such a remote place and in such a hurry; she would reconsider the situation and come up with a better idea. She then showed the most lavish hospitality to the Danish representative and sent him back home.

Carl returned to Lorraine. In May he made an official entrance into Nancy and swore on oath to preserve the rights of the citizens. As the coronation took place, Christina watched her son: although he was young, he carried himself upright, he was mature and wise in his ways. His eyes showed his strength of character and self-control. Art was to be promoted and the welfare of the people should come before his own personal pleasures. Carl outshone many a palatine, even many a king. Christina's thoughts took flight as the crown was placed on her son's head. Astrologers had predicted greatness for Carl. But how to be great when you were only the duke of Lorraine? Did it not demand deeper resources? Wasn't that what they had read in his stars?

Christina stared at the ducal crown, and found it too small and too poor. She glanced over at Claude, and sighed.

She was also present when, in Frankfurt, another crown was lowered onto the head of the new king Maximilian. Elsewhere, though, the state of affairs caused great consternation amongst the princes. In France, the soft hand of Catherine of Medici was proving ineffective and in the Netherlands the iron fist of Margaret of Parma and Granvella seemed equally disastrous.

Everyone was talking, voicing an opinion. Christina listened to it all, and thought back to Wilhelm of Orange's words at one of his grandiose parties: '. . . at the end of the day, we are all Christians'. She couldn't help seeing her old love in this man, although it was impossible to judge how much of this was simply her dwelling on old memories of René and how much was due to a genuine kindred spirit. Her heart warmed as she thought back to the young man with the dark blue eyes, who had been so intensely opposed to corseting women's waists and women's minds, to the corseting of mankind.

But René was in the Collégiale in Bar, a skeleton, carved in stone. With the onset of age and the disappearance of suitors, however, René was more than ever the only man in Christina's life. He was physical love and the longing of the body, he was the singing of swans' wings under high midsummer skies in Bruges, and for the moment she thought she could feel the wooden panels of a window pressed to her forehead as in an early morning she leant towards it and wept.

There was a mind and a spirit that lived on in her mind and her spirit, making her in tune with Wilhelm and his dream of the road to freedom.

The coronation brought an abundance of princes. Representatives of foreign powers had poured in, and among them was Schwarzburg. Later, when Christina tried to recall exactly what happened, she would find his actions as baffling as they were unbelievable. He had brought no news for her and nothing indicated that his presence in Frankfurt had anything to do with marriage negotiations. But all of a sudden he rose to his feet and announced triumphantly that his master the king of Denmark did not wish to marry the princess of Lorraine.

Christina had been speechless. The negotiations had so far, as was customary in such cases, been kept under a veil of secrecy. And now without warning she had been dealt this devastating blow.

Schwarzburg had behaved like a fool and a scoundrel. Everybody was disgusted at his behaviour; it was simply unheard of. And still he strutted around like a turkey cock, singing his own praises at the glorious part he had played. However strong the condemnation, nevertheless, the humiliation remained all too real and no amount of sympathy could compensate for the dishonour. Christina's daughter had been publicly rejected, and that was news that would speed into every corner of all the courts in Europe.

XXIII

The campaign against the Ditmarshes gave Frederik the Second *folie de grandeur*. He fell out with Hamburg over the right of staple for corn on the Elbe and was in danger of losing the respect of every other power. The final straw was when he detained the Swedish envoys in Copenhagen, kept back their passports and refused to let them leave. Such an act was totally illegal, and in the summer of 1563 war broke out in Scandinavia.

Christina took a longer look at the east and again began to consider Sweden.

A letter had arrived from a certain Charles de Mornay, a French Protestant in Swedish employ. He was close to King Erik, and on very intimate terms with his master.

Charles de Mornay had been in France, unsuccessfully seeking the hand of Mary Stuart for his Swedish king. It was on that occasion that he gave Christina to understand, through the de Guise family, that for its part Sweden wanted peace and alliance with Lorraine and refused to accept a Danish proposal to join together against all other states.

At the time Christina had not sent a representative to Sweden as invited, but now the project seemed interesting and she composed a new plan.

Hamburg, an obvious ally, must be contacted, as well as Bremen. The Ditmarshes were more than eager to start a revolt against Denmark, and could provide food supplies for the troops.

It would also be a good idea to approach the pope. Finally, the king of Sweden should be encouraged to launch a rapid attack on Skåne, while Christina with her allies pushed up through Holstein and Jutland.

'Erik the Fourteenth is a gifted man,' said Peder Oxe with one of his almost invisible smiles, adding, 'And he is not yet married.'

Peder Oxe was desperate to get home. No matter how much land she gave him, it was not Danish land with Danish sisters, brothers, sisters- and brothers-in-law as neighbours. Christina knew this and took it into account, but his plan was in no way desperate. It was completely in line with every other conquest she could remember.

On the 4th of October that year Grumbach broke the peace. He seized the city of Würzburg in the neighbourhood of his family estate of Rimpar, and bishop and cathedral were forced into a humiliating settlement.

Christina and Peder Oxe were highly delighted. Things were getting going and the prospects looked good. Denmark could wage war now, until the coffers were empty, and all its friends gone.

Carl and his young wife Claude lived permanently in Nancy now. While Christina was still waiting for news of the outbreak of war in the North, Claude told her happily that she was with child. Christina was overjoyed, but also anxious and full of sudden solicitude for the daughter-in-law whom she had not thought very much of till now.

She wondered whether Claude was strong enough to undergo a pregnancy and birth, and as her time drew near Christina spent hours on her knees praying for a happy outcome. So many young women suffered an early and often terrible death to bring children into the world, and the girl, with her huge belly, was small and frail.

But Claude gave birth to a son. She lived, and the child lived. Carl was a father and Christina had her first grandchild.

She held him in her arms and could not keep back her tears of joy. It was twenty years since she had seen Carl for the first time and now his son had come into the world. Carl entered as Franz had done to hear the witnesses swear that the child had been born of his wife's body.

Deeply moved. Christina went into the chapel, fell on her knees and gave thanks to God.

'He is to be named Henri after his maternal grandfather,' said Carl. This was no more than Christina had expected. Nevertheless she wanted to make her own suggestion. 'Why not Hans? . . . or Christian?'

Carl's laugh was deprecating. 'No, no; he's to be called Henri.'

Christina tried again; it was worth an attempt. But this time Carl did not laugh. 'I am not Danish, and Claude is not Danish, and we never shall be.'

'Are you sure?' Christina asked stubbornly. He knew perfectly well what was going on; he was as well-informed as she was and often spoke with Peder Oxe. What was he getting at?

But Carl grew agitated. 'It is here we belong, Claude and I and little Henri, and not in a bunch of frozen kingdoms halfway across the polar circle. I do not want my country and my dukedom to be notorious as Europe's hive of intrigues.'

Christina made no reply. There was nothing to say; but she was shocked to see her son opposing her for the first time. Did she create intrigues? Perhaps; but it was because others had intrigued, against her rights and her father's. Carl had a home, a fatherland; but she had none.

Christina passed it off. Naturally Carl was in an emotional state. He had become a father; that always bound one to what was closest. Moreover he was preoccupied with what was happening in France. Events there threatened to deprive Catherine of Medici of power, after a bullet had caused the death of the duke de Guise.

Carl was affected by the death of his relative. France was like a dance he had to keep time to, scherzo or andante. He did not understand Nordic rhythms; they were outside his sphere. Still, she thought, he was only twenty; there was plenty of time for change. Christina returned to the war in the North.

A constant stream of goods passed down the rivers of the Baltic: salt, copper, hops, corn. All of it had to be freighted through the Danish sounds and straits, north around Jutland

and down to Antwerp and the smaller harbours of Europe; and these supplies were vital.

But now shipping had been blockaded into the harbour of Danzig and along the coasts of Sealand. The Danish fleet lay in readiness north of Elsinore to prevent their passage; and this, surely, would force Philip to stir himself.

Christina wrote to Granvella to ask him to procure the necessary monies. Meanwhile Peder Oxe amused himself with his calculations.

'Figures are a good thing to have,' he said. 'In the end they decide everything. The Danish army numbers 30,000 mercenaries, the scrapings of every imaginable nationality. It costs 150,000 dalers a month to pay them. And it is,' he said with a little smile, 'it is about the same as the Danish state's annual income.'

Christina understood the perspective. Peder Oxe saw it; and Granvella too returned a positive reply, although he considered the sums she asked for would be insufficient. At last, thought Christina. At last they understood.

She decided to put the plan into action, and sent Peder Oxe off on a diplomatic mission. She provided him with detailed instructions for his negotiations with the Ditmarshes and Hamburg; also she gave him authority to commence discussions with the Swedes.

Summer came and Christina went hawking with her daughters. The falcon sat on her gloved wrist; she took off its hood, and let it fly after its prey.

She watched its soaring flight, and wondered whether the skies over Sweden were as high and blue as these. What was it like up there where for half the year the land lay in semi-darkness? Renata spurred her horse to a gallop, her black hair shining in the summer sun. Could she stand the cold and the dark so far north as Stockholm?

The whole thing was still only an idea, and depended so much on what this King Erik was like. His background was not encouraging. His father, Gustav Vasa, had made himself king, and had a long struggle to find a royal house that would demean itself so far as to send him a daughter as bride.

It was not a well-ordered court; on the other hand King Erik had close associates like this de Mornay, who had obviously grown acclimatised to the long winter nights. The crux of it was King Erik himself. A satisfactory spouse would make up for both bad weather and a primitive society.

Christina knew so little about the man himself. He was said to be highly intelligent; on the other hand there were murmurs about mistresses of low degree. Naturally a man of his age should have women. But the idea of another Dyveka sent a shudder through Christina. Renata should never be exposed to that.

Besides, there was the question of the demands he might make. He would claim his own share of Denmark–Norway, and then what should she offer him?

Ideas flew through Christina's mind. She had almost forgotten the hawk, when it flew back to her to be given strips of raw meat from her hand as reward for the partridge it had caught. She put the hood over its eyes, stroked its feathered back, and shared her daughter's pleasure in the day's sport. Meanwhile it was Sweden that was her concern now. They rode towards home.

Christina suddenly felt strange. There was a pressure in her chest. The sky turned white, and the earth turned white. She saw light, sharp and cutting. Her eyes hurt and she was dazzled as if the sun was in the field in front of her. She tried to shield her eyes; there were cries around her, Renata's and Dorothea's voices and questions; but she would not give in. She was just tired, they were close to the town, there was no need to ask for help for so small a thing. She would go on; Porte de la Craffe lay ahead. But it was white too, as were the walls and the towers.

Christina felt a sudden stab of pain in her head. The whiteness turned black and she fell to the ground.

They were all gathered around her bed, Carl, Claude, Renata and Dorothea. They were expecting her to die.

Christina did not want to die. The pain was still there, but she wanted to go on. There was so much to be achieved; and when was Peder Oxe coming back? Little Henri was to be baptised; she would not be cheated of that, even if he ought to have been given another name. And perhaps she would live to see Renata queen of Sweden, if this Erik turned out to be a respectable and honourable man deserving of so distinguished a bride.

Her vision blacked out again, and her hearing. She was shut into her own darkness with the pain; but it must not be the end. She was angry; she would not allow everything to disappear.

Christina saw light. Before she registered the faces around her she heard the rain. It was pouring down outside, and she was alive.

Not until some days had gone by did Christina realise for how many weeks she had been unconscious.

Peder Oxe had acted on his own initiative when he had been unable to consult with his mistress during her illness. Christina was satisfied with what he had done. The negotiations with Sweden were under way.

In November came a letter from the same Charles de Mornay who had presented himself previously. He requested her to send representatives to Stockholm, as King Erik did not wish to make peace without her approval. The letter's tone was reasonable.

Christina soon felt well enough to act and decided to send off a captain. He was to take a reply to de Mornay, and received detailed instructions as to her wishes.

Christina desired possession of Denmark including the dukedoms and rights up to the Sound. If the question of marriage to Renata was raised he was to say only that such a treasure was not easy to acquire. Finally the captain was bidden to build up a thorough impression of conditions in Sweden and to bring back an exact description of the Swedish king.

The captain set off and Christina busied herself with other concerns. She must send congratulations to Mary Stuart, who had married again, in Scotland.

Several years had passed since Mary had sailed back to the

land of her birth. In that time only one shadow had fallen on her. A young French poet at her court named Chastelard had expressed his love for the beautiful queen, and she had accepted his adoring verses with pleasure. One night he concealed himself in her bedchamber. It was an outrage, concerning as it did so distinguished a lady. Nevertheless he was merely sent away amid general merriment.

The next time he was discovered in his hiding-place Mary Stuart had him arrested and executed.

French poets were numerous, and serious crimes were indeed sometimes punished with death; but there was something sinister about this story. Chastelard went to the scaffold crying farewell to 'the most beautiful and cruellest of all princesses'.

Mary Stuart's letters were affectionate and touching, and Christina kept her impression of her as a golden roe-deer. But there had been the bird with a broken wing; there was a dead poet; and there were Nostradamus's ominous predictions.

Mary Stuart had married her second cousin, Lord Henry Darnley. He was a Catholic, descended on his mother's side from the English royal house. The marriage was a political stroke of genius with regard to England. Or so everyone thought, until the revelations of those few who had had the chance of meeting the bridegroom in person.

Words like 'fool' and 'idiot' were mentioned. Meanwhile in England Elizabeth still had not married. Whispers about the reason went the rounds.

It was the Earl of Leicester; and he had thrown darker shadows over his queen than ever the French poet had over the queen of Scotland. Elizabeth was deeply in love with the earl. But he had had a wife, Lady Amy, who in mysterious circumstances had fallen down a staircase and broken her neck. All this had happened in the second year of Elizabeth's reign, and some uncompromising things were being said in the streets of London about what had really happened.

But Elizabeth's perception of what her people would and would not tolerate surpassed her feelings as a woman. She did not marry the earl. He remained close to her and was still influential, but he did not acquire a crown. There had been one dead wife too many.

Christina was still waiting for money from Philip. She elected to ask her old friend Egmont for help. He was about to go to Spain with a demand from the Netherlands for the removal of the Spanish troops. A request for 300,000 would be a minor issue. Egmont, helpful as ever, promised to put her case in the best way possible.

When Egmont returned in April his reply was evasive, however. Christina set off to discover more, from a personal encounter.

The country she revisited in the early summer of 1565 had changed since she had left it six years earlier. The winters had grown colder and colder, the harvests had been ruined, and icebergs from the North Sea had been seen off the coast. Imports of wool from England had come to a standstill, putting thousands out of work in the big towns, and hunger and poverty were adding fuel to the Calvinists' fire.

Wilhelm of Orange fought, however, for freedom of belief; it was what he sent Egmont to ask for in Madrid.

King Philip had given Egmont a seat at his table – a rare honour. Egmont was praised for his bravery in the war, and he went home delighted and happy. He returned full of accounts of the magnificent building works at the Escorial – but with no mention of freedom for the Low Countries.

What had the king said? Egmont had no answer. He had had an exceptional experience; he, a Netherlander, had received what many a Spanish grandee would envy him. At first people queued outside his house. However they soon left, deeply disappointed and Egmont came to realise with bitterness that he had been disarmed by royal blandishments.

Wilhelm of Orange was furious. Christina merely sighed, gave up, and left the land of her childhood in the hands of poverty and Margaret of Parma.

On the 23rd of September Christina was at Blamont. There was still a hint of summer in the air as she received the

Swedish envoys, Hans Klasson, Lasse Knutson and Herman Bruser.

The Swedes were there to put forward a proposal on behalf of their king. Christina was to acknowledge King Erik as rightful king of Sweden, the Wends and the Goths; in return King Erik would acknowledge her, Christina, as rightful queen of Denmark. The heirs of Christian the Second must not demand Norway or the Skånian provinces or Gotland, while on his side King Erik accepted Christina's right to Denmark up to the Sound, together with the duchies. Also, an offensive and defensive alliance against the upstart in Denmark was to be formed, and Swedish ships should always have free right of passage through the Øre Sound.

Christina listened with a friendly smile and talked around their proposals. For why should she give an answer when she knew that they had better suggestions?

They had painted only half the picture. The Swedish gentlemen had been given secret instructions to implement, in the event of the first proposal producing a negative answer. A copy of those instructions had been on her table for a long time. Meanwhile she produced every imaginable objection.

It did not suit her to start a campaign now; it was too late. Besides, it had not been her intention to surrender Norway.

Christina retired to study the secret instructions.

They had been brought down through Europe to the Swedes by her own people. They had been sealed, of course; but the men had done their duty, and opened them, copied them and sealed up the document again invisibly. How naïve can people be, thought Christina.

Here was the proposal of marriage to Renata. The conditions were plain. Christina was to surrender all claims to inheritance in Scandinavia, even Denmark and the duchies. Renata was to have Vastergotland, apart from Älvsborg castle and fief, as a wedding morning present.

It would be marvellous to see her Renata queen of a united Scandinavia, taking up once more the possessions her grandfather had once lost.

There was only one small 'but'. It seemed as if King Erik

was not interested in this marriage. Or in any marriage at all. He had proposed to England, he had proposed to Scotland, and in Hessen and in Jülich; but was he serious? How much influence did his light-o'-loves have at the Swedish court?

If the marriage were to be merely a necessary expedient she foresaw a hard life for Renata. It was a great thing to be queen of the North; but the price might well be too high. Christina's mother had paid it. But her daughter must not pay such a penalty for those Northmen's ignorance of the dignity of princely rank and birth.

Precisely as expected, the Swedes returned. They had something to add, and presented the proposal she already knew about. Erik the Fourteenth requested the hand of Renata on condition that Christina relinquished all claim to inheritance of the Scandinavian kingdoms.

Christina summoned Peder Oxe, who as usual brought out his calculations.

Peder Oxe loved the information that came streaming in from his ever-increasing numbers of supporters, and he loved the arithmetical problems he built up with every newly acquired piece of knowledge. He sat there with his head hunched between his shoulders, staring at the pen's circumlocutions.

At present the Danish fleet was in harbour. The Danish king was minting money only one-third part silver, and he was obliged to mortgage one of his castles and borrow four hundred thousand dalers from the nobles, who had never fully committed themselves to the war.

Herluf Trolle had died of wounds he received down in Femarn ... marvellous ... marvellous ... and von Dohna drowned without a sound when his ship struck a fishing stake – even better. The treasures of the kingdom were being sold off, and the churches plundered of silver, all so that the king could pay his unruly mercenaries.

Peder Oxe calculated, and Christina knew what it was he was calculating. As he totted up his figures he tried, as an astrologer seeks to read the stars, to predict most accurately the exact date of financial collapse in the country he loved.

To know the day when with all honour and glory he would be called back to Denmark because he alone knew how to put her finances in order.

Christina could not blame Peder Oxe for his anticipations. They were human and understandable, they were much like her own. The problem was merely that Frederik would soon be where Peder Oxe wanted him, but Christina did not want Frederik to be anywhere at all. Peder Oxe claimed his share and his right – she claimed everything.

Peder Oxe's view of the Swedish marriage seemed clear. 'If I am asked to go back with the conditions I want I shall recommend the king to propose again to Lorraine. He will do so because he is in such great need that he will do everything I say. If I am not called back Denmark will perish, and then King Erik will have need of the Princess Renata in order to be able to call his conquests rightful possessions.'

Christina thanked Peder Oxe for his frank speaking. Though modesty was a virtue that could be exaggerated, this was not the case with Herr Peder.

He was feathering his own nest, and she could not blame him for that. His answers had their own inbuilt logic. But she dared not place her trust in his advice. Christina chose once more to let events take their course. She played dice and enjoyed the melodies of Thomas Tallis; meanwhile the early winter months went by.

Peder Oxe was a high-standing official in Lorraine, a ducal chamberlain. In his hands monies multiplied. At court functions many a beautiful noble lady glanced feelingly at the rich and mighty Dane who calculated everything on the basis of reason. He was often heard to say that no emperor or king had the power of the Fuggers or Medicis, banking houses that influenced the course of the world. They had the cash; they decided.

The prospect of going home made him as happy as a child. There was a soft spot in his mind behind all the arithmetic. He carried with him the recollection of the first twelve years of his life, with their sounds, smells and sights, and eleven younger siblings. It was something that could not be

323

repurchased with all the gold in the world, nor rediscovered abroad, albeit in the most beautiful country on earth.

Through these memories he possessed a part of his native land that was denied to Christina. He had watched the sun go down behind the green islands of the Småland sea, while she pictured the glowing sky behind the church spires of Mechelen. He understood the tongue that she had forgotten.

Those years again, those years that could not be changed. Twelve years of experience that could not be compensated for by the fancy that you remembered something to do with tar and stained wood and salt water slapping against a stern. The years that had given one a right based on a growing consciousness and memories, not on birth, inheritance and claims.

Peder Oxe wanted to go back and he had this to return to. When one day a safe conduct arrived, with an offer permitting him to reclaim his estates and position, Christina had to come to a decision.

Peder Oxe would save Denmark from economic catastrophe; but he would do this for the king she wanted to topple. She could keep him back; but then he would be of no value to her, and she would thereby acquire herself enemies in the Denmark where she had need of supporters.

Or she could let him go, and take away his Lorrainian lands from him. But that was not her intention, for all through the years Peder Oxe had been in Lorraine there had been a thought lurking at the back of her mind. It was not formulated, and it had never been expressed, for it was worthless as long as Peder Oxe remained in exile.

Frederik was well into his thirties. He called himself king, but he had not yet fulfilled his most elementary obligation, to supply heirs. And Frederik drank to excess, a habit which could cut short the strongest life.

What would happen if he were to die? Denmark would then have to find another monarch. One of his younger brothers? Perhaps. But perhaps not, for that was not as predominant a custom as the accession of a son.

Christina would allow Peder Oxe to go. When a ruler deferred so humbly to a nobleman, as Frederik had to Peder

Oxe, it made the nobleman indispensable, and put him in reality in the most powerful position in the land. Above king, above council of nobles, and in the strongest possible situation when a new sovereign must be appointed, should the present one drink himself to death without a queen and without children.

Peder Oxe was going home to Denmark. He would forget the honours she had awarded him; but not the land and fiefs, for all those she would allow him to keep.

The way to Peder Oxe's heart lay in land even if it was not Danish. As long as he had a fief under her control, as long as he was its owner – but only according to her decision – she held the power over Peder Oxe that would make him, when the time came to elect a new ruler in Denmark and Norway, point to her.

Christina duly announced to Peder Oxe that naturally he would remain a Lorrainian chamberlain and landed gentleman. Catching a flash of surprise in his otherwise controlled expression, she knew he understood. There was a little smile, an admiring affirmative smile, as he expressed his deep gratitude for her selfless generosity. He kissed her hand reverently and she realised she would miss her lengthy conversations with her talented compatriot.

For a moment she felt sad. But her spirits soon recovered. It was always possible that they would meet again.

Who knew how soon the king, no longer young, might die of drink? Who knew how soon she would be crowned queen of Denmark and Norway, without financial outlay and loss of human life, because Peder Oxe was in control of Denmark and she had taken care to keep control over him?

Peder Oxe left Lorraine. Meanwhile Christina did not intend to sit idle. The Swedish proposal was still on the cards; she needed to make contact with Charles de Mornay, and she must discover the truth about Erik the Fourteenth.

XXIV

When Charles de Mornay found himself the first person at court to be invited by the king to look round the newly finished tower room at Kalmar Castle he realised to the full how great a favourite he was with the king.

Erik the Fourteenth received him in the grey salon. The king was tall, blond and handsome, his hair cut close, his beard like a forked wheatsheaf on his black-clad chest.

'Monsieur de Mornay, come and see my chamber,' he said and opened the door to the little room. De Mornay entered.

The whole room was a work of art. There was wall panelling, in finely carved wood ornamented with Corinthian columns, and above the panelling were painted hunting scenes with wild boar, roe-deer, huntsmen and hounds. This part of the room was rather heavily Germanic in style; but the decoration of the window recesses was charming, in good Netherlands fashion.

Charles de Mornay was delighted. Not so much with what he saw – it bore no comparison with what could be found in his homeland – but at the honour of being the first to be shown what the German craftsmen Wulfrum and Schultz had been working on for so long.

Charles de Mornay had come to Kalmar five years earlier, in 1559. Then, as now, icy winds battered the fortress out on the point. As he took the narrow road to the south-western tower, he cursed himself for ever having ventured so far north. But the sight of the Swedish prince made him feel more at home. Not in colouring, not in stature, but in manners, speech and turn of phrase, the young duke was like a tropical plant in this ice-gripped land. He offered a welcome in excellent French, and Charles de Mornay felt an immediate empathy and affinity in mind and spirit.

The heir to the Swedish throne was the son of a man who had set the crown on his own head; his mother was a princess from one of Germany's least eminent principalities; and his half-siblings were of pure Swedish descent. Prince Erik was therefore the only person in his kingdom who could claim princely blood; also he lacked a fitting milieu and an adequate court. When his father took power Sweden had not had a king of its own for two centuries. The nobility versed in those Danish traditions that could have been adapted to Swedish usage had lost their heads on the scaffold during the Stockholm bloodbath, and the collapse of the Catholic Church had brought all learned scholarship and teaching to an end.

Old Gustav Vasa was what he was – a brilliant orator and agitator. He was fully aware of his own lack of education, and took care to summon as teachers to young Erik foreign disciples of Erasmus and Melanchthon. Nothing was too good for the self-appointed king's eldest son.

The prince fumbled his way forward. There was not a single person in his own country he could look to, no one who knew how to place musicians at a banquet or how to address a poet.

Who was high? Who was low? Of course there was rank and position to judge from, but there was also a lack of the elegance that stems from all those finer shades and natural irregularities that only the self-assured prince can permit himself. And at their very first meeting the prince confided to him that although his father considered silk suitable apparel he thought silver buttons sheer excess.

Mornay had arrived at a place where there was a use for him. He was aristocratic; he was a Protestant; he knew how things should be done; and he had met with a lord and master who wanted them done properly.

Five years went by, and Charles de Mornay and Sweden were now on intimate terms. He was familiar with the ringing sound of horses' hooves on the metre-thick ice of lakes and skerries, and with the high pillars of snow on birch and pine trunks. He was used to the reek from village chimneys and the sight of men slaving their hearts out dragging timber to the rivers in the spring thaw. He slowly learned to understand the language, and when he felt intoxication at the sight of green leaves breaking on the trees in mid-May he realised he was becoming a Swede.

But before that he had got to know the old king. It happened during the Vadstena affair.

Princess Cecilia, a tall, slender young lady with a taste for elegant clothes and handsome men, had been receiving nocturnal visits through her window from the count of East Frijsland. It was de Mornay who caught the young man in the act, clad in nothing but his shirt.

Gustav Vasa did not thank de Mornay for his initiative. He was furious with his daughter, with the count, and with de Mornay, who was condemned to a long spell of imprisonment as a punishment for his clumsy behaviour. The incident gave de Mornay the opportunity for reflecting on what it was that constituted kingly mores. On his release he discovered that Prince Erik had tried to shoulder all the blame, while the unfortunate young lady had run around shrieking in fear of her father.

In due time old Gustav Vasa died, and Erik was crowned king, as Erik the Fourteenth. He had arrived at this high number through intensive reading of Johannes Magnus's history of Sweden, according to which there had been no less than thirteen Eriks before him, including the legendary kings.

He also became His Majesty. The distinguished title had formerly been restricted to the German–Roman emperors, but in recent times the kings of Europe had also claimed this form of address, and Erik did not wish to lag behind his equals in the great world outside.

The coronation was to be on a scale worthy of a ruler by God's grace. Erik wished to be a king of the new era. He sought strong kingly power with which every outward symbol must match.

Again the problem of want of tradition presented itself. Everything was so new. Precious stones had to be brought from abroad; likewise silks and velvets and red English cloth. Orders went out too for aulochs, lions, camels and other animals not native to Sweden, all so that the populace and the world outside should recognise the king's might and eminence.

The king's agent did not succeed in finding the exotic animals – none were to be had on the market – but the jewels arrived, and the silks, and everything else; and with his perception of what others had that he himself lacked, Erik appointed barons and counts from among his courtiers. It was that kind of thing that gave lustre to the English court, and he wished to be no less glorious.

The coronation at Uppsala, followed by the entry into Stockholm, was a triumph. Sweden had acquired a great king, but there was no queen.

De Mornay was made privy to the political plans behind the courtship of England. Sweden had only one harbour, Älvsborg on the west; but it was enough to provide bait for the Swedish envoys. England urgently wanted trade with Russia, where goods could be bought for resale at a profit of several hundred per cent. But the route around the North Cape was long and difficult. A marriage between Queen Elizabeth and King Erik would provide an easier, cheaper and less dangerous way for the English, via Älvsborg and over the Gulf of Finland, while Sweden would escape from its claustrophobic sense of Danish envelopment.

Even though Elizabeth rejected the offer, de Mornay saw the statesmanship behind the proposal; and he applauded the king's ideas in many other connections.

De Mornay had a great admiration for King Erik, and there were no limits to his loyalty. He was aware of his master's suspicious nature, but felt that there were grounds for it. De Mornay saw what went on around the king. He heard the casual remarks of powerful Swedes, and the undertones implying that since a noble, not so long ago, had made himself king, such a thing might well happen again.

When a Herr Sture or a Herr Leijonhuved looked at their king, it was with an it-might-just-as-well-be-me expression. The king saw it, de Mornay saw it, and it went far to explain the king's untoward choice of feminine society.

There were a Karin Jacobsdatter, a Karin Pedersdatter, an Anna Larsdatter, a Britta and an Ingrid. They were women of the people, young peasant girls with healthy complexions who could neither read nor write. But with all their primitive manners they gave the king the security he could never have from an aristocratic young lady with a covetous family behind her. They were simple, knew their place, demanded nothing, and thus presented no danger.

But it worried de Mornay that their position at court was semi-official – they were not decorative, could neither comport themselves gracefully nor utter a sensible word, and did nothing for the king's reputation abroad.

It was essential to find a queen. De Mornay had tried Mary Stuart, while she was living as a widow in France. Her refusal came as no surprise. But it worried him that despite his own eager proposals the king regarded these solely as political missions. He did not evince the least desire for an intelligent, knowledgeable and distinguished wife, who could give him security of quite another exalted kind.

While in France, de Mornay wrote to the duchess of Lorraine, telling her of the friendly sentiments of the king of Sweden.

When the duchess's name had been mentioned at the French court, Catherine of Medici had exclaimed, 'That is one of the most glorious princesses of our time.' This had whetted de Mornay's interest in the Danish-born duchess, and no less in her daughters. The younger was deformed, he heard, so she was out of the running. But that still left the elder. Their mother was famed for her beauty, so the daughter must be a reasonable proposition. There was also a claim to the inheritance of the Danish kingdom, with all its harbours and with the Skåne, Halland and Blekinge, which King Erik had discovered in Johannes Magnus had of old been Swedish lands.

The claim was a serious nuisance to the Danish king, and

the gracious young lady was related both by marriage and blood to France and the mighty Hapsburgs.

De Mornay was delighted with his own idea. King Erik, however, was not. He was horrified, and reminded de Mornay that this Renata was the grandchild of the most loathed man in Sweden, of Christian the Tyrant himself, against whom his own father had marched.

De Mornay did not give up the idea, and when rumours came that Denmark had gone courting in Lorraine the king grew thoughtful. The duchess called herself queen of Denmark and Sweden and Norway. She could pass on her rights to her daughter in the event of a Nordic marriage. If she became a Danish queen there was that 'and Sweden'; but if she became a Swedish queen there would be an 'and Denmark and Norway'.

De Mornay had gone a step closer; and he came closer still after war broke out and the Danish Peder Oxe, journeying north, put out feelers for negotiations with the Swedes.

She was interested, that great lady in her little dukedom; accordingly she was urged to send representatives to Sweden.

But the king went back to his dreams of wedding the English queen. He cursed that earl who was in such high favour with her, and de Mornay began to suspect a practical motive behind the wish to marry Elizabeth. After all, she lived so very far away and surely would not dream of going to Stockholm. That would allow King Erik to strengthen his hand with a mighty and distinguished wife, and in day-to-day life go on amusing himself with his uncomplicated little playmates.

The king played the lute, enlarged his library, cultivated his literary interests and worked on the legal system. The law was to be written in Swedish, so that everyone could understand it; and he showed perspicacity in advancing the country's self-sufficiency in bronze ore, silver and timber. The prince and the state were one and the same and all concerns were his.

King Erik supported Grumbach and his intrigues against

Saxony. He was determined to gather as many friends as possible around him, in order to isolate Denmark. He sent emissaries to seek an alliance with Lorraine with the proposal that Denmark should be shared between him and the duchess. She should relinquish Norway and all the land east of the Sound.

But de Mornay continued to press him. Marriage was the best solution. Sometimes the king could be too hasty in his dealings with the nobles. A woman was needed, a high-born, distinguished woman. If the princess Renata possessed but half of her mother's virtues as they were acclaimed all over Europe the king would be saved from the dangers of his own nature, which saw too much, imagined too much and thus feared too much.

On that day when de Mornay was shown the king's newly decorated chamber at Kalmar Castle he also noticed the royal coat of arms on the outside of the door. It bore the three Danish lions and the Norwegian lion carrying the axe. He put the idea it expressed to the king. With Renata at his side he could not only conquer the whole of the North; he could also proclaim it his rightful property.

King Erik looked at de Mornay and a light came into his pale eyes. 'All of the North,' he said thoughtfully, 'All of it ...?' Doubt assailed him again, however, and he asked anxiously if the princess was really beautiful. He inquired too if she was wily, for if so he would not have her but would marry her to another after she had arrived in Sweden.

In the end de Mornay persuaded his master to send secret instructions to his emissaries. If the duchess of Lorraine could not accept the first proposal for a combined attack on Denmark in return for a share of the regained lands, they were to try for marriage; but in that event King Erik would demand the whole of the North.

De Mornay was in action. He advised on diplomatic issues; he lived the life of the court; he was entertaining, in his joking medley of Swedish and Latin; and he drank with his master, who generally preferred the company of foreigners, his servants and the people.

But Erik the Fourteenth still showed no desire for a woman of equal position. He kept on his harem of peasant girls, and de Mornay took note of something he did not like.

Her name was Karin Månsdotter. She came of peasant stock, a round-headed, broad-hipped girl, apparently just as shy and awkward as the rest. She began to learn to read and write and before long she was engaged in the very personal task of making the king's shirts.

What did she mean to use that learning for? No alphabet was necessary for the use to which she was put. Karin stayed as shy and gentle as ever; but slowly and surely she edged out the other girls until she had the king to herself.

De Mornay pinned his hopes on Lorraine. He hoped desperately that the duchess would accept, but the reply brought back by the Swedish emissaries in 1565 was very vague. And when spring came, little Karin's stomach was as bulging as her hips were broad. She was with child.

What kept the duchess back? Could it be the influence of that Peder Oxe? They said he was regaining favour in Denmark, and de Mornay feared that this might result in a new proposal from the Danish king.

King Erik would caress his Karin – but would send her out next moment and tell de Mornay he would marry Princess Renata even if he had to take an army to fetch her. De Mornay concocted a rapid plan to go to Lorraine himself. Since he was so close to the king the duchess would surely have more confidence in his own words, and would explain whatever objections she might have. The king seemed enthusiastic; but then hesitated, showed uncertainty, and called in little Karin again.

De Mornay could now speak fluent Swedish. He had a Swedish wife who had come up to all his expectations, and he was unquestioningly loyal to his king. He regarded Erik with fatherly affection, but also with a father's anxiety.

He had gradually grown familiar with the country, with the primitive castles, with the deep pine forests that were menacing and gloomy summer and winter alike, and with the seasons' violent changes from light, playfulness and gentle airs to cold, darkness and fear. But he could never grow used to not being able to read the Bible or any other book or manuscript during the long winter months, when the costly candles gave scant light even in the richest homes. He had felt an affinity at his first meeting with King Erik, but the fact remained that their characters had been formed under different latitudes.

The extremes of nature did not affect de Mornay. His mind was not scarred by the melancholy, so suddenly changeable to brutality that he had seen in these pale Northern people, or that he had seen in the king and which he feared would deprive him of common sense.

At the end of summer, while Karin Månsdotter's stomach grew great, Nils Hansson was sent to Lorraine. He swore to return both with the princess's likeness and with her consent. De Mornay sent up a fervent prayer that he would succeed, for King Erik's sake, for Sweden's sake, and for Nils Hansson's sake.

Months later de Mornay himself entered the field. The Danes under Daniel Rantzau were on their way to attack at Guldberg Enge and de Mornay marched despondently to meet them with his Swedish peasant army. A battle seemed likely. They faced the arch-enemy, and the battle must be won.

Christina grew more and more irritated with her daughter-in-law. The girl was always complaining that she was short of money and making pointed remarks about having to keep a smaller and less splendid court than her mother-in-law. If she was dissatisfied she should have brought more with her from France. What else had she imagined? She, Christina, was queen. Catherine of Medici herself acknowledged it, bowed to her as to an equal and addressed her publicly as such. Naturally she had a right to greater state. Surely there would be no discussion.

Besides, Claude was never properly stylish. She was decidedly unattractive with her prominent Medici eyes and blown-up Medici cheeks. And why should it have been the least interesting of the three French princesses that her son had brought home? Or any of them for that matter?

Christina could never accustom herself to having a

335

daughter-in-law from that bunch of children. The eldest son was dead, the next one, who was now king though a minor still, looking anything but strong. Altogether it was an odd set of weaklings Catherine had brought into the world.

But at least Claude could bear healthy children, with good strong Danish Oldenburg blood in them. She was nonetheless narrow-minded and moralistic, which seemed to be the fashion with the young; and she interfered in things which had nothing to do with her.

Christina was constantly forced to listen to remarks about this or that French prince, who would be the ideal husband for Renata or Dorothea, and to questions about when they were to be married.

Claude had no idea of what was at stake. To her the world consisted of France; Lorraine was merely a kind of country estate. She could not comprehend that there were other countries and other crowns, and when Carl made plans to beautify Nancy and buy works of art from Italy it was his mother he went to for advice.

Christina had naturally forgiven the unfriendly words that had once been spoken between herself and Carl. There could not be a more loving son. They could amuse themselves for hours planning new squares and deciding where to place fountains.

A suitor presented himself. This time it was to Dorothea.

The duke of Bavaria thought it would be a good match for his son Wilhelm. Christina was inclined to agree. It was perhaps not as prestigious as she might have wished, but he was an attractive young man. She had to take the girl's bad foot into consideration; and it was certainly a distinguished family.

She should probably accept. She would still have Renata in reserve, for her elder daughter was intended for something far more exalted than a dukedom.

Peder Oxe returned unexpectedly on a visit. He wanted to see to his lands. Christina found it incredible that he was permitted to visit Lorraine so freely.

Peder Oxe brought a message from his master. He said

the king of Denmark was mightily incensed over Schwarzburg's conduct in Frankfurt. It had been directly against all orders.

Christina nodded and smiled and Peder Oxe smiled too as he put forward the idea of renewed marriage negotiations between Frederik and Renata. Having done so, he had said what had to be said and could calmly return to the king, who really only wanted his Lady Anna, without an answer from the duchess, who would not dream of letting her daughter bear heirs to the Danish throne and thus bar the way for herself. Frederik had changed neither his life-style nor the object of his affections. It all seemed as promising as it could be.

But Christina had not dismissed the idea of a grand campaign. There were still two possibilities. She could wait until immoderate drinking put an end to Frederik's childless life; or she could conquer the attenuated country, using Hapsburg money.

Then there was Sweden.

She had to wait until the autumn of 1566 before an envoy came from the North. When he did, it was not de Mornay, as she had hoped. Nils Hansson presented himself as proxy, with orders to propose to Renata. Christina began to speculate.

This envoy, an extremely attractive man, tall and blond, never failed to speak of his master as his Royal Majesty. Christina had not thought of it before, but perhaps she too should use this title.

This was a digression, however. It was a marriage she was concerned with at present. With herself on the way to Denmark it might be a good idea to have Renata in Sweden. She was prompted partly by her lack of knowledge of the king as an individual, and partly because Sweden was rightfully hers to claim.

Why should she in fact share, if she could get the lot? Queen Margrethe had united the North; why could it not be done again? With the unrest that there was in the Netherlands, Philip must soon come. She would set off herself and explain the situation to him.

It struck Christina that the Swedish envoy was nervous. He was to take back with him Renata's consent to the marriage; meanwhile he stood there begging as if his own life was at stake. Surely it was not as bad as that? Could he not understand that now Peder Oxe was back in Denmark the situation had altered considerably? Christina waved him away with a half-promise of letting them know later.

She recognised the same fear in another Swede who turned up. Meanwhile de Mornay had been taken prisoner by the Danes, having lost a battle against Rantzau at Guldberg Enge. The news irritated her.

This latest representative was a member of one of the greatest families in the country. His name was Niels Sture. His hair was so fair it looked white. Christina gave the same reply. She would send a message in a few months.

This winter proved still harder than the preceding ones. Braziers were kept burning indoors as well as in the streets and squares. You could keep warm only in rooms that had closed stoves; and every year Christina felt the cold more.

She had grown old; now and again she felt too old. But indignation could still seize her, as when the duke of Bavaria sent a message to say that he did not want Dorothea for his son after all. He did not hide the fact that it was because of her deformity, and he had the insolence to suggest that Renata should take her place.

'Never!' cried Christina when Carl brought the message. Renata might be a queen at any moment. She only had to choose. If only de Mornay had not let himself be caught by the Danes she would have given Sweden her word. And if Renata were not to marry in the North there was always one of the emperor's sons. Besides, the contract with Dorothea had been practically finalised, and offers should not be refused on account of a small blemish like one misshapen foot.

Carl said not a word. The Shrovetide celebrations went on in Nancy's snow-covered streets. Meanwhile Claude returned from a visit to her mother with shocking news.

Mary Stuart's husband was dead. Catherine of Medici had been informed by her agents in London, which was seething

338

with talk of what had happened in Scotland. The Scots queen's consort had been murdered.

'They blew up his house with gunpowder,' said Claude stiffly.

'They did what?' asked Christina.

'The explosion was heard all over Edinburgh,' added Claude and went on, 'They say it was that brute the earl of Bothwell who did it, and that Mary loves him and wants to marry him. There was not even a proper funeral, and Mary kept on going to balls. It is more than the Scots will tolerate. After all, he was her husband.'

Christina was shaken. She was reminded of Catherine of Medici's thoroughgoing knowledge of herbs and medicaments of every kind, and what they could be used for. She asked Claude for her mother's comments.

'My mother just said, "With gunpowder!" I think she was amazed.'

The events in Scotland were the dominant topic of discussion during Lent. But the Easter celebration was overshadowed by something Christina had never experienced before. The day before Palm Sunday a family quarrel broke out.

It began when Renata burst into tears. Christina was completely unprepared for the flood of tears that streamed down the girl's cheeks. She rushed over to her to find the cause of this despair. But the girl merely held her handkerchief to her eyes and went on sobbing.

'But, dearest child!' said Christina, stroking the black hair. 'Oh, no,' she thought. 'I can't have her unhappy over anything.'

'She is not a child any longer,' said Carl coldly. 'Perhaps that is what is wrong. She is extremely adult, and she is extremely unmarried.'

Christina straightened herself beside her weeping daughter. Carl raised his white wine to his lips and looked at his mother over the rim of his glass. Christina looked at Claude, who was smiling at her husband admiringly.

There was a pause. Renata lifted her head from her lacy handkerchief. Her sobs had abated. It was dark outside and windless. The only sounds in the yellow room at the palace of Nancy were the hissing of logs and faint noises from the servants' quarters.

Carl slowly lowered his glass, and put it down on a chest of carved maple she had had sent from Antwerp as a present to him: 'You are playing for high stakes with your daughters' health. Late pregnancies tend to cause death.'

That was too much for Christina. How dare he set himself up against her? 'They are only . . . only . . .'

She halted, suddenly could not remember. How old were they now?

'They will soon be twenty-two and twenty-three,' came drily from Carl. He rose. 'Renata would be happy in Bavaria. Haven't you realised that? Does it matter at all to you? Or are you putting your power before her future happiness?'

He must be mad. Did he not know anything about the times he was living in? But as if he read her thoughts he said, 'I am tired of female power, tired of you forgetting what you were made for. I used to have a mother. I thought I had one. But she went rushing around, wielding power and travelling. I lay in bed at night, sometimes with earache or a sore throat. I said my prayers to others, and others had to bid me goodnight and sleep well. I was so little; I dreamed about my sweet-scented mother; I longed for her, but she did not come. I remember the longing but I don't remember her presence.'

Carl turned slowly away from the fire. She saw his eyes, those big brown eyes that were like a mirror of her own, but they expressed only a haughty anger. She had fought to keep him; for him she would have given up everything. She had thrown herself on her knees before the king of France, begging and weeping. Since then no one had seen her weep, and now they thought she did not possess the emotions that brought tears. She was strong, they said, and could stand anything; and therefore she would have to stand and bear this as well.

'Come along,' said Dorothea gently. She had stood up and put an arm around her mother's shoulders.

Dimly as through a mist Christina remembered a 'Come

along', but it was so infinitely long ago; and now it was her handicapped daughter, the deserted bride, who was the only one to understand.

'Mother,' said Dorothea quietly when they were alone, 'Let Renata have him.'

Christina looked up. 'And you?'

The girl smiled, pointed to her foot. 'He'll never have me anyway. Neither he nor anyone else.'

She said it cheerfully, evincing neither anger nor grief; and Christina understood why Dorothea alone understood.

An hour later Carl came to Christina's room. He was unhappy, apologetic. 'I didn't mean it – I spoke hastily,' he said. He was worried nonetheless about his sisters, and implored her to put the idea of a Swedish marriage alliance out of her head. 'Accept Bavaria. Make up your mind. Sometimes you make me think of a ship sailing up and down between two shores, just going on because the captain can't decide on which side to drop anchor.'

Carl went on, talking of the king of Sweden, whom he considered to be mad, and about Renata's prospects, while Christina just stared at him. How much did he know about her father; what had they stuffed him with at that French court? Did he have the comparison in mind, or was the expression he used merely a coincidence?

His voice was no longer hostile, and his expression was affectionate. But there was something he had to say. 'There is only one way to Denmark and that is through Frederik the Second's childlessness and speedy death.'

'Or through a Hapsburg army,' answered Christina reprovingly.

This was her affair, not his. She would hear no more, for with his French way of thinking he could not appreciate the value of her maternal forebears, nor what Philip owed her.

Carl stopped his pacing. He bent over her, took her hands and held them to his face as if for protection. There was something he was afraid to say. 'The emperor adhered to your claim to inheritance at Speyer. But at the same time as

341

that treaty was signed, secret instructions from him to Philip were drawn up.'

Carl looked at her and went on slowly, 'I have a copy of them. In them he is advised never to wage war against Denmark in order to obtain the claim. It is too far away. It is too dangerous for the Netherlands' supplies. There's the value of a Hapsburg family for you.'

That night Christina read the instructions. She held her candle to the text and her eyes smarted. But she read the words, coldly and soberly, as she looked treachery straight in the eye. Christina made no attempt to tell herself it was a fake. There was nothing to interpret, nothing to mistake. In Milan, and in Lorraine, she had done her duty towards the house of Hapsburg and its policies. But she would never receive anything in return.

She was surprised at her own equanimity. Had she instinctively been expecting this? There had been that lack of feeling, the absence of sorrow other than a formal expression, when her uncle had died in Spain. He had tried to help her in Lorraine, but it was for the sake of his own military interests, not for hers. She was merely the poor niece. To be used, not rewarded.

In the midst of all these thoughts Christina continued to feel surprise at her lack of shock. Perhaps it was overshadowed by something else, something that went deeper.

When she finally put the paper down she lay thinking of green shores. Two green shores beside a narrow fairway called Little Belt. She envisioned the ship. Her father was the captain and it was sailing up and down, up and down. Indecisive, irresolute, he could not make up his mind which side to make for.

She was her father's daughter. If she had been sailing up and down she would have to stop now. There was only one shore left, only one place to drop anchor in and go ashore. The emperor's orders had made the other vanish. She would have to wait for the death of the childless king.

When summer came Christina accepted the offer of marriage from Bavaria.

342

And while the people of Edinburgh demonstrated against their queen and openly called her the whore who married her husband's murderer, Erik the Fourteenth likewise made himself a murderer.

The unfortunate Nils Hansson was executed for failing to obtain Renata's consent. Worse, the king, mad with fury, personally plunged the knife into Niels Sture, and ordered his halberdiers to cut down all the man's relatives.

This eliminated her final doubts. The betrothal of Renata and William of Bavaria took place in Lorraine in August. The young pair swiftly came to know each other and Renata shone with happiness.

Now, all thoughts of angry words and treacherous instructions were to be cast aside. There must be feasting and celebration, a wedding to be renowned in history.

Bavaria, 1568–1578

XXV

Renata was married to Wilhelm of Bavaria in Munich in February 1568. It was a celebration that surpassed anything that had ever happened before. Princes from all over Europe came flocking to the town. Triumphal arches were erected, and there were tournaments and balls and popular festivals. While it was still going on, rumours began to circulate among peasants, servants and small tradesmen that the terrible Doctor Faust, who had sold his soul to the Devil, was still living and had been paid by three rich counts to transport them swiftly to join in the city's remarkable events. Doctor Faust had used his magic cloak and helped the three distinguished gentlemen to fly through the air all the way from Wittenberg to Munich.

Christina was amused at this story, which showed how successful the celebration had been. She knew very well that the Bavarian ducal couple had been overwhelmed at the sight of her court. As the bridegroom's parents they were responsible for the wedding and they had summoned experts and goods from all over the world to match up to her, while it fell on Christina herself to provide the bride's trousseau and appointments.

On her wedding day Renata wore a dress of heavy silk as blue as the winter sky over Bavaria. Her black hair was sprinkled with diamonds, sparkling as if the Milky Way had been brought down to earth for her veil.

Springtime and fertility were symbolised as well. Her dress was embroidered with flowers in gold and silver thread, which were then sewn in all their natural colours with precious stones; and over it she wore a coat lined with ermine and chequered with gold brocade and Brussels lace.

But most important were the pearls. These, the most precious of all jewels, were poured upon Renata. Christina had chosen every one of them. They must not be too dark nor too pink, yet not as cold as snow. They should have just the right velvety white, to reflect the bride's beautiful teeth. None must be smaller than a full-grown pea; and on her daughter's breast Christina had fastened the most exquisite pearl of all, delicate in its sheen and the size of a muscatel grape.

A murmur of astonishment arose from the assembled onlookers when Renata made her entrance as a bride. The most princely fell dumb at such a sight. Christina knew heartfelt satisfaction; and for long afterwards she was delighted to hear guesses about whether the dress had cost more than 100,000. Nothing had been too fine for her daughter's wedding. When she saw Renata beside the young duke, who was dressed all in white with gold embroidery and sables, she wept tears of joy. She prayed that they might be happy and blessed with beautiful healthy children, and that God would hold His hand over them.

Christina had come to a decision even before she had finished preparing her daughter's trousseau. She knew very well that it would occasion surprise, but she did not greatly care. She would go and live with her daughter; she would move to Bavaria.

Of course it was contrary to custom for a mother-in-law to move with her daughter, but then she was not any ordinary mother-in-law; and she could not be expected to tolerate Claude for ever more. Renata would have need of her; it would help her to have some support in her new country. Then, too, Christina felt that the political situation in Bavaria would be interesting for her, after sitting idle in Lorraine, where no one asked her opinion any more.

Since her clash with Carl he had been the most loving son imaginable. True, the expenses of Renata's wedding had brought a few groans from him; but Christina found it easy to shut her ears to them.

She and Carl were fully in accord when they discussed

works of art or town planning; but she failed to understand his political ideas. She could never get used to the Frenchness of his mind. He altered laws and decrees that she had made; for example heresy was being punished again with the stake. Carl pointed to the chaos that reigned in France because his mother-in-law had been far too merciful, whereas Christina fought to make him see that it was merely a case of lost souls. Surely in the long run people could not go on thinking that salvation was only a matter of grace.

It was no use. She was old, and old-fashioned. After the wedding the young couple moved to Landshut, and Christina and Dorothea went with them.

Landshut, on the river Isar, was a court of the muses. The melodies of Orlando di Lasso echoed through the old castle of the Wittelsbachs. Church music and hunters' choirs were often heard, and Duke Wilhelm sang and played the lute with them. There was commedia dell'arte, and the gallery of masks and the fool's staircase resounded to Renata's tripping steps and her laughter, light and lilting as if her pearls were transformed from substance to sound. She ran with her Wilhelm through mazes and labyrinths in the gardens, hid in pavilions and behind statues, played pell-mell over the lawns or watched the rare animals in the zoo.

Renata had taken her whole train of tumblers, Moors, dwarves and turban-clad black boys with her. They were in attendance on her together with musicians and clowns; they ran behind in her races, and shared her joys and occasional sorrows when a parrot died in its gilded cage or a rare plant would not put down roots and withered in its bed.

Christina was too stiff and slow for games in the labyrinth or running about. As the months went by she realised that she was sitting there with her lame daughter as an onlooker. Only through sight and hearing was she living Renata's life. It was a dissemblance, something she could only pretend to share in so as to assuage the pains of her body and the mirror's truth.

Christina liked Bavaria, though; she liked the country

itself and the correspondence she had with Renata's father-in-law about home and foreign affairs. She decided to move to a little distance away, and chose Friedberg.

They had beheaded Egmont and Hoorn in the square in front of Brussels Town Hall. Both men had been old friends of Christina, and she wept for them.

Thousands had been executed already in her old country, since Margaret of Parma gave in and the duke of Alba pushed through Europe and into the Netherlands with an army of weather-beaten veterans, to impose his bloody decree on the populace. Where was Wilhelm of Orange?

It took some time before Christina obtained an answer. He had turned tail. He had been the only one to suspect mischief, and he had fled to Germany. Even so, his fortunes were confiscated and his son was seized as a hostage and sent to Spain.

Christina was furious. If she had been regent in the Netherlands or in her rightful place in Denmark this would never have happened. She would have allowed the ships to pass and the Netherlanders to receive their supplies so that they did not starve, storm the corn stores and listen to demented Calvinists.

She wept again. She thought of Egmont's wife and children. Where were they now? And Wilhelm, now poor and calling himself a Protestant, still with his hunchbacked wife, who had lost his son as she had once lost Carl.

They were dead, Egmont and Hoorn, having been made guilty of all the misfortunes Philip had created.

'Well, well,' mumbled Christina, exhausted by indignation at last. Perhaps in time he would revise his ideas. Meanwhile in Denmark Master Frederik was still alive – but he was just as unmarried as before. Christina did not lose sight of her aim even though she was living in Bavaria, nor did she cease to collect information from Denmark.

There was always someone who had met somebody who had been there. Whether they had liked the country or not they all agreed that Peder Oxe held the most prestigious post in Denmark, second only to the king. In reality it was he who ruled the king, a fact that even the queen dowager had to accept.

When the Fuggers of Augsburg had had a representative in Copenhagen, he not only provided oral reports but also a written one, and Christina asked for a copy – written in large letters, for her sight was failing.

The Fuggers were having problems with King Philip, who would not pay his debts. Another banking house, the Mannlichers, were taking some of their business, and the Fuggers were looking for new clients. They sent a Herr Wusenbenzc to Denmark. He was to sell harquebuses and find out if the Danes would buy copper. Also he was to provide a complete report on the country, its inhabitants and its principal citizens.

Christina read the papers eagerly. This was not mere gossip at second hand, but an intelligent statement. However, Wusenbenzc was obviously influenced by Rantzau's views, and when he described the Danes as a 'wicked and malicious mob' she felt free to form her own opinion.

Such opinions, which stemmed from Holstein, made the factual details no less valuable.

The nobles in Denmark were neither faithful nor true to the king. Thus far, things were entirely satisfactory.

Wusenbenzc was speaking for himself, meanwhile, when he wrote that Frederik was 'a tall, strong, upstanding man, a prince possessed of great intelligence and good understanding'. Christina also read that this Master Frederik frittered away his nights with drink and loose women, and enjoyed being entertained by a German stable-boy who played the Polish bagpipes. What deplorable lack of style!

Peder Oxe was someone for whom Wusenbenzc did not care. There were reasons for that, perhaps, for it was Peder Oxe who decided whether or not the harquebuses should be bought, and something indicated that he had declined. Nor did the Fuggers succeed in selling any copper.

Wusenbenzc described Peder Oxe thus: 'This Oxe was governor and the highest gentleman and counsellor of all.' Then followed a remark that made Christina laugh aloud:

'. . . The one who has Peder Oxe has the king, the one who has Lorraine has Peder Oxe . . .'

Yes, indeed she had Peder Oxe. They seemed to have discovered that, even up there. For although she was in Bavaria she still held control over Oxe's lands; not even Carl interfered in that.

Christina read the sentence again and again with pleasure. There must be some Holstein gentlemen, certainly, who were not pleased to see Peder Oxe back in Denmark with a hook in his collar and a tether stretching right down to Lorraine and herself.

They had a man who called himself king; but they had no queen, and still no sign of one. Time was passing. The year was passing. She looked at her death's-head clock. The hand between the silver teeth had moved on. Mad King Erik's younger brother had seized power in Sweden; Erik, though, had managed to marry his light-o'-love. The war went on, while Christina waited and waited and kept firm hold of her long, long tether up to the real ruler in Denmark, to Peder Oxe, who had the king.

'Ex his una tibi' proclaimed the letters in black enamel round the hand. Still, the hour seemed to be taking its time.

Christina kept her eye on news from near and far. Her thoughts went to Mary Stuart, who had lost her crown, fled and ended up in captivity in England. She also pondered the desperate state of affairs in both France and the Netherlands.

Christina's sister was still alive, as disgruntled and dissatisfied as before. News came that the Scandinavian war had come to an end; and in the autumn of 1571 she was fifty.

'Una tibi', but not yet. She would relish another hour, the one that was his, for it was bound to come first. Christina was stubbornly waiting for the death of Frederik the Second.

A small item of news from Denmark affected her more than she would have supposed. Peder Oxe had married. What was this feeling? Jealousy? Perhaps.

She was the king's daughter, he only a nobleman. There was a gulf between them. But she had taken pleasure in his voice, his words, his talent, and his wise round eyes; and she had to acknowledge that there had been more. They were so unequal in rank and birth, but so equal in thought. And how they had laughed at the same things, hit on the same ideas and understood all that was left unsaid.

Christina would not admit that she had been in love with Peder Oxe. She was much too old for that, she told herself. But what a marriage they could have had, what a partnership; days ... and nights too ... the flight of thoughts brought a glow to her cheeks. She could recall the sound of his voice, 'marvellous ... marvellous ...' and she laughed a low intimate laugh, 'marvellous ... marvellous ...'

She sighed. Why couldn't destiny have exchanged their roles and let him be Frederik and Frederik be Peder Oxe? Then all the pieces would have fallen into place, and she would not be sitting here in Bavaria suffering this tedium of waiting.

Christina still had control over Peder Oxe's Lorrainian lands. Peder Oxe still had control over Denmark. What they had shared in Lorraine had been conversation and conversation only. But Christina missed him; she missed him as a man.

She went out hunting rarely now, lacking the strength. But she went on journeys, visited Carl in Nancy, and enjoyed seeing the increasing family of grandchildren. She was thoroughly enjoying herself among them one day when Carl made a joke. 'The king of Denmark is married.'

She had heard it so often. It was a standard remark, to say the king of Denmark had married, for that was what he did not do. Everyone knew that. Carl did not laugh. He was deadly serious, and repeated. 'The king of Denmark is married.'

'You can't mean it,' said Christina, already knowing this was not a joke. There was a moment's silence. She felt she could hear every sound all over the great house. Carl said slowly, 'The duchess of Mecklenburg presented herself at Copenhagen Castle holding her fifteen-year-old daughter Sophie by the hand and said: "Now get married." It was as simple as that. He did it; he married Sophie.'

Christina gave a piercing, inhuman scream. She seized a

porcelain dish and hurled it to the floor, then picked up the silver candlesticks and threw them at the wall. She shrieked, wanting sounds, din. It must be deafened, muffled, broken; this marriage must be wiped out, if she had to slay it with her own hands. She rained blows on the hearth with the poker.

She stopped. It had vanished as it had fallen upon her. Carl was shocked, but she did not care. She felt only emptiness, a strange, exhausted condition of nothingness.

She had had the feeling before but could not think when. It was as if the whole thing had happened before, and this was merely a repetition. It was odd really, that she could think such a thing at a moment like this.

Carl was talking, gently, cautiously, reassuringly. But she did not need that; she did not need anything any more.

Sophie of Mecklenburg, well . . . ah, well . . . She could go on hoping, of course, that there would be no children. A queen was no heir. But she was only fifteen and sure to be healthy and strong. It was too weak a straw to cling to; of course she would have children.

The Scandinavian war was over. In Sweden Erik's brother was on the throne; he too was a married man. In Denmark Frederik had a fruitful little bride at his side, while Peder Oxe's careful calculations had saved the country from economic ruin.

The actions of an over-zealous duchess had snapped a long, long tether. The other distant green shore sank into the sea. The chance she had had when Denmark was impoverished by war against the Swedes had been wasted. At one blow Christina was as old as her years.

Carl was affectionate and solicitous, good boy that he was. Naturally he loved her. How could she ever have doubted it? After all, she was his mother. He brought her diversion, in the form of talk and news from the world that had become so distant.

Claude's youngest sister was to be married. She was an impossible chit, whom Catherine found harder to control than the whole of rebellious France. There was hardly one man at the French court who could not boast of acquaintance with her bed and body. Now, however, it was to be Henry of Navarre who had the honour – or whatever it might be called – to give her his consent at the altar.

Christina could not really give her mind to such matters. It did not concern her. Except that she remembered how this Henry of Navarre's mother once did something she had always envied her for; she had thrown herself down on the church floor and screamed, and succeeded in getting the one she loved. She was dead now; but Christina couldn't help wondering if her son was equally stubborn.

Leave them to it. A sad and despondent Christina returned to Bavaria and to Renata and Wilhelm. There, everyone was full of the news from Paris.

Catherine had finally pulled herself together and cracked down on the Huguenots. Thousands of them had been drawn to Paris by the wedding. They thought it was to be a festival of reconciliation between the two denominations, this marriage between Catholic Marguerite and Protestant Henry of Navarre; but it had turned into a blood wedding. Once they had fallen into the trap the slaughter began, on St Bartholomew's Night. No count had been made yet of how many heretics had been wiped out, but the bridegroom was not among them, unfortunately.

Renata clapped enthusiastically and Carl wrote ecstatic letters. Now that accursed plague would be eradicated throughout France. It was said that down in Spain Philip was heard to laugh when the courier came from Paris.

There was jubilation at the Catholic courts and horror at the Protestant ones over the brutal killings. Christina felt she no longer understood the world. She could not keep up with it all; it was nothing to do with her. She merely gazed coldly at her daughter-in-law when Claude described the heaps of corpses lying in the streets as she, her mother and the whole court had gone from the Louvre to the Palais de la Justice in the August heat of Paris.

Christina had nothing to do with it, but she still felt impotence and disgust at what had happened. She was a mere spectator, a superfluous old widow whose opinion was never asked because it was worthless.

She could retire to a convent. Or she could go to her dower

house in Italy, where she could gaze out over the Po valley until it pleased God to take her to Him. What *was* she to do with herself? Why didn't she feel tired, like her aunt? Why did she never feel the urge to cultivate flowers in a walled convent garden?

A letter arrived, and Christina roused herself with a start. Everything came back, energy, willpower, vitality. Her role was not played out, after all. She read the letter again and again, with greedy enthusiasm.

Christina had recognised the hand at once. The letter was from Sweden. From Charles de Mornay.

It was a fresh appeal to Christina from one of the Scandinavian kingdoms. Charles de Mornay had been held prisoner by the Danes until after the war. Now he was in Sweden again with safe possession of his estates and position. But he needed Christina's help, to get King Erik back on his throne.

Why did he want to do that, she wondered? It looked like loyalty – a rare commodity these days. After all, Erik was stark staring mad. But that might still prove to be valuable.

King Johan wanted peace with the Danes. But Erik considered them the source of all evil and might conceivably start a new war. It was plain that many Swedes were dissatisfied with Johan – but then they were never satisfied, no matter who was king.

It was quite entertaining. Christina had always felt that de Mornay would be useful some day; and now he had made a suggestion that might put an end to the intolerable stalemate in the North. Christina hummed to herself. Anything might happen if the coup succeeded, and there were good men behind it.

De Mornay had contacts with Scottish mercenaries at Älvsborg, who were to be paid to participate. Another Frenchman from King Erik's time, Allard the horticulturist, had offered to supply a large sum, saying he knew of some treasure hidden by his master before his fall.

Of course, so many treasure hoards had been buried all over the place, and the fact was that they were seldom dug up again when it came to the point. On the other hand a man who knew about soils might well be better informed on the subject than most. Meanwhile, Christina glimpsed yet another royal younger brother, Duke Karl, like a shadow behind everything.

She herself was asked for money, a sum that she could well afford. After close consideration Christina felt it best not to discuss the matter with Carl – she could imagine his comments – even though Catherine of Medici also had her eye on the Swedish throne. But then Catherine had so many sons to provide for. She decided to offer a contribution. De Mornay could send for the monies.

What a lovely summer. The air was pure and cool over the mountains of Bavaria. It made you feel young, able to enjoy the pleasures of the chase or merely to listen to birdsong beneath the blue heavens. And then there were all the messages, full of news that came to her like welcome gifts. When autumn came and the nights grew darker she would sometimes get up and go out into the darkness. The only sounds to be heard were the steps of the guards and the occasional bark of a distant dog. Everyone else was asleep as she gazed up at the clear sparkle of the Pole Star.

In October a Scottish captain gave away information about the planned coup to the Swedish king. No one believed him, however, and the Scot paid with his life for his 'unjust accusations'.

The mercenary army was in Stockholm. It was to proceed to Estland. De Mornay meanwhile was obviously intending to go to Älvsborg.

When would they strike? And had the treasure been found? The road to Sweden was long and difficult in winter; nonetheless the time spent waiting was absorbing in itself.

'Marvellous ... marvellous ...', Peder Oxe would have said if he had been in her place. If he only knew what she was up to now. Christina had heard from various sources that the now mighty Peder Oxe enjoyed entertaining Danish friends with tales of his eventful years at her court. He had not forgotten her, then; and perhaps he would soon be reminded even more forcefully of her existence.

Claude was pregnant again. She had a host of grand-children, bright little things who came running to meet Christina whenever she arrived on a visit. But Dorothea, poor girl, was still unmarried. She was approaching thirty and an aunt. Her life had been ruined by nothing more than a misshapen foot. Could Christina not find a husband for her? Was there really no suitable prince for such a sweet girl? When all this was over and done with in Scandinavia Christina would devote herself again to searching. Some Italian prince, perhaps?

One night in April Christina stood looking at the stars. The coup had been exposed.

The battle between German and Scottish mercenaries in Estland had uncovered the truth. The king now knew every-thing. Duke Karl's implication had been glossed over; but de Mornay had been charged, and all was lost.

Not even a dog barked that night. The Pole Star was shin-ing among all the others; but its light was sharper in the North, where she was born. Had the night of her birth been a clear one, or had storms raged over the land? There was no one to tell her, and never had been. All those bonds were broken. All the shores were washed away. An injustice had never been revoked, and hope was dead.

Christina lowered her eyes. She had taken a farewell of the stars. She did not look up again, but went quietly indoors.

On the 4th of September 1574 Charles de Mornay was executed, on the Great Square in Stockholm. Christina had never met him, but she sat with his letters in her hands. It was strange, how it had been no more than a childish remark she had once made to her father when she said the land of Sweden was red.

It was the definitive end. Christina had finally given up all hope. Young Queen Sophie gave birth to a daughter and then a second daughter; next time no doubt it would be a son. But the feeling of having been robbed stayed with her. They had taken what was hers and there was no one to give it back. Even after she had received the knowledge of the secret instructions she had tried to get money from Philip, and had pestered Granvella. 'It might be possible,' she had thought only a few years ago. But she did so no more. Everyone had had their due except for her. She considered moving. But where? To her dower house at Tortona, south of Milan? Philip's Spanish soldiery were in charge there. Chaos reigned too in the Netherlands; and that left only Lorraine, with Claude.

Christina was weary of Bavaria. After seven years of marriage and a succession of pregnancies Renata had sunk into a depression. Fools and tumblers and hunting songs were gone; the muses had fled to Olympus. Wilhelm was burdened with economic problems and Christina's daughter always wore black. But Renata was not a widow, and even if she had been she had no need always to envelop herself in grief. The land was swarming with Jesuits meanwhile, and in Landshut nothing but plainsong was to be heard. The lute had vanished; it was gloomy; it was Spanish; the corsets pinched; the world was out of joint; and Christina was freezing.

In the new year death visited her family. Claude gave birth to twins; but they did not survive. Neither did she, and Carl was left a widower with five children. Christina went to Nancy.

For a short time she perked up. Of course he must not be left alone. When the mourning period came to an end he must have a new and lovely bride. She started to think of possible candidates.

But Carl forestalled her. He would never marry again. He had loved his Claude and could not love another.

Christina was amazed. It had been love? That was something that had never occurred to her. Carl was shattered by grief. She herself wept, at not having loved the Claude she should have loved because Carl loved her.

359

Another blow came when Peder Oxe died, in Denmark. He had been, after all, not much older than she was. Their good hours were a memory now, leaving nothing. Except for Dorothea, lame happy Dorothea, who had no time for sorrow but held on to laughter, and played and sang. One day she said she intended to get married.

Christina made no reply. What could she mean? To whom?

'Erich of Braunschweig,' said Dorothea, smiling. She wanted to marry Erich of Braunschweig. She was in love with him and wanted him, and he wanted her.

Erich of Braunschweig? Oh, but his wife was but newly dead, hardly in her grave. Hadn't there been talk of his treating her brutally? And he was a strange, roving character, without an aim in life. What could he give Dorothea? There was no money there either.

'Oh,' said Christina, at a loss.

'Yes,' said Dorothea as naturally as if she had no need to ask anyone for anything at all.

She had fallen in love; but where and when had it happened? At Renata's house? Yes, they had met there. But what had Carl had to say? Dorothea had told him of her decision. Again, just told him. Didn't she realise she had to ask them? This was sheer impudence.

Christina's swelling anger died down, however, to be replaced by confusion. Dorothea had simply come and told them. She was as lame as the tower of Pisa was slant; but she still stood there, just as it still stood. She, Christina, had searched the length and breadth of Europe for a husband for her and now she presented one herself. Shed no tears like Renata, asked no permission. That was the way to do it.

And Erich of Braunschweig? He had once given Christina his political support, but she had certainly never considered him as a son-in-law. Perhaps the rumours about his first marriage had been malicious gossip and he was now a good Catholic. He was not young, forty-seven, and had led a life like that of Albrecht of Brandenburg. Was Dorothea really sure? Was she prepared to knock about Europe? And perhaps he might want to go to Spain. Had she given thought to that?

Dorothea was sure; she wanted her Erich. Well then, that was good. Christina gave the engagement her blessing even though she had not been asked for it, and slowly recovered herself.

It was really wonderful. Now the dear girl would have a life of her own. But it was not merely that. She had done it as a matter of course. She shone with a light that was extinguished in melancholy Renata and severe Carl. She was the sick one, the youngest, the one who had least. But of the three of them only she possessed the vitality of Christina's own youth.

Even more perhaps. For she was marrying Erich of Braunschweig where she herself had rejected Albrecht. So inscrutable were the ways of the Lord, so unexpectedly did joy arrive when she had least expected it.

Christina had been shaken out of herself, and now she embraced her younger daughter. It was marvellous; and there would be feasting again, a wedding to celebrate in Nancy.

Dorothea was all joy. She stood at the altar, glowing, confident and happy, to be made duchess of Braunschweig.

The bridegroom? He was scarred and ravaged by his hard life but he looked at his wife with a devotion that was in marked contrast to his rugged appearance. Erich's face told of emotions he had probably never felt before.

Dorothea had come as joy; but perhaps too as something he had never been given before. She had released something in him that had been frozen and had prevented him from giving in turn. She had received the love she had never known before, and was ready to share his restless life no matter where it led.

There were celebrations. They were not as lavish as at Renata's wedding; partly because such celebrations could not be afforded more than once, and partly because the bridegroom had only recently been widowed and regard must be paid to that. 'My beloved, lovely Dorothea,' he called her. Nobody had ever called her that before. Glowing and lovely, she set off with him to the life Christina had once refused because her aims were too high.

Christina was left behind. She had all her grandchildren. The eldest girl had been named after her, which had pleased her. However, the girl's upbringing had been assigned to Catherine of Medici.

What kind of place was that for a child to grow up in? Catherine's second son was dead now, and the third was on the throne of France, under the name of Henri the Third. Europe was flooded with lampoons depicting the goings-on at his court, together with his little friends, les Mignons. He had married, true; but even so. And he was so fussy that he could not eat with his fingers, but used a little fork instead. What kind of nonsense was that? God had given people fingers to eat with; He had never told them to use the Devil's implement.

Henri was more interested in crazed notions than in his country. At the French court they had powder they sniffed up their noses. Christina had tried it once, and felt her head blowing up into a great cathedral. It was not enough to intoxicate yourself with wine; they wanted more. Also, the strangest rumours circulated. Henri really only loved the one woman he had always loved. And that was his youngest sister, Marguerite.

Christina no longer looked to the North. She never went out to gaze at the Pole Star, though once in a while she might give it a brief sideways glance.

When would that son be born in Denmark? Two daughters in quick succession, and then nothing more. That must annoy Frederik.

But then the Danish council of nobles decreed that after Frederik the man who married one of his daughters would be appointed king. Christina was filled with the old indignation. So they were prepared to use a daughter to continue the line. Now Frederik's son-in-law was to accede to the throne, even though her Carl was much nearer.

But it was all to no purpose; the waters had closed behind them. And the question was superfluous anyway when at last Sophie had a son.

362

At the age of forty-three Frederik had fathered his male heir. The child was named Christian. Christina counted. One day he would be Christian the Fourth. Frederik had waited for his Lady Hardenberg for almost twenty years, until he was presented with a fifteen-year-old bride. The marriage was uniquely happy. Such strange things could happen, and now he had a son as well.

There was nothing to be done. She shook off all such thoughts, and decided to go to her dower house in Italy. But first she wanted to make a stop in Bar.

Christina kneeled on the stone floor of la Collégiale. She kneeled before René; not weeping, merely looking at him in the dim light as she had done so often when in this town. This was the last time; she would never return again.

It was no use thinking of what might have been. It had not come about. But it was preserved, encompassed and lasting, like the heart in the bony hand.

She rose with difficulty, walked out into the light and continued her slow journey towards the sun of Italy.

Tortona, 1590

XXVI

Why be old for so long when she was allowed so short a youth? When Christina reached Tortona in 1579 she had been so feeble she had not expected to see a new decade.

But it was now 1590. Christina sat on the terrace, looking down on the roofs of Tortona in the heat haze. She wondered why she was still alive, when everyone else had died. Wilhelm of Orange had been shot down on a staircase. He had emptied life's goblet, and tasted the acrid drops of exile, but he had felt triumph in the end. He became a hero of freedom. The northern provinces tore themselves free of the Spanish yoke, and from the Orange hope of tolerance grew the little state of Holland.

Wilhelm paid with his life, struck down by a murderer's bullet just as René had been killed by a piece of shrapnel. They were dead, almost all of them.

When Mary was beheaded by the English, Christina had been shaken. After all, Mary was an anointed queen. They had accused her of intriguing against Elizabeth, but that was what was always said about the one who lost the game. She lost her lands and then her head; but perhaps she had gained something else, by dying with the myth of her beauty still fresh. The whore who married her husband's murderer was transformed into a martyr. Had Elizabeth thought about that when she set the executioner to work?

Some there were who felt sorry for Christina in her little dower house. But she was comfortable enough. She sat in the sun and looked out – though now and again she might swing her foot restlessly or drum her fingers, but then Dorothea would tell stories from the Escorial, where she was living while Erich was in the field with Alba's troops.

Dorothea had nine happy years with her Erich before he died. She claimed that the Spaniards regarded Philip as a great king. 'They are a proud people; they just have another way of thinking. They love a matador, but they like to fear and look up to a prince.'

'Very good; we will agree upon that,' was always Christina's reply when there was nothing else to be said.

Dorothea had also managed to get what she wanted. However, Philip could not cheat *her*. He did not dare return her letters, as he had returned Christina's because he had not known of any Christina who was queen of Denmark, Sweden and Norway. Christina might just as well title herself 'Majesty' for all the difference it would make to him. That would irritate him even more, and after all, she was still queen even if she were down here and not in Copenhagen. It had nothing to do with one's place of residence.

Christina had let out a deep, savage laugh when Frederik had died, back in her fatherland. So she had outlived him, even if it was too late. Far too late. Christian the Fourth succeeded to the throne when only eleven years old, and by all accounts he was well educated. In her heart Christina was pleased; her distant people once more had a king who spoke their language.

Perhaps everything was for the best in the end. It was cold up there anyway. Spring did not show itself until May; the capital did not even have a proper theatre; and the castle sounded as if it was frightful.

Secretly Christina wished Christian the Fourth good fortune with his throne and his country. Even so it did not give Philip the right to decide whether she was queen or not.

She was very interested too to hear all about the defeat of the Spanish Armada, first by English cannon and later by a storm in the Atlantic.

Apart from the affair of Mary's execution, Elizabeth and the English were both clever and lucky. A long time ago Elizabeth had stolen Philip's funds for supplying the troops in the Netherlands, and instead supported the rebellion. But now apparently what counted were the oceans. Philip had once helped to save the English queen's life. That must have annoyed him ever since.

Christina's eyes were failing and Dorothea often read aloud to her, especially from a book by Monsieur de Montaigne. So after all he had become a writer, the little official she talked to in the orangery on her return to Lorraine. But she did not agree with everything he said.

'Rubbish,' said Christina sharply. Children must learn in order to think, even though there was something in what he described as pedantic cramming. Or she ordered, 'Read on,' when Dorothea hesitated before such sentences as, 'Even on the world's highest throne we only sit on our backsides.'

It was disgraceful to write like that. Nonetheless Christina's thoughts leapt to the imperial throne, and the emperor who sat on it and who had cheated her so badly. Suddenly she was amused. Dorothea did not understand why. But that was understandable; she had no idea how it helped, to anoint bitterness with the salve of comedy.

He was really amusing, that Monsieur de Montaigne, and totally without respect; and it was good at last to hear something cheerful coming from war-torn France.

Christina's sister had long since gone to her rest. Catherine too had passed away the previous year, and all her sons were gone. She must have been quite doughty, thought Christina, looking down on the town. It had been a hopeless struggle for her to try to control France. Another woman ruler passed away. There was only Elizabeth left now, and she did not live a woman's life. Christina had always expected her to marry an Englishman; but she did not take a husband and had no children. Perhaps it was the price of power.

'Rubbish,' she thought again. Women were certainly quite as fitted. They should just throw off all their artificial indolence and get down to learning something, as girls had done in her childhood, when the pace of life was a gallop. That was what it was meant for. But it had been René who said that women made objects for themselves. Christina suddenly noticed the chill of evening.

The shutters were closed for the night. It was time to go in, and Christina supported herself on Dorothea's arm. The dear girl was the comfort and joy of her old age; but it was time the earthly life came to an end. It had been good on the whole. There had been aims she had not fulfilled, and defeats she had had to suffer, and opportunities she had not seized. Her children were living, even though she had lost Carl one ill-fated Easter and never really retrieved him again. And Renata painted the world black and could not manage to see the light that shone.

Christina's thoughts turned again to France. Carl's and Claude's sons were the only male descendants of the Valois house; but Christina could not muster the strength to think about crowns any more. Suddenly the image of a painting she had once seen came into her mind. Death sat astride his bloody horse and swung his scythe, while an army of skeletons advanced with coffins for shields. They cut down, they burned, they hanged. In his chequered tunic the fool overturned the backgammon board and tried to hide himself under a table. It was the triumph of death. A painting red with fire and blood. But it was not a true picture of the other world. It had been painted by a living man and seen through living eyes. Reproduced by the spectator who was able to feel both sorrow and pain. Montaigne was right. Death was good and right; only the fool hides. Death was the triumph of life.

' – Go away . . .' Dorothea's voice sounded in her ear.

Christina was in darkness, but she remembered what had happened. She had received extreme unction. The end was near; but they did not all need to shout so loud. She was not deaf.

Of course they meant well. They thought she was unconscious, that the Devil was trying to steal her soul. She could hold him off easily even if the road hardly led straight to Heaven.

She had not been a holy Birgitta. There were a few things in the corners of her life that indicated a stay in purgatory.

She could not feel her body, nor her breathing. But if only they would stop shouting like that she would be able to think more clearly. How bad was that purgatorial fire, she wondered? And how long would it go on?

God had created man, after all, and therefore René as well; and was it sinful to love what God had made?

That explanation was probably not good enough . . . and then there had been Albrecht too . . . and quite a lot more. The great accounting was at hand. She ought to be thinking pious thoughts . . . but it would scarcely help now. She felt troubled.

But eternal life waited on the other side. 'Come, come.' She heard Dorothea weeping. It was sweet of her to be sad. The rest of her family would merely feel relief. That was a good thing as well. She had lived long enough and been bored for long enough.

'O Lord, punish me not in Thy wrath,' sang the choir. The voices were fading. '– And chastise me not in Thy ire.'

Suddenly Christina saw a light, a high wonderful light above her. At last it was here. The hour, the moment. Her moment. 'Be merciful unto me, Lord, for I am . . .'

Christina reached up towards the light. Her final thought on earth was:

– Marvellous . . . marvellous . . .

Christina of Denmark died on the 10th of August 1590.

Bibliography

CHRISTINA

Hans Gram, 'Om Christine af Danmark; Kong Christiern II Datter, Hertuginde i Milan, og siden i Lothringen,' *Dansk videnskabsselskab's Skrifter, V,* 1751.

Julia Cartwright, *Christina of Denmark,* London, 1913.

Brantôme, *Oeuvres Complètes,* Paris, 1848.

Emilie Duvernoy, *Chrétienne de Danemark, Duchesse de Lorraine,* Nancy, 1940.

DENMARK

Erik Kjersgaard, *Københavns Historie Vol. 1,* Copenhagen, 1980.

Poul Colding, *Studier i Danmarks politiske Historie i Slutningen af Christian III's og Begyndelsen af Frederik II's Tid,* Copenhagen, 1940.

Poul Colding, *De Lothringske Praktikker mod Danmark i Syvårskrigens forste Ar,* Copenhagen, 1940.

Poul Colding, *Danmark-Lothringen 1565–66 og Peder Oxe's Hjemkomst,* Copenhagen, 1942–44.

L. Daa, *Frederik II's paataenkte Lothringske Giftermaal, og om Danmarks Forhold til de Grumbachske Uroligheder,* Kristiania, 1871.

Behrmann, *Christian den Andens faengsels- og befrielseshistorie,* Copenhagen, 1812.

Troels-Lund, *Michael Franck's rejse til Danmark 1590.*

Troels-Lund, *Peder Oxe, et historisk billed,* Copenhagen, 1906.

G. Jørgensen, *Dronning Elisabeth af Danmark,* Copenhagen, 1901.

Anne-Mette Eriksen, 'Noget slemt og ondskabsfuldt pakk,' *Kronik i 'Skalk'* no. 4, 1984.

J. Fr. Sick, *Nogle Bidrag til Christiern den Andens Historie under Landflygtigheden*, Copenhagen, 1860.

Claus Christoffersen Lyskanter, *Danske Historia, Danske Kongers Slaegtebog*, Copenhagen, 1622.

Mikael Venge, 'Når vinden føjer sig . . .' Spillet om magten i Danmark Marts-december 1533, Odense, 1977.

Mikael Venge, 'Anders Billes Dagbog fra rejsen til Speyer 1544,' article, Copenhagen, 1984.

Frede P. Jensen, *Bidrag til Frederik II's og Erik XIV's historie*, Copenhagen, 1978.

THE NETHERLANDS

Geoffrey Parker, *The Dutch Revolt*, New York, 1977.

J. H. Elliott, *Europe Divided 1559–1598*, Glasgow, 1968.

K. G. Koenigsberger and George L. Mosse, *Europe in the Sixteenth Century*, London, 1971.

Henri Nowé, *L'Hôtel de ville de Gand*, Ghent, 1949.

ITALY

Christopher Hibbert, *The Rise and Fall of the House of Medici*, London, 1974.

Marcel Brion, *The Medici, a Great Florentine Family*, London, 1969.

Lauro Martines, *Power and Imagination. City-States in Renaissance Italy*, New York, 1979.

Luisa Pierotti-Cei, *Life in Italy during the Renaissance*, Geneva, 1977.

Martin Kemp, *Leonardo da Vinci, the Marvellous Works of Nature and Man*, London, 1981.

ENGLAND AND SCOTLAND

Christopher Morris, *The Tudors*, Glasgow, 1955.

S. T. Bindoff, *Tudor England*, London, 1950.

Francis Hackett, *Henry the Eighth*, London, 1929.

John Bowle, *Henry VIII*, London, 1964.

Paul Rival, *The Six Wives of Henry VIII*, London, 1937.
Carolly Erickson, *Great Harry*, London, 1980.
James A. Williamson, *The Tudor Age*, London, 1979.
Jasper Ridley, *The Life and Times of Mary Tudor*, London, 1973.
Edith Sitwell, *The Queens and the Hive*, London, 1962.
Alison Plowden, *The Young Elizabeth, the First 25 Years*, London, 1971.
Antonia Frazer, *Mary Queen of Scots*, London, 1969.

LORRAINE AND FRANCE

Michel Parisse, *Histoire de la Lorraine*, Toulouse, 1977.
Lothringen, Geschichte eines Grenzlandes, 1984.
René Taveneaux, *Histoire de Nancy*, Toulouse, 1978.
Émile Auguste Begin, *Histoire des Duchés de Lorraine et de Bar*, Nancy, 1833.
Jean-Luc Demandre, *Bar-le-Duc et sa Région*, Colmar, 1983.
Nicole Reynaud, 'La Galerie des Cerfs du Palais ducal de Nancy', periodical article, Nancy.
Mark Strage, *Women of Power, the Life and Times of Catherine de Medici*, London, 1976.
Francis Hackett, *Frans I*, Copenhagen, 1936.

SWEDEN

Ingvar Andersson, *Erik XIV*, Stockholm, 1937.
Ingvar Andersson, *Erik XIV och Lothringen*, Scandia, Stockholm, 1933.
Carl Gustav Thomasson, 'Charles de Mornay', Article, Swedish Biographical Dictionary, Stockholm.
Roosvall-Hahr, *Svenska Slot och Herresäten*, vol. Småland, Østergötland, Stockholm, 1930.

GERMANY

Karl Vocelka, *Habsburgische Hochzeiten 1550–1600*, Vienna, 1976.
Ludvig Schrott, *Herrscher Bayerns*, Munich, 1966.
Abhandlung der historischen Klasse der könliglichen, Munich, 1902.

LITERATURE AND RELIGION

Jan Lindhardt, *Martin Luther, Erkendelse og formidling i renaessancen*, Copenhagen, 1983.

G. R. Elton, *Reformation Europe 1517–1559*, Glasgow, 1963.

Erasmus of Rotterdam, *Tåbelighedens Lovprisning*, Copenhagen, 1979.

Andreas Blinkenberg, *Montaigne*, Copenhagen, 1970.

Clementine Lipffert, *Symbol-bibel*, Kassel, 1964.

Martin Schwarz Lausten, *Religion og politik, studier i Christian III's forhold til det tyske rige i tiden 1544–1559*, Copenhagen, 1977.

CODING

Herbert W. Franke, *Die geheime Nachricht*, Frankfurt-am-Main, 1982.

MUSIC

Geoffrey Hindley, *The Larousse Encyclopedia of Music*, London, 1981.

ART AND PAINTINGS REFERENCES

Jane Roberts, *Holbein*, London, 1979.

Walter S. Gibson, *Bruegel*, London, 1977.

Timothy Foote, *The World of Bruegel c. 1525–1569*, New York, 1986.

Helen Langdon, *Holbein*, Oxford, 1976.

Michael Levey, *Holbein's Christina of Denmark, Duchess of Milan*, London, 1968.

Königliche Museen für schöne Künste, Brussels, Alte Kunst, Brussels, 1977.

Bevis Hillier's Pocket Guide to Antiques, London, 1981.

Larousse Encyclopedia of Renaissance and Baroque Art, London, 1981.

Dr Jane de Iongh, *Madama*, Amsterdam, 1967.

The Pleasure of Collecting, Caxton, 1974.

Jay Williams, *The World of Titian c. 1488–1576*, Amsterdam, 1982.

THE HOUSE OF VALOIS

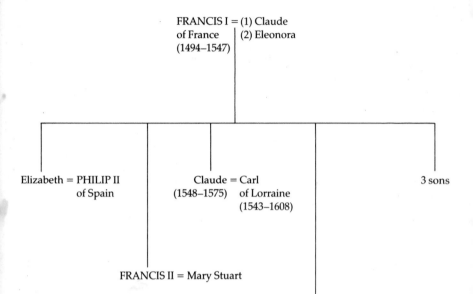

FRANCIS I = (1) Claude
of France   (2) Eleonora
(1494–1547)

Elizabeth = PHILIP II
of Spain

Claude = Carl
(1548–1575) of Lorraine
(1543–1608)

3 sons

FRANCIS II = Mary Stuart

Marguerite = Henry
of Navarre
(HENRI IV of France)